"It's all steampunk and circus wonder as we follow adventures of Elizabeth Barnabas. The double crosses along the way keep the plot tight and fun, and the conclusion sets us up nicely for book two."

The Washington Post

"Elizabeth Barnabus is a uniquely intriguing character who will take readers on a fascinating journey through the strange landscapes of the Gas Lit Empire. Rod Duncan's storytelling skill brings his fictional world to a mysterious, vibrant life which will entice readers from the first page. Enter his world and enjoy the ride!"

Stephen Booth, bestselling author of the Cooper & Fry novels

"Steeped in illusion and grounded in an alternative history of the Luddite Rebellion, Duncan's strong supernatural mystery serves ably as both a standalone adventure and the start to a series. Strategically placed steampunk tropes inform but do not overwhelm Elizabeth's headlong quest to find a missing aristocrat sought by the Patent Office, which is fixated on both achieving perfection and eliminating 'unseemly science.' A hazardous border crossing into the permissively corrupt Kingdom of England and Southern Wales provides ample excitement, and a glossary at the novel's conclusion hints enticingly at a much more involved story to come."

Publishers Weekly

"Rod Duncan's *The Bullet Catcher's Daughter* is a magic box pulsating with energy. Compulsive reading from the get-go, the blend of steampunk alternate history wrapped in the enigma of a chase makes for first-rate entertainment in this finely crafted novel."

Graham Joyce, author of Year of the Ladybird

"If I had a bowler hat, I'd take it off to the author of this beautifully crafted steampunk novel."
Chris D'Lacey, author of The Last Dragon Chronicles

"I'm saying it here and now: Elizabeth Barnabus might just be one of my favourite female characters of all time."
Why Words Work

"I haven't been this impressed by a book in a while... *Unseemly Science* is a beautifully written steampunk, alternate history style novel that manages to evoke the aesthetic without turning itself into a reflection of the rest of the trope out there. Elizabeth, the main protagonist, is a feminist heroine I can get behind – smart, intelligent, and void of the typical fantasy heroine. It's a slow burn mystery but so intelligently written and with a well-developed world, I barely put it down."
Adventures in Sci Fi Publishing

"The Gas-Lit Empire novels tell a great story, with a strong protagonist challenging rigid cultural norms, all in a richly built alternate history, uniquely designed."
Craig Newmark, founder of Craigslist

"A fine and well-crafted novel. As per the glossary, Elizabeth plays a key role in the fall of the Gas-lit empire. Cheers to that, as she is a captivating character. Angry Robot has picked a winner."
Koeur's Book Reviews

"I didn't predict the twists that *Unseemly Science* threw at me. Not only is this book much darker than its predecessor, it also keeps you in more suspense, which is a feat considering I compared *The Bullet-Catcher's Daughter* to a spy novel. A sequel that takes a macabre turn!"
Victorian Soul Critiques

"A detective story with a difference. Chapters begin with quotes from the legendary *Bullet-Catcher's Handbook*, phrases that introduce not only the idea of illusion that pervades the novel, but also the author's sly humour. Rod Duncan's talent has combined inventive plot and characterisation to create a smart, amusing and fascinating tale that had me reading long into the night."
Fantasy Faction

"The writing is as crisp, world-building deep, and characters as nuanced as the first book. This is a worthy second volume in what is turning out to be a fantastic series."
Online Eccentric Librarian

"Slipping back into the world Rod Duncan has created for his characters to play in was a bit like putting on a well-worn, comfortable, pair of gloves."
Frank Michael Serrington

"Rod Duncan has successfully written an absorbing tale from the perspective of a woman in the early nineteenth century. A cracking read."
Fancy Pans Café

"Duncan is an accomplished crime writer, and this detective story with fantastical elements shows his chops to great effect, and the steampunk elements don't overtake the story. The ending leaves so many wonderful possibilities for more adventures with Elizabeth!"
My Bookish Ways

"*The Bullet-Catcher's Daughter* is a unique and immaculately crafted novel that everyone should read, whether they're a fantasy novice or expert."
The Writer's Den

ROD DUNCAN

The Queen of All Crows

BEING VOLUME ONE *of*
The MAP *of* UNKNOWN THINGS

ANGRY
ROBOT

ANGRY ROBOT
An imprint of Watkins Media Ltd

20 Fletcher Gate,
Nottingham,
NG1 2FZ • UK

angryrobotbooks.com
twitter.com/angryrobotbooks
A nation of eels

An Angry Robot paperback original 2018

Cover by Will Staehle
Set in Meridien by Argh! Nottingham

Distributed in the United States by Penguin Random House, Inc.,
New York.

US edition ISBN 978 0 85766 700 7
UK edition ISBN 978 0 85766 699 4
Ebook ISBN 978 0 85766 701 4

Printed in the United States of America

9 8 7 6 5 4 3 2 1

THE QUEEN OF
ALL CROWS

THE AIRSHIP *AMERICAN FRONTIER*

For passengers on the AS *American Frontier*, at a cruising altitude of eight thousand feet, the moment the world changed was preceded by a vision of beauty: the shadow of their airship fleeting over moonlit cloud. Here and there the dark surface of the Atlantic was revealed in breaks between the white. From one such break came flashes like distant lightning. Passengers looked down in wonder through the cabin windows as bright streaks lanced up towards them. It was only when they heard the scream of bullets that panic set in. Impacts clattered against the engine and rear compartment. Then came the thuds of fatter, slower projectiles ripping into the canopy.

The great machine tilted back and began to fall. Every loose thing slid or tumbled toward the rear of the carriages. Smoke poured from the engines as they battled the inevitable pull of gravity. From a distance the end seemed slow, dreadfully slow, yet magnificent.

In the vast span of the civilised world, no gun existed that could have brought down an airship from such a height. And it was inconceivable that one could have been manufactured in the chaos beyond. Yet it happened. And the world changed.

Some would later argue that the downing of the American Frontier proved history to be a tide that no one could hold back. Others would cite it as evidence that change comes chaotically through the sparking genius of great minds.

Afterwards.

PART ONE

CHAPTER 1

Afternoon sun rendered every colour dazzling: the green and black of the Company flag, limp at the masthead; streaks of orange rust on the white-painted deck housing; the calm ocean, a teal blue; blood blossoming from the carcass of the whale.

A gantry of planks and rope had been swung out over the dead beast. Fires burned under try pots on the main deck. Gaffs, pikes and bone spades lay ready. And the crew waited.

"Get on with it, why not!"

The anonymous shout had come from among a knot of sailors gathered next to the starboard paddlewheel. The first mate shot them a warning glance, but no more. The slight figure edging out from the safety of the deck was the young scientific officer. Any sign of respect would have been transparent pretence.

The captain glowered down from the quarterdeck with ill-disguised impatience. He may have chosen the crew of the whaling ship *Pembroke*, but it was the Company that placed the scientific officer. All were subject to a captain's command, but only that one had a direct line of communication back to the board of directors in New York. Perhaps even to the International Patent Office. On such reports, the ship could be ordered to stop killing one type or another of whale, or be moved on to a different hunting ground.

This scientific officer was even less popular than the one the Company had called home so abruptly the previous year. This one carried a singular aloofness and had no stomach for the job, sins made flesh in the form of an ugly wine-stain birthmark. Ill-fortune is a contagion no sailor would willingly be near.

"Take your time, sir," the captain shouted.

Some of the sailors laughed.

The scientific officer wobbled and grabbed a rope for support, then began shuffling further out over the dead beast. Below, another wave washed the gash that had been left by the killing lance. More blood swilled into the ocean.

Such a creature. Such a death.

The sperm whale had rolled somewhat on its side, revealing the edge of a belly patterned with barnacles. At fifty foot, she wasn't large. But it had taken three harpoons to stop her. Somewhere in the fury of dragged boats and thrashing water, her calf had been left behind.

"Mr Barnabus?" called the captain.

The scientific officer turned, unsteadily on the plank. "Yes, sir?"

"Are your observations quite done?"

"They are, sir." It was a reedy voice.

"Then may I suggest you return to the quarterdeck to make report!"

Grinning, the men picked up their tools. Sunlight flashed from the surface of a blade.

Then a shout came from the lookout. "Steamer ho!"

The captain looked up, shielding his eyes against the brilliant sky. "Bearing?"

"Two points abaft the port beam. Heading straight at us, sir. And she's signalling."

They moved as one, the crew, to the other bow to stare at

the approaching ship. All but the young scientific officer, who clambered back to the safety of the deck, then silently opened the hatch and slipped unseen below.

Privacy was another reason for the crew's resentment. Scientific officers did no real work. They looked on, risking no danger, distant from the stink of blood and oil. They hindered rather than helped. Yet, despite all this, they enjoyed the unique dispensation of a cabin to themselves.

But privacy was the very thing. Without privacy it would have been quite impossible.

Scientific officer Barnabus bolted the cabin door, top and bottom, then, hands shaking, stripped off tunic and shirt and began to unwind the cloth that gave her the illusion of a masculine figure.

There comes a moment when deception is unbearable.

It had been the calf, not the mother, that had unsettled Elizabeth Barnabus. The thought of it had come to her unexpectedly as she stood out at the edge of the gantry. Under the gaze of the crew and unable to show a reaction, she'd felt acid rising in her throat. If the other ship hadn't been seen, she could still have done her job; climbed the steps to formally report the species, sex and size of the animal to a man who would have surely known all those things from a quarter mile out.

With the ritual complete, she would have been obliged to stand beside him on the quarterdeck and keep tally as blanket strips of blubber were minced and rendered. All that, she could have done, as she had many times before. She could have maintained the voice, gait and bearing of a man. But this unexpected release from duty had cracked the mask.

She lowered herself onto the narrow cot and closed her eyes, feeling the skin of her breasts pinching tight against the cold air.

The calf had escaped the harpoons but wouldn't survive.

Orcas would find it. Or sharks. It was the way of things. The knowledge shouldn't have disturbed her. She didn't want to consider why it had.

Picking up a hand glass, she inspected the false birthmark on the side of her face. It would do for another couple of days before she needed to apply the indigo dye and deepen the colours again.

A tin mug on the cabin shelf rattled against the wall. Elizabeth's eyes snapped to it. She'd not noticed the change, but the *Pembroke*'s engines were no longer idling. They were moving. The ship tilted with the start of a turn. She grabbed the binding cloth and began to wind it around her chest.

Other sounds she heard now; orders barked and feet running on the deck. And closer, booted feet marching towards her cabin along the narrow passageway outside. They stopped next to the door.

"Mr Barnabus?"

It was the first mate.

"Yes, sir?"

"You're wanted on deck. Quick now!"

She tucked the end of the cloth tight and reached for her clothes. "I'm coming."

"Captain's burning to know what business you have with the fleet."

"Business?"

"We're ordered to get you back. And in such haste we must cast off the whale."

Elizabeth returned to the deck, uniformed once more and steeled for trouble. Captain Locklight had a reputation for competence and measured judgement. But early in Elizabeth's voyage, he'd taken against her. His antipathy had grown as the months passed. At the best of times, being summoned would be the harbinger of some little humiliation.

The remnant of the gantry was being dismantled. The tools had already been stowed and steam billowed from beneath the try pots where fires had been doused. Junior officers had taken the watch on the quarterdeck. The first mate pointed to the prow, where Captain Locklight stood alone.

If the glances of the men had been insolent before, they were now hostile. Elizabeth started to pick her way forwards, but a pike clattered to the deck in front of her.

"Beg pardon," said the man who'd dropped it. He took his time to pick it up, his eyes locked with hers all the while. He rubbed his thumb over the edge of the blade.

She didn't blink.

Passing herself off as a man hadn't been the problem. That was merely a matter of disguise, movement and voice, things she'd been tutored in from childhood. Indeed, aside from the voice, presenting as a woman in polite company felt no less unnatural. Corset and binding cloth were disguises both. The illusion she had not mastered, could not master, was to pass herself off as a sailor.

She stepped forwards again. The men parted, staring as she went. But as she neared the captain they turned their backs.

"You wanted to see me, sir?"

Instead of answering, he stepped up from the deck onto the bowsprit – the spar pointing forwards over the water from the prow. Though one of his hands touched the rigging, he seemed to balance without its support. Gripping one of the ropes – Elizabeth could never remember their names – she hoisted herself up and followed him out, clearing the figurehead. The bow broke through a wave, sending up spray. She felt a mist of it on her cheek and her eyes stung.

"The wind's with us," Locklight said. "The engine's drinking fuel, but we're making good speed. We'll have you back with the fleet before noon tomorrow."

The prow dipped into a trough, pulling her forwards. The

rope bit into her palm as she gripped tighter.

"Are you enjoying your time with us?" he asked.

"It's an education," she said.

"That's a true word. There's always learning – some hidden thing to be seen. And this is your first tour."

"Yes, sir."

"Well, Mr Barnabus, I've never known a scientific officer quite like you."

He took another step out along the bowsprit. This time she didn't follow.

"I'll confide in you," he said. "I've a problem with the men. Two things make them follow my say – fear and greed. There's only so many backs you can flog. If I can't lead them to the whale, they don't get paid. They know that. They accept it. But to have them risk their necks killing one and then order them cut it adrift – that I've never done. Never had to."

Saying this, he turned and faced her full on. She tightened her grip on the rope.

"Can you swim?"

"Yes, sir."

"Of course you can. Though these waters are too cold for it. A man with some fat on him might last a few minutes. If his heart didn't stop directly. You've no fat on you."

"I'll not be going in."

"Well, that'll be for the best." His eyes flicked from her marked face to her feet, placed askew on the beam. "You didn't give me your report. Why is it you're always running away to that cabin? You might win more respect if you took time to walk among the men."

"It was a sperm whale, sir. Fifty foot. A female with calf."

"You will add it to the ledger."

"Yes, sir."

"A shame we lost the little one. A calf will stay by the dead mother. One time we caught three bulls that way. They must have heard its cries and come to rescue. Five whales in one day! But then, we'd still have had to cast them off. So it was no loss. Why d'you suppose it's with such urgency that you're wanted back at the fleet?"

"I don't know, sir."

It was the truth.

"Perhaps you'll be leaving us?"

"I really don't know."

"Well," he said, "we can hope. Maybe they'll next send an even younger man. With a yet more hideous face."

Elizabeth found herself faltering under his inspection. "Will there be anything else?" she asked.

"Yes, Mr Barnabus. I've held back from asking. But now it comes to it and I need to know. Why were you thrust upon us, and in the middle of a tour?"

"I don't know."

This was a lie.

"Would you use me for a fool?" He spoke quietly, for her ears only, though the crew would surely be straining to hear.

"No, sir."

"I say you would!"

She glanced over her shoulder. The crew's backs were still turned, but for the officers on the quarterdeck.

"Stand," he growled. "I'll have my answer. The truth, sir!"

"I cannot."

"You will speak. And frankly."

"I know I've pained you, sir. You've made no secret of it. You've ridiculed me at every call. So, frankly, if I did know this thing, why in heaven's name would I tell you now?"

Captain Locklight flinched. She began backing towards the deck, but his hand shot out and grabbed the collar of her tunic. She felt herself being pulled off balance as he drew her closer. Scrambling to find her footing, her hand slipped from the rope. If he dropped her, she'd tumble. There'd be no time to freeze. Her body would be broken under the paddlewheels.

"Best not wander the deck at night," he whispered. "You might meet me alone."

When her hand found the rope again, he released his grip.

"Go nurse your secrets," he said. "Perhaps that cabin is the best place for you after all."

CHAPTER 2

Secrets are a benediction, when held for the betterment of others, and lies should be embraced.

Thirteen months before the casting off of the whale, Elizabeth's dearest friend had been preparing for marriage. Indeed, Julia Swain was friend, student and confidante all rolled into one. If Elizabeth had had a sister, it would have been someone like Julia, she thought. The wedding would be joyous. She kept repeating it to herself. Julia would be happy. And that was all that mattered.

There would be two ceremonies; the first to take place in the church of St Clement Danes in London. That for the benefit of the groom's family, who were "social Christians" in the same way that some people are social drinkers. The second ceremony was scheduled for the Secular Hall in Leicester, to satisfy Julia's own parents, who were good atheists in every sense. Such was the mistrust that each congregation held for the other that the two families found themselves bound together in a happy conspiracy of small lies and shrewd silences.

On the evening before the first wedding, Elizabeth found herself promenading arm in arm with Julia along the embankment overlooking the Thames. They'd indulged in buying colourful dresses suited to the London fashion. Julia had chosen plain sapphire. Elizabeth's was emerald, with a printed leaf pattern along the hem. Both were Egyptian cotton. The skirts moved with a satisfying swish, attracting admiring glances from other promenaders.

As they walked, Julia became quiet. Contending emotions seemed to be battling within her.

"Don't worry," said Elizabeth. "Marriage will be all you've dreamed."

Julia's grip on her arm tightened. "Everything will change."

"Your love for him won't."

"Nor my love for you. If you'd not tutored me, the university would never have taken me on. And it was through you I met Robert in the first place."

"You're seeing too much good in me," Elizabeth said. "As always. You're worthy of your blessings. You studied hard. And Robert loves you for what you are. That's why I'm allowing you to marry him!" She winked, to show that it was mostly a joke. "And tomorrow you'll see a marvel. Tinker has a new set of clothes for the wedding. You'll not recognise the boy. It turns out his skin has a fairly human colour, once he's been scrubbed."

Julia's frown deepened. "Tinker needs you," she said. "And so do I."

"A peculiar family we make – you, me and a half-wild boy. Now at least you'll be respectable. And we'll visit so often, you'll be yearning for time to be alone with your husband."

Elizabeth expected at least a blush from this. But it was sorrow that racked her friend's face.

They had stopped next to the parapet and were staring out at the Thames. The reflections of coloured lights from the south bank marked out the wake of a cargo ship on its way up river. London was a hungry city. The business of feeding it never stopped. A sailor stepped up to the prow.

Then the boat was under one of the arches of Westminster Bridge and he disappeared into shadow. Thoughts of loss should have had no business on the eve of a wedding.

"I'm expelled from the university," Julia said, blurting the words in a rush as though she'd been holding them back for days. "They won't allow a married woman to study. We knew it would happen. But now it has. And..."

"Take them to law!" said Elizabeth. "Force them to have you back."

"It's the other way about. They could make a suit against me if they chose. The university has rules – which I signed up to. It's I who broke the contract."

"And are there such rules for all? Are married men expelled also?"

"We're different – however much you might wish it otherwise."

"Now you sound like your mother," said Elizabeth.

"You mustn't mention it to her!" There was a note of alarm in Julia's voice.

"She doesn't know?"

"Nor Father. Though he won't mind so very much."

That seemed to be the wrong way about. Elizabeth searched her friend's face for clues. Julia's father enjoyed shocking dour friends by boasting of how his wonderful girl was away studying law in London. He'd be devastated if she were to be expelled.

"What are you not telling me?"

"I'm following your advice," said Julia, who now would not meet her eyes. "You said I should never give in. You said it was up to me what I did in the world. The universities back home don't let women study, so I came here. And now in London they won't have a married woman as a student. But in the Free States of America..."

Elizabeth's hand shot to her mouth to cover the shock

and the unexpected stab of sorrow.

"Robert's practice has an office in New York," Julia continued. "After we're done with all this – the wedding and everything – he'll be flying out there. I'll follow just as soon as he's found a place for us to live. Columbia University has offered to take me. I'll be studying Patent Law. It's what I always wanted."

America. Under those broad skies even the impossible might find a place to hide, beyond the gaze of propriety or reason.

Elizabeth burst into tears. "I'm so happy for you," she said.

The arrangements took a month longer than expected. But at last the day of departure was fixed. Elizabeth left the boy, Tinker, under the watchful eye of a neighbour and accompanied Mr and Mrs Swain to wave off their daughter on her long journey.

Mrs Swain's eyes were wide as she stepped into the hangar of the St Pancras Air Terminus. It was only her second visit to London and everything must still have seemed brash to her.

A thin veil of smoke hung in the air, lit gold by beams of sunlight lancing down from windows in the high canopy. The vast scale of the arched roof would have been hard to comprehend but for three airships, which lay at berth side by side.

They found Julia standing next to a pile of tan suitcases. A private porter was harrying her for work.

"No thank you," she was saying.

"Oh go on," he said. "Wouldn't want a case to go missing." He delivered his threat with a smile. The man was a shark.

Elizabeth was hurrying forwards to intervene, but Julia leant closer to him and said something, whereon he glanced around and hurried off, ducking into the crowd.

Mrs Swain enfolded her daughter in a tearful embrace. Julia would have normally extricated herself. But perhaps understanding the magnitude of the parting, she endured. Her father kissed her on the forehead and then held her at arm's length with an expression that spoke of both pride and pain.

"What did you say to the porter?" Elizabeth asked, when it was her turn to be embraced.

"I told him he'd violated three separate bylaws of the terminus."

Elizabeth found herself laughing, in spite of it all. "He must have thought you the bait in a police trap!"

"Perhaps," she said. Then her grin dropped and she held both of Elizabeth's hands. "Thank you for coming. You will look after Mother, won't you?"

"As best I can."

"And you'll write."

Elizabeth buried the pang of impending loss with a grin. "I might just do that."

Julia glanced at the waiting airship. "I've been so busy with arrangements, I hadn't thought how it would feel to go. And now here I am."

"Don't think too much," said Elizabeth. "Things only become impossible when we think they can't be done. Your journey is a marvel. I'd always thought to go to America one day. But it's you who's doing it."

"Then come! You can stay with us. Robert won't mind."

"Robert is yet to understand what your goodness will cost him!" Then Elizabeth leaned close and whispered. "You know I'd be following you out on the next flight if I could. And you know what holds me here. But I hope. One day."

Julia said: "If it wasn't for your example, I'd never have set out."

"Then it seems I've done something to be commended after all."

They hugged each other, then. And when it was done, Elizabeth turned away to wipe her eyes.

The boatswain called for loading to begin. Everything was suddenly practical. Scales were hauled in. The cases had to be weighed and labelled. Elizabeth's father tried to insert himself into proceedings by checking that all the details had been correctly copied onto the manifest. But Elizabeth noted that it was Julia, her one-time student, who properly oversaw everything. And if she allowed her parents to help it was only to keep them occupied.

"You have gone beyond me," Elizabeth whispered, though no one could hear. "I'm so proud of you."

She watched her friend step to the barrier, joining the men who queued to have their tickets checked. Then she hurried after Julia's parents, who were heading to the next platform, where others had gathered for the best view of departing loved ones. Julia was already halfway up the steps to the alighting platform. At the top, a steward checked her ticket once more and directed her into the foremost of the two carriages. Elizabeth shielded her eyes but couldn't see beyond the reflections in the porthole glass.

A horizontal jet of steam had been hissing from the engine since they arrived. But in the last minute its pressure had increased, turning to a shrill whistle. Now it cut and, with a sharp exhalation of smoke, the engine began to turn. Doors slammed closed. Ground crewmen threw free the mooring lines. Then the propeller fired up with a dreadful roar and the airship began to slide forwards.

Elizabeth hurried to the end of the platform, waving in the hope that Julia could see her. The nose of the airship emerged from the shadow of the arched roof. Smoke came thumping out of the engine vents, the beat accelerating as it pulled away. The last detail she could see before it dissolved into the London haze was the name, the black lettering stencilled huge on the side of the canopy: AS *American Frontier*.

CHAPTER 3

Whaling ship *Pembroke* made contact with the first outlier before ten bells. The watch shouted and Captain Locklight ordered the helmsman to steer towards it. One by one, more of the fleet came into view; smudges of smoke at first, then discreet dots, which seemed to hover above the mirage of the horizon before resolving into the profiles of ships.

Elizabeth looked out on the scene as best she could through the salt-encrusted glass of her porthole window. She'd not dared to leave the cabin since the captain's threat. Indeed, she'd kept the door double bolted. A noise had woken her in the night. After that she'd not been able to sleep again until her pistol lay within reach. Locklight's anger had unsettled her. If the crew had woken to find her gone, she would simply have been marked down as missing; presumed fallen overboard.

People were changed by the wilderness of the ocean. But as they drew in among the fleet, it seemed that the restraints of civilisation might return. With breasts bound and her uniform buttoned, she emerged from the cabin, rolling her shoulders like a man as she stepped out into the sunshine.

The crew were rushing about their tasks and seemed content to ignore her. The unnatural act of cutting adrift the whale could not have been forgotten. But in the morning light she could at first see no anger. They had more pressing concerns. They'd been out of communication for three weeks. There would be news, perhaps. They could hope for deliveries from home, though home was a different compass point for each. And despite their recent loss, they were returning with one hundred and twenty barrels of oil. That meant money to spend, though not as much as might have been.

Elizabeth climbed the steps to the quarterdeck and stood, feet slightly spread, hands clasped behind her in the manner of the other officers. Waiting below had become unbearable. But here she felt exposed to their judgement.

With his eye to the helio telescope, the signalman was calling out the names and bearings of the other ships. Captain Locklight stood close to him, head angled to read from the calculation book.

Keeping track of a fleet was held to be the most demanding job on ship, but for the captain's. Every five minutes, each ship would use the helio to flash its name to all others in view. And every half hour each ship would signal the bearing of others within their knowledge, by which method the positions of all could be triangulated, though most lay beyond the curve of the horizon.

The fleet spread or gathered to match visibility. Rain or fog would have them close to a tight knot. But on this day of clear skies, the fleet might occupy two thousand square miles of the North Atlantic.

Captain Locklight straightened himself and turned to face her. "Seven and a half miles and we'll be back with *Mother*."

Other officers grinned.

"Why the bitter face, Mr Barnabus?" Locklight asked, before marching from the deck.

Feeling the gaze of the others on her false birthmark, Elizabeth stepped to the port bow and peered out at two of the distant ships, shielding her eyes from the sun.

"That's *Blackbird* and the *Port of Liverpool*," said the first mate, who'd come to stand beside her. He could be just as sharp in speech as the other officers if the occasion merited it. But he'd never gone out of his way to belittle her. It was a small mercy, for which she felt grateful.

"Are they heading away from the fleet?" she asked.

"Since as we're coming back, others must go out."

There was a sting in his words. His grey-green eyes were fixed on her, as if searching for clues in her reaction. Unusual for a sailor, he kept himself clean shaven.

"None of this was my doing," she said.

"Captain thinks it was."

"Blame *Mother*. The order came from her."

"That's the thing," said the first mate, dropping his voice. "They can't blame *Mother*. But someone must stand for it. And here you are."

"You don't believe me then?" she asked.

"I don't know. But it doesn't matter what I think." He pointed beyond the prow to where a column of engine smoke hung above a dark shape, bigger than any of the ships. "We'll find out soon enough."

Mother was more than a ship. Her three iron hulls lay side-by-side, bridged above the water by a crisscrossing of girders in compression and cables in tension, all topped by a wide deck. Viewed from the waterline, she could have been mistaken for a pleasure pier that had broken free and drifted a thousand miles into the ocean.

That was the only view Elizabeth herself had had of it. But on the wall of Locklight's cabin there was displayed an ornamental plate featuring an illustration of the leviathan viewed from overhead. From that angle, with its smokestacks and the upper parts of the paddlewheels encased in sheet metal, it seemed to her not so much a ship as a floating town;

which indeed it was. Asymmetry added to the impression, the portside hull being half as massive again as the other two.

It was from that side they now approached. With most of the paddlewheel cased in, there was no sign from a distance that it was moving at all. But as they drew to a quarter of a mile, Elizabeth borrowed the first mate's telescope and was able to see a faint frothing of the water next to the hull. The mother ship was turning. The movement was too slow to see, but when the half hour was called, the angle had changed, the stern rotating to face them. She felt the tilt of the deck shift under her feet and the whaler began to turn, bringing the bowsprit closer into alignment with the gap between *Mother*'s central and portside hulls.

The first time she'd witnessed the manoeuvre, it had seemed graceful. But that had been from a distance. A whaler steaming into the gap had been no different to a ship returning to harbour. She'd not understood why the sailors around her tensed as they watched.

But now she did.

The beat of the engine slowed for the final approach and the crew began hauling a rope to lower the crow's nest. The top of the mast slipped down inside the lower section, making clearance for them to pass below the crisscross of girders and cables that supported *Mother*'s deck.

Locklight had taken over at the wheel as they approached. Within seconds they were easing in between the iron walls. She watched the shadow of one giant hull sweeping towards her from the prow. The sheer scale of the thing had made their approach seem slower than it really was.

"Paddles dead stop!"

The captain's order was immediately echoed by the watch officer shouting into a speaking tube. The note of the engine changed. There was a rushing sound, like a canal lock filling. The paddles had become water brakes. Elizabeth staggered with the sudden slowing. At another time they would have laughed at her. Even the first mate. But everyone on deck stood fully alert and focussed for action should an order be called.

"Reverse, quarter power!"

The paddles began slapping the water again. This time Elizabeth was ready and braced for the abrupt change of momentum.

Ropes clattered down onto the deck from above. As crewmen took them up and began hauling in the slack, she looked up and saw that they'd been thrown from both sides.

"All stop!"

During the approach, they'd been wallowing, the waves hitting them abeam. But in easing between *Mother*'s iron hulls they'd entered a calm space, for a system of metal gauzes below the waterline served to dampen the swell.

The ropes grew taut as the men hauled them tighter around mooring cleats. There were two lines port and two lines starboard, holding them steady mid-channel, with a few yards of clearance on each side. The gap had seemed so much more from a distance.

A ratchet clattered above and a cargo net, bulging with crates, began to descend towards the main deck. It landed with a bump, and when its cable had reeled out enough slack for safety, the men jumped to work. The main cargo hatch had already been opened. As soon as the net had been emptied, they dragged it to the edge and dropped it into the hold. There it would be filled with barrels of whale oil, ready to be hoisted back up to *Mother*.

The first mate had extracted a leather document wallet from among the newly arrived crates. Gripping it under his arm, he climbed stiffly to the quarterdeck and presented it with all formality.

Elizabeth tensed as Locklight unbuckled it and began to

peruse the papers inside. He stepped away, turning his back on her and the other officers. They were all watching, like her, though there was no clue to be had from his stance or the angle of his head.

The deck tilted slightly and the ratchet clattered as *Mother*'s engines lifted the first load of cargo from the hold. Elizabeth became aware of the tightness of the binding cloth pressing in on her.

"Mr Barnabus," said the captain, turning. His face wore a cruel smile.

"Yes, sir?"

"It seems this is to be a sad day for us. Our scientific officer returns to *Mother*. We must say goodbye. You're riding the cargo net."

There was a proper way to travel from the ship to *Mother*. They called it the gig: a framework of protective struts within which an officer could sit, strapped in, whilst the hoist lifted him from the deck.

There was no time for that, the men said. The young scientific officer could ride like an ordinary seaman. If it hadn't happened so fast she might have seen the trick. But her caution had been thrown out of kilter by the speed and turn of events. The cargo net lay flat and open on the deck. They placed her sea trunk in the middle and indicated that she should go to sit on it.

"You'll be safe that way," someone said as she stepped out.

But she had only set foot on the webbing before the boatswain shouted, "Take in the slack!"

The ratchet rattled and loops of rope whipped taut. The corners lifted and she was upended, limbs poking through the net, her legs flailing above her. Then she slipped back, bringing a shoulder down sharply on the corner of the sea chest.

"Haul away!" called the boatswain.

The net rocketed up from the deck, pressing her stomach into her lungs so that the breath left her. Then she was swinging sideways and dropping. The impact of landing sent a second jarring shock through her back. Then the net relaxed, the cables fell slack beside her and she found herself lying flat out next to her upturned trunk.

Men were laughing. She had the impression of a crowd of faces looking down out of the dazzling sky. Then there was a smell of body odour and she was being dragged free of the net. Legs clothed in calico stood all around. Between two of the sailors she glimpsed the slight figure of a ship's boy. He reached out and touched her on the shoulder. The contact set her heart beating faster. Desperately, she tried to keep track of him as he retreated into the crowd, but he had already slipped away.

"Well? Make report, sir!"

The words came from above, shrill and impatient. Elizabeth got first onto hands and knees, then stood, legs unsteady. She found herself facing a man in officers' uniform. The rank marks on his shoulders were unfamiliar.

Trying to put the boy out of her mind, she said: "I'm Scientific Officer Barnabus of the whaling ship *Pembroke*. I was sent for." Her throat was tight. The words had come out higher pitched than she'd have liked.

"Welcome to the mother ship," said the man.

There was nothing welcoming in the tone of his voice.

From a distance, the mother ship might have seemed like a pleasure pier set to drift. But on its deck Elizabeth felt as if she was standing amid the factories of Manchester. The extraordinary expanse, the height of the deck housings, the chimneys and the columns of dark smoke all added to the impression. But more startling yet was the unnatural steadiness of the surface on which she stood.

The officer of unknown rank led her at a brisk march. From months at sea, Elizabeth had become accustomed to the whaler's tilt and ride. Now she found herself stumbling.

"Where are you taking me?" she asked.

He must have heard the question, but made no answer.

Attempting to stride like a man and cope with the unnatural steadiness, she followed him up a flight of grey painted metal steps that clanged with each footfall. There was no rust to be seen. Then they were across another deck. It was impossible to say how it should be named, such was the confusion of different levels and platforms. Up they climbed, stairway after stairway, traversing gangways between deck housings and an increasingly vertiginous drop. The final flight of stairs was the steepest, taking her to the highest point over what had to be the portside hull.

She'd barely had time to turn her head before the officer opened a metal door and snapped his fingers, pointing her inside. He didn't follow, but closed the door behind her.

Light streamed from windows on four sides. In the central position at the front an officer stood next to a line of speaking tubes. It seemed there should be a helmsman, but she could see no wheel. Other officers clustered around a chart table in the middle of the room.

"Your name?" one of them barked.

"Barnabus," she said. "Scientific officer of the *Pembroke*."

"What's your business?"

Before she could make answer, a desiccated voice said: "That's enough for today gentlemen." It had a smoker's crackle.

All straightened and clicked their heels. As they dispersed, she saw the commodore for the first time. He was so shrunken in on himself with age that without the braided epaulettes his shoulders might have collapsed to half their width. Liver spots showed through the dusting of white stubble on his cheeks and on the dome of his head.

He dismissed his officers with a weary flick of the hand. The door clanged open and they filed out.

"I'll take the helm," he said. His accent suggested the American northeast.

The man at the speaking tubes made a curt nod and followed the others out. The door closed and they were alone.

"So, Barnabus, what have you to say for yourself?"

"Say?"

"The trouble you've caused."

She'd been blamed for events beyond her control. She'd been scorned and tricked. And now came the questioning. "It was *you* who sent for *me*. Sir. They had to cast off a fifty-foot sperm whale."

If he'd caught the anger in her voice, he didn't show it. "The whalers are paid well enough. They'll recover from the inconvenience. And they've not discovered your secret?"

"They've not."

"I'll confess, when I heard there was a woman come to us disguised as an officer, I doubted the men would be so easily duped. But now I see you, I'm impressed."

There was an edge of ironic humour in the way he said this. Mocking, almost. As if he would have seen through the disguise easily enough. He must need her, she thought, or he wouldn't have called her back with such urgency. Yet here he was, playing a slow game. She glanced at the door, weighing the risks of turning her back on him and marching away.

"Is your voice naturally so?" he asked.

"Practice makes it possible."

He stared at her as if trying to identify a strange fish dredged up from the deep ocean. "I know your qualifications are false," he said. "But your certificates are genuine. That's curious in itself, don't you think? You've never been to sea before. But here you are, an officer of the fleet. You have all the disadvantages of womanhood. And yet you've been sent to me in disguise with instructions from the Board that I'm to play along."

"I'm not playing a game!" she said, louder now.

"Oh, we're all of us doing that, my dear. The question is, whose rules do we follow? I've been thirty-seven years in the fleet. In three years they'll give me a desk in Nantucket and pretty servants to polish it. I might run for senator; there'd be money behind me. But however far I climb, I'll still have the International Patent Office looking over my shoulder. They're the masters of the game. Even though we're far beyond the Gas-Lit Empire, we can't escape them. Their fingerprints are all over you, Miss Barnabus. I want you to tell me why."

CHAPTER 4

The nations had been bound together for nearly two centuries. Weapons and technologies that might have harmed the common man had been outlawed. The wild horses of progress and innovation had been tamed. Out of this order grew the Gas-Lit Empire; the slow ripening fruit of an age of reason. If the International Patent Office was the price men paid, so be it.

Not that the common man understood the Patent Office. It made judgements on which technologies should be permitted, granting licences or withholding them as it saw fit. People might read of court cases in which it had adjudicated. But its workings were mysterious. Its agents operated in the shadows, feared but not understood. A common man might claim to have seen one, but never to have known him.

Elizabeth Barnabus was an uncommon woman. She knew a Patent Office agent and strove to understand him. But she could never openly speak of him. He was the reason she could not follow Julia to the Americas. His name was John Farthing.

"Our lives are all secrets," she'd said to him once. "Take away the secrets and nothing would remain." Whereon he kissed her, putting the impossibility of their forbidden passion beyond thought.

At first they'd met at Elizabeth's home. But there were

only so many visits that could be explained away. Then they changed to a guesthouse. This they used on only three occasions. The landlord was polite enough to Farthing. But whenever Elizabeth faced this same man alone, as she was obliged to do, there was disgust in his eyes. And then lechery.

"You don't understand," she said afterwards. "I'm not safe there. Not safe from him."

So it was that she came to create an illusion to present a different sin on which they could be judged. She went to the Leicester Backs dressed as a man, walking with a bad man's swagger. She asked at inns and ale houses if anyone knew of a room, quiet and out of the way, where a chap could hold a game of cards or dice without risk of the constabulary breaking it up. It must be discreet, she said. The gamblers would need to come and go without being overlooked. There was no shortage of such rooms for hire in the Backs.

She put down a guinea in advance.

"Possessions and money are also forbidden to me," Farthing told her, when it was arranged. "And gambling is the worst of it. It's the very symbol of avarice."

"I don't see why they should be forbidden."

"A man with no attachments can't be influenced," he said. "And a man who can't own anything is impossible to bribe. It's the burden carried by every servant of the Patent Office. It's the vow I took when I became an agent."

"Don't you hear the songs in the music halls?" Elizabeth asked. "Haven't you seen the cartoons? Not all agents are so upright."

"I know they laugh at us."

"They only laugh to hide their fear, John. Don't you understand? You make your own laws to suit your needs. That's what scares us. People disappear, and years later we find out they've been serving hard labour in a Patent Office prison and it's all been fair because you passed some new law to make it right."

"The Patent Office is bound by treaty. You know that. We can't pass the bounds the nations laid on us. And agents are bound by oath – poverty, honesty, secrecy, celibacy. If all we did was make horseshoes or sell insurance, then surely there'd be no need for such rules. But we hold the peace of the world in our care. We safeguard the wellbeing of the common man."

"Now you sound like a brochure."

"It's what I believe."

"Well," she said, "If money and carnal love are equally forbidden, you'll feel no more guilt being suspected of gambling than from being suspected of what we really do. And for me it will be better. Think how much worse they'd look on me if the truth were known. A man's sins are never so harshly seen."

"I doubt that," said Farthing.

"Then read the newspapers! Any one of them on any day. A man repents of a dalliance as easily as taking off his coat. A woman might as well try to remove her own skin."

John Farthing was completely unlike her in background, beliefs and temperament. He hailed from the mountains of Virginia, she from England's rolling hills. He'd been born into wealth. Her father had died in debtor's prison. They both believed in goodness and decency, but had different views about how such virtues were best served. Her life was woven from white lies and shadow. Law and truth had been his first love.

"We could escape," she said to him one day.

"Where to?"

"Aren't there forests and mountains in Virginia? I've heard you can walk for a month and not meet another soul."

He held her tighter. "You can't escape from your own self," he said.

• • •

Months passed and the journey to the rendezvous became part of the rhythm of her life. Dressed as a man, carrying a carpet bag, which bumped against her leg with every other step, she made her way from the omnibus into the Backs. The trick, she knew, was to walk the centre of the road, to tap loudly on the cobblestones with the tip of her cane, to let her shoulders roll with each step. And though her frame was slight beneath the jacket and trousers, she knew better than to think small thoughts. Clothes may make the man, but the set of his mind makes him doubly.

The side passage around the alehouse was so narrow that in one place she had to sidestep to protect the carpet bag from grating on the dirty bricks. The flagstones were greasy and a fetid smell seemed to ooze from the walls. At the end of it she turned a sharp corner, entering a courtyard so dark that she had to reach out from memory to find the rickety hand rail that would guide her up a flight of exterior steps to the door of the room itself.

A candle burned on the card table. As she stepped inside, John Farthing rose from one of the five unmatched chairs that surrounded it.

It had not gone well the first time he'd seen her dressed as a man. But a routine had grown between them. Now he turned his back without her asking. She opened the carpet bag and began the transformation in reverse, removing the top hat, unpinning her hair, wiping the makeup from her face, laying her clothes and binding cloth on the card table and slipping a dress of simple cotton directly over her chemise.

She could have done it in a few seconds; the quick-change act practised from childhood. But the longer time allowed her to feel her way into a role that was new. And to allow him to do the same. When it was complete, she stepped up behind him barefoot and silent. She lifted herself and kissed the back of his neck. He turned in her arms until her chest was pressed against his and her face was up against the collar of his coat. The scent and warmth of him began to play its usual tricks and she felt her body respond.

"You're late," he said.

She pulled away to look at him. "I thought I was being followed. I had to double back."

"I mean to say that I was worried."

"I can care for my own protection."

He held her shoulders, adding an inch or two to the distance between them. "You begrudge my instinct of care?"

She was on the brink of answering, and sharply, but at that moment caught sight of herself, as it were, and put her cheek against his shoulder once more. "Please hold me."

So he did, relaxing into her. She raised her face to his and they kissed.

There was no bed in the small room. But there were bolts on the door and curtains over the window glass. She unrolled a blanket on the boards, and for a time, the texture and scent of skin and its heat drove away all other consideration. For him too, it seemed.

They couldn't do everything that she desired. But she could feel the urgency in him. It stood close enough to what she really wanted that she didn't care to ask whether it was love or if the difference really mattered. It was enough that the marvel and mystery that was John Farthing was focussed entirely on her.

Afterwards she draped herself half over him, her ear resting on his chest, listening as his heartbeat slowed. She didn't mind the cold as her sweat dried. Idly she stroked his shoulder, her finger tracing the mark tattooed there, the same mark worn by every agent of the Patent Office. She would have been happy to hold him for longer, together with the illusion that all was well.

"Do you know what would happen if they found out?" he whispered.

"They won't."

"For a dalliance – one night with a stranger – I'd be reprimanded. A black mark on my record. For a repeated offence, I'd be transferred. They'd send me to another office in another part of the world. We'd never be able to see each other again. They'd stop any letters from you reaching me."

"Offence." The word tasted metallic to her.

"But if they found out there'd been subterfuge," he said, "like this… If they knew it had gone on over years – it would mean prison. And if there was a child…"

"They won't find out!"

He shifted, reaching for his shirt, which lay near. It had fallen from the card table. He knelt and began scratching at the shoulder where the grimy floorboards had left a streak of dirt.

Elizabeth held out her hand for it. "Here. Let me try."

But Farthing shook his head. "It won't come off."

CHAPTER 5

The whaling ship *Pembroke* had been claustrophobic, Captain Locklight's anger unpredictable and dangerous. But now, on the mother ship, Elizabeth faced a new threat. Standing in the wheelhouse, high above the portside hull, the commodore stared her down. He'd accused her of working for the International Patent Office, something she could neither deny nor admit.

Folds gathered deeper on his brow. "Well?" he said at last. "Are you their spy?"

"I'm here for my own reasons," she said. It was a slight truth, but she could risk no more.

He turned to look out through the glass.

The urgency with which she'd been called back to the fleet suggested terrible news would be waiting. Yet now he played it slow, like an interrogator, using her own impatience to open her up. It was a game she too could play. Deliberately relaxing her shoulders and the muscles of her face, she began to insert a pause between each breath. One second. Two seconds. Think of something other than the danger. Breathe again.

Stepping across to stand beside him, she waited.

The grey ocean far below seemed like a corded cloth. The swell, marvellously regular, progressed obliquely towards them, the wind whipping foam from some of the crests. The asymmetry of the ship was clear from this angle. The gap between the portside and middle hulls was wide and without paddlewheels, allowing space for ships to dock. As if to compensate, the paddlewheel on the outer bow of the portside hull was of great size, rising higher above the deck than the others. It was an ugly craft, though she couldn't help but feel awed.

The commodore put his mouth to the left-most speaking tube and said: "Forward one fifth." Into each of the others he said: "Dead slow."

There was no tilt or change in momentum that she could detect but she felt a vibration through the floor. By imperceptible degrees the mother ship began to turn. Not until the bow was perfectly facing the oncoming swell did he again bend to the speaking tubes.

"Ahead one eighth."

When each engine room had responded and the ship's course was steady once more, he stepped to the map table and leaned against it, as if needing its support.

"We're the servant of three masters, Miss Barnabus: the Company, the ocean, and the International Patent Office."

It felt as if she'd passed a test of some kind.

"Which master do we wait on?" she asked.

"It has been all three. But since you are the only one who can tell me what the Patent Office wants, and you won't speak, I'm left with just the two. I'm ordered by the Company to tell you certain things – on the condition that you not repeat them. Under any circumstances. Do you agree to this?"

"Yes."

Saying it came easily. The word held her to nothing and they both knew it. He would record it in his logbook, no doubt. She would deny it, if it came to an inquest. But still it was a contract of sorts and strangely seemed to bring them closer.

He straightened himself, as if against the indignity of old

age. "Very well," he said. "Five days ago the *Iceland Queen*, a whaler, and the gunboat *Mary May* were sitting in fog a few hundred miles southeast of here. Something happened and only the *Iceland Queen* came back."

"What something?"

"The *Mary May* was lost."

When, after a moment, he didn't elaborate, Elizabeth asked: "How many of the crew got back?"

"None. We lost ninety-eight souls."

Illogically, she found herself glancing around the empty wheelhouse, searching for confirmation. Nor was anyone on the gantry beyond the glass.

"This can't be known," the commodore said. "Not even by my officers. We've lost ships before – southern outliers. But we've been able to put those down to freak weather. There were no witnesses so we could believe what we liked. This time, the whole ship's company of the *Iceland Queen* saw it happen. All those men – desperate to tell anyone who'll listen."

"And what did they see?"

"Nothing that makes sense. The only thing I can say for sure is that the *Mary May* was attacked. It was overwhelmed in calm water. It didn't have time to fire a shot. We've had hostiles out there since before I was around. They congregate in warmer waters further south. They were nothing that could threaten us. I'm talking about ragged men, half-starving, on the run from the noose. A nation of eels.

"We caught three men once, adrift in an open boat. They claimed to have been living among islands of seaweed for almost a year, eating nothing but crayfish, begging for water from passing ships. We're armed well enough against such men. They're a danger only to each other.

"But those waters now hold something different, which we don't understand. If a gunboat can be taken, what chance a whaler? There's a new power at work out there."

"Then why keep this secret?"

"What do you suppose happens to the whale oil we produce?" he asked.

"Such as we don't use gets shipped back to Nantucket," she said.

"You've seen these ships heading home? You've seen their cargo holds?"

"No, sir."

"*No, sir,*" he echoed. "It was the way of things once. We still send back a few barrels for show. Other than that we burn every drop here. It keeps the engines turning. It shortens our supply lines. The Company makes its money from what the Patent Office pays. In return we're supposed to do marine research. That's why there's a scientific officer on every ship. But it's only for show. Our real job is to hold the North Atlantic.

"We're a corporation armed by charter. But that doesn't make us an army. My men will only follow my say if they think the money's worth the risk. They might sail into a storm on the promise of a fat catch. But there are odds beyond which the bravest'll turn back.

"If word spreads that we were facing a power that can snuff out our strongest gunboat, none of my captains will steam south. We wouldn't be able to do the one job we're properly paid for. It'd be the end of the North Atlantic fleet. The end of the Company. Our real mission here and our links with the Patent Office – these are secrets known by many of the senior staff. But none of them can know the fate of the *Mary May*.

"I've had to take extreme measures to keep the secret. I ordered the *Iceland Queen* to stand off the starboard bow – out of hailing range. But we caught a crewman trying to signal to her with hand semaphore. He claims to have got no reply. I have him locked in solitary just in case. And the *Iceland Queen* – she's now standing two miles out, so there can be no repeat of it.

"I don't trust you, Miss Barnabus. You're tangled with the Patent Office in some way I can't fathom. I don't like telling you these things. But two orders from the Board came with you. The first is that I'm to keep you informed of any attack, and to do so without delay. Your fifty-foot sperm whale was the price of that."

"Two orders?" she asked.

"Yes. If we're attacked, I'm to dispatch you to investigate. We wait only for the swell to diminish and the light to fade enough for me to risk bringing the *Iceland Queen* in close. You'll be riding out to her tonight. If the ocean permits."

Though her paddlewheels were vast, the mother ship was not designed for voyages from one port to another. Each of her three hulls had been built in a different shipyard. The two smaller hulls had been constructed in Marseille and Glasgow. The larger of the three with its giant paddlewheel came from the shipyard in Belfast.

Had it been an enterprise of the Gas-Lit Empire, they would doubtless have done something similar, spreading the enormous workload to three different member nations. But the mother ship belonged to the Company, which had no such political objectives. The construction method had been designed for speed. When the Company wanted something doing, it wanted it fast.

The most hazardous aspect of the build had been joining the three parts together. There was no dry dock big enough to lay the hulls side-by-side. They were brought into alignment on an early August day. But it wasn't until mid-September that the conditions were deemed calm enough to attempt the operation. Even then, with an offshore breeze and the water seemingly flat as a millpond, movement between the hulls was such that a cable snapped and one of the marine engineers lost his arm.

When at last it was done, the giant floating platform began its slow westward crawl. The newspapers of the world proclaimed it the greatest feat of engineering that had ever been accomplished; a wonder of the modern world to eclipse the Great Lighthouse of Alexandria.

It was not so much a ship, as an outpost of civilisation deep in the wilds. For although the borders of the Gas-Lit Empire – and therefore the borders of law – stretched a mere twenty miles from land, the mother ship, and the fleet that served it, had brought a kind of order to the mid-most heart of the ocean.

During its twenty-four years at sea, new structures had been built on the wide deck. Walking across it, Elizabeth tried to keep track of her position, triangulating with repeated glances back to the commodore's control room far above and behind. They had passed the centre of the ship already and were continuing towards the starboard hull.

One question, at least, had been settled. The officer who led her across the deck was no longer of unknown rank.

"My steward will take you," the commodore had said.

There was something curious about the way the man walked. She dropped back, the better to observe him. It was, she decided, the overly deliberate swing of the arms that marked him out; a small man's affectation. Though her own legs were shorter than most men's, she could match him stride for stride.

Why he'd been chosen as escort, she had no idea. Nor did she know where she was being taken, for the commodore had given no indication of it. Direct questions hadn't worked on the steward, so she tried a new angle.

"You didn't tell me your name."

At first she thought he'd blanked this question like all the others. But then they ducked inside through a watertight hatchway. He turned to her and said. "Watkins. My name is Watkins." Then he set off down a set of iron stairs. Oil lamps were suspended from hooks on the wall, as they might have been on any ship. But these hung still and steady as plumb lines.

The land sickness was passing now, though she'd left the rolling deck of the whaler less than two hours before. She no longer stumbled like a drunken sailor.

Steward Watkins kept up a brisk pace as they descended two more flights. She wondered if perhaps they were below the waterline. But then she remembered the extraordinary height that they had been above it. Everything about the mother ship was outsized.

"What's this part of the ship used for?" she asked.

He glanced back over his shoulder at her. "Officers' quarters."

"How many officers are there?"

"I can't reveal that."

Though his tone of voice was still as strident, she sensed he wasn't being deliberately obstructive.

"Is that a commercial secret?" she asked.

"Yes."

"How long have you been aboard?"

"Five years."

"And how often do you get back to shore?"

"I've been aboard five years."

As she was digesting this, he turned along a side passage. Following him, she saw that the way was blocked by two marine guards. One stepped forwards, his hand hovering near the sabre at his belt.

"Restricted area," he said.

"I'm on orders from the commodore," said Watkins.

"And him?"

"We're both on orders from the commodore. We're to see the prisoner."

She expected the guard to demand written proof, but he turned and led them to an iron door, which he unlocked.

Watkins said: "I'll be waiting outside. Just knock when you're done."

"But who am I to see?"

"The captain of the *Iceland Queen*."

CHAPTER 6

Elizabeth kept her emotions hidden as she walked up Churchgate from the omnibus stop, heading into the Leicester Backs. Tears would have looked wrong on the face of a man. Edging down the narrow walkway between grimy walls, her eyes began to prickle. But it was only as she stepped into the room above the ale house and bolted the door behind her that they welled up.

When she turned to face John Farthing he was already looking away, following the custom that had grown up between them.

She dried her face as she wiped away the makeup, but it wouldn't do. In the time it took her to cast off the male guise, her cheeks had become rivers again. Instead of dressing as a woman, she threw down the last intimate garments and stood naked.

Perhaps he'd heard the catch of her breath, because he was already turning as she launched herself towards him. Trusting the strength of his arms, she let herself drop.

He held her. "Elizabeth? My darling. What's wrong?"

She couldn't answer, but pressed her mouth to his. And then, though she hadn't thought to do it, she unbuckled his belt and reached for him. He returned the kiss, uncertainly at first, as if startled, but with more pressure as her tongue touched his. His fingers inched down the lines of muscle in her back, as if questioning.

She whispered: "Yes."

Beyond that there was no more uncertainty. Her abandon had set the same fire in him. For a time she disappeared, and so did her sorrow.

It would usually have been him who broke the moment. But this day would be different. He lay holding her, contented for once, his face pressed into her hair. His breath came slow and even. She focussed on the angle of her hip as it pressed on the hard floor, the coldness of the autumn air, a sulphurous tang of coal smoke from somewhere outside. She dug her thumbnail into the soft skin of her upper arm, focussing on the physical pain. But no discomfort would be enough.

When his sleep had deepened, she lifted his arm from across her shoulder and rolled free. Clothes were scattered. They'd crashed about on the table and a chair before grabbing the rug from the carpet bag and taking their place on the floor.

She slipped the chemise over her skin and was gathering the rest of her clothes when he spoke.

"What's wrong, Elizabeth?"

"Julia is dead."

She was surprised to hear her own words come out so flat and factual. She watched their meaning take hold of him; his puzzled expression, then shock, then concern. He scrambled to his feet and held her. This time she didn't relax into him.

"I'm so sorry," he said.

"I found out today. Her father sent a messenger."

She felt his hand caressing the back of her head. "What happened?"

"It was three weeks ago."

"In America?"

"On the journey. There was some kind of accident. She was flying on an airship, the *American Frontier*, and..."

She felt the tensing of his stomach, the hesitation, then the speeding up of his hand as it stroked her hair. And then the too deliberate relaxing as he tried to cover the tell. She prised herself free from his embrace. He gave her an expression of sympathy, but she knew him well enough to see through it.

"Tell me what you know!" she said.

"The airship went down."

"What else do you know about it?"

"Only what was in the newspapers. Elizabeth, what are you..."

"It wasn't in the papers!" she snapped, not letting him finish. "I went to the library and searched. All they printed were obituaries for the dead. It was all vague – as if no one wanted to report it straight. And no article about the accident itself."

Farthing looked to the floorboards. "Then I must have heard people talking."

"Agents of the Patent Office?"

"Elizabeth, I can't always be open about what I hear. There are secrets I'm bound to keep."

"John Farthing! We're talking about Julia. My dearest friend in the world. If you know something about her death, you will tell me now!"

He turned his face away, as if by the force of a slap. "I'm bound by oath of office... to not speak of certain things."

"What about celibacy?" She knew the damage her words were doing, but couldn't stop. "Wasn't that an oath as well?"

He reached behind him for the support of a chair, then slumped down onto it. She held her breath. He lowered his face.

When he spoke, his voice was muffled by his hands. "There's a case open that involves the downing of the *American Frontier*. There'll be a file but I haven't seen it. I didn't know Julia was a passenger. I'm so sorry."

"How did she die?"

"I just don't know."

"But could you find out?"

He sat there, naked, still not meeting her eyes. "It's a different department."

"Get me the file," she said.

"I'm not supposed to have access."

"Bring it to me. I need to see it. Steal it if you must!"

Elizabeth took her time walking to the Swain household, a place of rose bushes, bay windows and neat brickwork on the hill overlooking the canal. She'd been dreading her first meeting with Julia's grieving parents.

Mr Swain welcomed her in the tiled hallway. He said a few words, which she couldn't afterwards remember. The sense of them was that he was sorry for any loss that she herself might have suffered in the tragedy. Then he took himself away to his workshop, his back held perfectly upright, his each step brittle. The maid showed her through to the drawing room, where Mrs Swain sat venting grief, as if tears were a medicine that might cure the world of pain.

Afterwards, not ready to return home, Elizabeth found a place next to the canal, away from the bustle of the wharf. There she sat, staring at the dancing reflections of trees on the far bank. A group of townsfolk came cycling along the towpath, laughing at some joke they'd shared. They didn't seem to notice her. As they passed, she felt the urge to call out to them, to tell them that Julia had died. The most true, honest, bright and joy-filled woman that they might ever have met was now gone. They would never have the chance to know her. But she held her tongue and she held her tears and then they were gone.

A rustling in the grass made her turn. It was Tinker, barefoot again; the boy could never keep a pair of shoes for long. He sat next to her, chin resting on knees. She'd been hiding her sorrow from him. He was just a scrap of a boy, after all. He'd been through enough of his own suffering before latching onto her as a surrogate parent. He had no business sharing the darkness that lay in her mind and heart.

"What shall we make for dinner?" she asked, food being his chief concern.

Instead of answering, he leaned over, laying his head in her lap. He took her hand and made it stroke his hair, until she would do it with her own strength, whereon he let go and she began to cry. He'd always had a way of seeing to the truth of her.

The days passed slowly after that. There was no body, so there could be no grave nor a funeral in the ordinary sense. The congregation of the Secular Hall had donated money for a memorial plaque. A meeting was scheduled to celebrate Julia's short life. Mr and Mrs Swain, each in their own way, threw themselves into organising. Having something practical to do seemed to bring them together. But whenever Elizabeth saw them, she felt the burden of the things she couldn't say. They might busy themselves with caterers and invitations. But there was more to be known, beyond the simple fact of the tragedy. And secrets had always been Elizabeth's domain.

And then, ten days into the turmoil of unresolved loss, a messenger arrived with a card written in John Farthing's hand: *I have it. Come now.*

It was evening by the time she reached the Leicester Backs but the sun had yet to dip below the roofscape. Two crows sat on the ridge tiles of the latrine roof. They watched as Elizabeth climbed the steps to the room above the ale house. She had never before come so early to the rendezvous. Inside, the south-facing wall radiated heat into the room. The windows were all sealed shut with old paint.

"Did you bring it?" she asked.

John Farthing wouldn't say anything until the door had been closed and bolted.

She'd expected the report on the downing of the airship *American Frontier* to be properly bound; a leather volume perhaps. But three box files lay open on the card table. Two of them were full of papers, the third half full. She flicked through one of the piles. Most were loose sheets but some had been pinned together. She sat, still dressed as a man, and tried to force her jittery focus onto the documents. At first he paced behind her, the floorboards creaking under his feet. Then he took one of the chairs and dragged it back to the corner near the door and sat.

She pulled out a sheet on which background data had been laid out. Twenty airships shuttled the North Atlantic every week, it said; more than that near the end of the financial year. Their main cargos were businessmen and information. It was the safest method of travel, and by far the quickest.

Accidents had been common in the early years of the twentieth century. But the technology of flight had developed, within limits set by the International Patent Office. Attention to detail had improved; the checking and rechecking of engines, the training of pilots and the precautionary principle in weather forecasting. In the final decade of the century no airships had been lost.

The raw data had been tabulated in fine copperplate on the following pages. Elizabeth brought her head closer to the table. It was written in brown ink, the lines closely spaced, which made for difficult reading. She placed the sheets side by side on the table, trying not to think about her lover just behind her. His chair creaked as he shifted.

Faithful to his promise, he'd borrowed the report from the Patent Office filing room. Stolen would have been the better word, but the plan was to get it back in place before anyone noticed it was missing. She knew it was distressing him. The betrayal of the vow sat like a heavy chain across his shoulders. Thinking of his pain began to overwhelm her, so she wrenched her mind back to her own raw wound, the death of Julia Swain, her dearest friend.

The chart on the table showed columns for the nationalities of airship, weather conditions at the time of loss, the manufacturers and model numbers of the engines, a demographic breakdown of casualties and more. Decades had been scored out as rows. At first she could make no sense of it. It appeared to show a single loss in the 1980s, no losses in the 1990s and three losses in the 2000s. But there were seven losses listed at the bottom of the chart that she could at first make no sense of. Then she realized that all seven had come in the two years since 2010. The *American Frontier* was the last of them.

Name:AS *American Frontier*
Date:12th/13th April 2012
Weather: Assumed fair
Visibility: Assumed good
Altitude:8,000 feet
Passengers: 40
Crew:8
Airship status: Total loss
Witnesses: None
Cause of loss: Unknown
Survivors: Nil

Farthing's voice broke her concentration. "If you plan to read every line, we'll still be here tomorrow," he said.

"You stole it for me. Shouldn't I read it?"

She knew her words would be poison to him, but couldn't stop them.

"It's not like a book," he said. "You don't work through it from page one. And even if you did, you wouldn't understand."

"But you do?"

"I do now. I've had to piece the clues together. These things aren't widely known, even among agents."

"Tell me what happened to my friend!"

"Her airship came down."

A fist of pain tightened around Elizabeth's chest. It had been holding her since the news came of Julia's death. For an hour she might forget. But it was always ready to renew its grip should she be reminded of her loss.

Farthing, sitting behind, wouldn't be able to see her anguish.

"The *American Frontier* disaster isn't the only subject of this report," he said. "Not precisely. It's about the Gas-Lit Empire and what will happen to it. The Patent Office isn't just agents and law courts. There are people you don't see: future-casters, who tell the judges which technology should be allowed and which forbidden. These papers come from their department."

She turned to face him. "Why are you telling me this? I need to know what happened to Julia!"

"This is the only way I can explain it," he said. "I'm so sorry."

He should have said something arrogant. Elizabeth wanted to lash out and he was denying her. John Farthing just sat looking at his hands, which lay interlocked in his lap. She took a breath, trying to calm herself.

"Then what do future-casters do? Do they predict the future?"

"No one can do that. Their job is to identify moments of uncertainty."

"Everything's uncertain."

"No. The future can't be predicted. But that's not true

for uncertainty itself. Think of this: there's a high chance of the government in Carlisle being the same tomorrow as it is today. One of the guardians might die, though it's unlikely. We could predict the chance of that happening in any given day, but not the outcome if it did. There'd be an election. It might even change the balance of the government. But these changes aren't usually important. They modify the detail. But the system is the same. In twenty years time, who would even remember?

"When the Gas-Lit Empire was first formed, the world was all chaos. But as more nations joined, peace and stability spread. We came to the Long Quiet. It's then that the science of future-casting began. The future-casters never tried to say what would happen tomorrow. It's been their task to chart scenarios in which degrees of certainty about the future fall away to nothing."

"Chart?" she asked.

"Yes."

"They're making a map?"

"Of a kind, yes. They're making a map of future situations where the equilibrium of the world could flip. Moments beyond which we can't see. It's called the Map of Unknown Things."

When he'd started, his words had been laboured, as if each sentence had to break his vows afresh. But as the discourse developed, he'd spoken with more conviction. Now it was a flood. The dam of secrecy was being washed clear.

"Consider what might the world be like if we'd not done this."

"Full of marvellous inventions," she snapped, frustrated at not getting the information she needed.

"Full of war machines," he said.

"Have you seen this map?"

"It isn't something that can be drawn out on a sheet of

paper. It's vast, continually updated and maintained; an equation of mathematics, economics, history and psychology. It identifies scenarios of danger. These are given to the judges and agents. We use our influence to steer the world away from them, maintaining the Long Quiet."

The tension of concentration had become almost unbearable. She'd asked for answers to a question that she didn't understand. He was placing pieces of a completely different puzzle in front of her. She stood, knocking over her chair. He flinched as it crashed to the floorboards.

She started pacing. Five steps took her from the hot sunbaked wall to the north-facing one. She touched her forehead to the bricks, focussing on what little coolness they had to offer.

"Will you please tell me what this file means."

"I'm so sorry for your loss," he said. "If I could change anything, I would. But this file is about more than that. The downing of the *American Frontier* has pushed the world towards something that mustn't be allowed to happen. At any cost.

"When the future-casters work through their predictions, there's one scenario they keep coming back to – the most impenetrable future, where certainty falls away to nothing. That scenario is this – communications are cut between Europe and America. It's the biggest unknown in the Map of Unknown Things. The most dangerous moment in history."

"I thought the Patent Office had ended history!" Again, her words came out too sharp.

"Listen to me, Elizabeth! If the Gas-Lit Empire fell, the world would be plunged into a perpetual war."

"You contradict yourself. You said you couldn't predict the future!"

"We predict change. What can peace change to but war?"

"How can you know it would be perpetual?"

"Can you name a year before the coming of the Great Quiet when there wasn't war in the world? We've protected you from that for almost two centuries. We've steered you away from the unknown things."

"You? We?"

"You're still not listening! Airships are going down over the Atlantic. We can't intervene because it's beyond our mandate to operate outside the Gas-Lit Empire. We're impotent. And if air travel were to be cut, we'd be blind as well."

"So what happened to Julia? What happened to these other airships?"

"They were shot down."

"At eight thousand feet?"

"Some were flying even higher. It seems impossible. But, unregulated, technology is always turned to the science of destruction. Weapons are being developed out there beyond our power to stop them. We don't understand what they are. But they threaten to cut Europe from America.

"The waters near the middle of the North Atlantic Gyre have for over a hundred years been home to renegade sailors. Pirates, you might call them. Away from the trade routes, they could exist, no trouble to the Gas-Lit Empire, constantly fighting each other. When news of them dried up some twenty years ago, we assumed they'd finally torn each other to pieces. Now it seems we were wrong. A single warlord has come to ascendency. A floating nation has been born. News dried up because all our informers had been neutralised.

"We've tried to place spies since then. All but one were killed."

"How do you know they were killed?"

"From the one spy they didn't find. We learned of the others from her report."

It took a moment for the significance of the word to hit home. "Her?"

"Yes," he said. "All the men we sent were killed. The floating nation is entirely female. They allow no men to live."

At first, she couldn't speak. The world he was describing was so different from anything she could have imagined that she found herself doubting him. She searched his face but found only sorrow.

"Their barbarism is no reflection on your sex, Elizabeth. The wilds make animals of all who live there. Men and women."

"Then Julia might be alive?"

"She'd have had to survive the airship coming down."

"Send me," Elizabeth said. "You must send me as a spy!"

John Farthing shook his head. "You have no idea what chaos lives out there. It would mean your death. I cannot think of it!"

"But the woman you sent survived! Please, you must help me go there. Ask your masters in the Patent Office. I can be their spy."

"Our spy sent just one message. Then she was gone as well. You cannot go. I couldn't bear to lose you."

CHAPTER 7

Deep in one of the three bellies of the mother ship, Elizabeth stepped into the cabin where the captain of the *Iceland Queen* was being held. The door closed, plunging her into near darkness. The only thing she could see was the tiny yellow bud of an oil lamp flame. And then, as her eyes adjusted, she made out its reflection in the wood panelling behind it.

There was a creaking sound; a man turning on a cot, she thought. She blinked, trying to clear her vision. A hand reached from the shadow and turned up the wick of the lamp. As the flame grew, she saw him swing out his legs and sit. His face came into the light, sallow and gaunt.

"Scientific Officer Barnabus," she said, holding out her hand.

"Captain Woodfall," said the man, not taking it. "What's your ship?"

"It was the whaling ship *Pembroke*, sir. But I'm recalled. Tonight they're sending me to the *Iceland Queen*."

He was on his feet before the words were fully out of her mouth. In two paces he'd crowded her back against the door. "What business have you on my ship? And why am I held prisoner?"

"How long have they kept you here?" she asked, trying not to let her fear show.

"Two days. No. Dear Gods, I can't keep track! It's three. I came aboard to pass my report." His voice had grown stronger, filling the cabin. "Where's the *Iceland Queen*?"

"Standing two miles out," she said.

"Why've they put me in here? No one will say. And now they send me a scientific officer!" He lifted the lamp from its hook and held it close to her face. "A disfigured one at that. Is this for humiliation? Tell me!"

She felt for the door handle behind her. Steward Watkins should be standing out there with the marine guards. But Captain Woodfall's anger was already ebbing. He sighed and turned away. Elizabeth took a breath to steady herself.

"You scared the commodore," she said. "Whatever it was you told him, he doesn't want others to know. But you're to tell me."

"How can he want to keep me quiet *and* send you to hear it?"

"If you won't tell me, you won't," she said. "But I'm as lost as you. And as alone."

"Make them let me out!" he said.

"You think I have that power?"

"I don't know what you are," he said. "But the only power they've left me is to choose to speak or to hold my tongue."

Elizabeth was tired. Such sleep as she'd had the night before had been uneasy. Through the transfer to the mother ship and the interview with the commodore, her heart had been pumping hard. Captain Woodfall's anger had given it another boost. But now, in the dark, stuffy cabin with his aggression turned maudlin, weariness reached up from her stomach.

"Should I go?" she asked.

When he didn't answer, she edged past him and lowered herself onto the cot.

He seemed suddenly unsure of himself, like a boxer whose

opponent climbs out of the ring without a punch being thrown.

"What's the weather doing?" he asked.

"It's clouded over. But there was sunshine this morning."

"Is it not morning still?"

"It's two in the afternoon," she said.

He put down the lamp. The cot creaked under him as he sat next to her.

"Visibility's fair," she said. "They told me it was ten miles this morning. Though I couldn't say for my own part."

He stared at the floor. The silence gathered around them. She waited, sensing the pregnancy of the moment. There was a water jug and bowl on the stand opposite. A shaving brush lay next to them.

"How's the ocean?" he asked, at last.

"First thing, there were white tops on some of the waves. The wind's dropped since then."

"I wish I could feel it," he said. "And see the horizon."

"How many heard you talk to the commodore?" she asked.

Captain Woodfall shook his head. "There'd been no position report from the *Mary May*. He must have known something was wrong. He'd sent the officers out before I got there. His chief concern was to find a story to cover the truth. We agreed to tell them that the *Mary May* had been sent back to Southampton for engine repair. And the *Iceland Queen* had fever onboard and would be quarantined.

"That must have been all he wanted – for the officers to hear me say it. Because no sooner was it done than he set his steward to bring me here. I was to wash and rest, he said. But when I tried to leave I found they'd locked the door.

"Are you really a scientific officer?"

"No."

"Then tell me what you are."

"I can't."

"Hell's teeth, man! Will you not try to give me cause to trust you!"

He wanted to tell the rest of his story. She could sense it. He was close to giving it all.

"How much food is there on the *Iceland Queen*?" she asked.

For a moment he made no answer. But she could see the thoughts turning in his head. He sat straighter. "It's water that'll run out first. We had twelve days' supply. Less the time I've been here. That makes nine."

"Then that's all the time the commodore's got. After that the secret turns sour. He'll have to bring her in. Or send her back to port. Either way, there'll be no point keeping you locked in here."

Captain Woodfall rubbed his face, as if he were a man trying to sober up. She could hear the rasp of his palms against stubble.

"Unless it rains," he said. "How's the barometer?"

"It's set fair," she said. And then: "Where were you when the ship was lost?"

"Three hundred and twenty miles southeast of the fleet." This came in the same quiet tone, though it was the first real information he'd offered.

"The commodore said you were in fog?"

"Yes. It started out as a haze. But through the afternoon…"

"What?"

He turned to face her. "Who are you really?"

"I'm someone who'll help you if I can. But I need to know what you saw. Why were you in that part of the ocean?"

"Hunting minke whales. We'd had sightings down there."

"And why was there a gunboat with you?"

"There often is when we head to those parts. Commodore's orders. You can't have sailed south yourself or you'd know that."

"I haven't," she owned.

"Then have you sailed in fog, Mr Barnabus? Thick fog?"

"Yes."

"So you know the way it swirls, like a living thing? Whoever you really are."

"Yes," she said.

"Icebergs can be carried so far south. It's rare, but in the fog you get to thinking that every shadow's a wall of ice. The whole crew comes up on deck, but for the engineers."

"I know," she said. "You don't want to wait below for the sound of the hull being split."

"So you are a sailor," he said.

"Not a real one."

"A spy then. Are you working for the Patent Office?"

"The commodore believes I am."

"Is he right?"

"Not entirely."

Captain Woodfall took in a deep breath and let it out slowly. "You've given me little enough, Mr Barnabus. But I've a feeling you'll be as much a piece of grit to the commodore and to those bastards at the Patent Office as you are to me."

"Does that mean you'll tell me what you saw?"

He nodded. "But it'll bring you no good.

"We were in fog. Thick and reeling. We'd had no sight of the horizon for an hour. The only fixed thing was the *Mary May*. One moment it clears and her deck cannons come into view. Then another billow rolls in and all you can do is listen for her. Even our own ship's bell sounds muffled, like it's coming from under the water.

"And there's something happening. One of the starboard lookouts calls me over and points down at the water. He's seen a shadow, he says, though he can't tell me what it was. A movement is all he can say.

"Everyone's crowding over to look. Someone shouts that there's a whale passing below. So we all rush over to see it come out from under the port side. For a second I see it too – a great grey shape heading towards the *Mary May*, and bubbles rising from it. But the fog closes about us and it's just white after that, droplets of water drifting in front of our eyes.

"I hear a noise, then. A dull boom, like an explosion in a deep mine. The wind turns back towards us and it brings the sound of screaming men. A window opens in the fog and I see the outline of the *Mary May*. Her stern has tilted clear of the ocean. Water must have been rushing into her, because the full length of the ship starts to slide under. I just watch it happen. I don't know what to say or do. Then she and all her crew have gone under."

He stopped speaking as abruptly as he'd started. One of Elizabeth's hands was gripping the blanket beneath her. She realised she'd been holding her breath. "The commodore made me think it was pirates," she said.

Captain Woodfall's voice dropped to a whisper. "The commodore wasn't there. It was a sea monster that took the *Mary May*. It dragged her down to hell."

Whatever the truth of his story, there was a sickness hanging heavy in the air of Captain Woodfall's cabin. Once out of it and on the deck, Elizabeth breathed deeply, trying to clear the last traces from her lungs. Then she begged to be taken closer to the edge of the deck, where she could see the swell as it rolled in steadily from the southwest. The wind had dropped and there were no more white crests.

Impatient as ever, Steward Watkins allowed her less than a minute before urging her on. "We'll get you across to the *Iceland Queen* tonight," he said. "If it's no worse than this." He then escorted her belowdecks, following a confusing path, which she quickly gave up trying to remember.

"How do you find your way?" she asked.

"By seeing clearer than you." This he said quietly, though

there was no one else to hear.

She was about to ask what he meant by it, but he threw in an extra step, pulling ahead and shifting to the centre of the narrow corridor, leaving her no option but to follow behind.

They were descending, she knew that much. But each corridor and stairway looked the same.

"Where are you taking me?" she asked.

He stopped in front of a door bearing the number 253, which had been stencilled in yellow paint.

"We're here."

"Where?"

"Your trunk is already inside. You'll find water and soap."

"What about food?"

"I don't know about that."

"You're a steward!"

The word seemed to sting him. "I'm the commodore's steward."

He opened the door and stepped to one side so that she could enter. It was a bare cabin with no porthole. They were below the waterline, she thought. Iron plates made up the walls. A double line of rivets ran from floor to ceiling. Another line ran horizontally across the hull wall at eye level. Her trunk lay in the middle of the floor; next to it, a washing jug and folded cloth. She turned just in time to see Steward Watkins closing the door. And then she was alone.

Unlike her cabin on the *Pembroke*, the door had no bolts. She hefted her trunk across to block it. There was nothing to wedge it against. But it would give her warning if someone tried to get through. Perhaps five seconds' grace, if they were determined.

The heat and tightness of the binding cloth across her chest had left her feeling unclean. Once she boarded the *Iceland Queen*, there was no telling how long it would be before she had the privacy to strip again. So she took the risk, straining to hear any sound in the corridor as she poured water and washed the sweat from her skin.

Captain Woodfall had seen the *Mary May* lost with all its men. That much was the truth, she thought. But the story of a monster seemed more the dream of an unsettled mind. Indeed, any person of sensibility would be unsettled by the cries of a doomed crew. The rest of it, he could have imagined. That didn't explain how the ship had been lost. But it enabled her to push the madness of his vision from her mind.

Feeling cleaner, she dried herself, wrapped the binding cloth and dressed.

Through the whole process there'd been no sounds from the passageway. Unblocking the door, she turned the handle and peered through the crack, opening it inch by inch until the steward's face appeared directly in front of her.

"Yes?"

"I didn't know you were here," she said.

"Evidently."

"I'm finished now. Washed, I mean."

"And?"

"I should like to take a turn around the deck."

"That's out of the question."

Elizabeth opened the door fully and tried to pass him, but he sidestepped, blocking her way.

"Commodore's orders," he said. "What do you really want? I don't trust you."

She couldn't tell him her reason for wanting to explore. But saying nothing felt dangerous. She sensed an acuteness of perception in Steward Watkins, which was beyond anything she'd encountered in the other sailors.

"Must you stand here all the while?" she asked. "It'll be five hours till sundown."

He didn't answer, but folded his arms and met her stare.

It was Elizabeth who looked away first. Though he was slight, she couldn't risk trying to force her way through. If they grappled, he'd discover her secret quickly enough. She had tricks and illusions to escape from most traps, but the bare cabin offered nothing to help her.

"I need to eat," she said, trying another tack.

He shook his head. "I'm sorry."

"I have a medical condition," she said, warming to the lie.

This seemed to disquiet him. He glanced down the passageway, as if fearing someone might overhear.

"If you keep me without food, I could faint. It could kill me."

"These are my orders."

"You'd be responsible. What would the commodore say when you told him?"

"But I can't leave you here."

"Then take me with you. We can go to the galley together."

When she saw the flicker of relief in his eyes, she knew she'd won the first battle.

Several galleys were needed to feed the crew of the mother ship. But at that time in the afternoon, the fastest service would be had in the starboard hull, according to Steward Watkins. And getting the excursion over with quickly was clearly a priority. Before, he'd been content to walk in front of her, but now he hovered close and a few inches behind. She experimented by tilting one shoulder a fraction, as if readying herself to run. His hand darted out.

"What are you doing?" she asked, as if offended.

"I'm sorry. I thought..." His hand dropped to his side.

The tallest of the above-deck structures had been built on the mother ship's portside hull. Those on the starboard hull were less extensive. The central hull had been sparsely built on by comparison. As they approached it, Elizabeth scanned the superstructure for doorways. She could see none, but there were access hatchways in the deck itself, for the purpose of maintenance, she supposed.

"How many crew do you have?" she asked.

"It varies."

"Are there sleeping quarters in all of the hulls?"

He took a moment before answering. "There are."

"Even the central hull?"

"Why does it matter?"

"It doesn't."

Having passed through a gap between two of the central structures, they continued on over the wide deck towards the starboard side. The buildings of the starboard hull came between her and the sun. Details which had been obscured in the glare now became clear. Some parts were painted orange, others white or green. A gang of sailors were hard at work, scrubbing and mopping one of the upper decks. Black smoke drifted forwards from two great chimneys. The ship could be making little headway, if any.

"What about you?" she asked. "Where's your cabin?"

"I... That is to say, I'm billeted near the commodore."

"And where is he stationed?"

"He has rooms in each of the hulls."

"One man has many rooms?"

"You wouldn't understand. He never sleeps for more than two hours. He barely rests at all. But if there is a cot nearby, sometimes he can be persuaded."

There was something in the way Steward Watkins said this that caused Elizabeth to turn. He maintained a rigid forward gaze. Who was it that persuaded the commodore, she wondered.

"Through here," he said. And then: "What is your medical condition?"

"Hunger," she said.

• • •

On the whaling ship, when mealtime was called, those crew not on watch would crowd together below decks, holding out pewter plates and mugs. The cook and his assistant would ladle out the stew or pudding and slosh the spiced tea, bitter and sweet. Then the jostle of conversation would die as all set to the important task of eating.

The canteen of the mother ship could not have been more different. Knots of men sat eating and talking in low voices. Five great copper pans steamed at the side of the room. Elizabeth peered into them. The first four she recognised as savoury foods. The fifth smelt powerfully of oranges.

"Tell them what you want," Steward Watkins said.

So she pointed and watched as a cook's assistant filled a plate.

"Put it on my account," said Watkins.

The cook's assistant nodded and noted something down in a ledger. Behind him was a serving hatch, and beyond that more copper pans in a wide galley. Standing between two of them was the ship's boy. He was staring intently at her. She met his gaze and made the slightest of nods. Then he was gone.

She seated herself on a bench before a narrow table. Steward Watkins sat facing her.

"Must you pay for your food?" she asked.

"Of course."

"And you can come here any time?"

"When you're not on duty. Now eat. I wouldn't want you to get ill." This he said in an arch tone, as if he was beginning to doubt her story.

So she dipped in her spoon and began. The meal, potato and fish chowder, tasted better than anything she'd eaten in months. The mother ship was more frequently supplied than the rest of the fleet, even though it remained far from land. In a sense, the mother ship *was* a piece of land – or a substitute for one.

She tilted her plate to scoop up the last of the juices. "Thank you."

"For what?"

"You paid for it. It's on your account."

"The commodore's account," he said. And then: "We'd better get you back to that cabin."

"Why the hurry?"

"Orders."

"Hasn't this been some little diversion for you? Better surely than standing in that passageway."

"Indeed no! You ask questions all the time. It puts me on edge. All of the time."

"I don't believe my questions disturb you," she said. "It's the answers you're afraid you might let slip. But I'll offer you this deal – you walk me around the deck and talk to me about whatever feels safe. I'll ask no more questions."

"If I knew what was safe all this would be easy."

"Then let's walk in silence. I've been confined in a whaling ship. And now there's an expanse of deck wide enough to play a game of ball. One time around the outside and I'll be satisfied."

"I can't disobey the commodore."

It seemed unnatural to leave her dirty plate and cup on the table. But Watkins indicated that it was the thing to do. In leaving she glanced back and saw the cook's assistant gathering them up.

The shadows had grown longer whilst she had been eating. She crossed the decking between the starboard and centre hulls without once feeling the sun on her back. Steward Watkins had begun to inch ahead in his eagerness to have her in the cabin once more. He had already begun to step into the gap between two of the central buildings when she turned aft. He jolted after her.

"What are you doing?"

"Going by a different way."

He seemed ready to make a grab for her. She felt the balance of authority wavering between them. If he did launch towards her she would have to put out an arm for him to grab. Even then he might be able to feel through the disguise. No man would have wrists so delicate.

She took a step backwards. He followed. It seemed he too was reluctant to grapple. She turned and set off in her chosen direction. He fell into step behind. She breathed more easily again. Whilst she remained outside, there was a chance for her to see that ship's boy again.

He had been there in the crowd of sailors who had hauled her free from the cargo net. And he'd been there in the galley. He would surely have followed them out. She glanced around, eyes seeking out the doorways and deeper shadows.

They had reached the end of the superstructure above the central hull. Steward Watkins shifted closer to her shoulder, edging her around towards the port side of the ship once more. Hearing the metallic squeak of a hinge she glanced behind her. There was no boy to be seen. But there was an open doorway and a small hand, beckoning.

"What's that?" she asked, pointing in the opposite direction.

And when Steward Watkins turned, too polite to not look along her arm, she stepped back in the direction of the beckoning hand and was through the doorway before he could react. The door slammed closed, shutting out the sunlight. There was a screech of something heavy being pushed across the metal floor. Then a child's sticky hand grabbed hers and she found herself pulled deeper into the dark.

CHAPTER 8

Having informed all who might notice her absence that she was visiting relatives, Elizabeth set out south for the Big Smoke. The one person she hadn't spoken to about the trip was John Farthing. But he was away on Patent Office business and they weren't due to meet for another ten days. That would give her time enough to make the journey and be back without him ever needing to know. Unless her offer was accepted. In which case, she would have to face the ordeal of telling her lover she'd betrayed him.

But not yet.

The address she'd been sent proved to be a smart Georgian townhouse near the Strand. The number 67 moulded in blacked iron had been affixed to the door, but she could find no name plaque. Perhaps the neighbours had guessed the purpose of the building from the comings and goings. If so, they would surely have shuddered. But a passerby would never know that number 67 belonged to the International Patent Office.

She pulled the bell handle and heard the jangling inside. There was barely time for her to step back and glance up at the frontage of the building before the door was opened by an elderly gentleman dressed in charcoal grey.

"Elizabeth Barnabus," she said.

He nodded and made room for her to step inside.

The house proved deeper than she'd expected. The doorman led her along a doglegged corridor, then up a narrow staircase. They would once have been servants' stairs, she thought. The Patent Office owned many buildings scattered across the land. Most, like this, were anonymous. And their functions were a mystery.

The doorman left her in a wood-panelled room, sparsely furnished but with a luxury of height and ornamental plasterwork around the edges of the ceiling. Looking out from the window she saw a flagstoned yard. Two fruit trees had been trained espalier style over one of the garden walls.

The click of the door opening made her turn. A younger man stepped inside, also dressed in charcoal grey. His red hair and apple complexion seemed too exuberant for his clothes.

"Thank you for coming, Miss Barnabus," he said, offering a plump hand, which she took.

"You have me at a disadvantage."

"You may call me Agent Sorren."

"Thank you for seeing me, Mr Sorren."

"Not at all. Service is our duty and a pleasure."

This was disingenuous. No ordinary citizen could expect such an audience. Indeed, few would want one. The International Patent Office might have been established to safeguard the interests of the common man. But its powers were wide and its agents haughty. Working from the shadows, they were supposed to use their powers only to stifle unseemly sciences and cultivate peace. But power and shadows do not mix well.

"We found your letter in the general pile," Agent Sorren said. "It could easily have been missed."

"I sent four," she said.

"Ah. Well, quite. If you'd addressed them to a named individual, all would certainly have been seen. You did once have a case officer. Two years ago. An Agent John Farthing?"

"I didn't want to involve him."

"Indeed." He nodded, still smiling, though she thought the expression false. "No matter," he said. "You'll understand we get many strange letters; offers of help from psychics and priests. The asylums are full of people who believe themselves the very centre of the world. Such men are drawn to us."

"Well, they would be," she said.

"But your letter was different. I'd be grateful if you could tell me what you know of the airship *American Frontier*."

"My friend was on it."

"Forgive me. I should have offered my condolences from the start. But people die in accidents every day. Their friends seldom believe the truth of things is being hidden. What set you to such a proposition?"

"There have been seven airship disasters in two years," she said. "The same number as in the fifty years that came before."

"That's a remarkable statement, Miss Barnabus. How did you come by your information?"

"I read it. In a newspaper."

"It wasn't in the newspapers."

"How strange," she said.

His eyes were disconcertingly pale and steady. The moment stretched.

"Have you told anyone else about your... research?"

It was a dangerous question. "One," she said. "A lawyer in New York. The husband of my dear friend who was lost."

"Ah. Indeed?"

They had not moved since shaking hands. Though in close proximity, she could detect no scent from Agent Sorren. No perfume. No body odour. No remnant of soap or tobacco.

"We have a file on you," he said, indicating its thickness by the spread of his thumb and finger. "I read it, of course, in preparation for meeting you. I must confess, there was something in it that I found hard to believe. And harder still now having met you. It stated that you are able to effect the likeness of a young man."

She felt her mask of composure turning brittle. Julia had known the secret of her double identity. And Tinker, the boy had seen through it. But it was only John Farthing who could have told the Patent Office. The feeling of betrayal made her stomach clench.

Agent Sorren's pale gaze was fixed on her. She turned her back on him and stepped to the window, trying to get her breathing back under control.

"You've been in and out of our interest for many years," he said. "And your father before you. I must confess, I'd been expecting someone less well presented. You were raised in a travelling show. Yet you carry yourself like a respectable citizen. There's much in your history that I don't understand. But enough that I do. You're a singular woman, resourceful and intelligent. So when you write to us offering help, it's clear you're not just another escapee from the asylum. And being able to appear as a man could perhaps make it possible."

She unclenched her hands. The palms were slick with sweat. "Do you want my help or not?"

"Perhaps. But if we were to accept it without knowing where you obtained your information – this would be a concern."

"I read it in a newspaper," she said again, keeping her voice flat, hiding the churn of emotions.

"Offers such as yours must go before a committee. If you'd only let me know the truth, I could argue your case. Otherwise, I'll have to recommend against you."

"I can argue my own case," she said.

"Very well," he said. "But you do so at your own risk."

• • •

Agent Sorren marched ahead, leading her towards the front of the building, then up a wider staircase. He stopped before a pair of double doors and turned to instruct her.

"You will remain standing unless told to sit. If dismissed, you will leave immediately and without objection. Remain silent unless invited to speak. And behave with servility at all times."

He knocked twice and waited. Presently a voice from within called "Enter", whereon he swung the doors open and gestured for her to follow.

This room was far larger than the last had been. At its head lay a dark wooden table, behind which sat five men. Two chairs had been left in the space facing them.

It took all of Elizabeth's will to not turn and run. She could see none of their faces. Each man was bent forwards, studying papers on the table in front of him. But John Farthing she would have recognised from the slightest glimpse. He sat on the left hand side, bent deeper than his colleagues.

Agent Sorren escorted her to one of the vacant chairs, in front of which she stood, dumbly. Then the central man, who seemed older than the others, glanced up and made a downward motion with his hand. Agent Sorren sat and gestured for her to do the same.

Elizabeth's thoughts were in turmoil. Farthing might not realise she was there. A reaction of surprise when he looked up could give away their secret. That would mean the ruin of them both. But these imaginings were swept away by a more obvious, a more painful truth. He'd known she was coming, even before she received the invitation. He'd already known when they last met in the room above the ale house. He must have been waiting for her to say it, but she never did. She felt her face reddening at the memory.

"Present yourselves," said the eldest man, looking up from his papers.

"Please may it be recorded that I am Agent Sorren, in attendance with and representing Miss Elizabeth Barnabus. She offers her services in the gathering of information regarding the recent loss of the airship *American Frontier*."

"Very well. Let it be so recorded. Also record that I am Senior Agent Lopez, presiding officer, and that this is a tribunal of irregular deputisation constituted under the provisions of the Auxiliaries Charter, section twelve."

The man sitting next to Farthing opened a ledger and began to write.

Having paused for the secretary to catch up, Senior Agent Lopez continued: "We've had the opportunity to peruse copies of Miss Barnabus's letter and other papers relating to the case and her background. We chiefly wish to ascertain where she sourced her information. Have you questioned her on this?"

"Yes, sir."

"Was she forthcoming?"

For the first time, John Farthing looked up from the papers on the table. His eyes met hers. The contact lasted a fraction of a second, but she could too easily read his anguish through the mask of cool efficiency. It felt as if lightning had penetrated her chest.

"No, sir," said Agent Sorren. "She did not reveal that information."

Farthing looked down to his papers again.

"Very well," said Senior Agent Lopez. "Miss Barnabus, you see here before you a tribunal assembled to consider your offer. It has the power to accept or reject on the part of the Patent Office. Or hold you in detention pending the resolution of any outstanding questions. I am the convener. Agent Farthing, I believe you have already met. For the record we need to say that he was your caseworker on a previous investigation. Do you have anything to say?"

The recording secretary stopped scratching in the ledger and looked up, waiting for her to speak. Everyone but Farthing was watching her.

Her mind churned. If she refused to say where she'd discovered the information, she might be held in detention. But were she to admit the truth, Farthing would surely be imprisoned. And stripped from the role to which he'd devoted his life.

"Do I need a lawyer?"

"You're not charged with any offence."

"You said I could be detained."

"Agent Sorren is here to represent your interests."

She took a breath but Sorren cut in before she could speak.

"Thank you, sir. I've briefed Miss Barnabus on our procedures. Her wish is merely to be of assistance."

"How generous of her."

One of the other men sat forward and cleared his throat. "The woman has offered help. But what qualifications does she have? This is a waste of our time as far as I can see. And how could we trust her, anyway?"

The secretary nodded agreement as he wrote. "She's a woman. What useful skills could she have?"

"Very well." said Senior Agent Lopez. "What about you, Agent Sorren? Do you recommend that we accept Miss Barnabus's offer?"

Elizabeth glanced across to Sorren. His pale eyes were downcast.

"No," he said.

"It seems that no one will speak for you," said Lopez. "Will you not consider revealing your sources?

"No."

"Very well. I am empowered to detain you pending a resolution of this outstanding question."

Elizabeth took a deep breath and stood, making her chair

legs scrape on the floor.

"Sit down," Sorren hissed. There was panic in his voice.

Her pulse pressed against the constriction of her corset. "You want skills!" she said. "How many others have been able to find what I've discovered? Who else beyond your agency knows that airships are being brought down?"

No one answered.

"You want someone whose discretion you can trust. But when I protect my sources – in the face of your threats – you count it against me! Would you think me more trustworthy if I betrayed that trust? And what skills do you think I employed to get this audience? You want qualifications – though you know they're near impossible for a woman. Consider that my qualification! But I'll give you more here and now – if any of you dare take my challenge! Test me on the law and I'll test you. We'll see whose knowledge is greater! Which one will go against me?"

She cast her gaze from one to the next. Their eyes were wide with shock. Sorren had scrambled to his feet. His mouth hung slack. If a beetle had crawled across the carpet and started reciting Plato, it could hardly have amazed them more.

Anger had spurred her. But a gambler's instinct also. She'd already proved herself unnatural in their eyes; a woman sparring with a panel of agents. Doubt was incubating in them. She could feel it. Any one of them would have called her bluff if she'd been alone with him. But in the tribunal they risked humiliation in front of their peers.

Lopez made a rumbling sound that turned into a clearing of the throat. "Please remain standing." He looked to the recording secretary. "We will take our vote. All those in favour of accepting Miss Barnabus's offer, please indicate."

No one moved.

"All those against?"

John Farthing raised his hand. She felt pain, like a knife

piercing her skin.

"One against and three abstentions," said Lopez.

The recording secretary looked up, confused. "Three?"

The senior agent nodded. "I've yet to cast my own vote. I found myself ambivalent. And yet..." A smile had begun to spread across his face. "...and yet, her performance was quite magnificent. She beat you all, though we won't record that in the minutes. Indeed, she has won me over."

"Then the votes are tied," announced the recording secretary. "But Agent Lopez's seniority carries the motion."

She had won her case, but it felt as if she'd lost something far greater. Her legs wobbled and she dropped back to the chair. The agents filed out from behind the table.

"Come," said Sorren, when they were alone again. "We've paperwork to complete. And a letter to draft to the North Atlantic Trading Company. They'll provide the means of it. We'll have to arrange for you to visit with them. I presume they'll need to see with their own eyes that you can appear as a man."

He beckoned for her to follow.

"I don't think I can stand," she said.

The weeks that followed were consumed with planning and preparation. She threw herself into weaving the two cover stories: one to explain her sudden disappearance to those who knew her, the other a fabricated past for the young scientific officer she was about to become. There were books of terminology to learn, as well as the anatomy of North Atlantic whale species. She spent her evenings in the Natural History Museum in Kensington, allowed in after hours and tutored by order of the Patent Office.

Through all this, she tried to not think about John Farthing. She was now helping the Patent Office. That put her in closer alignment to his ideals than ever before. She knew that, in some senses, she'd betrayed him by making contact behind his back. Balanced on the other side was his betrayal of her. The ability to switch between male and female gave her what little agency she had in a world dominated by men. But only so long as it was kept secret. He had given that secret up. His guilt was surely the greater.

Standing in a museum storeroom one night, between shelves stacked with the bones of whales and tissue samples in formaldehyde, she found herself rehearsing what she would say when she next saw him. She tried to remember the tenderness of his expression. But when she pictured his face, it was clothed in sorrow.

Thereafter she couldn't concentrate and left early for her lodgings. She resolved to take a trip north to confront him. They would each say their piece. She would state her regrets and he would apologise.

Walking from the museum, she began to construct a story to tell Agent Sorren. Tinker was being looked after in Leicester. Though he could fend for himself better than most adults, the boy would be missing her. He deserved a visit. A few days away would in any case freshen her mind. Her studies and preparation would benefit. All this was true enough.

But when she got back to her lodging house, she found a letter waiting. A commission had been secured for her on the *Pembroke*, a whaling ship of the North Atlantic fleet. She would depart on a supply ship heading out of Liverpool in four days. She must set out immediately.

The next morning, Agent Sorren met her at the air terminus and delivered an envelope of documents into her hand.

"Degree certificate, identity papers and passport," he said.

Of necessity, she'd developed a connoisseur's eye for forgeries. "Are they good?" she asked.

"They're genuine."

It seemed that it paid to be with the Patent Office.

"And there's one more thing. You've not been told this until now because, honestly, I didn't know it myself until yesterday. It is the greatest secret we're giving you. It can't ever be written down. This is the phrase to be uttered by your contact or by yourself. One will say: 'I watch for the Pleiades.' To which the other will reply: 'I watch for the Pole Star.' By this will you know each other. If a man speaks this line to you or responds when you say it, then you can tell him all you've learned. Your message will find its way back to us."

"Then my contact is a man?"

"Forgive me," said Agent Sorren. "I was wrong to assume. Nothing but this phrase has been told to me."

Elizabeth arrived at the Company dock in the male guise she would need to maintain, perhaps for months. She presented her papers for inspection at the main office. A man behind a large desk brought out a magnifying lens to inspect them, but would hardly look her in the face. She felt vindicated by his reaction. But also alone.

"Your sea trunk arrived this morning," he said, sliding the papers back without ever looking at her properly. "You'll find it in the parcel office."

Other than a clerk's desk and vacant chair, the parcel office was filled with shelving racks. Daylight streamed down from high, narrow windows, each crisscrossed by iron bars. All the packages waiting for dispatch were wrapped in identical brown paper, tied with twine. Seeing no one in attendance, she cleared her throat.

John Farthing stepped out from behind the rearmost shelves.

So unexpected was the revelation of his presence that for a moment she couldn't breathe. Somewhere outside a steam whistle sounded. She managed to swallow and then inhale. She'd had a speech prepared for when she saw him again. If only she could remember it.

He too seemed paralysed. "What's happened to your face?"

Her hand went to her cheek where she'd painted the mark. "It's... That is..."

But he was already stepping towards her, arms open, and she found herself rushing towards him. They held each other.

"...indigo," she said, mumbling the word into his shoulder.

"What?"

"My face. It's supposed to be a birthmark."

"But why?"

"So people don't look so closely. Please don't make me cry. I'll make a mess of your jacket."

He held her even closer. "You don't have to go. You don't have to do it. No one can force you."

"I'm helping the Patent Office. You should approve."

"But I don't want to lose you."

"Is that why you voted against me?"

"I was voting *for* you," he said. "For your safety. For your life."

She pulled herself free of his embrace and touched her hands to her flattened chest. "They knew about this," she said. "My disguise."

"Yes."

"You told them! How could you do that?"

"Without it you'd have been no use as a spy. Not in the North Atlantic."

"I thought you didn't want me to go!"

"But going is your heart's desire. And if I hadn't told them, you wouldn't have been given the chance."

"You still betrayed me."

"You betrayed me first. I didn't tell them until they showed me your letter. I'm begging you. Don't leave."

"Agent Sorren said that no one else could do this."

"He was manipulating you."

"You think I'm so biddable?"

He laughed then, though there was no humour in it.

"Will you keep an eye on Tinker?" she said. "I've sent him to stay with Julia's family."

"Have you thought what'll happen when he finds you've gone? He'll think you've abandoned him."

"I don't know why he ever came to me," she said, trying to make it seem more right than it was.

Farthing's eyes admonished her. "You make your own rules. You're probably more like him than any adult he's met. He may be feral, but sometimes you seem half wild yourself. How could he fail to love you?"

"I didn't ask for the responsibility."

"No one ever does."

"Will you look out for him?"

"As best I can."

"I couldn't have told him," she said, trying again to make it seem right. "He'd have done something stupid, like following me. I can't take him into that danger."

She held John Farthing tight, desperate to feel him one more time, though there were layers of clothing and disguise between them.

"Will you not give me your blessing?" she whispered.

"I cannot," he said.

And with that tender ill-grace, they parted.

At last, the ship's steam whistle called her to the quayside. She joined the line of new recruits and climbed the gangplank. Once on deck she hurried to the side of the ship to scan the faces of those who'd gathered to wave off loved ones. John Farthing was not among them.

The mooring ropes were untied and thrown free. The dark waters of the harbour churned. The ship began to turn, tilting slightly as it pulled away from the dock. The crowd on deck began to disperse as others sought out their berths below. But Elizabeth stood gripping the safety rail long after the Company dock had been swallowed in Liverpool's hazy air.

She received only one letter from him. It was addressed to Scientific Officer Edwin Barnabus, and took the form of a communication from a reform school. She recognised his handwriting, although the signature at the bottom was a made-up name. It reported in brief and unsentimental language the news that the boy, known as Tinker, had run away.

Though his whereabouts are unknown, the last sighting of him was in the Liverpool docks. We assume he may have stowed away on one of the Trading Company's boats, heading into the North Atlantic.

CHAPTER 9

She had the impression of stacked barrels in the gloom. Behind them, the door clanged as Steward Watkins tried to get in. There were sounds of exertion and a scraping noise. But the boy had already led her out of the small storeroom. They were in a metal passageway. By the time they reached the flight of stairs, her eyes had grown accustomed to the low light and she could reach out for a handrail.

Down they went, quickly at first. Then he slowed, made a "Shhh" sound and stopped. There was no more noise of Watkins struggling with the door. The boy let go of her hand. She could see him now. Placing his feet silently, he led her across a landing and through another door, which he eased closed behind them.

They continued down after that. She lost count of the levels, but the air became hotter. It smelled of lubricating grease. The boy opened yet another door and she followed him into a space small enough to be called a cupboard. He struck a match and put it to a candle stub before pulling the door closed.

Then he hugged her. He buried his face in her side and held her tight enough to make her ribs flex. She cradled his head in her hands.

"Oh Tinker," she said. "I've missed you so."

He sniffled and she thought he might be crying, though it was something she'd never seen him do in her years of fostering. Then he pulled back as suddenly as he'd launched himself at her and turned to busy himself with domestic arrangements.

The floor was strewn with blankets, spoons, empty food cans and whalebone figurines. The detritus he scooped into one corner. The blankets he scrunched into an approximation of two chairs. The candle had its own tiny shelf which had been fashioned out of wax.

"It's my place," Tinker explained, when they were seated.

From the labels on the empty cans it seemed that he'd been living mainly off tinned peaches and various flavours of jam.

"It's very nice," she said.

"You going to stay?"

"I can't. They'll send me off to the *Iceland Queen*. Tonight."

There was a flicker of a frown, then it was gone and he grinned. "That steward'll be bloody mad!"

"Tinker! Language!" But his grin was infectious and she found herself giggling. "Is that the way they speak in the galley?"

"Don't work in the galley," he said.

"But I saw you there."

"I don't work nowhere."

"Everyone works on a ship."

"Not me." There was pride in his voice. "They all think I work somewhere else."

"Then what were you doing in the galley?"

"Fetchin' jam for the commodore."

Elizabeth considered the genius of the boy. Wherever he went he would be seen as running an errand from somewhere else. She'd not got a straight answer from Watkins about the size of the crew, but there had to be thousands. A boy with Tinker's wits could lose himself in such a crowd. With a place to hide and his name on no timesheet, he would have more freedom than anyone else on board.

"I saw you was docking," he said. "Was going to get in the net and stow on your whaler. But then up you come."

"There's nowhere to hide on a small ship like that."

"I'd have found a place."

Indeed, if anyone could have managed such a vanishing act, then Tinker could. She found herself staring at an oil smear on his face.

"No one goes the places I go," he said. "I've seen the commodore's cabin. And the ice rooms. And the oil tanks. And the gun room. And all the galleys and galley stores. And all the engines but one. And the..."

"What one haven't you seen?"

His grin widened. "The hidden one."

"If it's hidden, how do you know it's there?"

Not breaking eye contact, he turned his head and pressed his ear to the wall. She copied him. Her heart beat twice before she felt a tingle of vibration on her cheek and heard a low, distant thrum. Seconds passed before the sound repeated. It was unmistakably a steam engine. Something large and slow.

"For one of the paddlewheels?" she asked.

He shook his head.

"Do you know where it is?"

However far they had already descended, Tinker now led her three flights deeper. There were no more side doors. The slight curve of the left-hand wall suggested they were walking next to the hull itself. The right-hand wall was perfectly straight, so that the further they went, the narrower the passage became. Tinker could stride out normally, but she found herself having to sidestep. Every few yards they came to a sturdy joist, to pass which she had to bend low.

The temperature had increased. As had the noise. She could

feel the beat of the hidden engine through her boots. The curve of the wall became more pronounced. Soon they were both obliged to lie flat to worm under the projecting girders. She wasn't usually aware of claustrophobia, but when one of the brass buttons on her officer's tunic became jammed under the joist it was all she could do to extinguish the spark of panic. Having backed up a few inches, she breathed out, expelling all the air from her chest, and then started forwards again.

She felt Tinker's hands gripping hers. She squirmed her shoulders and he pulled. Suddenly the crawl became easier and then she was through and scrabbling to her feet. She found herself standing in the narrow triangular space behind the prow and in front of whatever it was they'd been skirting.

She looked down and was horrified to see dark greasy marks over the sleeve of her uniform. A wooden fish crate lay on the floor. Tinker shifted it across to the vertical wall and stood on it. One of the rivets in a line was missing, leaving a hole the size of a penny. To this Tinker put his eye.

Seeming satisfied, he pulled back and made room for her to look. She took his place and peered through. At first she couldn't resolve what she was seeing. Behind the wall lay a huge void. Lamps, evenly spaced down the walls, revealed its breathtaking scale. In the centre, mounted on an axle so that it was suspended in the middle of the space, was a great drum, from which a cable was slowly unspooling. And what a cable. Smooth and black, it seemed to her perhaps as thick as a man's thigh.

"See? Tinker whispered.

"How do you get in there?" she asked.

"Can't. Locked doors."

From the drum, the cable rose up, changed direction over a free-running wheel, and exited through a hole in the roof.

"Where does it go?"

"Doesn't."

"But it has to."

"I bin all round it," he said, patting the wall. "And over the top. Doesn't come out nowhere."

A movement on the floor below the drum caught Elizabeth's attention. Two men in boiler suits were heaving another length of cable behind them. The final foot of it was sleeved in metal. When it was level with the drum, they let it drop and returned the way they had come.

"It's got to be going somewhere," she said.

Elizabeth Barnabus stood near the mother ship's port bow and watched the lights of the *Iceland Queen*. It had started closing just before sunset. There'd been helio signals back and forth. Whatever message the commodore sent had caused it to get up steam and head directly in, but now it waited, two hundred yards off. The mother ship hadn't changed its angle to the swell, so it didn't seem that a docking was being planned.

"You!"

Steward Watkins's shrill voice made her turn. He was storming towards her across the deck, his face a mask of rage. "We've been searching for three hours!"

"And now you've found me."

"Where did you go?"

"For a walk."

"You abused my trust."

"What trust?"

His eyes swept over her oil-stained uniform. She saw his contempt. The Company was its own law out in the deep ocean. Men could be hanged on a commodore's say. But not on the say of his junior officers. And the Patent Office would be watching.

"There's something I've been meaning to ask," she said.

"How is it *you* were set to watch over me? A steward."

He recoiled slightly. She saw him double blink. Then he looked away, to compose himself, she thought. When he looked back at her, his gaze had hardened.

"You'd better hope that I'm more faithful to my orders than you. I'm to be your pilot."

The steam launch was narrow enough for her to grip both sides. This she did so tightly that her fingers ached. Cables snapped tight and lifted the boat from its cradle. Then the boom shifted and they lurched out from the safety of *Mother's* deck. For a second they swung in the air. Then someone shouted "Release." There was a clunk followed by a whirling of gears, and they dropped. She felt her stomach lift within her, then they were decelerating. The hull slapped into the water.

In months of steaming the North Atlantic, Elizabeth hadn't seen the ocean surface so close. If she'd dared to let go, she could have reached over the gunwale and dipped her hand.

Watkins pulled back a lever and the paddlewheels started to turn. The waves had seemed small from the deck above. But as the launch emerged from the shelter of the mother ship's hulls, the roll and pitch became so violent that she had to brace herself for fear of being tipped over the edge.

With an oil-fired engine, they had no need of a stoker. It was just her and Watkins and the ocean. They climbed to the top of the largest wave yet and she saw the lamps of the *Iceland Queen*, dirty yellow against the last grey of dusk. Then with a sickening change of angle they pitched over the top, sliding into the next trough, shrinking her horizon to a few yards of vertiginous water.

The nose of the launch began to turn and Elizabeth glanced back to where Watkins sat, leaning his weight against the push of the rudder.

"Enjoying the ride?" he shouted.

If he let go, they would be swung around and the swell would hit them on the beam. They'd be awash in seconds. The mother ship was already too far behind to be able to help. She might have expected to see some sign of Watkins gloating after the way she'd treated him. But his expression was all focus. Feet spread, he raised himself from the helmsman's seat and stared forwards as if trying to glimpse the *Iceland Queen* over the wave top. The launch's own lamps gave his narrow face a stone-like quality. Paddle spray seemed like a halo behind his head.

Then he lowered himself and the tension eased from his face. The next wave was shallower than the last and when Elizabeth turned she saw the full length of the *Iceland Queen*, which had turned side-on in the swell. Though it rolled, its hull was giving them some slight shelter.

The launch may have been small, but it was fast. They passed over more wave crests and troughs, then began to turn into alignment with the ship.

"Be ready to catch the harness," Watkins shouted. "And be quick to strap it on. I can't risk slowing."

A man on the deck above them was swinging a rope. He let it fly and it clattered across the launch. She grabbed, but as they dropped into a trough it whipped out of her hand. She grabbed again, catching the harness before it slipped over the side.

They were rising as she slipped it around her waist and pulled the buckle tight.

"Thank you," she shouted to Watkins.

But then the launch dropped again. The rope snapped tight and she shot into the air. The side of the *Iceland Queen* came at her. Her hands and knees took the worst of the impact. The wave passed and she dropped. The water took her under. Then the harness pulled tight and she was out again, dragging air into her lungs against the shock of the cold. She hardly felt the next impact with the side of the ship. Hands were pulling her up and over the gunwales. Coughing and spluttering, she dropped onto the deck of the *Iceland Queen*.

PART TWO

CHAPTER 10

"What are we to do?" asked the first mate of the *Iceland Queen* as soon as they were alone. He seemed young for such a rank. His eyes were dark and too large for his face.

"There are orders," said Elizabeth, unbuckling the document wallet from her waist. He whipped it from her hand as though it was a lifeline and he unable to swim.

Elizabeth's clothes were still dripping onto the floor of the captain's cabin. Her hands and face had stung from the sudden cold after she came out of the water. Now they prickled as salt began to crystallise on her skin. She pulled a chair and sat to remove her shoes, draining the water from each. She would have stripped the woollen stockings as well, but the delicacy of her feet would have been too obvious.

The first mate had been reading. "Commodore says we're to pull away. We're to stand a mile off. But no word of how long for. Where's Captain Woodfall? Why isn't he sending the orders?"

"He's safe on *Mother*," she said. "Warm and dry." It was true, after a fashion.

The first mate wrinkled his nose, as if sniffing for danger. "When's he coming back?"

When Elizabeth didn't answer, he drew a second letter from the document wallet and passed it to her. On the envelope a shaky hand had written: *For the attention of Scientific Officer Barnabus.* She broke the wax seal. The paper had remained dry inside the case. It crackled as she unfolded it.

You are to determine the sequence of events leading to the loss. You are to compile a list of possible causes. Your list should include human error and mechanical failure. Every crewmember must be questioned. I have instructed that you be given a cabin for your sole use. You have twenty-four hours to complete your report. You must destroy this paper.

She read the message three times, dwelling on the last line and the lack of date and signature. The commodore had gone out of his way to avoid using the name of the *Mary May*. The words made easy sense in context but would hardly constitute evidence in a law court. Though her own name had been printed on the envelope, it had been omitted from the orders themselves.

"What took the *Mary May*?" she asked.

"Explosion in the forward battery," said the first mate.

"Is that what Captain Woodfall thought?"

"You've spoken to him?"

"Yes."

"Then you know as well as I."

The builders of the *Iceland Queen* had given the captain's cabin a luxury of space. A man could put in five full paces crossing it, though he'd need to bend to pass beneath the ceiling beams. A row of glass windows graced the outward sloping stern wall. It was to these that the first mate turned. He stooped to look out. Elizabeth could see the lights of the mother ship catching the waves.

"What set the explosion?" she asked.

"A spark from a boot nail. Or someone could have taken a candle into the magazine. We'll never know. And what does it matter? If you've a room stacked with barrels of black powder, you know the risk."

"Did you not see something below the water?"

"I did not."

"A whale, perhaps?"

"No."

"Your captain did."

"Then why ask me?"

"What did he record in the log?"

"You can read that for yourself. This cabin's to be yours. Now, if you'll excuse me, I'm ordered to move the ship."

The cabin door was thick oak. Once its three iron bolts were shot, she stripped and arranged her things to dry. The binding cloth she stretched out in front of the open window. Even should one of the deck hands dangle by a rope outside, he wouldn't be able to see in.

There was a drinking glass on the captain's chart table. The dark residue in the bottom smelled of vinegar and herbs. A cork rested loose on top of the ink bottle. A pen rolled with the tilt of the ship. Under the glass she found the beginnings of a letter.

My Dear Susan,

I hope this finds you well, and the children, and that good fortune smiles on the community.

She turned the sheet but found no more. A small silver tray on the table was dusted with ash, as if it had been used for the burning of papers. There was no sign of a log book. Below the table were three sliding drawers. Two contained Atlantic charts. But the bottom drawer, deeper than the others, was locked.

Her final act before turning in was to reread the commodore's orders, then slip them under Captain Woodfall's thin cot mattress.

Twice in the night she woke to the squeak of the door handle being turned. There was no knock and the bolts did not rattle. Whoever it was remained just outside for perhaps half a minute before the creaking of the boards betrayed his retreat.

The next time she woke, light was streaming through the binding cloth. With each tilt of the ship came a distant clanging, a loose chain touching a metal plate, she thought. She turned onto her back and lay listening to it and to the slow thrum of the engine. A bell should have been rung for the changing of the watch. There should be the sounds of men moving about and orders being shouted.

The binding cloth and most of her clothes had dried. The uniform jacket was still damp where the broadcloth was folded double for cuffs and lapels. But it would serve well enough.

Before venturing out, she tested the sliding drawer with a letter-opening knife. It wouldn't budge and she dared not apply more force for fear of leaving its tip jammed in the lock. She had a set of lock picks concealed in her trunk, but that was two miles away on the mother ship. It might as well have been in Jamaica.

The passageway outside was empty. So was the main deck. Doubling back, she went to seek out the galley, following her nose, for there was a scent of roast meat in the air. On her way she found one of the crewmen. He lay flat on his back with his head propped at a sharp angle against the wall. At first she feared he might be dead, but a slow, rattling in-breath gave the lie to that. She crouched next to him. He was ripe with body odour and she could smell the ardent spirits in his sweat. Prodding his stomach had no effect.

There were three more men on the floor of the galley itself, dead to the world. The bench and basin had been left in a chaotic state. In the midst of the unwashed pewter and steel lay a tray containing the remains of a leg of pork. She wrenched a cook's knife from the beam overhead and cut a sliver from the roast. Having tasted it and satisfied herself that it hadn't been lying long, she carved a larger strip and began to eat with purpose.

A cask on the table seemed to have been the source of the alcohol. It had been left for empty but she tilted it and managed to coax a trickle of dark rum into the palm of her hand. The water butt was three quarters full. She dipped the ladle and drank a full measure, then repeated the process, but not from thirst. The state of things on the *Iceland Queen* meant that there could be no certainty about anything, least of all when she might next be able to eat or drink.

It was in the heat of the engine room, in the belly of the ship, that she found the first sober men. Two engineers stood before a bank of controls and gauges; an old man and an apprentice with an untidy dusting of hair on his upper lip. A flywheel clicked as it rotated. A regulator spun. The boom and hiss of the engine came as slow as the breathing of a giant. The hull walls defined the shape of the engine room; wider at the ceiling, sweeping together as they neared the floor.

"You're the one from *Mother*, then," said the old man. He didn't seem impressed with what he saw. "Why are you here?"

"To find out what happened to the *Mary May*," she said.

"Then you've come to the wrong place. We were the only ones belowdecks when she went down."

"You're the only ones who can stand upright this morning!" she replied. "What kind of ship is this?"

"A ship without a captain."

"Then can you tell me nothing?"

"Only this: we were down here the whole time. There was nothing for us to see."

On the whaling ship *Pembroke*, the men had clung to discipline. That had puzzled Elizabeth at first. They'd watch one of their number being flogged at Captain Locklight's order. They'd flinch at every stroke. But they never questioned his right to rule them. Locklight's cruelty only seemed to make them respect him more. It was months before she came to understand. A sailor might resent the lash, but in part of his mind still welcome it. He feared what he might become, so far from civilisation. And here on the *Iceland Queen* she was seeing what lawlessness could do. But for the resolve of the chief engineer, the ship might already be lost.

From the angle of the sun she guessed it to be not long before nine in the morning. That meant her allotted time was already half spent. To find one person who would speak frankly with her would be a victory, let alone the entire crew. Not that the commodore wanted it, she thought. All he needed was plausible distance; a suitably phrased report with someone else's signature on the bottom. Someone other than himself for the board of directors to question.

She had no intention of being that person.

The fleet had seven more gunboats. If they were sent south, together, they might be able to face up to the pirates. There would be a chance of capturing one of the pirate ships and discovering the nature of their weaponry. That was the only way the truth could be discovered. It was also the best chance of discovering what had happened to Julia.

On the way up from the engine room Elizabeth came upon three ordinary seamen carrying water jugs. They swayed as they walked and had the pallor of men who regretted the excess of the night before. They touched their forelocks as they passed, but kept their eyes from meeting hers. She waited for them to descend to a lower deck before setting off to follow.

By this method she found the main body of the crew, asleep in rows of hammocks so closely arranged that they touched, swinging together as the ship rocked. The three she had followed were filling beakers for others who were awake. She could not tell if it was water or the hair of the dog that bit them. They straightened somewhat on seeing her.

"Who saw the *Mary May* go down?" she asked.

They cast uncertain glances at each other before one said: "We all did, sir."

"And what exactly happened?

"It was dragged to hell by a monster."

She found the first mate behind the wheel on the quarterdeck. He nodded to acknowledge her greeting but then continued to stare out at the horizon.

"Your men are drunk," she said.

"Yes."

"All of them."

"Yes."

"You don't use discipline?"

"It'd do no good after what they've seen."

"But you said it was an accident. An explosion."

"They think different. And that's all that matters. If there was something for them to do, I could take their minds from it. A whale to chase. A storm to fight. But this – the waiting. It's the worst thing."

"Are there monsters in the sea?"

"Somewhere. In the deeps. I'm certain of it."

"But this wasn't one?"

"They'd been staring into the white for hours," he said. "When there's nothing to fix on, it plays tricks with you.

Maybe one of them saw a mackerel shark swim under the boat. I don't know. Maybe the captain saw it too. But I'll tell you this – half the men who'll swear on their eyes they saw a monster weren't even looking into the water. Oh, they all believe it now – since they've had time with nothing to do but stew together below decks. They've grown the story between them. But if it hadn't been for the *Mary May* going down, it'd be forgotten already, just like every other shadow."

He glanced up and looked directly at her. There was fear in those over-large eyes. But not fear of a monster below the water, she thought. He was a man given leadership when he didn't want it. Whatever the crew believed they'd seen, it had left them unbiddable. She'd assumed Captain Woodfall's despair had come from being locked away. But now she wondered if that dark humour might have come from him trying to deny a truth that his eyes had seen.

For all his fear, the first mate had had the courage to say what he believed, though it ran counter to everyone else on board. She respected that.

"I never asked your name," she said.

"Ryan," said the first mate.

She shook his hand. "Scientific Officer Barnabus," she said.

It is a fine skill to open a lock leaving no sign of your work. Opening it when you no longer care is merely a trial of strength and requires a more substantial pick. She raided the whaler's tool store and selected a bone spade for the job, resting the long iron shank over her shoulder as she marched back to the captain's cabin. With the chart table turned over, she lifted the spade and crashed it down on the underside of the locked drawer. The noise left her ears ringing. The blade had cut into the wood. It screeched as she wrested it free. On the third blow, the oak cracked down the middle. Pressing on the shank with all her weight, she levered out a section.

There was a bundle of letters in the drawer, a bottle of laudanum – half empty – a hefty purse of gold coins, a document wallet and the ship's log book, bound in brown leather.

The first letter was from the captain's wife. She unfolded it and read.

Last night I dreamed that you had returned to us, my dear Henry, just as you were in October, the same smile of parting, and this morning I can do nothing but think of you.

Elizabeth flicked through the rest of the bundle. All had been addressed in the same hand. An image of John Farthing came unwontedly to her mind. Stifling a pang of longing, she retied the bundle of letters and slipped it back inside the ruined drawer.

Next she opened the log book, flicking through to find the account of the disaster. But there was nothing. The final entry stated: *Fog. Visibility 80 yards. Turned into the swell. Bearing 195°. Proceeding dead slow. Watch doubled.*

She slumped back against the chart table, the hope of discovery draining from her. And yet a picture was forming. She unstoppered the laudanum bottle and sniffed. It smelled of the same herbs as the residue in the captain's drinking glass. Having witnessed the loss of the *Mary May*, he turned the ship around and steamed back to *Mother*, making no record in the log book.

The document wallet was empty. There was wax on the flap; the remains of a seal bearing the commodore's mark. Her mind flicked to the paper ash she'd found on the silver tray.

For months she had been focussed on keeping secrets from the people around her. Now she could feel the presence of other people's secrets. The commodore had two sets of secrets;

those he kept for the Company and those he was keeping for himself. He had spoken too easily of the Company's relationship with the Patent Office; their mission to keep the Atlantic open. He didn't know she would see the strange unspooling drum in the belly of the mother ship's central hull.

Whatever secrets the commodore nursed, his steward would surely know them. There was a strange intimacy between the two men. Though Watkins' rank was low, the guards had taken his word as carrying the authority of the commodore. And there could be few stewards with the seamanship to pilot a small launch between ships with such finesse. But perhaps most tellingly of all, the commodore had seen fit to keep a captain in solitary confinement for fear that he might mention what he'd seen. But he'd allowed his personal steward to keep Elizabeth's company, despite what she'd been told.

The image of the thick black cable came back to her, unspooling from its drum by inches, being fed out of the chamber. It did not emerge from any side, Tinker had said. Nor from above. But the boy hadn't searched below.

All the mysteries seemed tangled in what lay below.

When she was freshly arrived on the *Pembroke*, before the crew turned against her, a harpoon man had shown her how to listen to the cry of the whales. He held the shaft of an oar against the bottom of the whaleboat and had her press an ear flat to the paddle. Nothing in her studies had prepared her for the sound. She'd found interest in the collections of the Natural History Museum. But this strange and unearthly music had stirred something deeper.

A thought took hold of her. She jumped to her feet and hurried from the captain's cabin, abandoning the ruins of the chart table to whoever might look in. This time she knew where she was going and the question she would ask.

This time, on entering the engine room, she listened before speaking. Flywheel and regulators rotated slowly, clicking softly. The low boom of the engine came slower than a heartbeat.

"How fast does it turn when you're on one-eighth power?" she asked.

"Just as you see," said the old engineer. "That's how we are today. Enough to keep us pointed in the right direction."

"And when the *Mary May* was sunk?"

"It was the same."

She placed a hand on one of the in-curving walls. One sheet of iron was all that separated her from the ocean. And from all that swam in it.

"Do you ever hear the song of the whales?"

"Yes, sir," said the apprentice. "When it's quiet."

"Did you hear anything just before the *Mary May* went down?"

He glanced at the old man, who nodded, as if giving permission.

"There was a noise," the apprentice said. "It passed under us."

"A whale?"

"No, sir."

"Some other fish?"

Again, that conversation of looks between the two of them. This time it was the old man who answered: "It was a machine," he said. "I'd swear it. Though I never heard its like before."

CHAPTER 11

The idea of the helio was simple. In the daytime it reflected the rays of the sun. In the darkness it directed its own light through lenses so as to be flashed over many miles with undiminished brilliance. But the marvel of the technology lay in its gimballed mounting, which perfectly counteracted the movement of the ship. It was a means of aiming, without which the helio would have been useless.

Perhaps reasoning that it could equally have been employed to steady a gun, the International Patent Office banned its use. But the ban had jurisdiction only within the Gas-Lit Empire. Thus the Company could manufacture helio machines in workshops on the mother ship, far from the borders of any nation.

With the other officers of the *Iceland Queen* drunk, it was left to First Mate Ryan to mount the helio on its stand. He primed it with a measure of methylated spirits, from which the main burner ignited. Next he pumped pressure into the oil chamber. The flame roared and the quicklime at its focus began to glow, becoming brilliant as it heated. Swivelling the mirror into place, Ryan looked through the sighting telescope and took aim at the mother ship's control room.

The shutter chattered as he sent three slow flashes. He repeated the signal over and over until three flashes came back.

"We're ready," he said.

It was just dusk and a band of yellow still hung in the sky above the western horizon. The commodore had offered Elizabeth twenty-four hours. That time had slipped past.

"Signal this," she said. "Report written. Send launch to collect officer Barnabus."

The helio chattered with each opening and closing of the shutter. Though Ryan wasn't a signalman, he worked with marvellous speed.

"Done," he said.

"Is that it?"

"We must wait for their signoff."

So they waited. The yellow streak in the sky faded to cream, then to grey. The constellation of Orion became visible above them in a gap between the clouds.

She was about to question him further, but saw the angle of his shoulders change. Eye to telescope, he began writing on his notepad. Even with the naked eye, she could see the flickering of helio light on the mother ship, but not clearly enough to have been able to read the sequence of flashes.

At last, Ryan took his eye from the telescope and stood tall. He twisted a valve, releasing the oil pressure with a hiss. The flame died and the brilliant light began to fade.

"You're to remain on the ship," he said, reading from the pad. "They're sending us a new captain. And new orders. Do you think we'll be going home?"

Home was the one place Elizabeth knew they couldn't be going. She'd been placed in the fleet in the hope that it would help her infiltrate the "nation of eels". The fleet might be far beyond the border of the Gas-Lit Empire, but the commodore would never go against the desires of the Patent Office. He might send her into danger, but he'd not bring her back to *Mother*. And if the worst thing happened – if the *Iceland Queen* suffered the same fate as the *Mary May* – then the ocean would claim all those inconvenient witnesses that had so worried him.

"They'll be sending you back to face the monster," she said.

Ryan hesitated before answering. "I don't believe you."

"Then why do they give us a new captain? You know Woodfall. He'd refuse to do it."

"He could be ill?"

"He thinks it was a monster took the *Mary May*. He drank laudanum because the fear of it was too much for him to carry. He couldn't order the crew to steam south. But a new captain might."

"The crew wouldn't do it."

"Under a new command? A new hand at the lash?"

But Ryan shook his head; more in an attempt to dispel fear, she thought, than in disagreement.

"You said it was an explosion in the magazine."

"I said I didn't see a monster."

Elizabeth regarded him. He was an honest man. And honourable. She imagined he would have thrived if all was orderly. But he was ill equipped to cope with the overthrow of reason.

"I'm scared too," she said. "But I've a way of making things safer for us. When the launch comes, I may tell you to do something. If it happens, you must act immediately and without question. Do you understand?"

"Yes." He seemed almost relieved.

Perhaps the hangovers had softened. Or perhaps fresh rum had been found to soften the edge. Either way, the crew set to work with a level of energy she hadn't previously witnessed, hanging lamps off the starboard bow, preparing the *Iceland Queen* to receive the mother ship's steam launch.

First Mate Ryan had let the officers know that a new captain was on his way. The news swept through the ship, leading to a frantic bout of cleaning and the destruction of incriminating evidence. By the time they steamed in closer to the mother ship, the *Iceland Queen* was almost presentable. To a casual glance.

"Could you point out three troublesome men," Elizabeth whispered to the first mate.

"Only three?" he asked, with the first smile she'd seen him wear.

"Troublesome, but they must be able to handle a small craft."

The first mate pointed. "Him, him and him over there."

"Keep them in sight," she said.

With the ship turned so that the swell was hitting it abeam, it began to wallow. Elizabeth held tight to the gunwale. One of the watch officers shouted and pointed into the dark. It took several more seconds before she too made out the shape of the approaching launch, heading directly for them. As she'd guessed, there were three figures aboard.

At the last moment the boat turned parallel to the *Iceland Queen* and came alongside. Someone threw down a coil of rope. Then a team of men hauled it back until two sea chests came crashing over onto the deck. One of them was hers. She watched as two more lines were thrown. The men in the launch gripped the ropes rather than securing themselves with harnesses. Each timed his jump so as to be lifted clear of the small boat and arrive dry on deck.

Elizabeth grabbed Ryan's arm. "Get your three men onto the launch and have them take it back to *Mother*," she said.

Then she leaned over the gunwale and shouted to Steward Watkins, who was at the helm of the little boat. "Climb up! I've the report for you!"

He seemed bewildered. But men were already clambering down, so he gave up his place at the helm. So graceful was his jump from launch to ship that he could have been a trapeze artist.

"What's the meaning of this?" he demanded in that shrill voice. "Where's the report?"

Elizabeth drew him away into the lee of the wheel housing. The light of a wildly swinging storm lantern made their shadows dance.

She leaned in close and whispered: "The *Mary May* was sunk by a machine."

"I need it in writing!"

"Then I shall write it."

He must have sensed the trap because he spun and ran back to the gunwale. But too late. The launch was already slipping away from the *Iceland Queen* and heading into the dark.

Elizabeth had but a moment of satisfaction before the other two men from the launch stepped towards her. The first was Captain Woodfall, as she'd expected. His expression showed bewilderment. The commodore was indeed getting rid of all the inconvenient witnesses. But then the second man came into the illumination of the swinging lamp: Captain Locklight, master of the whaling ship *Pembroke*, her old tormentor.

"Scientific Officer Barnabus," said Locklight, spitting the words. "It seems I'm fated to command you again. And straightways you're mixed in a strange business. Tell me, man, why is it the launch is sent back without the commodore's steward?"

CHAPTER 12

There is a moment when the last outlier dips below the horizon, when there is no more view of the fleet and the ship finds itself alone. It means a different thing to every man on board. But no one is untouched by it.

From land, the horizon seems to be a straight line. But in the heart of the ocean it is revealed as a circle. And nowhere more so than from the crow's nest, high above the deck. Elizabeth had never before climbed the mast. She had a good head for heights and had scaled buildings in the past; scrambling over rooftops to escape pursuit. But never before had she suffered from vertigo. Rooftops remained steady. The top of the mast swung wildly. It was the same movement as the rolling of the deck, but amplified tenfold.

"You get used to it," said First Mate Ryan, who was wedged into the small space next to her. "First time I took watch in the crow's nest, I was sick. Luckily the wind took it and it landed in the ocean."

"If you mean to make me feel better, it's not working."

He laughed. "What's your history with Captain Locklight? He seems to have the measure of you."

"I served under him on the *Pembroke*. He hates me."

"Well, he's licked the crew into shape. And faster than I'd have thought."

It seemed to Elizabeth that Captain Locklight had been aided by the crew's previous disobedience. Every ordinary seaman had committed some misdemeanour during Woodfall's absence. And the officers had failed to keep order. When he pulled one man from the ranks and accused him of drunkenness and theft, every other man sweated cold. And when that man was lashed, they all of them felt the cords cutting into their own skin.

By the time six men had been punished, all the rest were jumping at the captain's command. They couldn't obey him fast enough. Some food was still being stolen, they said, but other than that, discipline had been completely restored. And when the captain didn't punish them, they loved him for it. His humiliation of the strange scientific officer with a wine stain birthmark seemed merely to cement their loyalty.

"How long will he keep me up here?" she asked.

"You know him better than I," said Ryan. "But you must try to enjoy it. It's the best place to be on a day like this."

"Is that why you came up to join me?"

"To tell the truth, I wanted the chance to talk – where no one else can listen. I don't understand what happened the night he came aboard. Why did you keep the commodore's steward with us? And why didn't Captain Locklight call for the launch to take him back? He could have done it."

"Locklight may be cruel, but he's not stupid. Whether you believe in monsters or not, the truth is we're going to a dangerous place. Do you see how the commodore put all the witnesses onto this one ship? Everyone who saw the disaster and everyone who's heard about it. If we were to sink and all be lost, how convenient would that be?"

"And the steward?"

"Watkins isn't who he seems. I can say that much. He's the commodore's most trusted servant. I have a feeling – a guess – that the commodore won't want to lose this particular steward. Keeping him with us seemed like a good idea. And look…" She turned and nodded in the direction of the two ships that followed a mile astern. "It seems to have worked."

"He was always going to send an escort," said the first mate.

"Two gunships? Are you so sure?"

Ryan's expression said that he wasn't.

"Captain Locklight seems to agree with me," she said. "He was quick enough last night to have us steam away from the fleet. We've been getting helio messages from our escort since sunrise. But I've not seen any replies sent back."

Ryan nodded. "They want the commodore's steward transferred over to them. The same signal repeated over and over. Locklight said to ignore it."

For a time the first mate was silent, content, it seemed, to stare out at the extraordinary expanse of the ocean. He rested his forearms on the railing that surrounded the tiny lookout post. Elizabeth was gripping it tight enough to make her hands ache.

"Captain Locklight can't hate you so very much," the first mate said.

"How do you figure that?"

"We are a ship with two scientific officers, yet you're the one given the cabin."

Elizabeth concentrated on the horizon and tried to relax her breathing. It had been months since she was last seasick. "That wasn't his choice," she said. "It's the commodore's orders."

Ryan turned to look at her. "Then I'm surely in the presence of greatness!"

When the bell chimed for the end of the watch, a junior officer climbed up to replace her. Exhausted, she clambered back down. Missing the final rung of the ladder, she jarred her leg and went sprawling onto the deck. The crew of the

Iceland Queen were already learning to laugh at her.

How easily Captain Locklight had fallen back into the same pattern of belittling her in front of them. Yet this mission was different. It was not whales they chased, but knowledge. A special bonus was to be paid to every crew member once they returned. It would be doubled should they bring home any of the wreckage or news of what had taken the *Mary May*.

Elizabeth was still surprised that the crew had not rebelled. But they might yet, she thought. Fears might be convenient to forget with the promise of a fat bonus. After all, they were sailing with good visibility and two gunships in view. But if the fog rolled in again, how quickly those sailors would remember the screams from the *Mary May*. As for the *Iceland Queen*'s previous captain, she'd seen nothing of him since he came on board.

Elizabeth slid the bolts and leaned back against her door, alone at last. Her cabin porthole on the *Pembroke* had opened, making it possible to dry clothes overnight. But this cabin was closer to the waterline and the porthole was not designed for opening. Two hours of tension at the head of the mast had left her clammy with sweat. She had a spare binding cloth hidden in her sea chest. That might keep her going for another couple of days. But they were moving ever south and the mercury had already started to climb.

Having laid her tunic and shirt on the bunk, she unwound the cloth and wafted it in the still cabin air. It was a fine cambric and would have been quick to dry in better conditions. There was some small draught through the cracks around the edge of the door, so she contrived a means of draping it there to make the most of a bad job.

Then she knelt by the trunk and swung back the lid. She'd been about to remove the contents so that she could raise the false bottom and extract her spare binding cloth from the compartment below, but her things had been disturbed. She tilted her head. The chest had been hoisted by rope from the steam launch and dropped hard on the deck. But the chaos of her clothes seemed more the work of a hand than of gravity.

She'd been careful to hide any item that might give away the secret of her sex. But the thought that someone had been searching her possessions was itself disturbing. Catching a hint of engine grease in the air, she brought her head low and sniffed, tracing the smell back to the trunk's catches. Whoever it was, he'd spent time around the paddlewheel axle or the engine.

Item by item, she emptied the trunk. There was a dark streak on the shoulder of one of her shirts. But it was when she got to the false floor that she felt a stab of fear. She'd left the end of a yellow thread trapped between the board and the wall of the trunk. Panicking, she felt along the edge, searching for it. But it had gone. The catch was a button hidden beneath the upholstery. Touching it, she detected the thinnest smear of grease. It clicked as she pressed it. She lifted the board. The cavity beneath was little more than two inches deep.

The spare binding cloth had been moved. It might not have meant anything to an untrained eye. The menstrual rags would not have been so easily mistaken, for it was never possible to completely bleach them between use. The code book she'd been given by Agent Sorren seemed untouched. She flipped through its pages but could find no finger marks. She'd also concealed a small bundle of papers: notes from Julia and love letters from John Farthing, which she'd read from time to time, when she felt the need to weep. All lay undisturbed beneath the code book.

She'd kept only one other article in the hidden space; a brick of dried, compressed beef. A high density food; it had been her insurance against the aftermath of shipwreck. Whoever had gone through her things had taken it.

• • •

She found Captain Locklight balanced on the bowsprit, with the *Iceland Queen*'s figurehead below him and spray flying. He stood with one hand touching a rope, just as she'd seen him on the *Pembroke* the day they were called back to the fleet. That time she'd been summoned. This time she'd gone to seek him out.

She stepped up from the deck, putting herself his level. "I was surprised to see you come on board, sir."

"I wasn't surprised to see you," he said.

Gripping a rope, she inched out towards him. She would never be able to match him for balance. But positioning herself in that way was a statement of a kind. She would meet him on his terms. And no one would be close enough to listen in.

"Did the commodore tell you I'd be here?"

"He didn't need to. All that time on the *Pembroke*, you were hiding. Now you're revealed. A Patent Office spy, come to seek out the monsters that are dragging down our ships."

"I can tell you this," she said. "It's an underwater machine that took the *Mary May*."

Captain Locklight's focus was suddenly intense. She felt his eyes searching her.

She looked away. "The engineers heard it pass under the keel."

"Who made the machine?"

"That's what I'm sent to discover."

"At last, a word of truth from you, Mr Barnabus. But I fancy, not yet the whole truth."

"What about you?" she asked. "Why are you here, sailing into danger?"

"I'm following orders."

"You told me that men follow orders for fear and for greed. I've seen you use both. But what about you? I can't believe the commodore threatened to lash your back. And what use is money when you're dead?"

On the *Pembroke*, he would surely have struck her for such insolent talk. But the scales of power were swinging free and yet to find their balance. He turned away, as if to stare out at the horizon ahead of them.

"What trickery did you play when I came aboard?" he asked.

"Keeping Steward Watkins with us?"

"Don't play games," he said. "We're beyond that. Tell me straight – what happened to my belongings?"

When she didn't answer, he turned to shoot her a cold glance. "Why did you steal from me?"

"I didn't!" she said, baffled.

"Then tell me this," he said. "Who was it took all the books from my sea chest?"

CHAPTER 13

The dining table had been set up in the captain's cabin and the officers summoned to present themselves in dress uniform. It was an uneasy gathering for all, though it was Woodfall, sitting next to Elizabeth, who seemed to be suffering the most. His was the indignity of seeing the *Iceland Queen* passed on to the command of another man, and yet having to remain on it as it sailed towards a thing that he couldn't admit he feared. He seldom raised his eyes beyond the rim of his plate.

The ship's previous scientific officer bristled whenever he looked at her. Since her arrival he'd been evicted from his cabin, in accordance with the commodore's orders, and was obliged to bunk with the crew. First Mate Ryan had taken some of the blame for the disorder and drunkenness that preceded their southward voyage. The junior officers seemed unsettled by the mission, as well they might be, and by the change in command.

The commodore's personal steward had also been granted a place at the table, though his position wouldn't ordinarily have allowed it. It was to him that Captain Locklight addressed his first question:

"How does it feel to be waited on, Mr Watkins?"

"I should be on the mother ship," he said.

"And yet Mr Barnabus thought otherwise. So here you are.

We should drink the health of our disfigured scientific officer, don't you think?"

He lifted his wine glass and when even the old scientific officer had complied by doing the same, he drained it in one go. It was his third, to her counting. He held it out to be refilled by the cook, who was hovering near the table with a fresh bottle.

"How are we provisioned, man?"

"We're run out of butter, sir," said the cook.

"And beyond that?"

"We'll stretch to three weeks for food."

"And water?"

"Less than a week, sir. Unless it rains."

"Then we shall pray for the heavens to open. Indeed, fortune does love us all!" He raised his glass again. "To wherever you send your prayers – to God, the Company or the Patent Office!" On this last part, he nodded towards her.

This time she was obliged to drink with them, but allowed only a taste to pass her lips. It was not good wine. Perhaps the crew had found the better stuff. It was a miracle that any alcohol remained after the last few days.

In the months she had sailed with Captain Locklight she'd witnessed his many moods which, good or ill, were always fierce. But never had she seen him possessed of such a dark humour. It animated him, making his movements jerky. He was easily ten years older than Captain Woodfall, she thought. But helplessness and fear had drained the younger man of his energy. He looked more fit for a retirement home than a whaling ship.

"How would you rate our chances of finding wreckage from the *Mary May*?" Locklight asked. When no one seated would meet his gaze, he turned to the cook. "A good chance, do you reckon?"

The cook's face reddened from the unexpected attention.

"Aye, sir. We'll find it."

"Good man! See it before me and I'll give you twenty silver dollars."

The cook beamed. "Thank you, sir!"

"First to catch sight of wreckage will get that from me on top of the bonus from the Company. You can tell the rest of the crew. We're going to make good money on this voyage!"

A terrible bitterness lay below the captain's display of enthusiasm. Elizabeth could feel it. A sickness, even. But the other officers seemed too intent on their own individual miseries to notice. The cook was mesmerised.

"We should drink to the silver and gold we'll make," announced Locklight. "And not with horse piss." He pulled a key from inside his jacket and tossed it for the cook to catch. "I have a mind there's a few bottles of something stronger and sweeter in my trunk."

"Yes, sir."

"Good man. And pour a measure for yourself!"

Elizabeth watched the cook scampering to the captain's sea chest. As he knelt to open it, she looked back to the captain and saw the dark coals of his eyes were flicking around the table from one officer to the next. First Mate Ryan was watching the opening of the sea chest. The others were staring at their plates.

"But it's empty, sir," said the cook.

"Ah," said Locklight. "That must be my mistake. Then go search for something that escaped Captain Woodfall's chaos. Something strong."

When the cook was gone, Locklight thumped his fist on the table, hard enough to make the cutlery jump. "You will stand tall in front of the men, God damn you! You will tell them from your bearing that they'll return, rich, to their families from this voyage. When the time comes, I *will* remember your actions – every one of you. Your obedience. Your conduct.

And your thievery."

The cook's locked store yielded two bottles of good brandy. The captain made them drink toasts to the success of the voyage. Scared into compliance, the officers joined in. And though it was plain to Elizabeth that they were only acting their enthusiasm, by degrees and with the help of the alcohol, their spirits caught something of Locklight's mood, so that by the end of the dinner, they were thumping on the table and shouting huzzahs when he required it. Not Woodfall, though, whose mood had sunk lower with every glass. Elizabeth raised hers when ordered, though she didn't let a sip pass her lips. And when a tray of sponge cake was served they were all too far gone to see her slipping three extra pieces below the table, where she wrapped them in a clean handkerchief.

During her time at sea, Elizabeth had decided that engineers were a different kind of sailor. They had their own technical schools and their qualifications were measured on a different scale. They served the end of their training on board under the care of the senior engineer. Regular sailors respected them, but left them to themselves.

The *Iceland Queen's* senior engineer was the old man who'd told her that the monster was a machine. It was he that she found on duty in the engine room, together with his apprentice.

"I've brought you cake," she said, holding out the bundle she'd sneaked from the captain's cabin.

"Why?" asked the senior engineer. He held a grey rag in one hand, with which he'd been wiping the glass of a water-level dial.

"To say thank you for what you told me," she said. "It was important and I'm grateful."

He nodded towards a small workbench. On the wall behind it, spanners and screwdrivers had been strapped in rows of ascending size. She placed the bundle, untied the corners and opened it out. The smell of lemon zest rose up to her. The apprentice stepped forwards for a closer look.

"Why three pieces?" asked the senior engineer.

"So I can eat with you. It seems to me you know more about the running of a ship like this than any of the so-called sailors on deck."

"We may do," he acknowledged.

"And it seems to me you don't get paid the respect you deserve. When Captain Woodfall was taken off the ship and all the crew were getting drunk, you kept the wheels turning down here. They'd have been drifting without a hope if it wasn't for you."

After a moment's consideration, he nodded. A click of his fingers and a gesture had the apprentice running to fetch three stools. When they were all sitting and each had a square of cake in hand, he said: "Thank you." Though whether it was for the cake or for the sentiment of her words, she couldn't tell.

"How did you get that mark on your face?" blurted the apprentice.

"I was born with it."

This seemed to disappoint him, as if he would have preferred an accident to be the cause. "Is that why you came to sea? To hide from people?"

The idea seemed curious. There were people enough on board a ship. And cruelty to spare. But then, the engineers were cloistered like monks.

"Don't mind him," said the chief engineer. "He doesn't know better."

"It was a fair question," she said. And then, to the apprentice: "We are all of us hiding from something."

She watched them eat the cake. The apprentice demolished his in three large mouthfuls then sat blissfully chewing with his eyes closed and cheeks bulging. The chief engineer broke small pieces, taking time with each, watching her as he chewed.

"Why don't you eat yours?" he asked.

"I've just come from the captain's table," she said. "Now I come to it, I find my stomach's full." It was a lie. Such had been the tension of the banquet that she'd only been able to pick at the food on her plate. "If I wrap it up and leave it here, perhaps I could come back later?"

He weighed this for a moment before saying: "I don't see why not." And then: "You're right. They don't listen to us down here. But I don't reckon they listen to the scientific officer, neither. Seems like you might have some stories to tell if anyone would listen."

She wrapped the cake and left it hanging from a peg on the wall. "To be clear of the rats," she told them. But in reality it was to be clear of their view. For the place she'd chosen was a yard into the passageway and sunk in shadow. The hook might once have hung a lamp, she thought.

Having said goodbye and taken her thanks from them, she headed out and up the steps, treading heavily enough for them to hear her go. Only when she was back to the door of her own cabin did she stop, hold her breath and listen. No footsteps had followed. No shadow was out of place. So she turned and retraced her path. And when she came to the final flight down towards the engine room, she placed her feet on each step so as to make no sound. Then, halfway down, she sat in the shadow and waited.

From time to time, she could hear the engineer and his apprentice moving about in the control room. Whenever one of them approached the passageway she would get to her feet. If they discovered her she could pretend to be on her way back down. The third time it happened the shadow of one of them loomed into the space at the bottom of the stairs. She stood, ready to give her explanation, but the shadow pulled back. She counted ten before lowering herself to sit once more.

The engine control room was merely one part of the space they occupied. There was a walkway behind the bank of dials and levers. Beyond that would be the fuel tanks, the boiler and condensers, the funnel inlet, the great cogs that geared down revolutions of the engine, and, somewhere forward, the axle of the paddlewheels, running clear across the ship.

She had seen Captain Locklight's trunk hauled aboard. It had taken two men to carry it below decks. Having spent years in the company of conjurors, she knew better than to believe the obvious truth, that it was full and heavy. His trunk might already have been empty and the men feigning the weight of it. But then, the emptying could only have happened on the mother ship. And the crew of the *Iceland Queen* could have had no message to prepare for such a deception. Also, they had no motive.

Therefore, the captain's trunk had been full when brought aboard. There'd been perhaps two minutes between it being carried below and Locklight following it down. Time enough for an expert with a pick to have it open. And if there'd been others to help carry, the trunk could have been stripped of its books.

Before leaving the captain's cabin she'd stepped across to the trunk and crouched for a moment to examine the lock. It was made of brass and had the name Chub engraved on the front. Not something an amateur could pick. But there'd been scratches where a knife blade had been inserted underneath the lid. Whoever had taken the captain's books hadn't bothered with subtlety. He'd levered the metal wall of the trunk, bending it until the bolt popped free from its catch.

But the question that had most perplexed her was why anyone should wish to steal the captain's books. What was it that made them so valuable as to be worth the risk of a lashing and dishonourable discharge? Indeed, where on board a whaling ship could such a quantity of books be hidden?

It wasn't until she turned the question around that the answer had come to her. The books had not been taken because they were valuable. They'd been removed because they had no value. They did not need to be hidden, merely thrown overboard. The thief was illiterate. And he'd had no use for the contents of the trunk. He only needed the space the books had previously occupied.

There was a clanking sound from within the engine room, as if someone had begun to use a soft hammer against metal. Every few beats, it stopped and she heard the chief engineer giving instructions. They were disassembling some part of the machinery to be cleaned.

Keeping her eyes on the foot of the stairs, she stood, tensed and ready. The hammering continued. She began to count the seconds. Before a minute had passed, she saw a new shadow move across the floor. And then Tinker stepped into the passageway, reaching up towards the small bundle of cake. She was down the remaining stairs and had grabbed his arm before he had a chance to lift it from its hook.

His first reaction was to pull away. But then he saw her properly. She put a finger to her lips and eased him back into the shadow, up the stairs and away.

CHAPTER 14

Men never watch the sky so keenly as when the fresh water is running low. There might have been barrels of it to spare on the escort ships, but Locklight had kept them far behind as he crisscrossed the ocean in search of wreckage. With the superior speed of the *Iceland Queen*, he could keep control of the distance. Perhaps he wished to stop them taking back the commodore's steward. Or perhaps it was for some other reason that Elizabeth had yet to fathom. Either way, he seemed content with the thirst of his men.

By noon on the fourth day of their southward journey, there'd still been no rain. Nor did there seem prospect of it. The captain ordered them onto half measures.

For Elizabeth, the problem was doubled.

"Drink it slowly," she whispered to Tinker, in the privacy of her cabin.

But he'd already drained his beaker and was holding it out for more.

"You're going to have to do without," she said.

He'd been stealing food and drink until she caught him. A little bit from here and a little bit from there. The dried meat that had gone missing from her own trunk had all been eaten. Not that food was the problem. Her own portions were easily big enough for the two of them. But the captain had placed a guard next to the supplies of fresh water. And when a man is thirsty, he doesn't leave his share lying around where it might be spilled. He drinks it in one go.

If she reported the stowaway Tinker would be given a ration of his own. But he'd also be locked in the brig; the most dangerous place if the ship were to sink. There would be a prison sentence waiting for him, if they ever made it back to land.

Unless rain came, there would be no option but to divide her own meagre ration two ways.

"Why did you do it?" she asked.

But like all the other times, his response was a shrug, as if to say it was obvious. Which, indeed, it was. The boy would follow her into hell, if she chose to go there. It might have been easier to be angry with him if only she wasn't doing the very same thing; following a loved one into the wilds at the cost of all else she held dear. She had even abandoned her lover. What she would now give for a touch of John Farthing's skin, or to breathe the scent of him.

When first she stepped onto the *Pembroke*, she'd been faced with a moral dilemma. Her reason for being there was the possibility of coming into contact with the pirates who had shot down Julia's airship. Then she would try to find the means of transferring across to their world. If Julia were alive, Elizabeth would find her.

The pirates were women. They might accept her into their ranks, if she could prove her usefulness. But her crewmates were men. She couldn't escape the thought that the outcome she hoped for might well lead to their destruction. Perhaps Locklight had been correct in accusing her of aloofness. But keeping to herself had been the only way she'd been able to cope with such an inner conflict.

Now here she was with Tinker. The pirates killed men, she'd been told. But what would they do with a boy? She'd thought of trying to disguise him as a girl. But it takes years of practice to make the illusion convincing. His voice was still high, though it couldn't be long before it broke. From time to time when he opened his mouth his words came out as a squeak. It was movement that would have given him away. And that too easily.

A childhood of malnourishment had left him small, however. He looked younger than his years. She hoped that might be the saving of him.

He was tracing lines on the floor with his finger. He had the strange gift of acting as if any extraordinary situation was normal. Yet the threat of a bath or a clean shirt would have him struggling like a wild thing.

"How did you get out of the trunk?" she asked.

"Kicked the lid."

"And that popped the lock? You were lucky. If the captain had found you, you'd have been lashed for sure."

"Wouldn't have found me."

"How would you have escaped?"

He shrugged, as if to say he'd have found a way.

She was about to say something cautionary – she hadn't decided what – when the sound of running feet snapped her attention to the passageway outside the door. Whoever it was passed quickly. But there were other sounds, more distant, that had her sitting up straight. Footsteps on deck. The shout of orders. She couldn't make out what was being said. Tinker must have heard it too. He was sitting crosslegged on the floor, his head cocked.

Then she heard the ship's bell. Three mournful chimes.

"We're in fog," she said.

Stepping out onto the deck was like entering an alien world. She could see the housing of the paddlewheels, but everything further forward had been swallowed by the swirling grey. She could smell the moisture and taste it, but it did nothing to quench her thirst.

The bell was struck again; three chimes sounding eerily distant as if somehow ringing from a world below the surface of the water.

She climbed the steps to the quarterdeck. The officers were a huddle of shapes until she drew closer. First Mate Ryan was there with others she recognised but couldn't name.

"Come join us," he whispered, making space for her to step into the circle.

The others looked at their boots or at each other or over their shoulders; anywhere but at her.

"Barnabus is safe," said Ryan.

Whereon one of the others, who she recognised as the old scientific officer, hissed: "He was on the *Pembroke*! He's the captain's man."

Ryan put his arm over Elizabeth's shoulder. "Anything you can say in front of me, you can say to Mr Barnabus."

"What's happening?" she asked.

"We're cut off from the escort," said Ryan.

"He's put us here on purpose!" whispered the second mate.

"You're blaming the captain for the weather?"

"No," said Ryan. "But as soon as the lookout called the fog bank, he had us change course and go full speed towards it. He's left the gunships behind."

The second mate nodded. "They'll never find us in here. And this is just where we need them."

"The fog can't hurt us," said Ryan.

"The monster lives in the fog," hissed the second mate. "Locklight is going to get us killed."

As if summoned up by mention of his name, the captain emerged from the swirl. "Gentlemen. I find you in conference."

All but Elizabeth jumped, straightening to attention. She edged back as the circle opened to accommodate the captain.

"Mr Barnabus, are you leaving us?"

"No, sir."

"No, sir," he echoed. "Then tell me, pray, what is the subject of your discussion?"

"The weather, sir."

"How very English. And what do you think of our fog bank?"

"It's thick, sir."

"Then I suggest you lead the crew by example. All of you. Get to your stations and keep watch."

The other officers were away before Elizabeth could move, dispersing into the gloom. But when she turned to go, Locklight took hold of her shoulder and pulled her back.

"Tell me what they were really saying."

"They're scared," she said.

"Of course they are."

"Why did you leave our escort behind?"

"I fancy we could do with another pair of eyes in the crow's nest, Mr Barnabus. Jump to it, man!"

Only the lower half of the mast was visible. The four cables that held it steady angled up steeply into nothing. The ladder was slick from the fog. Two rungs up, her foot slipped and she dropped back.

"Watch how you go."

She couldn't tell which of the shadow figures on the deck had spoken the words. Nor did she recognise them. Most were standing at the gunwales. A few moved across the deck like ghosts. She began climbing again, making sure to grip with two hands whenever she lifted a foot. The sounds of men whispering to each other became muffled. At what felt like halfway up the mast she looped an arm through the ladder and stopped to rest.

The arches of the wheel housings loomed up towards her.

The deck itself had become little more than a darker shadow in the grey. The bell chimed three times. It was impossible to say which direction the sound came from.

A drop of water clung to the iron rung in front of her face. As the ship swayed it crept one way and then the other. Inching her head forwards, she caught it on her tongue. There were one hundred and forty-three rungs from deck to crow's nest. Not enough to fill a beaker. A tablespoon, perhaps. It would be better than nothing.

She took another step, careful to hold the sides of the ladder instead of the rung, and was rewarded with a bigger drop than the last. She let it run onto her tongue and continued her climb. It wasn't enough to slake her thirst, but by the time the crow's nest began to emerge from the fog, her mouth no longer felt dry.

At the bottom of the mast, such light as there had been seeped in from all directions. Here it was brighter and she had the definite sense that the sun was above them somewhere. With a final effort, she clambered into the crow's nest, dropping the trapdoor back into place after her.

"Glad to see you!" said the watchman. "Swear I'd have gone mad if I'd been left alone a minute longer."

"Why?" she asked.

Instead of answering, he reached down and helped her to her feet. There was only white in front of her and water droplets drifting. Compared to her last time at the masthead, the ship was barely swaying. But now there was nothing to see below and no horizon. She gripped the railing. Her eyes jumped from place to place as if with a will of their own. There was nothing to fix on.

"Why did he bring us here?" the watchman asked.

When she didn't answer, he said: "We'll not find the wreckage in the fog. And the monster will take us."

"There is no monster," she said.

"But I saw it."

"On both sides of the ship?"

He nodded, though without so much certainty.

"What colour was it?"

"I... You could ask Bill, the cook's mate. He saw it clear."

"And what shape was it?"

"I saw bubbles rising."

"And that makes a monster?"

Before he could answer, the fog around her turned brilliant white. She felt a sudden warmth and saw the dazzling blue of the sky directly overhead. Quite suddenly they were standing in full sunshine. Below them and spread all around were billows of white, like an ocean of cloud. Holding on tight she looked over the edge. The wheel housings were emerging, their paintwork more brilliant than she'd ever seen it before. The quarterdeck was bathed in sunshine. Officers were shaking hands. Then the entire ship was free of the fog and the men were cheering, as if they'd just sailed into harbour.

"There's our escort," said the watchman, pointing back. "Thank God. But we're safe again."

Elizabeth followed the line of his arm and saw the ships following, dark smoke rising from their funnels. She imagined the panic as their captains watched the *Iceland Queen* heading for the fog bank. And yet in the fog they'd been quite hidden.

"If you still think it was a monster, how did it find you?"

"We was in the fog. It lives in the fog."

For Elizabeth, a new thought was beginning to coalesce. "Was it a fog bank like this one?" she asked. "Did you sail into it?"

"No, sir. It grew around us."

"So, where did the monster live before it formed?"

CHAPTER 15

Were a clean-shaven scientific officer found to be without the means of shaving, questions would surely be asked. Therefore, Elizabeth kept a brush, razor and strop in her trunk against the chance that it would one day be searched. She'd bought them secondhand for the appearance of use. The blade hissed over the leather as she prepared it.

"Why?" asked Tinker, his lower lip protruding in a sulky pout. He was sitting on her bunk, stripped to his underwear.

"It's so you'll seem younger."

"Why?"

"So they'll not treat you like a man."

"But I am a man."

"You're a boy."

She lifted his foot and placed it on her trunk. Then she began brushing lather onto his outstretched leg.

"When's your birthday?" she asked.

"Don't know."

"Good. And how old are you?"

He frowned, as if trying to remember whether it was truth or falsehood he was supposed to be answering with this time. "Nine."

"Very good!"

Once more: "How old are you?"

"Nine."

"Tell me the truth now. How old?"

"Fourteen."

"No! For the hundredth time, no! Whatever I say, however I plead, or anyone else, until we're back home and safe you'll be nine years old. For once I thank the heavens you lived so many years half starved. You have the frame of a nine year-old."

So saying, she slid the razor flat over his leg. Fine hair came away with the foam, leaving smooth skin behind. By way of a bonus, the soap had left him cleaner than before.

He cast her a baleful look.

"Remember when you first saw me dressed as a man?" she asked.

He nodded.

"Remember how you knew it was me? No one else could see it, but you did. This is going to be the same. We're going to make you look younger. Everyone else will think you're nine years old. But I'll know the truth."

All the while she spoke, she continued to glide the blade over his leg, the rhythm of her speech matching the movement. "Sometimes we need to hide. It's always been the way of it. We're outsiders, you and me. We put on our disguises. But who we are underneath – that doesn't change. They can't take away who you are. You've seen behind my disguise. I'll see behind yours."

She took a cloth and wiped away the last of the foam. The lower part of his leg had been transformed. He ran his fingers over the smooth, pale skin.

"I'm teaching you how to lie," she said. "And I'm teaching you to pretend to be what you're not. But we use it to help people. That's all. You understand?"

When he nodded, she began to lather the rest of his leg. "You're learning new skills. Think of it as growing up."

"Must you do everywhere?"

She laughed and handed him the razor. "Not me. It's your job now."

He examined it. "I don't know how."

"Try it. It's easy."

She'd been brought up as a chameleon; taught to slip between being a boy and a girl. Then between man and woman, even as she was discovering what those two words meant; man and woman. They were masks. Not that in being masks they lacked power. The reverse was true.

She took his hand and guided the blade onto his leg. His first few strokes were tentative. But after a couple of tries he was making long, smooth sweeps from thigh to knee.

It seemed ironic that it should be now she realised how much of a young man he'd already become. It was easy to miss with Tinker.

She tried to remember the day her father told her she'd need to bind her chest when passing herself as a boy. He hadn't laid out the reason. That would have been her mother's job, if her mother had still been with them. But Elizabeth had known. Perhaps at first she'd blushed. Later, in the privacy of the wagon, she wrapped herself for the first time, hiding the new swell of her breasts. Looking at herself in the glass, she'd felt pride.

"If you weren't already a man, you wouldn't need to do this," she said.

Tinker wiped his leg with the cloth.

"You've made a good job of it."

He seemed pleased with her praise.

"And, once this is done, I've another job for you, but... it might be dangerous."

At the mention of danger his smile broadened into a radiant grin. And at the thought of it, she felt her own smile grow heavy.

• • •

On their fifth day of searching the ocean the lookout spotted another fog bank and shouted it down from the crow's nest. As before, Locklight ordered the helmsman steer towards it. The officers whispered as he stalked around, his movements jerky with whatever evil humour it was that drove him.

Instead of climbing to the quarterdeck, where she'd risk another confrontation with the captain, she joined the men on watch near the prow. They seemed grateful for her presence.

"Will the monster take us?" asked one of them.

"No," she said.

It wasn't that they believed her. But her certainty seemed to calm them. Somehow she'd achieved a level of respect that the men of the *Pembroke* had never given her.

"Here, sir," said another of them, handing her a beaker.

She sniffed it.

"It's water, sir. See?"

He stepped aside and she saw that one of the mast cables came down to the gunwale there. A man was holding a small marlin spike against the underside of it. A trickle of water dripped from the tip. This he was collecting in another tin mug.

"The rope catches the fog, sir," he said. "Takes a few minutes. But once it starts to run we get to tap it."

It was only a mouthful. She drank it in one go and handed it back. "Thank you."

"Why won't the monster take us?"

They'd given her water. She owed them an answer in return. But telling them it was a machine wasn't going to satisfy. They wouldn't believe her. Nor would they believe that it couldn't find them in the fog. Though to her it was the truth. Their eyes were fixed on her, expectant.

"The *Iceland Queen* has no guns," she said. "It only takes boats with guns."

One of them was nodding. Then the others, as if it made sense. And why not? The monster *had* spared the *Iceland Queen* before, swimming underneath the hull to attack the *Mary May*. Grinning, one of them touched his forelock and said: "Thank you, sir!"

She walked away, marvelling at how easily they'd accepted a story she'd made up on the spur of the moment. Marvelling also at how closely it fitted the facts.

Few can recognise their own sickness until they witness its work in the heart of another.

On the whaling ship *Pembroke*, officers had gathered around Captain Locklight, magnetised by his charisma. The reverse was starting to happen on the *Iceland Queen*. Excuses were made to avoid him. An officer hurrying to take the watch, on seeing the captain in his way, might change course or turn around entirely.

From a distance, Elizabeth observed him standing alone next to the starboard wheel housing. Fog concealed the detail of his features, but his posture spoke of torment. He was driving them on and she could detect in him no thought of return. Whatever his goal, it had come to match her own.

She remembered her meeting with John Farthing in the room above the ale house; her demand that he steal from the Patent Office. In pushing him to break another oath, she'd understood the damage she was causing. But she'd not understood her own self.

It wasn't until she was standing next to the captain that he looked around and saw her.

"Barnabus! What do you want, man?"

"I thought you might like to talk."

"You thought wrong."

"Did the commodore tell you that I work for the Patent Office?"

"He didn't need to. It's plain as that birthmark."

The fog had begun to thin already. She had to squint to look into the brightness above. A tear of blue sky opened in the white, then closed again.

"The men think they'll be safe once we're out of this," she said. "They're wrong. We're only safe when we're in it."

"Tell that to the crew of the *Mary May*."

"That was a different fog," she said. "There was a haze that day. The two ships steered closer and closer as visibility dropped. By the time the mist had thickened into fog they were sitting at hailing distance. Whatever attacked them – it must have been watching through the day. The more hazy the air, the closer it came. It didn't need to find them in the fog because it was already there."

"How do you know this?"

"The same way I know it was a machine, not a monster. I kept asking questions till I found the right question to ask. And I kept thinking. By steering full speed into a fog bank, you're hiding from it, whatever it is."

Sunlight flared before dying and flaring again. Then the veil thinned to nothing and the sky became brilliant blue. Suddenly there were shadows and colour.

She stepped to the gunwale. Locklight followed. Behind them, the edge of the fog bank was at first indistinct. But as it receded it took on the appearance of a cliff face.

"Turn around and head back into it if you want to be safe," she said.

He didn't answer. But neither did he walk away.

So she said: "Why is it you care so little for life?" She knew straight away, from his eyes, that it was the right question.

"My son was on the *Mary May*," he said. "Why would I want to live?"

From the crow's nest came the call that one of the escort ships had been sighted. Seconds passed and the captain's eyes didn't leave her. Nor did he blink. Then he seemed to wake. He strode back towards the quarterdeck. Then he was running.

"Where's the other escort?" he shouted.

"We've no sight of her yet."

Elizabeth rushed after him, enforcing the strict male gait, though instinct was telling her to throw away restraint and run.

"Signalman!" the captain shouted. "The helio! Get to the helio!"

Elizabeth clambered up the steps and watched as the signalman adjusted a mirror. He steadied the machine, eye to telescope, aiming it towards the escort, which was perhaps three miles distant. He flicked the lever, making the shutter flap open and close. Three slow flashes then a pause. Three more flashes. Elizabeth could see no response with her naked eye.

But the signalman said: "They've answered, sir. We're set."

"Then request the location of..."

But the signalman held up his hand, interrupting. He had no notebook, but she saw the man's fingers moving, as if writing with the ghost of a pen. "They want to know the location of the other escort ship, sir. It went around the far side of the fog bank. We should have it in view."

Elizabeth snapped around. Others were moving to the gunwale, as if a few extra paces would reveal the missing ship. The horizon was a perfect line, unblemished by the black dot of a ship or a column of smoke.

"They must have gone into the fog," said First Mate Ryan.

"They'd not chase us in there," said Steward Watkins.

Elizabeth looked around and was surprised to find him standing close behind her. She'd not seen him on deck for days.

"Why not?" she asked.

"They'd not risk colliding with us."

"The steward's right," growled the captain. "They'd skirt the fog bank and wait on the other side."

"Then the fog's still between us."

"Perhaps."

She followed the line of everyone's gaze. All were staring at a small patch of sea where the edge of the fog bank met the horizon. It was impossible to say how distant or close it was. The sky above the fog showed no trace of engine smoke.

There was a scampering of feet and she turned to see Tinker rushing towards her. One side of his face was dark with greasy stains.

"I heard it!" he shouted.

Everyone turned at once. Locklight grabbed Tinker by the shoulder. "Who the devil are you?"

The boy squirmed out of his grip and jinked past Ryan, who was also trying to catch him.

"I heard the machine," gasped Tinker. "Getting louder."

"Who is that boy?" The captain was shouting now.

"No time to explain," said Elizabeth. Then she grabbed Tinker's hand and they ran.

CHAPTER 16

For the first time in months, Elizabeth moved with no thought to the sway of her hips or the rolling of her shoulders. She just ran, swinging herself down the steps by the handrail and pelting towards the hatchway. She could hear Tinker's footsteps behind, but didn't look back.

After months of waiting, the moment had come. And now she had no time.

All the crew were on deck, but for the engineers. She sprinted the empty passageway and barged through the door into her cabin, leaving it swinging. On her knees, she threw back the lid of her trunk and began scooping its contents to the floor.

The door crashed open a second time as Tinker dived into the room.

"Tell me everything," she said. She'd got to the bottom of the trunk already. Clicking the hidden catch, she released the false floor and lifted it out.

"Did what you told me," he gasped. "Hid behind the oil tanks. Kept my ear to the hull."

Elizabeth grabbed her pistol, a bag of shot and a small powder horn from the secret compartment. Taking a deep breath and letting it out slowly, she began to load the gun.

"Didn't hear nothing till just now."

"What does it sound like?"

"Like a wasp," he said. And then he hummed a single note; high pitched and wavering.

She was about to instruct him on what to do if they were rammed from beneath the water, but a small noise made her snap her head around. Something had scraped across the outside of the hull. Then a figure was clambering past the porthole. Beads of water from the fog made the glass unclear. She saw a russet sleeve, a shoulder, a double-breasted jacket, then legs clad in grey and black sea boots. A scabbard hanging from the belt swung around and tapped the porthole.

A man, it seemed. But the pirates were supposed to be women. She felt a wave of nausea rising from her stomach. She told herself she wouldn't be sick. It was only fear. She could banish fear. She would hide among the men as she'd hidden all along. She wedged the pistol inside her jacket, buttoning it back up with trembling fingers.

Shouts of alarm came from above.

"You're a stowaway," she said. "You're nine years old. You'll give yourself up to them. Don't try to run or hide. And whatever happens, *you must not try to help me*! Do you understand?"

He nodded. His eyes were wide with fear or excitement.

Her breath was coming in short gasps as she marched out through the hatchway and onto the deck. The men were all at the starboard bow, leaning over to look down into the water below them. Tinker kept close behind as she advanced up the steps to the quarterdeck. The officers were staring over the side, the same as the men.

Locklight pointed his finger at her and then beckoned with a single sweep of his arm. She ran to his side.

"It's under us," Ryan whispered. "We saw it pass."

She coughed, trying to clear her throat. "Someone's climbing the side of the ship."

"Don't play the fool!" barked the captain. "You've still to answer for the stowaway." He glared at Tinker.

Elizabeth shielded her eyes and looked to the escort ship, which was closing fast. Smoke billowed from its stack. It would take fifteen or twenty minutes to reach them.

She'd begun to turn her head back towards the captain when the sound of metal straining against metal screeched and the deck juddered under her feet. Everyone staggered. For a fraction of a second there was only stillness and uncertainty. Then the ship heaved a second time.

Elizabeth fell. The deck was tilting. The portside gunwale dipped into the waves and water began pouring in through the scuppers. Tinker was sliding towards it. She grabbed his wrist.

Locklight remained standing, though all others who hadn't found something to cling to had fallen. "Launch the boats!" he shouted. "Launch the boats!"

Elizabeth began to crawl up the slope of the deck, dragging Tinker with her. She reached for the safety railing and pulled herself upright. One of the whaleboats had broken free and was floating askew off the submerged port bow. Sailors were diving in and swimming towards it. The other whaleboat swung from its awning, high above the sloping deck.

"The axe!" shouted the captain, pointing to where one was fixed to the gunwale just above her. "Bring it to me!"

She clambered towards it, hand over hand, and hefted it from its fitting. Then the ship jolted again and she found herself sliding back down past him. Her feet crashed against the submerged gunwale. The shock of the cold took her breath.

Then the axe was being prised from her grip. The captain was next to her in the water.

"We're being dragged!" he shouted. "It's trying to drag us under!"

He splashed away from her. A wave sluiced the water clear and she saw what he was heading for: a hook caught on one of the scuppers. Another wave brought the water rushing back. It surged up to her waist before sucking away once more. The captain raised the axe and when the hook was again revealed, he struck. There was a cable angled down into the ocean, tight as a piano string. The axe bounced from it.

He hacked at it again. Then the next wave rushed in. Reaching Elizabeth's waist. The water pulled her as it curled along the deck. Her feet slipped and she fell. Her head went under. She grabbed one of the mast cables and held on until the wave was spent. Coughing and spitting salt water she tried to scramble to her feet.

The floating whaleboat was full of sailors, but more were swimming towards it. Then the other whaleboat dropped and crashed, tumbling over the deck, taking men with it. It landed upside down but some of the swimming men struck out towards it.

Tinker cried out. She saw him sliding down the deck towards her. Then another wave came up and took her. In the chaos of bubbles, dragging water and stinging salt, she grabbed blind and then grabbed again, catching the thick fabric of his coat, holding on to it, though it seemed it would be ripped from her grasp.

Somewhere a whip cracked. She found herself being catapulted skywards, the deck surging up, the water pouring away. She coughed and retched. Tinker lay next to her. She held the collar of his coat in her fist. Her fingers were so cold that it took effort to let go.

"There's one more cable," Locklight shouted.

She scrambled to her feet. The deck was still tilted to the port side, though not as steeply as before. The quarterdeck was clear of the waves but the prow was being pulled down, submerging the bowsprit.

"We're the only ones left," he said. "You're going to have to cut it."

He was cradling his right arm. The breaking cable must have caught him because there was blood on the sleeve.

She struck out across the deck towards the second safety axe. But before she'd made it halfway, the *Iceland Queen* lurched again, the prow rising up. It came to her that the cable holding it down must have snapped. She ran to look over the edge. The ship was floating true again. The second whaleboat had been righted and many of the crew were safe. Others still swam, clinging to the sides of the boats, for there was no more room for them to clamber in. One body floated, face down.

She was about to call the boats back to the ship, but the click of a gun hammer being cocked made her turn. The figure dressed in russet and grey stood with pistol levelled at the Captain. Locklight brandished a knife in a clumsy, left-handed grip. Elizabeth reached into her jacket. But as her fingers closed around her pistol, the figure in russet shifted its weight from one hip to the other. It was a movement distinctively female.

Elizabeth drew her own gun and took aim at Locklight, advancing towards him. She pushed the muzzle against his chest.

Aghast, he said, "What are you doing?"

"Drop the knife," she said.

As it clattered to the boards, three more figures were scrambling onto the deck, women clad in men's clothing. Only when Elizabeth was sure they'd seen what she'd done did she bend slowly to place her pistol on the floor. She kicked it away and raised her hands.

The woman in russet and grey stooped to pick it up, the aim of her own gun never wavering. "We have the ship," she said. "Quick now."

One of the other women reached over the side and started beating the *Iceland Queen*'s hull with a metal object. It made a harsh clanging noise. She kept up a regular rhythm as the others aimed their guns at the sailors in the whaleboats. "Come no closer!" they shouted.

The Company gunboat was still a mile off, but closing fast.

Locklight rounded on her. "You snake!"

"I saved your life!" she said.

"You'll hang for this treachery! You'll..."

But whatever he was about to say remained unspoken. A shadow was rising between the *Iceland Queen* and the whaleboats. The ocean began to shift as if above an upwelling current. Then a machine broke the surface. In size and curve it was like the back of a whale, in texture like the hull of a wooden ship or a vast barrel, banded with iron.

The rhythmic clanging stopped. A hatchway on the crest of the machine fell open. And out swarmed the pirates, taking up positions on its back, guns aimed at the crew in the whaleboats.

Lines were thrown, then; from the underwater machine to the ship and from the ship to the whaleboats. Water churned around the rear of the machine and it started to move, turning in a tight circle, heading back towards the fog bank. Elizabeth felt a judder as the slack was taken up. Water ran from the towline as it pulled taut. The deck tilted and they were moving. Then the whaleboats full of crew were moving also, dragged in train behind, and the men clinging on in the water.

She felt the drop in temperature and smelled the moisture in the air. The pursuing gunboat was still out of range. It would arrive too late. The white closed in around them.

The woman in russet stepped closer, gun still aimed, one finger pressed to her lips. The *Iceland Queen*'s engine was still idling on slow revolutions. Muffled by the fog, it was a vibration more felt through the feet than heard through the ears. The underwater machine made a different kind of noise; a barely audible hum, sounding just as Tinker had described it.

She staggered as they began to turn. Even should the gunboat risk following them into the fog bank, it wouldn't find them now. The *Iceland Queen*'s engine stopped altogether.

Since setting out from Liverpool, the only moments of silence had been in her dreams. There'd always been an engine turning somewhere. She listened to the slap of a wave against the hull. The hum of the underwater machine had stopped also. She could hear voices off the port bow – the men in the whaleboats. She was waiting for them to start shouting, but then they too fell silent.

The woman in russet backed away, beckoned with her gun. Locklight, Elizabeth and Tinker followed her down the steps to the main deck. One of the other women dropped a rope ladder over the side and stepped away as the crew began clambering back aboard. Seeing the guns, they raised their hands. When more of the pirates followed them up the ladder, there were still seven men missing, to Elizabeth's count. Then the four engineers were brought up from below. She'd seen one dead man for certain, which left two unaccounted for.

The woman in russet started along the line of captured crew. Her features were not masculine, but there was a strength about her that reminded Elizabeth of a classical statue. Her dark hair had been tied back.

"You're taken captive," the woman said, her voice clear but not loud. The accent strange. "You're prisoners of this war."

"There is no war," said Locklight.

"Who are you?"

"I'm captain of the *Iceland Queen*."

He'd begun to lower his hands, but the woman stepped up to him and pressed the muzzle of her pistol against the middle of his brow.

"Make an order, then. If it be followed, I'll believe you're a captain as you say."

Elizabeth didn't move. But she saw the man on the other side of Locklight edging away from him.

The woman drew back the pistol. The muzzle had left a mark on his skin. It seemed she would walk away, but then her hand whipped around, catching him on the side of the head with the stock. His knees folded and he dropped to the deck. His mouth fell slack. For a moment Elizabeth feared he was killed, but then he inhaled; a sickly rasping breath, like a gutter drunk.

"Captives you are," said the woman, stepping back again. "Captives of a war you will lose."

"May we ask who you are?" said Elizabeth. She could feel the man next to her leaning away.

"We are the Sargassans. Our nation rules this ocean. And who are you?"

Elizabeth swallowed. Willing her voice to return to a pitch she'd not voiced for six months, she said: "These men know me as Edwin Barnabus. But my real name is Elizabeth. I beg for asylum in the Sargassan Nation."

She heard the ripple of shock as it whispered around the crew of the *Iceland Queen*. One man let out an oath. Elizabeth kept her eyes focussed on the woman in russet. All her sacrifices had been for this moment. She braced herself. If the woman struck her down, she would be in the worst possible place; a prisoner despised by all other prisoners.

Next to her feet, Locklight shifted and groaned.

The woman spat towards him, then nodded and said: "The Sargassan Nation will hear your claim, Elizabeth."

"Then please hear mine also," said a reedy voice further

down the line.

"And who are you?"

"My name is Fidelia. But these sailors know me as Watkins. I was lately steward to the Commodore of the Company fleet."

PART THREE

CHAPTER 17

The skill of making toast was chiefly to maintain the optimum distance between bread and stove, and to do so for the optimum time. On land it would have been easy. But with the movement of the ship Elizabeth's first attempt had ended up catching fire.

They were heading southwest, as far as she could determine. The waves were cutting across their path at more or less forty-five degrees. It made for an uncomfortable ride. The ship tilted aft, then port, then forward, then starboard. The cycle repeated every ten seconds to her counting. In the galley, which was her new home, everything that was not fixed down had already fallen. Pans, cleavers and ladles hanging from hooks, swung away from the wall then around in a loop and back to clang against it, each with its own dull note, keeping rough time like a children's orchestra. With every forward lurch, Elizabeth had to fight gravity to stop the bread plunging into the coals once more.

Then came the cheese. She kept her fingers well clear of the blade and thus ended up with thicker slices than she would have liked. But surveying the plate when it was done, she wasn't unpleased.

Only a day had passed since the Sargassans had seized the ship. But already a kind of routine had set in. The crew had been locked up, officers and men together, all squeezed into one of the cargo holds. Two times a day the cook was released under strict watch, to prepare food for the captives. In this, Elizabeth assisted. She was allowed to help in carrying the food down to the men. Each time, she'd seen Tinker, sitting towards the back. Their eyes would connect for a fraction of a second; an acknowledgment too brief for anyone else to notice. At such moments, she felt the swell of pride in her chest. Who was she to teach lying to such a boy?

The others, stunned by the revelation of her sex, had grown more hostile on each visit. Several times she'd stolen down to eavesdrop on their conversation, hiding just out of view. She'd not been able to make out many words over the sounds of the waves and the engine. But she'd picked up anger from their tone. And she'd heard them speak her name.

Alone among the male crew, the chief engineer had been kept at his post. Two Sargassans stood to guard him at all times. And also to learn, she thought. He too ate from what the cook prepared.

After twenty-four hours, the underwater ship had been left far behind. This may have been because it couldn't keep up with a paddle steamer at full speed, the *Iceland Queen* in particular, for it had been one of the fastest ships in the Company fleet. Or perhaps because it had some other mission. Elizabeth knew well enough not to ask such questions. Nor did she know how many Sargassans there were to crew it. But eight women had transferred to the *Iceland Queen*.

They cooked for themselves for the most part. She'd come to the conclusion that this was from fear of poisoning, for they seemed suspicious of every word or act, as well they might. The only one who would accept food directly from her was Siân, the woman in the russet coat. She seemed to be their leader, for she'd taken up residence in the captain's cabin. But there were no salutes, and all of them went by their first names. Such informality might have seemed out of place on a ship. But Elizabeth had detected a sharp kind of discipline at work in all they did. Siân would sometimes write and sign orders, then hand them to members of her crew. These scraps of paper were received like precious gifts.

Elizabeth knocked once, then opened the door, manoeuvring into the cabin with the plate as level as she could manage. Then she stood, feet spread for balance, waiting for instruction.

Siân was bent over the chart table, consulting with Ekua, a small woman of dark skin and close-cropped hair. Both wore Hessian boots and grey breeches. A line had been marked on the sea chart. Ekua measured along it with a pair of dividers, whispering the result in a voice too quiet for Elizabeth to hear.

After the capture of the *Iceland Queen*, whilst they were still wallowing, enveloped in fog, fresh supplies of drinking water had been hauled across from the underwater boat. Even with that they wouldn't last long. But Siân had shown no concern over the matter. Elizabeth wasn't close enough to see the detail of the sea chart, or where the line ended.

The two women concluded their conference with a nod. Siân held out her hand, palm upwards. Ekua let her own palm slip over it before leaving. Elizabeth had seen the same ritual between others. It was always the senior woman who made the first move and the junior one who completed it.

"Did you find any?" Siân asked her.

"Yes, ma'am," said Elizabeth, stepping forwards to hand over the plate.

Siân lowered her nose to it and inhaled deeply. "We learn to take what food we get. But we rarely get what we best desire." She placed the plate on the chart table. It seemed a casual move, but she'd perfectly covered the line they'd been measuring. When the plate began to slide with the swell, she held it secure with her hand.

"You should no more say *ma'am*. It's a *gone* word. We've left it behind. Do you understand?"

"Yes..." She had to hold herself back from saying it again.

"Your given name – that you can keep. Or change it if you fancy. But the family name is a gone word also. You're made new when you come to the Nation. You're the property of no man and you bear no man's name. If the Nation takes you in, you mustn't be saying the name of an oppressor. We're free. Are you smart to that?"

"Yes."

Siân took a bite from the toast, closing her eyes in an expression of bliss.

"It is very fine," she said, when it was swallowed.

"When did you last have cheese?" Elizabeth asked.

Siân hesitated before making reply. "When we last took a ship. I can't make you out, Elizabeth. You ask little questions, but often they'd call up big answers if I weren't guarding myself." She reached out and tested the hem of Elizabeth's jacket, feeling the broadcloth between finger and thumb as might a tailor. Then her hand moved up to the fake birthmark. "What is this?"

"It's indigo. I had to paint it on every few days. It'll fade now. A few weeks and it'll be gone."

"Many women come to us disguised," Siân said. "But I've never before seen this."

"Men see the disfigurement," Elizabeth explained. "They don't look at the person behind it. I might have used false hair on my face. But it takes time to maintain. Time every day. And I wouldn't trust the illusion to months of close living. So I chose this."

"How long did you pass yourself as a man?" Siân asked.

"I've done it most of my life. Off and on. First it was my part in a circus act. Then there was an aristocrat who took a fancy to me. I ran but he kept searching. After that I'd always be hiding. Sometimes I'd be a man and sometimes a woman. Whichever was safer."

All of this was true. And thus easy to keep track of. The danger came in making a lie and then having to remember the detail of it on each new questioning.

Siân's hand shifted to the insignia on Elizabeth's shoulder. Her finger traced the design.

"Men do have a fancy for ranks and medals. What is the meaning of these marks?"

"It's the badge of a scientific officer."

"Of course it is. Curious a ship so small should merit one scientific officer. Let alone two. And a steward. What do you say of Fidelia?"

"I didn't know she was a woman."

Siân nodded slowly. "That's what she said too. And the commodore having the keeping of her. It often happens that way. A woman is hidden, pretending to be a steward. But then, the captain she serves – he knows it. It being for his pleasure she's kept."

"No one knew about me."

Siân seemed to consider this as she took another bite of the toast. Elizabeth felt sure that some of what she'd said had been believed. But every question was a new test.

"There are some who dress as boys from very small." Siân held her hand low, as if touching the head of a child. "They keep on with it after they're free – it being mostly who they are. And there are some who walk as men only to hide. Put them in a cabin with a man's clothes and a woman's clothes laid out – they'll choose the dress and be happy for it. But I can't figure which kind you are. Which clothes would you take if you wanted to be most yourself?"

Elizabeth thought before answering. "I'd take the dress."

"Are you sure of that?"

"Which would you take?" she asked.

"I was freeborn. There were no tyrants to rule me. It's not the same."

It wasn't really an answer and Elizabeth wanted to ask more. But there'd been a sharp edge in Siân's words. There was much about the ways the Sargassans treated each other that she didn't understand. It would be easy to overstep and not know she'd gone too far.

"I've never lived without tyranny," she said, trying to match the grit with which the Sargassans spoke about the world of men, hoping it would deflect further questioning.

Siân's expression didn't change. "What happened to that aristocrat who wanted you?" she asked.

For a moment, Elizabeth thought about creating a lie. But then she said: "He died."

"From old age, perhaps?"

"No." This she said with conviction.

At which, and for the first time, Siân smiled. "Your fate's not in my gift. But when we land, you'll see the Nation for yourself. It'll all come clear then. And, if you pass the Test, I'll be the first to welcome you into the free world."

No barrier had been put up between Elizabeth and the commodore's steward. It was just that they'd been kept busy on different tasks in different parts of the ship. On those few occasions when they had been together, there was always a Sargassan present to watch and to listen. If Elizabeth prepared food in the galley, the woman she now knew as Fidelia might be keeping lookout in the crow's nest. And when Elizabeth was set to work scrubbing the deck, Fidelia would be helping to make an inventory in the storerooms.

But on returning from the captain's cabin, she found Fidelia in the galley, leaning against the wall, working an apple with a bone-handled pocket knife. A single long spiral of peel dangled below. With a final cut it dropped. Then she sliced the apple and held out half.

"I wouldn't want you to die of hunger," she said.

Elizabeth took it. "Thank you."

She opened her mouth to ask a question, but Fidelia made a small shake of the head. Immediately, Elizabeth was alert. Though the passageway outside had been quite empty, the galley's narrow window light had been left propped open. Fidelia pointed to it and then put the same finger to her lips. Someone was standing up there, listening in. She'd stumbled into another test.

"We are free," she said, for whatever audience there was. "How do you find it?"

"I like it very well," Fidelia answered, though without a smile.

"Can I get you anything?"

"No, thank you. I found the apples already. I'm sent to prepare a feast of them."

Elizabeth's mind churned with questions. There were so many things she wanted to know and to say. If they backed each other up, they'd both stand a better chance of passing whatever tests lay ahead. But they'd been given no opportunity to confer.

Meeting Fidelia's eyes, Elizabeth said: "I never guessed you were a woman." She kept her tone of voice bright.

"Nor me, you," said Fidelia. From her expression, this seemed to be a lie. As a confidant of the commodore, she might well have been let in on the secret. The relationship between commodore and steward had bothered Elizabeth before and it bothered her still. Siân had said stewards were often mistresses. But intuition told her that wasn't the whole story.

She unhooked a sack of flour from the wall. "The bread's nearly gone. Will you help me make fresh?"

She emptied a generous heap onto the table. Two weevils

scurried from it. With deft fingers, Fidelia picked them out and flicked them away before making a hollow in the top of the mound. Elizabeth spooned in a starter from the crock, following it with warm water until the hollow was full. But instead of dipping her fingers, she took another handful from the sack and scattered it onto a clean stretch of table. Using the handle of a wooden spoon, she wrote in the flour: *What will the commodore do?*

Fidelia smoothed the words over with her palm and took the spoon. But as she began to write her answer, a small noise came from the passageway outside. Not the tread of boots, but the telltale breath of fabric brushing against the wall, as if someone were edging along it. Whoever it was came stealthily.

With two sweeps of her hand, Elizabeth scooped all the flour towards the centre of the mound, obliterating the newly written words.

Ekua looked in from the doorway. "We're getting hungry," she said. Her tone was easy but her eyes darted around as if searching for evidence.

Fidelia picked up the bowl of apples and followed her out.

Elizabeth stood in the galley alone, wondering at the words she'd glimpsed in the flour before they'd been wiped clean. What would the commodore do? *He'll send out the whole fleet to get me back.*

CHAPTER 18

After two days of steaming southwest, Elizabeth could no longer dip a jug fully under the surface of the fresh water. By the morning of the third day she had to tilt the cask and scoop with a mug. And then, when that was no longer possible, she found herself bending half inside it, bailing with a soup spoon into a cup.

That last mouthful she kept for herself. Then it was dry.

Finding the captain's cabin empty, she climbed out onto the deck. The sky was deep blue above and too bright to look into without squinting. The only cloud was a streak of white near the northern horizon. The ocean had grown calmer the further they steamed. With the engine no longer battling against the swell, their speed had increased. A fine spray from the paddlewheels caught a rainbow on the shadow side of the ship.

She found Siân and Ekua on the quarterdeck, conferring with two of the other Sargassans. Fidelia was standing back, just out of their circle. A large canvas bag lay between them. Elizabeth had seen it hauled across from the underwater ship, but had been given no intimation as to what it contained.

"The water barrel is empty," she announced, once they'd acknowledged her. "When shall we have fresh supplies?" It was one of those "little" questions that might have returned a big answer, but in reality never did.

Siân said: "You can help us. This job needs many hands."

Ekua and one of the others got down and delved into the bag. First out were four coils of thin rope, which they placed on the deck, side by side, as if the precise arrangement was important. Then came a bundle of long wooden spars, taller than a man, and numerous shorter ones. Finally they heaved out a great quantity of pale blue canvas, which Elizabeth took to be some kind of tent. But when the spars had been slotted into pockets in the fabric, it began to take the shape of a huge kite.

"Sit on the wing," Ekua said, snapping her fingers and pointing.

Elizabeth jumped to the task. Fidelia took the opposite side. And just in time, because the wind was trying to lift it. Ekua worked fast, inserting the shorter spars crosswise, stretching squares of canvas. The last of these formed a series of open-ended boxes between the two wings, pushing it proud of the deck.

With this new sail area, the kite began to twitch. Siân fastened ropes, one on each side, and then something that looked like a trapeze artist's harness. Ekua followed just behind, testing the knots. When everything had been assembled, she stepped to each of the Sargassans in turn and embraced them with a hug and a kiss on the cheek. One woman she kissed full on the lips. It seemed to Elizabeth a kind of ceremony, for everyone knew their part. The lip kiss surprised her, though; not that such a thing would be done, but that it would be done in open gaze.

Ekua put on a pair of goggles and a tight-fitting leather hat. Then she sat on the deck and buckled herself into the harness. The others looped ropes twice around the stern railings at the very rear of the quarterdeck.

"The Unicorn will sail," Ekua said, with gravity, like a priest intoning the first line of the Lord's Prayer. The words made no sense to Elizabeth, unless it was a reference to the kite itself.

"Ready?" Siân asked.

"Ready," said Ekua.

The others took hold of the kite.

"Get off it now!"

Elizabeth obeyed, rolling from the wing as Fidelia did the same on the other side. The entire structure bucked, jumping from the deck, turning as it lifted, passing over the railing and coming to the limit of its short rope with a sound like the thump of a slack drum. There it danced, suspended over the water behind the ship. The ropes of Ekua's harness were long enough to have remained loose. But now she began to adjust them, standing as she brought them shorter, climbing up to sit on the railing, where she took in the last of the slack.

"Ready?" Siân asked for the second time.

Instead of answering, Ekua made a circle of her thumb and first finger. The others began to let out the ropes. The kite eased away from the stern and she swung free, dangling beneath it. At first it seemed she might be dunked in the ocean, but the kite began to climb again as they let out more rope. Out and up it went until it was level with the crow's nest. They continued to pay out the rope turn by turn and the kite went higher still, twice as high as the mast. More perhaps; it was hard to tell. Ekua was a dot, swinging below it. Elizabeth felt a kind of awestruck horror as she watched. The solemnity of those parting embraces had been real.

"Why?" she asked. "What's she doing?"

"She's going to show us the way."

Only two of the ropes had been used, the others lay where they'd been placed on the deck.

"We keep them for a day of stronger winds," said Siân.

Elizabeth had to shade her eyes to look at the kite. From

such a vantage point Ekua would be able to watch over a great expanse of ocean. It was said that from the top of the crow's nest, a sailor with a keen eye could spot another tall ship from twenty miles, should the air be crystal clear. Ekua's view would be far wider. The Sargassans seemed to have no means of signalling at night from ship to distant ship. They'd marvelled at the *Iceland Queen*'s helio. Yet here they were, sending an observer hundreds of feet into the air, something the Company couldn't do. The technology was simple, yet to Elizabeth it seemed breathtaking in its audacity.

All on deck were staring at the kite; a dot in the vast sky. She could feel their excitement. Then one of them exclaimed: "She's moving!"

It took a moment for Elizabeth to understand what was happening. The kite had dipped and was swinging around towards the starboard side of the ship.

"She can steer it?"

"She shows us the way!" cried Siân. And then, to one of the others: "Bring us around. Ten degrees to port!"

Elizabeth gripped the railing as they began to turn and the deck tilted under her feet. She watched the ropes shift back into alignment with the ship. The kite lifted once more, attaining its greatest height. Then it was descending again.

"Bring her in," called Siân.

They began to haul, three to a rope, keeping time, coiling each line on the deck as they went, loop after loop.

"Where are we going?" Elizabeth asked; a big question this time.

"Home," said Siân. "We're going home to Mother."

Ekua, Siân and the other women took to standing near the prow whenever they could, staring at a smudge of haze hanging low in the sky directly ahead. As the hours passed, the haze resolved into a column of smoke, and then into several separate columns, which Elizabeth supposed to be ships. And somewhere among them would be the flagship of the floating nation.

The world she had come from seemed the opposite of the world she was entering. The Company was an outpost of the Gas-Lit Empire. By contrast, she'd been told that the Sargassans were a nation of eels, an assemblage of runaways and pirates. The Company dominated the ocean through the statement of its mighty presence. The Sargassans kept hidden, attacking from below the waves. She'd had to disguise herself as a man to be commissioned as scientific officer. Now she'd had to reveal herself as a woman to avoid being imprisoned by the Sargassans. Yet, for all these oppositions, it seemed that both sides had chosen to call their flagship "Mother".

"Have you ever been free?" asked Ekua, when Elizabeth went to stand with them at the prow.

"When I was a child."

"Siân said you were born in a travelling show?"

"It's true."

"And you did magic?"

"Yes."

"Did your mother teach you?"

Elizabeth thought before answering. "I don't remember my mother." Then, to avoid more questions coming, she asked one of her own: "Were you always Sargassan?"

Ekua shook her head. "I was born Ashanti. When I was twelve, my father decided to take me to London. It was the best thing he ever did for me. Our ship was wrecked off Cape Verde. I thank all the gods of the ocean that I came to be free."

Elizabeth had yet to make out the profiles of ships ahead, though the columns of smoke were ever more distinct and it seemed they couldn't be far. "Siân said that when we arrive, I'm to be tested. What kind of test will it be?"

The women glanced at each other; an unspoken

consultation. Then Ekua said, "The prisoners will be hungry. You best go feed them."

It was Lena, a woman of Scandinavian appearance, who did much of the guarding duty. She wasn't large or conspicuously muscled but she walked with the flow of a dancer. Or a knife fighter. Elizabeth had seen enough of both to recognise the signs. No movement happened by chance. It was she who escorted the cook to the galley, then stood in the passageway to watch as he organised the meal. Even in stillness she was a study in precision.

"There's no water," Elizabeth said.

"Then what would you have me do?" asked the cook.

"There are apples. And there's still hardtack from yesterday."

"You mean there's no water for no one? Or no water for us below?" Anger edged his words.

Elizabeth patted the side of the cask. The hollow sound was answer enough.

"We'll die," said the cook.

Elizabeth shook her head.

"Then are we to make land?"

Elizabeth glanced at Lena. Finding no clue in the woman's impassive expression, she said: "Water will come."

"And what happens when we do make land? Will they kill us then?"

"No! Surely not."

"There's talk. They're saying we'll be roasted in fires – that they're cannibals." This he hissed under his breath.

"Where's all this talk from, then? Is it dreams? Or has someone had a vision down there in the hold?"

"It's talk. That's all."

"Then put it aside! Let's make the best of things. We've a good supply of meat."

"With no water?"

"It's what we have."

She selected the best looking of the hams from the store room and hefted it back to the galley. Salt crystals on the skin crunched against the table as she laid it down.

When the cook reached for the knife, Elizabeth saw Lena adjust her stance. It was no more than a shift of balance but it told a story. When he set to carving the joint she returned to her original balance.

The serrated blade cut easily through the cured meat, revealing pink flesh below the outer surface. Ordinarily the cook would have been the one to measure out the stores and make sure no one took overmuch. There'd be times when this put him on the wrong side of the crew. As a fellow prisoner his role had been reversed. She saw him cutting the slices extra thick. They might thank him for it at first, but there'd be no water until they reached the Sargassan fleet. Hunger might be better than the thirst they'd suffer after so much salt.

When it came to sorting the apples, the cook picked up the keg, looked inside and shook it. "There's few enough left," he said. "I'll take the lot."

Lena didn't object and Elizabeth was happy to let it pass. She was left to carry a load of meat and hardtack, which had been heaped together on a large wooden tray.

Their first stop was the engine room. The chief engineer nodded a greeting towards her, but didn't smile. The cook delved in the barrel and handed him two apples. Elizabeth held the tray for him.

"No water?"

"I'm sorry."

"And we're burning through the oil," he said. "We can't keep up this speed for long."

"I'm sure they know what they're doing."

"Do you think so?"

He selected a small slice of the ham and a larger square of hardtack. "Be careful who you make alliances with, Miss Barnabus."

"That name's gone," said Lena. "Her name's Elizabeth now."

At the door of the cargo hold, Lena peered through the grille, checking left and right before turning the key. The cook went in first. Elizabeth took a deep breath before following. There were too many men in too small a space and the slop buckets were never emptied soon enough. The smell had grown worse by the day. The insults too. They'd called her traitor at first. Now they muttered worse things whenever she was within range of hearing.

The cook squatted and lowered the apple cask to the floor. He reached inside it and seemed to select one for himself before standing. There'd been an awkwardness to his hand movement in the barrel. A premonition prickled at the back of her neck.

"You're a whore!"

The words had come from the back of the room, spat with such hatred that they caught in her mind, distracting her from the thing that she should have been thinking about as she knelt to place the tray of food next to the cask.

She felt the move before it happened; a shift in the rank air, a hiss of shifting cloth. The cook barged her shoulder and she went sprawling. Hands grabbed her wrists and one of her ankles. She was being dragged. She twisted one arm free. But they still had her. Someone grabbed her hair.

No words were said, but in that fraction of a second the prisoners all scrambled back from the door. They hauled her to her knees. Something cold pressed against her neck. She glimpsed the cook's hand and a flash of polished steel before they yanked her hair again, pulling her head up. The blade's serrations pricked the underside of her jaw.

"Back off or she's dead!"

She couldn't see who'd said it.

Lena was standing just beyond the doorway, a pistol raised. She shifted back half a step, then flicked her left hand forwards. Elizabeth felt her hair released. The serrated galley knife clattered to the floor. The cook dropped and twisted onto his side. The handle of a throwing knife projected from his face. He brushed at it, as if it was no more than a speck of dirt, though the blade was buried deep in his skull.

Then he was still and everyone else had started to move.

Elizabeth felt her arms grabbed from behind. Locklight snatched the galley knife from the floor. Lena aimed the gun at him. He froze. Then she raised her aim above his head and fired. The gunshot reverberated from the metal walls, disorientating. Locklight rushed towards Lena, but she slammed the door closed before he could reach her. The sound of voices came back first; shouts sounding like whispers. Sulphurous gunpowder smoke hung in the air.

The knife was at her throat again. They pushed her up to the door, ramming her face to the grille. Lena was reloading her pistol, standing beyond any attempt to grab through the bars. Her movements were unhurried, tamping down the shot, tipping a pinch of black powder into the pan, cocking the hammer.

Someone was wailing. "They're going to kill us! They're going to kill us all!"

A low boom reverberated around the hold. A sharp line of daylight broke in from above as the cargo hold covers swung away. The hands that had kept her pressed to the door now wrenched her away from it, twisting her around. Silhouettes interrupted the square of sky above.

"We'll kill her!" shouted Captain Woodfall.

A shot sounded. He crumpled. There was blood this time, spreading from a hole in his chest.

Two of the other men dropped to their knees and raised their hands. But Locklight hauled Elizabeth sideways along the wall to the corner of the hold, keeping his body behind hers. The serrated knife was at her throat. They might still shoot him, but it would take a steady hand if the bullet wasn't to go through her body first.

"What do you want?" called Siân from above.

"Let the crew free," shouted Locklight. "You can keep me. I'm a captain. I'm a valuable hostage. And keep the *Iceland Queen*. In return, you get this *woman* back alive."

"I give you a choice," called Siân. "Kill her if you've a fancy for it. She's not yet one of us. But know that if you do, I'll use that same knife and cut the balls from every one of you. Either way, you'll be alive – if you don't bleed too bad. I give you one minute to decide."

The silhouettes moved back, leaving the sky as an empty square.

"It's a bluff," hissed Locklight. "We wait and we press our bargain."

"She said they won't kill us," said Ryan.

"That's not what she said!"

The two men who'd previously surrendered now lowered their hands, but didn't get up from their knees, as if caught between two thoughts. The bass rhythm of the engine vibrated through the hold, measuring away their allotted time. The cook lay still. A line of blood was creeping from Woodfall's body, following the join between two metal plates in the floor. When it had all but reached the feet of one of the sailors, Elizabeth spoke.

"I know you hate me. And you may not believe this, but I'll say it anyway – they're not going to let you out of here, except on their terms. Nor would you if things were the other way about. Any threat they make, I believe they'll carry out – to the letter. But I'll make you this promise, yield as they've asked and I'll argue your case when we get wherever it is we're going. If they'll let me." Then, turning her head to look back at Captain Locklight, she added: "I'll argue for your loved ones too, if they're still alive."

She could feel the trembling in his arm; Locklight, the man of iron. Taking his hand, she eased it away from her neck and unpeeled his fingers from the galley knife. Then she stepped to the door and offered it through the grille, hilt first.

"And the other one," Lena said.

The men backed away as she approached the dead cook. Fighting nausea, she braced one hand against his still-warm forehead and gripped the handle of the knife with the other. It took strength to wrench it free. Only then would Lena turn the key and let her out.

Whilst she'd been held – the whole thing could have lasted no more than a couple of minutes – Elizabeth's experience had flowed with a kind of super-real clarity. Almost a calm. The trembling set in as she left the hold. By the time she was climbing the stairs, she'd broken out in a sweat and her stomach was squirming into a knot.

"The knife... It must have been... He'd hidden it in the barrel..."

Lena stroked her hair. "You're a warrior, Elizabeth."

"Two men died."

"It was their choice."

Elizabeth's stomach heaved. She dropped to her knees and threw up. After that she retched three more times. Sitting on the step, she placed her face in her hands. There was no fresh water to wash away the taste. Lena brought her a cup of sea water.

"Swill and spit," she said, then wiped Elizabeth's face with a damp cloth. "They did what men do. It's not your fault."

"I should have taken more care."

"No woman's been left dead by their hands."

She swilled and spat again. They sat together for a time as Elizabeth's sweat dried.

"Can you stand yet?" Lena asked.

Elizabeth nodded.

"Then come up top. There's something you should see."

On deck, Siân and Ekua beckoned her over. She followed their gaze and saw an island immediately ahead. But not an island like any she'd seen before. It spread, wide and flat. Low trees grew everywhere. Smoke rose from the chimney pipes of houses. But the most unnatural sight were the landlocked ships that seemed to form part of the island itself. Every one of them was upside down, keel pointing to the sky.

CHAPTER 19

In her long and lonely nights of preparation in the Natural History Museum, Elizabeth had studied charts of the Atlantic Ocean. She'd tried to memorise the islands of the Caribbean, the crinkled coastline of Central and South America, charts of ocean depth and the directions of prevailing winds. Geography was an imperfect science. But during the 1950s and 60s, great efforts had been made to map the unexplored reaches of the world. Airships carrying the most sophisticated surveying equipment had crisscrossed the oceans, identifying countless islands and sand shoals. But Elizabeth knew of no land mass marked in the middle of the Sargasso Sea.

Small boats began following them when they were still half a mile out. By the time the prow of the *Iceland Queen* swung around for the final approach, a flotilla was all but surrounding them; sails of blue, maroon, brown, pale green and yellow. It was a marvel that none of the boats collided. Lena and Ekua waved and many arms waved back. Siân stood on the quarterdeck, directing the engine room and steering the ship as it slowed.

Elizabeth had looked to each of the small boats, hoping against the odds to catch a glimpse of Julia. Now she scanned the crowd that had gathered on the jetty ahead, examining each face.

Fidelia slipped in beside her at the gunwale and whispered: "We must help each other."

Elizabeth glanced around. For once they were unwatched. "They'll question us," she whispered. "Say we both came on this mission desiring to escape."

"And if they ask the men?"

"The men can't claim to know our secret thoughts. And, it'd be our word against theirs. But you shouldn't have told them you were steward to the commodore."

"Someone might have known my insignia," Fidelia said.

There was another question that Elizabeth wanted to ask, but she didn't know how to frame it. According to Siân, Fidelia must have been the commodore's mistress. Indeed, it would explain the strange intimacy that she'd enjoyed, as well as the message written in the flour on the galley table. But it felt wrong.

"Why will the commodore send the fleet to get you back?"

Fidelia bent in closer and whispered: "Because I'm his granddaughter."

The words were a revelation. But at the same time, Elizabeth felt as if she'd always known, in some part of her mind. Suddenly everything fitted into place: the skills of seamanship, the absolute confidence of the commodore in the trustworthiness of his steward, the concern she'd expressed for his wellbeing.

Fidelia seemed about to say more, but Lena was striding across the deck. She stepped between them and put her arms over their shoulders.

"Feeling better?" she asked.

"Yes," said Elizabeth, smiling to cover the shock of the revelation.

"Now you'll see what marvels we've made. How do you like our island?"

"I like it very well," Fidelia said, her voice artificially bright.

Up on the quarterdeck, Siân shouted. "Dead slow!" The ship continued forwards, water sloshing around its paddles, which had become water brakes. And then: "Reverse one quarter!"

Elizabeth gripped the railing against the sudden lurch.

"All stop!"

Ropes were flung across the gap and hauled tight.

"We've landed," Fidelia said.

"Not quite," said Lena, pointing in the direction of the island.

Elizabeth looked along her arm trying to see what she was indicating. There were trees and houses and a quantity of machinery of unfamiliar design. A wave coursed along the side of the ship. The jetty rose and fell with its passing. And then the trees and houses of the island shifted also.

"It's all floating," Elizabeth said. "Everything's afloat!"

"Welcome to Freedom," said Lena.

Fresh guards came aboard and the eight Sargassans took their leave of the ship. Elizabeth found herself separated from Fidelia as they walked. With every step the floating jetty bobbed underneath her. And with every step she was leaving Tinker and the other captives further behind. The thought gnawed at her as they climbed a short flight of wooden stairs to the island itself.

She could feel the movement of this also, but it was more from the ocean swell than from the weight of people walking over it. It felt as if there was a great mass of island below her feet and below the waterline.

Her first impression of Freedom Island was a smell of sewage and decaying seaweed. Flies buzzed around them. Their path was a boardwalk, held up by stilts above a ground surface that seemed mostly a tangle of tree roots. Peering over the edge of the boards she saw objects gripped within the matrix of roots. Mostly they appeared to be bales of vegetation. But there were also barrels of different sizes and logs. In one place she saw a riveted metal cylinder that could have been the boiler of an engine. Everything below was green and slick with algae.

Smaller walkways branched from the main path, joining clusters of huts, also held up on stilts. Women on every side-path and around every house applauded as they passed. Some of them rushed up to take Siân's hand, placing it on their own foreheads, as if asking for her to bless them. Elizabeth searched the faces. Each new group of women might have contained her lost friend. But none of them did.

Most of the women were of African or European descent. Dresses were worn, but only to the knee. Many wore breeches and boots in the manner of Siân and the other sailors. Two of the women she saw were heavily pregnant. Therein lay yet another question, for there were no men. She hadn't expected there to be. But the revelation of it was still a shock.

There were children though. Some of the younger ones might have been boys, though they wore their hair in the fashion of girls and their outer garments seemed something between smocks and dresses. A thought of Tinker flickered in her mind. But his safety would come only if she could secure her own, so she forced her focus back onto the bizarre island.

The walkway turned, joining a wide, straight deck. It ran perhaps a quarter of a mile, which was the entire length of the island. The huts on either side were open fronted, giving them the appearance of shops. Indeed, it could have been mistaken for the main street of a jungle town, had it been possible to ignore the ripples of the ocean swell passing under them and away.

Women issued from the shops to follow on behind. Glancing back, Elizabeth saw that the procession numbered some hundreds.

The outer island had been squalid. But as they approached the centre, buildings became more substantial in construction and size. Fine soil lay between them instead of tangled tree roots. Lettuces, cabbage and beans were growing in every space, as well as fruit trees and other vegetables she didn't recognise.

In the very centre of the island stood a wooden sailing ship, beached, as it were. Unlike the others, it lay the right way up, though without rigging or masts. Lines of coconut palms had kept it hidden from distant view. Wide steps led up to the deck. As she climbed, Elizabeth found herself being shifted within the group so that by the time they'd reached the top step she was shoulder to shoulder with Fidelia. The eight Sargassans formed a wall around them. Siân led them onto the deck and when they were at last facing the quarterdeck called out in a strident voice.

"Siân, daughter of the Sargassan Nation, is returned with a great prize."

The procession of followers had stopped short of the ship's deck. They waited and watched from the steps and the wide boardway.

The main hatch opened and a red-haired woman in a fine dress of sky blue emerged. She climbed to the quarterdeck and turned to look down at Siân. The resemblance between the two women was striking.

"Gwynedd, daughter of the Sargassan Nation, will hear you," she said. "What is your prize?"

"I bring the paddle steamer *Iceland Queen*. I bring a cargo hold full of prisoners. And I bring these two women."

"Let the women present themselves."

Elizabeth felt a hand pushing her forward. She found herself standing next to Fidelia at the front of the group.

"Do you come to us of your own free will?" asked Gwynedd from the quarterdeck.

"I do," said Elizabeth.

Fidelia nodded.

"Do you wish to join the Sargassan Nation, renouncing all former loyalties, ties and agreements?"

"I do."

"And do you understand the absolute bond you seek to join?"

Elizabeth hesitated. She could feel the pulse throbbing in her neck. Neither had Fidelia spoken. The silence of the crowd pressed in on her.

"Well?" Gwynedd demanded.

"No one has taught us," Elizabeth said, her voice sounding small.

A murmur moved across the crowd.

Gwynedd folded her arms. "If you wish to be free, you must first undergo the Test. Should you pass, you will become part of the Nation. That means being bound to every woman here as a sister, sworn to protect and to obey. Even unto death. Do you understand this?"

"Yes," they both said.

"Until then, you are our guests on Freedom Island. Your Test will be tomorrow."

Ekua led them down the steps from the ship and along the main boardway. But before reaching the path that would have taken them back to the jetty, she took a right-hand turn between two of the shops and out behind them into an area of trees. Elizabeth caught glimpses of women here and there, but there was none of the applause that had accompanied the triumphal procession from the *Iceland Queen*.

The final walkway was so narrow that they were obliged to go single file. A cluster of five stilt huts lay at the end. Each was capped with a gently sloping roof, thick with vegetables. From a distance the roofs looked like small patches of farmland. But coming closer, Elizabeth saw that they were of corrugated iron construction and that the plants were growing in pots, densely packed on top.

Ekua stopped on a small deck between the houses. A woman working one of the roof gardens stood and picked her way between the plant pots to the edge. In one hand she held a trowel, in the other a quantity of dark green leaves.

Ekua shielded her eyes to look up. "I've brought you a guest. She's to take the Test tomorrow." Then, turning to Elizabeth: "You'll be collected in the morning." Without waiting for a response, she turned and led Fidelia back the way they'd come.

The woman on the roof clambered down a rickety ladder at the side of the house.

"Welcome," she said.

"Thank you. My name's Elizabeth."

The woman didn't take her hand. Her smile seemed more from embarrassment than warmth. "Come," she said. "I'll fetch water."

Inside the hut was a single room, without windows or lamps. As Elizabeth's eyes started to adjust, she made out a crude iron stove and two barrels. The rest of the room's contents hung from ropes suspended across the space above their heads. Herbs, vegetables, dried fish, pans and pots, gardening implements, fishing nets and folded hammocks, all swayed with the shifting of the island.

The woman reached up and took down a wooden cup. This she dipped in one of the barrels before offering it two-handed. Elizabeth drank, cautiously at first. It was the freshest water she'd tasted in months. She drained the cup and passed it back, hoping for a refill. But the woman hooked it below the rafters again.

"What is the Test?" Elizabeth asked.

The only answer was another embarrassed smile.

"Can you tell me your name?"

A shake of the head.

"Will you be able to tell me that if I pass the Test?"

"Yes."

"And if I fail?"

Back to the embarrassed smile. "I'm sorry," she said. "But if you fail, you die."

CHAPTER 20

The clothes on Freedom Island displayed an eclectic mixture of fabrics, colours and styles. Some costumes might have come directly from the streets of New York, Paris or St Petersburg. Others from Kumasi, Timbuktu and Mogadishu. But all showed signs of long use and repair.

The woman who would not give her name wore an ochre-coloured dress. The material seemed homespun. As Elizabeth watched, she cooked up a stew of vegetables and fish, which she served in wooden bowls. They sat together outside the stilt hut and ate in silence. Elizabeth dangled her legs over the edge of the decking. She'd been given a dented metal spoon to eat with. The woman used one made of wood.

There were no voices or sounds of activity from the other huts in the little cluster. As it grew darker, no lights were lit. Indeed, she could see no lamps anywhere. The deck, she now saw, had been tied to its stilts rather than fixed with rigid struts. On finishing her soup, she got up to investigate. The huts too were suspended, though on thicker ropes. She'd grown used to the gentle undulation of the island and hadn't wondered how the buildings remained standing. But now she saw the method and realised what a problem it had overcome. Just as there were hammocks in the hut to allow for a gentle sleep on an ever shifting island, so too the buildings rested in cradles of their own.

Wondering what else she might find, she asked: "Am I free to explore?"

"I'm sorry" said the woman. "You must stay."

Once the sun had fully set, Elizabeth lay back and looked up at the sky.

"The stars are beautiful," she said, trying to find common ground with her host. But she might as well have tried to open an oyster with kind words. The woman excused herself and went inside to string hammocks between the beams.

A breeze rustled the leaves and brought the sound of distant machinery; low and rhythmic, like the cogs of a windmill.

All the International Patent Office and the North Atlantic Trading Company knew about these people might be written on one side of a sheet of notepaper. From that standpoint of comfortable ignorance it had been easy to talk of spying missions and contacts. The Sargassans had indeed evolved a strange pattern of technology. Wooden bowls and wooden spoons, an island tied together by tree roots, huts empty of furniture; all this seemed primitive. She'd seen the way they marvelled at the gimballed mount of the helio on the *Iceland Queen*. They had no such signalling technology. Yet they could pilot a kite hundreds of feet into the air and keep watch over a vast expanse of ocean. They'd created an underwater ship. They'd acquired the means of shooting down aircraft flying at eight thousand feet.

John Farthing had told her that technology unregulated would always be bent towards the sciences of destruction. And so it seemed. Yet what choice did these women have? Beyond the Gas-Lit Empire was a world of danger and constant war; this Farthing had also told her. If the Sargassans had not developed the means to protect themselves, their nation would have been snuffed out.

A nation of eels, they'd been called. Indeed, they had

attacked the *Iceland Queen* and sunk the *Mary May*. They'd imprisoned the crew, including Tinker. Yet Elizabeth was becoming aware of a disturbing doubt. She had stepped into a society where women were the agents of their own destiny. The eight Sargassans who'd brought them back to Freedom Island had spoken with passion about their nation. Elizabeth hadn't trusted their words. But they'd also spent their time at the prow of the ship, gazing at the horizon, yearning for that first glimpse of their island home.

She focussed her mind on the airship *American Frontier*, picturing her last glimpse of Julia climbing up to step aboard. It was the Sargassans who had shot it down. They were murderers. In a few hours they would turn their tyranny against her, forcing her to endure a test of life or death.

Yet the woman who had been left to guard her lay snoring inside the hut.

The moon had risen, its light turning the many tones and colours of the island to black and white. The shadow of the hut lay over the boards where Elizabeth lay. If anyone was watching from a distance, they wouldn't be able to see her. She sat up and looked around. There was no one and no sound but the creaking of the island itself. Getting to her feet, she stood, keeping her back pressed to the wall.

The more she'd discovered about the Sargassans, the less certain she felt. If Julia had come to the island, she too must have been tested. If she'd passed the Test, she might be very close, perhaps on a ship or a fishing boat. She could even be in one of the underwater craft.

Placing her feet, Elizabeth stepped away from the wall, crouching as she moved from the shadow of one hut into the shadow of the next. In ten paces she was at the boardwalk that could take her back towards the centre of the island. She stopped. The way ahead was flooded with moonlight.

She peered over the side of the boards. It would be easy to

let herself down to the layer of tangled roots below. The green algae might be slippery, but she could go on her hands and knees if necessary. She could crawl underneath the boards, in shadow and perfectly hidden. It might even be possible to travel underneath the wide deckway, right across the centre of the island.

On the *Iceland Queen* the Sargassans had left little to chance. It seemed wrong that on their island home, they'd make it so easy for her to go wandering.

Placing her feet once more, she retraced the path of shadows back to the hut. She'd been left the hammock nearest the doorway, from which it would have been easiest to escape into the night. She climbed into it and lay looking up to the herbs and dried fish and pans dangling below the roof.

She hadn't seen anyone waiting under the boardwalk. But that is where she would have waited, if she'd wanted to catch a runaway.

The smells and sights of the island had been so overwhelming at first that Elizabeth hadn't focussed on its sounds. There were many hundreds of huts and miles of decking, all suspended by rope. She'd counted the hulls of six upside-down ships – landlocked, so to speak – and trees grew everywhere. Through shift and give, every part of the island seemed to whisper to its neighbour. Any one of these sounds might hardly have been heard above a gentle breeze. But laid over each other, and in the stillness of the night, they combined to make a low, mournful voice. She listened to it as she lay awake. Sometimes it seemed like a giant, whispering over and over again a word that she couldn't understand. And sometimes it was like a monster breathing in sleep. The swaying of her hammock kept time.

In the night she opened her eyes and saw a bar of moonlight on the wall where there had been blackness before. Her first thought was surprise that she'd been able to sleep. The open doorway had been troubling her. It was an invitation. But before she slept, or in her dream, she wasn't sure which, it had come to her that this *was* the Test. There would be no examination and no ordeal. All she had to do was obey when she seemed to be unwatched.

After that she slept more deeply. In one of her dreams she saw John Farthing, as she had many times before. She wanted to go to him, but this time he was far away and looking in the other direction. Again and again, she tried to approach, but he was always walking away from her.

The second time she woke it was to daylight, the smell of wood smoke and the ache of thwarted longing, which she couldn't quite place. The woman who would not give her name was bent low, brushing out the hut with a bundle of twigs.

Elizabeth sat up and said, "Good morning."

The woman's smile seemed more genuine than it had been the previous night. She took down a bowl and tipped three small fish into it from a pan on the stove. Elizabeth accepted the food. No cutlery was offered so she set to eating with her fingers. It lacked much flavour beyond oil and salt, but she was glad of it, and of the water that was offered once she'd finished. This time she asked for more and drank three large measures.

In the morning light it felt less as if she were a prisoner, more a genuine guest. The warmth and openness of the woman was surely a sign that she'd chosen well to not go wandering.

"I have work," the woman said. "They'll come to fetch you soon."

"Do you think I'll pass the Test?" Elizabeth asked, hoping for confirmation.

"The Unicorn will sail," the woman said. Then she took

down a fishing net from under the rafters, slung it over her shoulder and walked from the hut.

Elizabeth watched until she'd disappeared behind the trees. It wasn't just the hulls of the landlocked ships that were upside down on Freedom Island. The behaviour of the Sargassans was constantly unexpected. So much of what they said and did made no sense.

At least the chamber pot was familiar. Alone for the first time on the island, she took the chance to use it unobserved. Not knowing where to empty it afterwards, she followed her nose to a small outbuilding behind the cluster of huts. This proved to be the privy. But even here she found strangeness. A rough wooden ladder gave access to the land of tangled roots below the platform. From what she'd seen of the island, anyone could walk freely into any building, for all were open. But the space under the privy drop was guarded by a small door and an iron padlock.

The sun was high by the time they came for her. Two women, wearing swords at their belts, marched her along the narrow way, one in front and one behind. On reaching the broad deckway, they took up positions on either side. Neither spoke.

On the previous day, women had come out to applaud their progress. Now they turned their backs. Conversations fell silent. Toddlers were scooped up and older children sent inside.

Logic told her that she had nothing to fear, that she had already passed the Test. But the solemn mood began to infect her. Nothing could be certain in a world of such strangeness. A smile of embarrassment might not mean the same as it did in London. Nor a smile of warmth.

On the previous day a great crowd had followed them to the ship at the centre of the island. Now they climbed the steps alone. Nor was there anyone on deck to receive them.

The guards marched to the hatchway, leading her inside to a lamp-lit passage and down a flight of steps. At the door to what should have been the captain's cabin, they parted, making room for her to pass.

Elizabeth's breath came faster and shallow, as if there wasn't enough oxygen in the air.

"What should I do?" she asked.

The guards wouldn't meet her gaze.

There being nothing else to do, she knocked on the door and listened. The only sound was the creaking of the ship as it moved. She glanced back. The women were now standing shoulder to shoulder, filling the width of the passage, barring any possibility of escape. Each kept a hand to her sword hilt. Elizabeth knocked again. But this time, instead of waiting, she opened the door and stepped through.

The room was tall and wide, as if all the cabins of two floors had been cut into one. The only light was the circle cast by a chandelier, which swayed left, then right, with the movement of the island. Stalactites of wax hung beneath its candles. What should have been window glass had been replaced by carved wooden boards. At the head of the room, on a throne atop a dais under that one circle of light, sat the queen of the Sargassans, bent backed, lined with age and wrapped in furs. Elizabeth had no doubt of her station.

It was a scene unexpected, bizarre and somehow terrifying. Despite her resolve and reason, Elizabeth found herself trembling. She advanced towards the foot of the dais. There'd been no indication of what was expected, but she found herself kneeling.

"What is this, my children?" the queen intoned, her voice all on the same note. "There is someone in my way."

A movement made Elizabeth start. Figures were stepping out from the shadows around the walls of the room. By their gait they seemed women. But they wore black facemasks and tall black hats.

"Who is it, Mother Rebecca?" The chorus of their whispers made a ghostly drone. "No one should stand in your way." They took another step as they spoke.

"I know not, my children," intoned the queen. "I am old and cannot see."

The masked figures stepped forwards again. Elizabeth's fear turned to panic. She willed herself to stay kneeling, though her skin was crawling and every nerve was screaming at her to run or fight.

"Shall we kill her for you, Mother Rebecca? Shall we remove her from your path?"

The circle of figures was closing. Each held a short dagger.

The queen intoned another line: "Is this an enemy come to slit your mother's throat?"

"We shall bring her low," they replied. "Nothing will stand in your way!"

"Or is she a friend, come to give your mother aid?"

"Test her, Mother Rebecca! Put her to the Test!"

They were near her now, to the sides and behind, like a fishing net drawing closed. Their daggers were raised, ready to plunge.

"Will you face the Test?" asked the queen.

Elizabeth tried to speak but her throat had constricted and her tongue seemed huge in her mouth.

"She will face the Test!" chorused the masked figures. Then all at the same time, they stepped back and back and back until they were once more in the shadows around the walls of the chamber. But two had remained and taken up positions on either side of the throne.

"Stand," commanded the queen.

Elizabeth's breath was coming in short gasps but she managed to get to her feet.

"Would you obey the Sargassan Nation in every order and

to the letter?"

"Yes," she said, finding her voice.

"Don't trust that word," spat the figure on the left of the throne. "Her answer came too quick. She'd promise the moon to save her blood. It means nothing!"

The voice sounded like Siân's, though it was muffled by the mask.

"If I order you to your certain death," said the queen, "would you obey?"

Elizabeth tried to steady her nerves and think. She would die for her friends but not for any nation. It wasn't a truth that seemed wise to admit. She counted to five in her head before speaking, not repeating the mistake of answering quickly and glib.

"I would obey."

"More lies," hissed the figure on the left. "It's what she thinks you want to hear. Such a creature will never speak truth!"

There was a whisper from the shadows; a wordless sound of disgust. Elizabeth glanced over her shoulder.

"Are you distracted?" asked the queen.

"No, ma'am."

"That is a gone word! You don't speak it here!"

"I'm sorry."

"Then listen to your third question. If the Nation ordered you to kill your dearest friend, would you obey?"

She'd tried the answers she thought they wanted. Both times they'd called out her insincerity. She'd not stolen away in the night, taking that as a test. The queen's questions could be the same. Each had an obvious answer and a truthful one. If it was a test of honesty, she should answer with truth. Yet the Sargassans spoke of their nation with religious fervour. They might be so immersed in their cause as to regard anything but complete self-sacrifice as treachery.

"Speak," said the figure on the right of the throne. The voice sounded like Gwynedd's.

An image of Julia flashed in Elizabeth's mind. "I couldn't do it," she said. "I couldn't kill my dearest friend."

"Treachery!" hissed the figure on the left. "She'd betray the Nation. She'd betray Mother Rebecca. She's failed the Test."

"Give her one final chance," said the figure on the right. "Give her the Test of Casks."

"Very well," said the queen.

The two figures bent behind the throne, each lifting a carved box, which they placed on a step of the dais in front of Elizabeth. One of the boxes was white, ivory perhaps. The other was wooden and black.

"Each box houses a future," said the queen. "One is the home of freedom. The other will deal you death. You must choose your fate. One box to be taken. One box to be opened."

Through the questioning, panic had clouded her thoughts. But presented with a puzzle of objects, she found her focus returning. It was more a conjuring trick than an inquisition. It felt like familiar ground.

She knelt to examine the boxes. A feather had been carved on the lid of the white box and a fish on the lid of the black. The designs continued around the sides of each. A feather might represent the air; a fish, the water. They were people of the water. And yet also of the air. They lived at the junction between the two.

"Is there no clue?" she asked.

"They are what they are," said the figure on the right. "You must make your choice."

Elizabeth picked up the white box and turned it. It was whalebone, not ivory. Though a feather was carved on the lid, the whale lived below the waves. And though a fish was carved on the other, it was made from the wood of a tree that lived in the air. However she looked at the symbols, there was a different way to see them. Bone might mean death. But then what was dead timber but the bones of a tree? She replaced the box.

There was a kind of symmetry about everything. Two masked figures. Two boxes. Air and water. Black and white. Water and air. It came to her that the symmetry must continue inside each box. It being a puzzle no logic could solve, both boxes would contain a message of life. Or both would contain a message of death.

"You must choose," said the figure on the right.

The Test of Casks was another trick in an island full of tricks. She felt sure of it. There would be no difference between the contents of the boxes. She reached out and touched the box of black wood. She'd hardly removed her hand before the figure on the left had taken the other box away.

"You have chosen the ebony box," said the queen. "Now open it and read your fate."

Both boxes were life or both were death. Elizabeth repeated the thought. *Both are the same. Both are the same.* There was no more tremor in her hand as she opened the black box. A folded sheet of paper lay within. She took it and read aloud: "You have chosen the image of the fish. You will be weighted down with chains and thrown into the ocean to drown."

She stood. "The other box – show me the message in the other box. I demand to see! And let me open it myself!"

The queen nodded. The white box was placed in her hands. Elizabeth opened it and removed the paper.

You have chosen the wood of the life-giving tree. You will live freely in the Sargassan Nation.

The masked figures advanced from around the walls. Hands grabbed her arms from behind and the paper tumbled to the floor.

• • •

The cell of the condemned was a square stockade somewhere near the edge, where the island was thin and the waves shifted the ground with particular intensity. The wooden stakes were half again as tall as Elizabeth. Each had been roped to the next, leaving slivers of light between, which opened and closed with the passing of the swell. Putting her eye close, she could make out the waves splashing some twenty paces distant. Between the stockade and the very edge lay a desolate landscape of barrels, logs, crates and what appeared to be bales of seaweed, all lashed together with coarse rope. A layer of green algal slime covered every surface. Saplings grew immediately around the stockade. Each planted in a hessian bag of soil and anchored with a stake. The trees on the landward side were larger and had already begun to spread their roots.

When Elizabeth grew tired of peering at the world beyond the stockade, she lay on her back and stared into the jagged square of sky.

The island must have started in what had become its centre, growing outwards over decades. The ship in which her trial had taken place was the nucleus, she thought. Everything had spread from there. The kind of landscape she was seeing at the edge must have been the way it all used to look. It didn't matter if the ropes rotted over time. Roots took over the job of binding the island. The trick must have been finding a tree that would grow in salt water. Some kind of mangrove, perhaps.

The vision and force of personality required to drive such a project would be a rare quality indeed. Viewed in that way, the ship was not the nucleus. Rather, it was the queen of the Sargassans and the sheer force of her will.

Terror had nearly overwhelmed Elizabeth during the Test. More from the queen than from the masked figures. She'd felt all the physical effects: the sweat, the drumming heart, the tightening of breath. Where the body leads, the mind will follow. Her thoughts had fogged. She'd made mistakes with her answers.

Strangely, the panic that had gripped her when she'd still some hope of living had been driven from her by the certainty of death. There was nothing left to do. She'd already tested the ropes and the door of the stockade. The stakes were too tall to climb. And if by some miracle she *had* found a way out, the guards who patrolled beyond would be there to catch her.

There had only been a narrow line of shade when they threw her into the condemned cell. Through the afternoon it grew, moving across the enclosure and higher up the walls. At sunset the light turned golden. The sky near the horizon faded to a pale duck-egg blue and the first stars began to shine directly overhead.

She wondered what Fidelia had been able to do or say to avoid sharing her fate. Each question in the Test had been like a trick. To answer truthfully was to condemn one's self. Yet to answer any other way was to be accused of lying. Perhaps they would have let her live if she'd been consistent, choosing to be honest or dishonest all the way through.

If Julia had survived the downing of the airship and been captured, she must also have endured the Test. Elizabeth had no doubt that her friend would have answered each question with total honesty. It was a simple but uncompromising streak of Julia's personality, which somehow managed to be maddening and endearing at the same time. Perhaps honesty was what the Sargassans wanted. If so, Julia could still be alive.

The throne room was a stage, that much was certain. The Test had been theatre. And Elizabeth had played the starring role. But she still wasn't sure who the audience had been. Not the queen, who'd been the director of it all. Perhaps the masked figures, who'd served as the chorus.

The Test of Casks had confused her at the time. Both fates would be freedom, she'd thought. Or both of them death. But it wasn't so. It was only afterwards that she'd understood. It was the simplest kind of conjuring. No sleight of hand was needed and no gimmick. The trick had been all in the queen's words: *You must choose your fate. One box to be taken. One box to be opened.*

Elizabeth had tapped the wooden box. But was she asking to open it or to have it removed? They could interpret the gesture as they wished. Whichever box she touched, she would have been left with the fate of death. But if they'd already decided to kill her, why go through such an elaborate charade?

The door of the stockade creaked open. She hadn't heard the approaching feet. Her host from the night before stepped through. Someone else closed the door behind her. The lock clicked.

"I've brought you food and water," the woman said.

Elizabeth accepted a bowl and cup. This time the spoon was wooden. "Thank you."

Instead of leaving, the woman sat down and crossed her legs. Elizabeth drank, emptying the cup in one go. The bowl was full of the same kind of fish stew as on the day before. But this time it was more strongly spiced.

"Now will you tell me your name?" Elizabeth asked.

"If you'd become one of us. But there are no names beyond the Nation."

"Did you go through the Test?"

The woman smiled that embarrassed smile again.

"I'm to die tomorrow. Won't you tell me something? What harm could it do?"

Instead of answering, the woman pointed towards the stockade door. It was a tiny gesture, a secret, not intended to be seen by anyone else. Her hand hadn't even moved from her lap. It was the first hint of division that Elizabeth had sensed among the Sargassans. It was nothing more than a thread of hope. But Elizabeth felt a premonition. Something more was coming. Just as the lack of hope had calmed her, this set her heart beating heavy and irregular. Her chest felt tight.

The woman looked up at the stars, which were now forming thickly. "I watch for the Pleiades," she said.

CHAPTER 21

There are moments to be still and moments to act and those who can tell which is which are the ones who survive. The woman's words repeated in Elizabeth's head: *I watch for the Pleiades*. They were the words Agent Sorren had told her to listen for, by which she would know her contact. *I watch for the Pole Star*, she was supposed to reply.

Instead she dipped her spoon and took another mouthful of the fish stew. "It's good," she said. "But the pepper makes me sweat."

"I made it specially for you."

"You are very kind."

"It's really nothing."

The woman held her gaze.

"Do you ever get tired of eating fish," Elizabeth asked, concealing her turmoil with another spoonful of the stew.

"Sometimes," the woman said. She still seemed to be waiting for Elizabeth to make the coded response. But why hadn't the woman spoken the night before? They'd been sitting alone together. They'd even mentioned the stars. It would have been the natural moment to make contact.

Elizabeth looked up into the night sky.

"Do you have something to say to me?" the woman asked. The answer came to Elizabeth all in a rush. The horror of the Test *had* been a piece of theatre. And the audience had been herself. Its entire purpose was for her to see herself fail utterly and be condemned. For all its spectacle and costume, it had been merely a preamble to this moment; sitting in the stockade under the cold stars and being tempted to reveal herself as a spy of the International Patent Office.

"I think you should go," Elizabeth said, holding out the empty bowl and cup.

The woman leaned close. "I can help you."

Elizabeth's certainty increased. "I'm beyond help."

In the same move as taking the bowl and cup, the woman placed a key in Elizabeth's hand. "Save yourself," she whispered.

They both stood. The woman turned to go. All the Patent Office spies in the Sargassan Nation had been found and killed. And then the last one, a woman, had gone silent. That was what John Farthing had told her.

"I can't take this," Elizabeth said, holding out the key.

"But they'll kill you!" hissed the woman.

If it was theatre they wanted, it was theatre she would give them. "Where would I run?" she asked, her voice louder now. "If I can't find freedom here, I'll find it nowhere. Let them kill me. I'm done with this world." So saying, she placed the key in the woman's hand and turned away.

Two guards came for her at dawn and marched her back towards the main deckway. Lamps shone from some of the wealthier houses in the centre of Freedom Island. But there were few people about to stare as they passed and no one followed.

More guards were waiting on the ship's deck. But instead of leading her down to the throne room they stood to attention, waiting for something, Elizabeth thought.

"What's happening?" she asked.

No one answered. Their mouths were set level and stern. But the eyes that looked on her seemed to be smiling. There would be no execution. A more subtle game was at play.

She turned and saw two more guards climbing the steps from the deckway. Fidelia walked between them, her face white with terror. The same charade was being played out for her. Instinctively, Elizabeth held out her hand. Fidelia took it.

"Don't worry," Elizabeth whispered as they came together in an embrace. "This isn't what it seems."

"It's time," said one of the guards.

Elizabeth could feel Fidelia's tension through the clammy grip of her hand as they stepped together towards the hatchway.

There was no executioner waiting in the throne room, nor any guards. The queen of the Sargassans sat on her throne. On her right hand side sat Gwynedd, the woman who looked so like Siân. Elizabeth scanned the shadows around the walls. This time there were no masked figures.

"Come closer," said the queen. Furs wrapped her, as they had done the previous day, but this time she smiled. "You, child." The queen gestured to Fidelia. "Come sit here."

Fidelia obeyed, climbing the steps to just below the throne. "Am I not to be killed?"

The queen placed a hand on Fidelia's head. "You are to become one of us. But what will you become? What, exactly? Today we decide."

Confusion and relief played over Fidelia's face. Then amazement. She looked directly at Elizabeth, her expression questioning.

"What was your work before you came to us?"

Fidelia swallowed before answering. "Steward," she said, her voice breathy, as if she'd yet to recover from her terror.

"We have no need for stewards. What else might you do?"

"I can... pilot a boat."

"Can you fight?"

"I could learn."

"Oh, I'm sure you could. You were steward to the commodore, they tell me."

"I... That is... yes."

"You must have overheard many things." The queen's gnarled hand began stroking Fidelia's hair. "How many ships does the Company have?"

"I... don't know."

It was a subtle interrogation; the most subtle that Elizabeth had ever witnessed. She had no doubt that the queen would have picked up on Fidelia's hesitation.

"How is it you don't know, child?"

"The ships came and went from month to month," Fidelia said, more certain now. "But I'd say there were always more than twenty-five. And less than forty."

It was a clever answer. A wide enough range to not betray her grandfather, the commodore. Yet narrow enough to seem believable ignorance.

"Among those ships, how many were made for war?"

"I've seen five with my own eyes," Fidelia said.

There was art in this evasion. Elizabeth remembered how the same quickness of mind had been used on her when she first went to the mother ship. Yet these were most likely questions the Sargassans had the answers to already. With underwater ships, they could have been in among the fleet for years and no one would have been any the wiser.

The queen continued to stroke Fidelia's hair. "What did you think to our Test, my dear?"

"I was frightened."

"Everyone is frightened. That is its purpose."

"I don't understand."

"It is a test of doing, not saying."

"But I failed it. You said I'd be killed, or I wouldn't have run away."

"You ran and we watched. Those who run are of two types. We call them the gazelle and the lion. Both are creatures of action. The Test was to tell which creature you are."

"But what was the Test?"

"There was a boat. You could have taken it."

"A child was asleep in it."

"There was a pistol. You checked that it was loaded. We watched you through every step. There was a knife. You didn't take it. You picked it up. Then you put it down again. You ran but you didn't try to kill. By this, we know your nature. You are a gazelle."

"Then did I pass or fail?"

"It is a different kind of test. No one fails – but for a very few. By your action I know to make you a sailor but not a warrior. We'll have use for you, Fidelia. Good use in the time to come."

Fidelia's eyes were cast down. "Thank you," she said, though the words seemed to be difficult for her to form. Few find comfort in admiring their own enemy.

"Come here, child."

This time it was Elizabeth's turn. She climbed the dais to sit on the floor next to the throne, turned so she could look up at the queen. Mother Rebecca's hand rested on her head and began to stroke. Elizabeth understood well enough what was happening. Having pierced the illusion of her first visit to the throne room, she knew another piece of theatre was in play. But it is one thing to recognise a drama, another to stay free of its grip. She dug a fingernail into her palm, banishing the pang of affection for her lost mother.

"Some who take the Test will run," Rebecca said. "These are the brave ones. The courageous. Women of action. But when offered the key, some won't take it. Or in taking it, they won't dare unlock the door. We call these the sheep and the dogs. The sheep are those women made meek by fear.

They too will take their place in the Nation. They will become fishers and tailors, cooks and cleaners. The dogs are those women who do not run because their instinct is faithfulness to the rule, even though it seems a tyranny. The dogs will become scribes and messengers, assayers and negotiators."

If Julia had been there, sitting at the foot of the throne, Elizabeth had no doubt which quality would have shone through. Every particle of Julia's being was faithfulness.

"What skills do you bring to us, Elizabeth?"

"I can read and write," she said, trying to follow the same path her friend would have taken. "I could be a scribe or a messenger."

"These are fine skills," said the queen. "Yet not uncommon."

"I have knowledge of the law as they know it in London and Carlisle."

"How came you by this knowledge?"

It was a dangerous path, this gentle interrogation. Trying to follow Julia's steps, trying to speak only truth, so as not to be caught in a lie. Mother Rebecca's hand smoothed back her hair.

"I was born in a circus," Elizabeth said. "I would have stayed there, but a cruel man wanted to have me. He took my father to court. Sent him to a debtors' prison. After I ran away, I taught myself the law from books so I'd never be caught the same way again."

"Yes, child. Siân told me your story. But do you have skills, aside from books and letters."

"I can make a disguise."

"There are many here who've passed themselves as men. But I think you have a greater skill that you're not telling us. What did you think of the Test?"

Elizabeth looked up and found herself caught in Mother Rebecca's gaze. "I was scared," she said, borrowing Fidelia's answer.

"That is its purpose. But do you think it works?"

"I... That is... yes. It's a clever test."

"You didn't run, my dear. So you may be a sheep or a dog. Which is your defining quality? Are you faithful or are you meek?"

"Faithful," Elizabeth said, without hesitation, trying to match what Julia would have said, but feeling like a small creature being slowly skewered.

"Not meek then, for sure. But the thing that confuses me is this – when you were a girl, you ran away. You crossed from one nation to another. You hid as a man. Or as a woman. Whichever was safer. You survived through action. Yet when you took the Test, you chose to stay, waiting for the executioner. We offered a way out, but you didn't take it. When you were a child, you were defined by action. What caused such a change in you, Elizabeth?"

No wonder the Sargassans had rooted out every Patent Office spy. The queen may have been old, but she was sharp and her interrogation was subtle. Elizabeth was already being opened up by it.

Gwynedd had been sitting silent all this time. Now she spoke. "You can tell everything to Mother Rebecca. The more you tell her, the more she can help you."

Elizabeth looked up at the old woman who stroked her hair, resisting the impulse to think of her with affection. Even in the queen's name there was a subtle force at work.

"You divide people into lions, gazelles, sheep and dogs. But there are more than four types."

"Then choose an animal for yourself," said the queen.

"Perhaps I'm a fox."

"What are the qualities of the fox?"

"It's the animal that knows it's being watched," said Elizabeth. "It thinks and it waits."

"What would a fox do if we gave her the Test?"

"She'd know she was being tested. She'd understand that the key was a trick. She'd refuse to take it. And she'd say so in a voice loud enough for everyone to hear."

"But this is a rare type," said Mother Rebecca. "We call her the crow – the animal that watches its watcher. How did you know you were being tested?"

"I didn't. At first. It was the Test of Casks that gave you away. Once I'd figured that for a fool's choice, I thought back and saw that all the questions had been the same. Any answer I gave could be argued as wrong."

"Then you are a crow indeed, my child."

"Are there jobs for crows on Freedom Island?"

Mother Rebecca put a finger under Elizabeth's chin and lifted her face. "Crows are dangerous. It's difficult to choose their fate. Their words and actions may not match their thoughts. The farmer kills the crow to protect the other animals. Tell me this, child, why should I not kill you?"

"Because you're not a farmer," said Elizabeth. "I think you're a crow as well. You're the queen of all crows."

CHAPTER 22

From above, she'd thought the tree roots would be slimy. But having let herself down under the cluster of stilt huts, she found them to be quite dry. Nor was she prepared for the intense smells of decay and salt and sewage she found there. It was almost overpowering. But that was how the island was grown. Every bit of human waste was mixed with seaweed and rotted down until it became the fine, nutrient-rich soil in which they grew their crops. Compost hardly seemed like advanced technology. But the Sargassans had made a science of it and had created a wonder. So central had it become to their way of life that night soil could be exchanged for goods or food.

After the interview with Mother Rebecca, Elizabeth had been sent back to the hut of the fisherwoman where she'd spent her first night. Fidelia's status had been resolved. But Elizabeth's was still ambiguously poised, half in and half out of the Nation.

She looked up at the hut above her, where her host was sleeping. The new moon had set early. Buildings and walkway were revealed as irregular silhouettes against the stars of the Milky Way.

Looking at things from unusual angles had been the basis for the two careers in Elizabeth's life. The intelligence gatherer and the conjuror each turned things around; one to find the truth and the other to hide it. From this new perspective, squatting below the huts, the island seemed more grown than built, the work of trees and worms rather than carpenters and architects.

That first night on the island she'd held back from taking this path, reasoning that a guard would have been stationed there against her escape. Three days had passed. What was the chance that a guard still remained? With such logic she had talked herself into the adventure. But in truth, her decision had been driven more by emotion. Days of being watched and tested were taking a toll. Mother Rebecca made the rules for each encounter. Elizabeth was growing desperate to make rules of her own.

Instead of setting off directly under the walkway, she shifted out into the faint light of the stars and stepped barefoot from root to root. At the next cluster of huts she ducked down again and waited. If a guard had been stationed to keep watch, a response would surely follow. Better to be found and stopped so close to the hut than further into the journey. So far, she had only committed an indiscretion. What followed would be a crime.

She held her breath and listened for footsteps of pursuit or any movement under the walkways. But the only sound was the breathing of the island itself: the creak of ropes and the distant clank of machinery.

Crouching in the shadow, she was surprised to catch herself smiling. Whatever came of the adventure, it would be a path that she had chosen. She set off parallel to the edge of the island, but then the walkway above her joined another and changed course, heading more towards the centre. Though the boards above were wider and offered more cover, the ground level had started to rise. There'd easily been four foot of clearance between the huts and the ground but by increments she was forced to bend lower and then go down on hands and knees. Roots were replaced by soil. The air became more wholesome. By the time she reached the main deckway, there was a cool, grass-like vegetation under her knees but only a few inches of clearance above her head.

It was here that she made her first discovery. Under the very centre of the deckway, running parallel with it, she found a line of roughly cut wooden planks projecting up from the ground and almost meeting the deck above, so that it was impossible for her to cross. She crawled along, searching for the end of it. Stakes had been driven into the ground every few yards, to which ropes were tied. The ropes crossed over the barrier like giant stitches. Having found no end to the line and having made no sense of it either, she gave up and crawled back to the edge.

Turning left, she started to make her way along the line of the deckway, counting the walkways that branched from it as she went. It was impossible to make out any of the island's landmarks from below. After four branching points she risked putting her head above the boards. The scene was deserted, the houses dark. After two more side paths she found the one she wanted and began crawling out once more towards the island's edge.

The space above her head increased. When the tree roots became uncomfortable under her knees, she found there was enough space to stand once more. She advanced, bent low, straightening as the walkway descended towards the edge of the island and the floating jetty. It was there, directly beneath the final flight of steps that Elizabeth stopped and peered over the cluster of fishing boats, which were moored three deep. The familiar profile of the *Iceland Queen* lay beyond them.

Two women were strolling on the jetty some twenty paces out, coming closer. One was smoking a pipe. The scent of sweet tobacco came to Elizabeth on the breeze. The other woman was speaking in a low voice, saying something about her cousin, who was ill. Then they turned and started back, away from the island once more.

When they were halfway towards the *Iceland Queen*, Elizabeth stripped off her jacket and trousers, placing them beyond the reach of the waves that splashed over the island's edge. Then, dressed only in her shirt and knee-length bloomers, she let herself down into the water.

The first shock of immersion made her draw in breath, but kicking out to swim she began to get used to the cold. Her head was low. The guards would have no chance to see her behind the fishing boats. But there was a gap before the ship itself. She stopped at the last boat, gripping the rudder, keeping her head just above water. Peering around the hull she could see the guards strolling back towards the island. They were close enough for her to make out a brace of pistols in each belt. And swords.

She waited until they were well past before striking out again, swimming for the prow of the *Iceland Queen*, putting the ship between herself and the guards. A wave curled along the length of the hull, splashing against the paddlewheel. It pushed her back then sucked her forwards. Though she'd been at sea for many months, there had been no chance to swim. Sailors in northern waters never did. She found herself out of practice. Her muscles started to feel like wood. She grabbed for one of the downward-sloping paddles on the front of the wheel but another wave pushed her back and it slipped from her grip. She grabbed again as the water boosted her forwards. This time she had it.

She clung on, catching her breath as three more waves rolled past. Then, on the fourth, she used its lift to grab hold of one of the higher paddles. Swinging her legs around, she managed to get a foot into the ornamental fretwork on the face of the wheel housing. After that it was a straight climb to the top.

At any stage on her night-time journey she could have been stopped by a vigilant guard; under the boardwalk, at the jetty, or here on the ship itself. Her plan had simply been to go as far as she could and then turn back. But no watch had been set on the deck of the *Iceland Queen*. She dropped, light footed, and padded across to the cover of the cargo hold, against which she pressed her ear. The only sounds were the waves and the clank of rope against the masthead.

The hatchway below the quarterdeck was unlocked. She stepped into the dark; memory and touch guided her down the steps and along the passageway. But as she descended further, a faint glimmer made her slow. Somewhere between her and the internal door of the cargo hold a lamp had been left burning.

She had come further than she'd ever expected. But this would be the limit of it. The prisoners could not have been left unguarded. There was frustration in being thwarted so close to her goal. But no real harm. She couldn't have rescued Tinker this way. If she'd opened the door, the other prisoners would have poured out. Men and women would have died as a result. But she wanted to see him. She wanted to look through the grille and know that he remained unharmed; to reassure him that she hadn't forgotten.

She found the lantern hanging from the wall on the final descent. It had been left on a low wick, casting only enough light to reveal the turn at the bottom of the steps. She stopped just behind it, held her breath and listened. The silence was so complete that she risked another step down, shifting to the other wall to keep her shadow tight. On the final step she peered around the corner, incredulous. The hold had been left unguarded.

Taking the lamp and lifting it to the grille in the door, she let its light spill into the hold itself. But she'd guessed the truth already. The hold was empty. The prisoners had gone.

She didn't sleep well after creeping back into the stilt hut and climbing into the hammock. The prisoners had to be somewhere on the island. She would have heard the arrival of any ship large enough to transport them away. But each time she began to drift off, her fears gathered once more and the only way to dispel them was to wake. She still felt unsettled when the guards arrived in the morning to escort her back to the centre of the island.

Before, she'd not been able to take in the detail of Mother Rebecca's ship. Too much had been unfamiliar. She'd half-seen the figurehead below the bowsprit and thought it a white horse. This time, she looked more closely and saw the golden horn projecting from its forehead. She would have stopped to stare. She would have marched to the stern to read the name plaque for confirmation. But the guards pushed her on, up the steps to the deck and then down through the hatchway.

Siân sat in her place on the left side of the throne and Gwynedd on the right. When Elizabeth had first seen Gwynedd, she'd been struck by her similarity to Siân. With familiarity the differences were becoming clearer. Gwynedd was less well muscled. Her cheek bones were not so angular and her expression revealed less of her thoughts. Siân seemed more controlled by zeal for the Sargassan Nation and its queen. She was quicker to anger and quicker to smile.

A carved wooden stool had been left for Elizabeth on the lowest step of the dais.

"Mother Rebecca has granted that today you may ask questions," said Gwynedd.

"Thank you," said Elizabeth, for it seemed that gratitude was expected. And then: "Is there anything I shouldn't ask?"

Siân and Gwynedd both looked to the queen, who made

a dismissive gesture with one of her bony hands, as if to say they would worry about that later, should the problem arise.

There was so much she wanted to know. What had happened to the men of the *Iceland Queen*? Was Tinker still among them? Had any survived the downing of the *American Frontier* and, if so, where had they gone? But the tragedy of the questioner is that she reveals more than she learns. To ask any of the important questions directly would have been to give away her most precious secrets. Indeed, the pattern of Mother Rebecca's leadership was becoming easier to read with each encounter. The Queen of the Sargassans created theatre. She knew all the elements that would occur and could read truth from the reactions of the participants. The honour of being allowed to question her was merely a fresh stage in the interrogation. But Elizabeth was a lock that wouldn't easily be picked.

"State your first question," said Mother Rebecca.

Elizabeth pointed to Gwynedd and Siân. "Are these two women sisters?"

The queen paused before answering. "They are cousins."

"Your granddaughters?"

"Yes, child."

"Where are their parents?"

"Gone."

"Siân told me she was born in the Nation. And I've seen children…" Here Elizabeth hesitated, hoping that the question wouldn't need to be stated in full.

Siân was sitting a fraction forward, eyes narrowed. Gwynedd had looked away. But Mother Rebecca's expression didn't change.

None of them spoke to help Elizabeth, so she said: "If the Nation is only women, where are the fathers?"

"Where do you think?" asked Rebecca.

"Are they sent away?"

"Of course they are. Indeed they cannot live with us."

"Why not?"

"Because they're men!" growled Siân.

Gwynedd's eyes flicked to her cousin, across the throne; a glance that might have been irritation. Elizabeth wasn't sure.

Rebecca placed a hand on Siân's shoulder. "The question is fair and I'll answer," she said. "You've lived among men. Were you justly treated?"

"No," said Elizabeth.

"No," Mother Rebecca echoed. "They think they know justice. But if a man wants something, he uses his strength to take it. This is his nature. He is taught to use it from boyhood. It cannot be unlearned. You told me that you ran away and hid from a man who desired you. Why didn't you go to him to explain that you weren't interested? Why didn't you reason with him? Because you knew what he'd do if he once had you in his reach. And why did you disguise yourself as a man? As a man, more chances were given you. More opportunities. Don't marvel that I know what you haven't told. It's the same story for many who are now here on Freedom Island. In all of history has there been a year when women were given justice? Tell me."

"I... don't know."

"There was not. If ever a strong queen stood tall, men rushed to pull her down. Think of Boadicea. They whipped her. They raped her daughters. They sent all the armies of Rome to wipe out her name."

"Can't men learn to be different?"

"Can a shark learn to eat seaweed? Through all of history we've been oppressed. Now we start again. Separate. Without men. In this way we've shown we're the stronger sex. We think more clearly. Men are dominated by base desires and their need to show themselves as powerful. We are able to use our emotion and character and intelligence and loyalty and deadly intent, all in balance with each other. Their pride will always rule them. That's why their civilization can't progress. By making ourselves separate, our civilization will surpass theirs. And soon.

"You'd not keep a hawk and chicken in the same cage. Nor can we tolerate men to live among us. If any of us wish to have a child, they can choose a man from among the prisoners. But once the work of it is done, he can't any more live with her."

"What if the baby is a boy?"

"There are tribes we trade with who'd happily foster him. If the mother wishes, she can raise him. Until his man-nature starts to show."

"There was a boy on the *Iceland Queen*, a stowaway. I should like to know he'll be looked after." Elizabeth said this with as casual a manner as she could manage, as if it were of no greater importance than any other comment she'd made.

"What is his name."

"He calls himself Tinker."

"And what is he to you?"

"It's more what I am to him. He attached himself to me."

Mother Rebecca shifted under the furs as if trying to find a more comfortable position. "How old is he?"

"I'd say eight. Or nine maybe."

"That's too old for a boy to come to us. If he was raised outside, he'll have learned the thinking of men. He'll believe himself above us."

Elizabeth was trapped and knew it. If she were to leave it at that, Tinker would be shipped out to wherever the other prisoners were going. But if she pressed his case, the depth of connection between them would become clear. Her concern for him could be used against them both.

"He's more wild than raised," she said.

"Why does it matter?" asked Mother Rebecca.

"I feel responsible."

"How commendable. But don't worry, child. I'll see that the boy is cared for well enough."

CHAPTER 23

The queen's ship might once have been described as a frigate, though it was hard to be precise because the masts and rigging were long gone. They'd been the first things sacrificed in the building of the island. That's what the Sargassans said. Miles of rope had been unwound to begin the baling of seaweed and the binding of flotsam.

"They thought she was mad," Ekua explained. "Making a raft out of a good sailing ship. She told them it was a Nation, not a raft. Named it Freedom Island there and then. And that when it was no more than a hulk. When one of the men went against her, she killed him. They were too scared to go against her after that."

"There were men?" Elizabeth asked.

"There'd been men on the *Unicorn*. But they were never part of the Nation."

"Did she kill them all?"

"No."

Elizabeth had still not discovered where the men of the *Iceland Queen* had gone. But other information was being pushed at her. It was as if Ekua and the others had been instructed to educate her, and as quickly as possible. No reason for the change had been offered. Nor had anyone told her that she'd properly become a Sargassan. Ambiguity hung heavy in the air.

"Where did the men go – those she didn't kill?" Elizabeth asked.

"Somewhere. I don't know."

"If the ship had been made into a raft, how did they leave?"

"They were against her – that's all that matters." Ekua's voice was becoming sharp with frustration. "Mother Rebecca saw the future – an island, a great nation of free women. The men didn't want it, so she had to send them away."

They'd been touring the main boardway, looking into shops, which mostly sold vegetables and fish, though one had been full of metal wares, pewter tankards and plates, cutlery and nails. With the gentle shifting of the island, all the goods had swung on their hooks and clanked against each other. Yet the day was calm.

"How do you manage when there's a storm?" Elizabeth asked as they walked away.

"We learned it the hard way," Ekua said. "The island was ruined every time at first. It's weakest at the edges and back then it was all edge. When parts broke off, we had to go out and pull them back. After one winter there was nothing left but the ship, and that wallowing with no sail to keep it into the wind. So we started over. The first time we built it, it was fixed in place with nails and timber. Then we learned to let all the parts move. The secret's in the ropes and the tree roots. It took us five years to figure that."

"Us? You saw it all?"

Ekua smiled. "I'm not that old! But I'll be here for the next time."

The next time. Elizabeth turned the phrase in her mind. Though the history lesson was interesting, the most fascinating revelations slipped out as if by accident. They were instructing her in the myth of their own creation. But woven through it was a golden thread of destiny, running from the building of the island to the moment of the telling and then on to a future they could all see when they closed their eyes. They would build new islands. They would conquer new oceans.

Connected somehow with that glorious future was a phrase: *The Unicorn will sail*. Each time she'd heard it spoken, the context had been destiny. It had made no sense until she saw the figurehead of Mother Rebecca's ship and learned its name: the *Unicorn*.

"The first years were all hardship," Ekua said, continuing the history.

"What did they eat?"

"Fish and seaweed."

"But where did they get the materials to build the island?"

"The ocean brought it all. Everything that floats in the mid-waters of the North Atlantic ends up here."

Hardship and determination were more believable than destiny. It seemed unlikely that the ocean would provide all the things they'd needed: barrels and rope and logs, and at such a rate that an island could be built faster than the storms could wash it away.

"When we were on the *Iceland Queen*, you told me we were going home to Mother. But now we're here, you say its name is Freedom Island. What should I properly call it?"

"You ask the strangest questions, Elizabeth! The island is our home. But Mother Rebecca is the Nation."

"What of Gwynedd and Siân?"

Ekua shot her a quizzical look. "What of them?"

"Siân seems first when it comes to fighting. Gwynedd in counselling the queen."

"Perhaps."

"Which of them has the higher position?"

"You have us wrong! We do different jobs, but we're all of us equal in the Nation."

"But I've seen people bowing to them," Elizabeth said.

"Respect costs nothing."

Elizabeth would have pressed her further, but Ekua turned abruptly, setting off along a narrower walkway, and all she could do was follow.

Freedom Island had zones of development. In the centre was the *Unicorn* itself, clustered around with the most prestigious buildings. None were more than a single storey, but she'd seen conspicuous quality in the carving of their lintels and luxury in the width of their doorways. Beyond the centre were shops, in which some trade was conducted in barter. Closer to the edge came poorer housing interspersed with machinery.

"This is the secret of our wealth," Ekua said.

They were looking at hundreds of panes of glass arranged on the ground, each angled gently, like a sloping roof. From a distance it had appeared to be a sprawling field of cucumber frames. Closer now, she saw that lines of guttering had been arranged below, some painted black and some white. Condensation ran from the underside of the glass.

"What is it?"

"We're making water. Fresh, sweet water from the sea!" Saying this, Ekua beamed with pride. "The waves under us make the seawater flow along the troughs. The sun warms it. It evaporates and condenses onto the glass. When the drops get big enough, they fall into the fresh water troughs. Our storage tanks are always full. All from little drops.

"Long ago, when Mother Rebecca was young, she made sweet water this way and sold it to the sailors who passed. That's how they lived back then. As the island grew, we made more. So however many came to join us, there was always enough to drink."

Elizabeth didn't doubt the evidence of her eyes. But the origin story left out as much as it revealed. If they'd had fresh water, why didn't the sailors take it by force? How did they protect themselves right back at the beginning? The future-casters of the Patent Office believed that the chaos beyond the Gas-Lit Empire should snuff out any spark of civilization before it could develop. But something had enabled the Sargassans to gather sufficient strength to survive.

"The beginning of the Nation was the water trade?"

"There's more," said Ekua. "Come."

She followed along another walkway, which took them further out towards the edge. The ground movement was enough to make Elizabeth stumble. More than once she had to swing an arm to keep from falling. The sound of machinery was louder here. Structures that seemed like waterwheels were positioned between the trees. Wooden frames held them clear of the ground so that there seemed nothing to power their movement. Yet they turned on their axles, slowly, creaking and clanking in time with the movement of the island itself.

As they approached one of the wheels, Elizabeth made out a crank arrangement, the drive for which was a metal rod connected to the ground.

"This is the secret of our power," said Ekua, reaching out to let her fingers brush against the turning wheel. "The thing that is our weakness – that our island is in constant motion – this has become our strength. The swell shifts the ground. That turns the wave mills. And the wave mills make galvanic energy, which we channel through metal ropes."

The next wheel they came to was stationary. Four women worked on it, adjusting the crank arm.

"It's like the sail of a boat," Ekua explained. "If not trimmed to the conditions, the mill won't turn. However high the waves come to us, the machine must be changed to match. A fraction out and the wheel doesn't turn. Or worse, it breaks itself to pieces. But perfect alignment makes great power."

Elizabeth had seen the workings of mills before, by which some natural force could be harnessed to drive a saw or loom. But the wave mill had no machinery. The only thing attached to it was a curious rope, leading away from it like a washing line, supported above the ground by pairs of sticks.

"What is it for?" she asked.

"Follow the galvanic rope and you'll see."

They followed another walkway across the landscape of roots, parallel with the line of the galvanic rope. Other ropes trailed across the island from other wave mills, converging at a hut next to one of the upside-down ships.

"Don't touch anything," said Ekua, before leading her inside.

Elizabeth sniffed the air. There was something in it that made the inside of her nose tingle. "It's too dark to see," she said.

"We can't have a flame here," said Ekua. "But be patient. Your eyes will get used to it."

And so they did. The galvanic ropes all converged at a curious machine of barrels and copper pipes. The whole thing looked like nothing so much as a brewery or whisky still.

"Do you make alcohol?"

"No, sister. Listen."

Elizabeth did. "What am I listening for?"

"Put your ear close to the vat."

It was the faintest of sounds, less than a whisper. It reminded her of a mug of sparkling cider, the breath of escaping bubbles.

"The wave mills make electricity flow along the ropes. And here, we galvanise the sea water, splitting it into hydrogen and oxygen. That's what you're hearing. We store the gases inside the hulls of the upturned ships. When hydrogen and oxygen are brought back together, all the energy of their separation is released. They burn with a flame that makes no smoke. It leaves only water. That's how we drive the submarine ships."

It was an answer to a question that Elizabeth hadn't even considered.

The moment stretched. Ekua seemed content to stand in the dimly lit building, staring at the strange machine, though it had no moving parts. Elizabeth was glad of the pause. Much information had been fed to her, yet she'd had no time to think about it or put it in order. The galvanic rope had somehow brought to mind the unspooling drum of cable, hidden in the mother ship's central hull, though the leviathan was driven by oil, not electricity.

Then she thought of Tinker, who had led her to the place where she could look in on that secret chamber.

"Where are the men from the *Iceland Queen*?" she asked, trying to make the words sound casual, not expecting a straight answer.

"I'll show you," Ekua said, taking her hand.

They followed a galvanic rope away from the field of wave mills towards another machine, quite different in appearance. A low, wide drum rotated slowly on a horizontal axle. Drawing closer, she made out rungs on the barrel. That's when she knew what it was, for she'd seen illustrations of convicts undergoing reform by hard labour.

But only when Ekua led her around to the other side of the drum did she see the men of the *Iceland Queen* clambering endlessly up the ladders of the treadmill. Each was kept in his place by a chain. Other men sat or lay on the ground nearby. They too were chained, waiting their turn.

Perhaps seeing her horror, Ekua said: "They must earn their keep as we all do. We may fight or fish. They make electricity."

The men on the mill could only focus on the task before their faces. If they stopped for a moment, they'd fall and be left dangling by the chains. The men waiting their turn seemed too exhausted to move, let alone notice that their one-time crewmate was watching. Locklight lay on his side. His face and captain's uniform were covered in grime.

But nowhere could she see Tinker.

The sound of footfalls on the boardwalk made her turn. A messenger was approaching at a run.

"Mother Rebecca will see Elizabeth," she called. "You're summoned to her presence!"

CHAPTER 24

Two of the three chandeliers had been lit, driving most of the shadows from around the edges of the throne room. Mother Rebecca sat, fur-draped as ever. There was no sign of Siân this time. Elizabeth would have felt safer knowing where she was.

Gwynedd was standing, pointing to a carved wooden panel where a window should have been; a design of interwoven snakes. Next to her, looking along her arm, stood a child. Elizabeth's heart beat twice before recognition hit. Dressed in a yellow smock, hair clean and brushed out to its full length, it seemed the slight figure of a girl. Then it turned and she saw Tinker's face staring back at her. He didn't run to her and wrap his arms around her waist. But he yearned to. She could see it. And so could they. Gwynedd looked to Mother Rebecca, who nodded.

"We've been getting to know each other," she said, as Gwynedd led the boy from the room.

No threat had been spoken. But no threat could have been more compelling.

"Where's he being kept?"

"Here with me. On the *Unicorn*. I told you I'd look after your boy."

"Is that why they've told me so many secrets?"

"Sit next to me," Mother Rebecca said, gesturing to the stool on the right hand of the throne. It was the place where Gwynedd usually sat.

Elizabeth didn't move.

The queen closed her eyes, fatigued it seemed. "When two crows meet, each becomes the other's puzzle," she said. "We hide our intentions. Yet we may be an answer, each for the other. This is my hope. The boy lets me say this. I know you won't hurt me, when he's in my care."

"You'd harm a child?" Elizabeth asked.

The queen's eyes opened. "I'd slaughter ten children if it saved a hundred more. Now sit!"

This time, Elizabeth obeyed, and from this new angle saw that a pistol rested on the furs in Mother Rebecca's lap. The emblem of the turquoise leaping hare inlaid in the stock was unmistakable. It was Elizabeth's own weapon, taken from her by Siân when they were on the *Iceland Queen*.

Mother Rebecca regarded Elizabeth's gaze. "It's a pretty thing," she said. "Where did you get it?"

"My father gave it to me."

"You're attached to it?"

"He told me to always keep it near. And to use it without regret."

"Siân would say your father had selfish reasons for what he did. And Gwynedd would say there was good in him."

"What do you say?" Elizabeth asked.

"That it doesn't matter which is true. It only matters what people think. Did your father teach you to do magic in that circus?"

"Yes."

"Real magic or tricks?"

"There's no difference," said Elizabeth. "It only matters what people think."

Rebecca stroked the gun. The skin over her finger joints was cracked, as if it would no longer stretch with her movement. One of the cracks was weeping.

"Could your father catch a bullet from the air?" she asked.

"I never saw him do it. But he could make me disappear and my brother appear where I'd been."

"You had a brother?"

"The audience believed so."

"A brother, a father, a rich man who desired you – it seems your life was full of men. Did you have lovers?"

Elizabeth felt herself blushing.

Rebecca nodded. "I watch you, my child. I see you attracted by the freedom you could have with us. It pulls you. But I see you also attached to the world of men. You think to yourself, surely you could have both – that not all men are oppressors. You think of your father and your lover and hope that others might be so good. Don't marvel that I know what's in your heart. Understanding is the power that's kept me here." She patted the arm of the throne. "How else could I have done all this? My granddaughter, Gwynedd, thinks there are men who might be reformed."

"And Siân?"

"Siân is of a different mind. She knows evil in the way a child knows to say the sky is blue. It is a learned thing. Believed but not understood. How old were you, Elizabeth, when you ran from your home?"

"Fourteen. But not all men are like that."

"Some have a veil of civility. You've glimpsed behind it. But I've seen more than you. When I was fourteen, I lived behind that veil. I witnessed the animal nature of men – that part of them they might keep hidden. There are five of us still alive who saw what I'm going to tell you. The others wouldn't believe it. I am the warrior queen. I am purity itself. They'd kill you if you tried to tell them.

"The *Unicorn* was once a floating brothel. This hall is where the men would come to choose a girl. They'd sit just where we are now, on this very throne, like kings. We were paraded out, each to take a turn across the floor. They'd choose and pay and we'd be taken and done with in whatever way they desired. One man ruled the *Unicorn*. All we earned went to him. He called himself the Crocodile and had crocodile skin tattooed all over his body. I don't know what his real name was. He kept a twenty-eight gun frigate standing a hundred yards off. Girls were safer than piracy, he'd say. He didn't need to chase the money. It came to him. Men wanted to hand him their gold.

"One day the Crocodile took me for his own pleasure. Afterwards, when he was asleep, I found the knife he kept hidden in his boot and I slit his throat with it. He tried to call for help. But I'd cut deep into his windpipe. All that came out were bubbles of blood. I watched him die. Then I took his pistols. When I pointed them at the guards, they just put up their hands. We had control of the ship. But the frigate was still there. It could have sunk us in one volley. The *Unicorn* was a hulk even then. The masts must have gone years before.

"So we cleaned and dressed the Crocodile, tied a cravat to hide the wound and sat him in a whaleboat as if he were alive. Then we rowed it over to the frigate, just like it was him ordering us to pull the oars.

"It's their weakness, Elizabeth. Their fatal flaw. They think us so far below them that we couldn't do the things we've done. The sailors helped us up onto the deck. Imagine it. They reached down and lifted us on board. It was far from their dreams that we might be strong enough to fight them. And they, so complacent from years of drinking and rutting and taking money. I shot one of them in the fat of his stomach. It was a bad wound, Elizabeth. He rolled on the ground, screaming. They could have rushed us. We had three loaded guns between us and there were ten of them. At close quarters they would have had us. But their man is dying in front of them, and they're all imagining it's them next. They put up their hands and we had them.

"He kept screaming till there was no more strength in him. And after that he just looked from face to face of his crewmates, eyes wide. It took him five hours to die.

"That day, I told the others we'd no more be the property of men. That was the beginning. The first plan was to run the brothel for ourselves. But some of the men who came, they saw what had happened and they tried to take over. They held one of the girls under a knife and said to the rest that we should yield. I shot her through the forehead. And once she was down, I shot him too.

"I tell you so you'll understand. This is how we knew that we couldn't have men among us. There was a slave trader who'd come from time to time, bringing new girls. We sold him our prisoners. Men kept coming to us, thinking the *Unicorn* was still a brothel. Each one we took captive and sold them to the slaver. With that money we bought weapons, until we were strong enough."

"Slaves," Elizabeth said, horrified.

"Are you shocked?"

Elizabeth didn't answer directly. Rebecca's suffering and the barbarity of the brothel keeper so appalled her that her mind recoiled from picturing the events. But the story carried the power of sincerity. She had no doubt that it was true.

"I'm sad," Elizabeth said, at last. "No child should see such things."

"I was never a child. Besides, you've seen the same darkness."

"I ran from it."

"So would I. But there was nowhere to run. Nor for the others. That's what the Nation is – a place for us to stand and face the enemy. I've built it with these hands, Elizabeth. And this heart. It's taken all that I am."

She reached out. Elizabeth took her hand. If Rebecca had been a slave trader, who in the same situation would have chosen differently? The other paths would have led to death or slavery for herself and her friends.

They sat that way in silence. The air had cooled and freshened over the days that she'd been on Freedom Island. But in the throne room a charcoal brazier radiated warmth, making the air stuffy.

Rebecca's grip on her hand tightened. "The time of hiding will soon be over. We'll announce ourselves. They'll see us and quake. By the ferocity of their attack, you'll know the depth of their fear. But we'll be strong. There's a ship coming to us – the beginning of a trade route. We'll have new kinds of weapons. Then, should all the worlds of men combine, they'll not be strong enough to defeat us."

"Where will the ship come from?"

"From the metal works of Patagonia."

Elizabeth suppressed a shudder. Contending claims by different member nations had prevented the southernmost stretch of South America from becoming part of the Gas-Lit Empire. Little was known of those lands, but they'd become bywords for barbarity.

Mother Rebecca bowed her head, as if to rest from the weight of the story she'd told. The skin of her hand felt like sandpaper. Elizabeth wanted to be rid of her touch but couldn't bring herself to let go.

Even in the very centre of the island, it was possible to sense the motion of the waves. There was more sound to it than movement. A low reverberation creaked through the wooden hull of the *Unicorn*.

"Show me some magic," Mother Rebecca said.

At last Elizabeth's hand was released. She looked around the throne room. When it was a brothel there would have

been playing cards and dice and cigarettes and wine glasses.
All the usual props of the close-up conjuror. But after what
Mother Rebecca had told her, it felt wrong to ask for any
of them. Instead she stepped to the brazier and selected a
charred twig from the floor.

"I'll need a flame for this magic," she said, reaching to twist
a candle free from one of the chandeliers. "And I need paper.
Any small scrap will do."

Mother Rebecca shifted, sitting forwards and delving under
the furs. Which is when Elizabeth set up the trick, dipping
her thumb next to the candle wick and pressing a crumb of
charcoal into the hot wax as it solidified on her skin.

It was done by the time the old woman had found a leaf
of notepaper.

Elizabeth placed the candle on the floor between them.
Then she took the paper, holding it up next to the charcoal
twig for Mother Rebecca to see. "This is soul-reading magic,"
she said. "I want you to think about an object or a person that
is dear to you. Use your mind to picture it. Your thoughts will
come to me through the flame of that candle."

Mother Rebecca nodded, then closed her eyes. An
expression of concentration formed on her face. "It is a
person," she said, then opened her eyes again. Her gaze
was suddenly so intense that it took Elizabeth a moment to
compose herself.

Moving deliberately so that Mother Rebecca could see
what was happening, she positioned her hands behind her
back. "The answer has come to me. I'm writing it now on the
paper."

After a moment of fumbling, pretending to do just that, she
brought the paper around to the front of her again, holding
it up in one hand so Mother Rebecca could only see one of
the blank faces. With the other hand she cast away the twig.
From thereon the trick was simple enough. She would ask

the name. Then, having heard it, she would secretly write it with the grain of charcoal stuck to her thumb on the side of the paper hidden from her audience's view.

"Who were you thinking of?" she asked.

Mother Rebecca said: "The woman who is to lead this Nation when I'm gone."

"And will that be Gwynedd or Siân?"

"I do not yet know."

Afterwards, Elizabeth would think about the change that had come over the guards; their new deference towards her. "You saw Mother Rebecca alone?" one of them had whispered as they descended the steps towards the boardway. Elizabeth hadn't answered.

Her mind was turning over the strange interview, which had seemed as much courtship as inquisition. The revelation of slave trading had shocked her. But more shocking still was the understanding that, in Mother Rebecca's place, pushed to such extremes and desperate to save her friends, she would have done the same.

Her thoughts shifted to the strange way in which the interview had concluded. It had been in Elizabeth's power to write the name of either granddaughter. One of them was too eager for combat. The other, too prone to compromise. If Rebecca believed in the power of soul-reading magic, Elizabeth might have pushed her one way or the other. Siân would surely drive the Nation towards an outward-facing war. She would hunt down enemy ships until all men had been driven from the ocean. Gwynedd would compromise away the hegemony of the seas. Mother Rebecca had been right about one thing. The nations of men would strive to restore what they thought of as a natural balance. Gwynedd's negotiation would become a whittling away of power. In twenty years who would remember what the Sargassans had built? The dream of a place where women could choose their own destiny would have been snuffed out.

But Mother Rebecca might not believe in magic. If so, any name that Elizabeth wrote would have been seen as a political statement. Indeed, the entire episode could have been another theatrical charade, a disguised test to determine Elizabeth's true character.

All this had flashed through her mind as she held up the paper, her thumb poised to write. To act on impulse is said to be a weakness. But to be able to act on instinct is taken as a strength. In reality the two were the same. They could only be judged by outcome.

Elizabeth offered the leaf of paper. Mother Rebecca took it, turning it in her hand, over and over. Both sides were blank. There'd been a moment when Elizabeth thought she read sorrow in the creases of the old woman's face. Then her expression had become one of terrible fatigue.

"I'm tired," she'd said. The gesture of dismissal was little more than a tremor of her desiccated hand.

They'd reached the last narrow stretch of boardwalk leading to the cluster of huts when a messenger caught up with them. Panting for breath, she held out a slip of paper, which the guards took. Elizabeth watched their expressions change as they read. There was a moment when they each seemed to be waiting for the other to speak. Neither would meet her eyes. Then the one holding the paper said: "We're to lock you in the stockade. I'm so sorry."

CHAPTER 25

The women accompanying Elizabeth still seemed to be an honour guard. Whenever she glanced back, they dipped their gaze in deference. But they kept closer than they had before the message. Close enough to grab her, should she try to run. As she stepped inside the stockade there was another apology. In the last moment before the door closed, she was sure they bowed. But it was still a prison.

Her freedoms and privileges, gradually won, had been snatched away. In the last few hours she'd come to know more about Mother Rebecca than did most of the Sargassans. It hadn't helped her. She didn't even understand the nature of the displeasure she'd caused. One thing was certain, though; she knew too much for them to ever let her go.

That evening, it was Fidelia who brought the stew for her supper. There were lumps of white vegetable half-floating in the broth. Elizabeth tried a piece and found it not unlike potato, though more fibrous.

"I hope you like it," Fidelia said. "The fish were my catch. They taught me to throw a net and haul it in again. It was all small fish. I don't know the name of them. We had enough to fill three buckets by the end. The rest are being dried and smoked. They think a storm's on its way. In two days. Or three. The small boats won't be able to go out so there'll be nothing fresh."

Elizabeth focussed on eating. Though it was bland, the root vegetable was satisfying her hunger in a way the stews of the previous days hadn't.

"So you're to be a fisherwoman?" Elizabeth asked.

"They're testing my sailing skills. That's what they said. And every Sargassan needs to learn how to fish – whatever they end up doing." She hesitated before continuing. "They tell me you spoke to Mother Rebecca again."

"Twice."

"Who else was there?"

"Gwynedd."

"I heard you were alone with the queen. That's what the fisherwomen told me."

"That was the second time I saw her."

"They can't believe it. They say only the closest advisors see her alone. Was there not even a guard?"

Elizabeth remembered the pistol lying in Mother Rebecca's lap. It had been loaded when Siân took it from her. It might be loaded still. She could have grabbed it. The old woman wouldn't have been able to stop her. She could have threatened the queen and demanded whatever she wanted. It would have been a fool's game. There were too many ways such a plan might go wrong. Too many unknowns. But it still surprised her that she hadn't thought of it at the time; the gun lying there in easy reach. It had almost been an invitation.

"What do you think of these people?" she asked.

Fidelia glanced around the walls of the stockade. There was no telling who might be listening beyond. "I'm glad to be here," she said. Her eyes told a different story. She was lying for the benefit of the guards. But there was something more in her expression; a grudging admiration.

"What will you think if they kill me?" Elizabeth asked.

There was no answer.

"A ship is on its way from Patagonia," Elizabeth said. "It brings powerful new weapons. Soon no one will be able to attack the Nation and live. If the Company were to send the entire fleet, every one of their ships would be sunk."

Fidelia's eyes grew wide with horror.

From the confinement of her prison, Elizabeth heard but could not see the arrival of the ship. The rhythmic thump of the engine came to her on the breeze, growing louder until she could hear the splash of the paddlewheels. After it stopped – it couldn't have been more than a hundred yards distant – there were three long blasts from its steam whistle and she caught a tang of oil smoke on the air.

After that, the rhythm of the island changed. She felt it in the footfalls of people passing outside the stockade, and in the pitch of their voices; though she could seldom make out the words.

A guard brought news with the evening meal.

"They're back," she said. "We have our trade deal. It's all we wanted and more." She might have been saying that a Messiah had come, so fierce was the light in her eyes.

"I'm happy for you," Elizabeth said.

Whereon the guard seemed to remember herself. She flashed an embarrassed smile then picked up the empty bowl and cup from the noon meal. Backing away, she dipped her head in a parting gesture that had become familiar. Elizabeth listened and heard the metallic click of the padlock after the door had closed; a muffled sound, as if the guard had taken pains to lock it quietly.

I'm happy for you, Elizabeth had said. She was surprised to find truth in the words. She had many reasons to hate the Sargassans. They'd been the cause of death to hundreds. They held her and Tinker captive. They'd shot Julia's airship from the sky. And yet, when Mother Rebecca held her hand and told the story of her life, it wasn't hate that Elizabeth felt, but kinship.

Watching the stars wheel overhead, she thought about Julia and John Farthing and Tinker. If she'd only accepted the loss of her friend, she would have better served her lover and the boy. And yet, it had never been her nature to let go where there was still a chance. Perhaps there is truth to be found when hope has been used up.

Her relationship with Farthing had always been impossible. He'd sworn the oath of the Patent Office agents: obedience and the celibate life. But still she'd clung to a dream in which one day they'd lose themselves together under the wide skies of Virginia. She'd created a subterfuge so that they could maintain the illusion that all was well. Their love had been doomed from the start. But now it came to her that, even had she known it, she would still have done things just the same. There was contentment in that thought.

She closed her eyes and for once sleep took her easily.

Elizabeth woke in darkness to a new sound. Abrupt and terrifying, it ripped through the night air, fast as the beat of an engine, yet unmistakably the report of a gun. It was impossible to imagine how a weapon could be fired and reloaded with such extraordinary speed and regularity. When at last it ended, many women cried out, as if in victory. The sound of their celebrations continued until the stars began to fade.

The guards came for her in the early light. It seemed that much of Freedom Island was sleeping off the excitement of the night before. The houses of the outer island were dark. But as they turned onto the main boardway, she made out a scattering of lights in windows and doorways. The *Unicorn*'s lanterns shone dull yellow.

On seeing her, the guards on deck stood straighter.

Elizabeth ducked through the hatchway and climbed down to the throne room.

She knew something was different as soon as the door opened. All the chandeliers were lit. Masked figures stood around the edges of the room. The guard pushed her inside. The door closed heavily behind her.

A low stool had been positioned directly in front of the dais. She stepped towards it. But after two paces realised that what she'd taken for a stool was an executioner's block.

She half turned, about to run for the door, but the masked figures had closed ranks behind her, forming a wall. They advanced, driving her on, closer and closer until she stumbled and was pushed down to her knees. A hand pressed on her head, bringing her neck towards the notch in the block. In panic she pushed back; a single, violent thrust. The one who'd been holding her crashed to the floor. But other hands gripped her shoulders, stopping her from getting to her feet. A sword rested across the arms of the throne.

The queen of the Sargassans looked down on her. "The judgement is made," she said, in a voice like dried-up leaves. "You are a remarkable woman, Elizabeth. But I have no way to trust you. You've seen our secrets. You've seen our rites. We cannot have you live among us. Nor can you be released. Therefore will you be sent on to whatever follows this life. It will be clean and quick."

The masked figure standing to the left of the throne reached out and took the sword. It was a curved blade, wide and half as tall as the woman who held it. That must be Siân. Elizabeth's mind whirled from thought to thought. Siân's place was on the left. Gwynedd was the merciful one. How many were in the room? Could she reach the queen before they grabbed her? The sword's pommel glinted with green and red gemstones. Its holder descended the dais. Could she grab the sword itself? Could she hold it to the queen's throat?

But hands pushed her down. There were deep cut marks across the top of the block, almost aligned, meeting at sharp angles. Her neck fitted snug in the notch, the wood cool and smooth. Bracing her hands against the block, she tried to throw them back, but there were too many of them this time.

The executioner's feet moved, planting on the boards next to her, slightly spread and angled, ready to make the blow. Elizabeth could still see the curved blade, the tip of which rested on the floor. She kicked back, savagely, catching something. One of the hands lifted from her but two more replaced it, pushing her down so hard that the notch pressed against her throat. Her head seemed too full of blood. Or too empty. The pressure was strangling her. A ring of blackness was closing in from the periphery of her vision. The sword blade lifted.

Then someone screamed. There was a push on her side that wasn't the pressure of hands. She could feel body heat and a head next to hers, another neck resting over the block. Though her sight was almost gone, she knew the scent of the woman who knelt beside her. She knew it without any doubt or hesitation. Who else would willingly share her execution?

She pushed back again. This time the hands gave way and she righted herself. People were shifting back. She could hear the shuffle of their feet. The blackness retreated and she found herself on her knees facing the figure who'd a moment before lain next to her. The mask clattered to the boards and Elizabeth saw Julia's face.

"I knew you'd come for me," Julia said. "I knew you'd come."

PART FOUR

CHAPTER 26

The bullet rolled with the swaying of the island, away from where Elizabeth sat and then back towards her. Away and back. She had stripped down her pistol to its component parts and laid them out in order, except for the screws, which she'd dropped into a wineglass for safekeeping, just like her father had taught her when she was a child. Now she took the soft cloth, dipped it in light oil and worked it against the walnut stock in small circles.

"It was clean already," said Julia, who'd hardly left her side in the twelve hours since the execution that wasn't an execution.

They were sitting in a house that had been given for their use. Situated near the centre of the island, it was close to the *Unicorn* itself, being three doors down and opposite across the main boardway. Like everything on Freedom Island, it appeared to have been constructed from salvage. No two boards were quite equal. But the location spoke of prestige. Quality ran through the building from the finish of the joinery to the materials themselves.

Away and back. Away and back. The bullet was rolling closer to the far edge of the table each time. At last it dropped and Julia caught it. Elizabeth looked up and saw the frustration written on her friend's face.

"Cleaning it helps me to think," she explained. "I'd been hungry for information all this time. Now all of a sudden I have too much of it to take in."

"What is there to say but that we're prisoners?" Julia asked.

"They gave me back my gun," said Elizabeth. "Why is that? Tell me again about the *American Frontier*."

Julia dropped the bullet into the glass with the screws. "There's nothing more to say."

In the hours since reunion, their questions had concerned the practical history of how each had come to be in that place. Elizabeth had kept her own answers general enough to be innocent, avoiding mention of the Patent Office. Julia was incapable of sustaining a lie, even to save her dearest friend.

"You told me they fired through gaps in low cloud. How big were the gaps?"

"How could I know such a thing?" Julia asked.

"Then, how much of the sea was covered? Half would you say? A quarter?"

"Less."

"Then you might well have flown clear across them and never been seen. It was chance that you were shot down. Except that from their view, they'd positioned themselves under clear sky. And Atlantic flights follow the same timetable each week."

"I can't hold such a dispassionate thought," said Julia. "The pictures come to my mind when I don't want them. It makes my heart jump as if it were happening over again. The sound of the bullets – they howled like banshees. And the feeling in my stomach as we dropped. You know the men screamed? Did I tell you? I didn't know that men would scream."

"You did tell me." Elizabeth put down the cloth and took Julia's hand. "Let's talk of something else. The Test – I haven't asked you about that."

Whereon Julia recounted her experience, which proved

just as Elizabeth had imagined; Julia's resolute honesty, guiding her to a truthful answer in each case. She'd accepted the key and used it to escape from the stockade. But she gave herself up as soon as it became clear there was no way off the island without doing harm to one of the Sargassans. There'd been no others taking the Test with her. Julia had been the only woman on the *American Frontier*, all the other passengers being men of business.

Elizabeth had put together the story of the airship disaster from those fragments her friend had been willing to recall. And from information about the weaponry, which Ekua and Siân had given freely.

The howling bullets were not designed to ignite the gases in the airship's canopy. When fired they were sleek and pointed like miniature javelins. As such, any holes they made would have been pinpricks in such a mighty craft. But towards the top of their trajectory they slowed, allowing small blades to spring out like fans. On hitting the envelope, the bullets slowed further and the blades sprung fully out, so that when they exited on the other side, they ripped wide circles in the fabric, allowing the buoyant gases to pour out.

The pilots battled, but must have known that at such a rate of descent, they would land in the ocean. Their only power was to minimise the speed of impact, which they did. Once down, they sent up distress flares. The Sargassan ships found them easily enough.

The men had been locked in a cargo hold and Julia given freedom to roam the ship. She watched as the *American Frontier* was stripped of everything that could be salvaged: engines, fuel, structural members, window glass and the entire cargo of legal documents and banknotes.

Back on Freedom Island, Julia had been tested and found, according to Mother Rebecca's classification, to be entirely faithful; one who would act but do no harm. Thinking of it, Elizabeth felt a rush of pride and affection. Her own life was woven from half-truths and compromise. She'd never had the space for simple virtues. Perhaps that's why she so admired such qualities in her dearest friends: Julia and John Farthing. Among the runaways, stowaways and pirates of the Sargassan Nation, Julia's transparent honesty must have shone through.

Also her knowledge. A woman trained in the law would be rare enough in London or New York. In the middle of the Atlantic, there could surely be no other. Until Elizabeth arrived. In the space of a year, the Sargassan Nation had acquired two legal minds. In all the tests and questioning, she'd not thought along that angle. The queen of all crows wasn't going to accept the conjunction as mere coincidence. From the start, Mother Rebecca must have known the two arrivals were connected; so similar in age, accent and knowledge. The drama of the execution had been the final test of it. By placing her neck on the block, Julia had revealed a depth of love and loyalty that no words could ever have proved.

But by the same act, Elizabeth's real motivation had been exposed. She'd come to the Sargassans to find her lost friend and lied to conceal the fact. The revelation should have resulted in a doubling of the guard on the prison stockade. Instead she'd been promoted to a high status residence. Her gun had been returned, together with powder and shot.

Mother Rebecca now had Tinker, Julia and Elizabeth on the island, each a hostage for the others. She could send any one of them on a mission and be confident of a faithful return. The only way they could escape would be all together. Which would surely be impossible.

Elizabeth slotted the stock and barrel together. It was a beautiful fit. Then the flintlock. Dipping into the wineglass, she began screwing the pieces in place.

"Tell me about Richard," Julia said.

Elizabeth had so far managed to avoid talking about Julia's new husband. "He was well when I last heard from him," she said.

Julia stood and began to pace the room.

"Was he... That is, did he..."

"He loves you."

It was true. And yet not the whole truth. When news came of the loss of the *American Frontier*, Elizabeth had searched for a way to believe Julia could still be alive. But Richard had been unable to cope with the limbo of uncertainty. He had thrown himself headlong into a chasm of grief. It had quite swallowed him. In his last letter he'd written that he did not expect there could be another like Julia in the far span of the world. Nor did he believe he would ever recover from the loss. By the time Elizabeth steamed from the port of Liverpool, Richard had already initiated the process of obtaining a death certificate. Her fear was not that he would find some other woman to marry, but that the blackness might consume him entirely.

"Is he happy?" Julia asked, a tremor in her voice. "I wish it were so. And yet I hope it's not. I'm a horrible person, Elizabeth."

"Your feelings are just as nature would make any of us in the same place. He does love you. I know that more clearly than ever I did. And yes, he's sad. But let's not dwell on it. Come tell me about Patagonia. How was the journey? You must have crossed the equator. I never dreamed either of us would travel so far."

"It was long," Julia owned.

"And Patagonia – is it as fierce and wild as the stories say?"

"I saw little enough. Just the port and the inside of the lord's palace. The windows of the coach were blacked so we couldn't see."

"And what was your part in it all?"

"To read the agreement. In English, at least. They'd drafted first in the Welsh language. After that it was translated. They had a lawyer on their side also. We had to make the text so that there could be no cause for argument later. It meant writing the whole thing without punctuation, worded so it would still stand. That way the meaning couldn't later be changed by the adding of a comma."

"Did it take long?"

"Three days. Each night we were returned to the ship. Then it was finished and the lord put his mark on it. The most frightening part was the trade itself. There were so many men. And guns everywhere. You hardly dared breathe for fear a movement might be mistaken."

"If they have such guns, what do they need from the Sargassans?" Elizabeth asked.

Julia's brow creased in a puzzled frown. "Do you not know? The Patagonians need workers for their mines and furnaces. They can make guns in their workshops. And engines and cylinders to hold compressed gas. But they can't make men. What the Sargassans bring is slaves."

The house had cots rather than hammocks. The woman who brought the food for their evening meal said it was a sign of great honour. And the fact that there were candles, which she lit for them.

"Our mother loves you," she said, with the warmth of a benediction. It might have been expected to gladden their hearts.

When their bowls were empty, she gathered them up to take away. Elizabeth didn't offer a hand, but the woman took it anyway, touching it to her forehead.

"The sun shines on us," she said, though it was night, then turned to go.

In the dark of the bedroom, with the faint smells of salt and seaweed and herbs and the whisper of the island's movement, Elizabeth shifted again in her cot. She had focussed all this time on following Julia's path. That single objective had blotted out other considerations. But now she thought about Ryan, Locklight and the others. Even the treadmill might be better than Patagonia. Mines and metal works were dangerous places, even for free men. The crew of the *Iceland Queen* would be shipped out as slaves, just as the men from the *American Frontier* had been sold before them. She wondered how many still lived.

As a child, Mother Rebecca had sold her captured oppressors. In doing so she'd saved the women of the *Unicorn*. The men themselves had forced her into desperate straits and had paid for it in full measure. There'd seemed a moral balance to it. Enough to absolve the queen of guilt.

"Are you awake?" Julia's voice was a whisper.

"Yes."

"I never used to have trouble sleeping," said Julia. "I think I'm afraid."

Elizabeth reached out in the dark towards the other cot. "Who could frighten the woman who'd put her own head on the executioner's block? You're the bravest person I know."

Julia's hand found hers. "Well then, I don't know what I feel."

"It's called uncertainty," said Elizabeth. "You can't name it because it's unfamiliar to you."

"That's not true! I've been uncertain about lots of things."

"Never about the goodness of your own intent."

"I drafted a contract for the sale of slaves." There was a gulp of air that might have been a sob.

"What if you'd refused?" Elizabeth asked. "They'd have killed you for sure. And then someone else would have done the drafting. But still... you could have made a stand. And now you're worried that it would have been better to die. But nothing would have been made better by it. The slaves would still have been sold. And I would have lost you. Alive, you have a chance to help them. And me. You did the right thing. It's just not so easy living with it."

Perhaps those few words of reassurance had been all that Julia needed. Her breathing slowed. Her grip slackened. When the sleep was deep enough, Elizabeth got out of bed and placed Julia's arm under the covers. Intending to explore more of the island, she slipped from the room. But as she reached the front of the house, the thought of leaving her friend brought her up short.

And there it was, more binding than any lock or chain.

She lowered herself to sit just inside the door. The deckway lay beyond, and the *Unicorn*. The breeze in the palm trees made a sound like the rustling of dry papers. Closing her eyes, she lay down on the boards.

"Damn you, Mother Rebecca," she whispered.

An explosion jolted Elizabeth from sleep. She'd been dreaming of guns and slaves so vividly that she couldn't at first decide what was real, nor how she came to be lying on the floor of the house. Moonlight shone on the palm trees beyond the doorway. A breeze rustled the leaves; a sound like dry paper. She remembered leaving her cot. And then the events of the previous day came pouring back.

Julia.

The reunion itself seemed like a dream. She turned, about to creep back to her friend's bedside. But a distant boom made her pause. Thunder perhaps. The Sargassans had been talking about a storm. She stepped out of the house and looked up. The sky was milky with stars.

Then one of the buildings down the boardway detonated, shattering into flying splinters. She was ducking as the sound of the explosion hit her. Women were shouting. Elizabeth staggered back inside, realization coming all in a rush. "Cannons! Take cover!"

Julia met her half way. Elizabeth grabbed her friend's hand and hauled her out of the house. Everyone was pouring onto the boardway now, running, though there was no way to know from which direction the cannon fire had come. More booms sounded in the distance. She pushed Julia to the edge of the boards. There were only a couple of feet of crawl space below the planks. But it would do.

"Get down!"

Julia resisted.

A cannonball hummed overhead, coming from behind the *Unicorn*. Another one landed somewhere close. There were children among the crowds. For a moment, Elizabeth couldn't move.

Julia broke free from her grip and was running towards the little ones. "Get them under the boards!" she shouted.

One of the women nearby understood and began shepherding the children to the edge. Then others had seen and were doing the same. The walkway began to clear.

There was no time for Elizabeth to be proud of her friend. Yet the feeling hit her like a wave, breaking the spell of fear that had rooted her to the ground. She took off, running in the direction of the cannon fire.

"Wait!"

Julia was following. Elizabeth pelted on, along a small walkway, then onto a smaller one still, adjusting her stride as she came closer to the edge of the island so the movement of the waves didn't throw her.

The dark shapes of two ships loomed, far out to sea. Lights flickered on one of them. She counted the seconds till the sound of the guns reached her. They had to be more than a mile out. Beyond the limit of any accuracy. But the island was a big target. A cannonball landed between the houses ahead, disappearing into the ground. Another hummed across the sky. She looked back and saw it take the roof off one low building and crash into the wall of another.

The floating jetty lay directly ahead, to which the *Iceland Queen* was moored. There were figures on the quarterdeck. Elizabeth clambered up the gangplank and ran to join them. Julia followed close behind. Lena was there with three other warriors.

"What's happening?"

One of the women offered a telescope. "We'll have them!" she growled.

Elizabeth braced her feet and levelled the glass, trying to keep steady against the shifting of the deck. The image of the ship that had been firing came into view. Twisting the eyepiece, she brought it into focus. The deck guns flashed again. The paddlewheel housings on either side rose higher than the quarterdeck.

"I think it's the *Ajax*," she said. "Twenty cannons. But these are the long guns. There are only four of those. She's fast."

A cannonball came down close, smacking into a boardwalk near the island's edge. Another arced across the sky, set to overshoot.

Elizabeth trained her view on the other ship, which she didn't recognise.

"We've had no shots from that one," said Lena.

"Looks like a whaling ship," Elizabeth said, passing the telescope on to Julia.

Lena's face was set with anger. "*Sealion*'s on its way. It'll be three more minutes. But they'll ram it from underneath. You'll see. Their ship's going to go down like a stone."

Two more booms followed in quick succession. The cannonballs came down somewhere in the middle of the island, hitting wooden structures to judge by the sound.

Smoke was rising from one of the earlier strikes.

"It's changing course," said Julia.

Lena grabbed the glass and trained it on *Ajax*. Even with the naked eye, Elizabeth could see the darkening of the funnel smoke and the ship heeling over as it accelerated into the turn.

"She's racing like the devil," whispered one of the others.

"Do you think they spotted the *Sealion*?" asked Julia.

"Well they're making a run for it, sure enough. They can't get away. They mustn't."

They were all of them leaning forwards, as if that would help the undersea boat to get to its target in time. Elizabeth's emotions were in turmoil. There could be a hundred men on *Ajax*. If it sank, they'd drown. Or be sold into slavery. Them and the crew of the whaler. But if they got away, the Company would learn the location of Freedom Island.

Elizabeth took back the telescope. *Ajax* had straightened out. Underwater ships were slow, she'd been told. The whaler might not escape. But *Ajax* was already beyond the reach of the Sargassans. She should have been glad. The men had escaped drowning. But her feelings were all dread. When the Company returned, it would be in full force. Then who would be the slaves?

"It's a fight to the death," said Lena.

Fast feet approaching down the jetty made everyone turn. The runner stopped next to the *Iceland Queen* and hailed them. "Council of war! Mother Rebecca calls you to come!"

Elizabeth looked to the others on deck, expecting one of them to move, but they were all looking at her. So was the messenger.

CHAPTER 27

The Company whaler had been captured. They shouted it across the island, many mouths taking up the cry. Every other woman Elizabeth passed was ready to tell her the good news. Some cheered overloud as if trying to cover their fear; a celebration of no joy. Others stood dumbly, staring at ruined buildings.

The messenger had urged her to run. But she walked, trying to order her churning thoughts. Julia was following close behind, though she'd not herself been summoned. She'd been trying to say something at first, but Elizabeth's mind was in turmoil and she hadn't been able to take it in.

Ideas were in play as well as lives. The vastness of the Gas-Lit Empire, stagnating under the weight of its own rules. The nascent vitality of the Sargassan Nation; a dot in an ocean of chaos. A hegemony of masculine power and the single matriarchy to exist in the wide span of the world. Slave traders. Her mind kept returning to that ugly truth.

A line of porters hurried towards them along the narrow walkway, carrying cargo. Boxes and bales of edible seaweed balanced on heads, kegs suspended from shoulder poles. Julia manoeuvred Elizabeth onto the deck of a small house to let them pass. The boards bowed under their feet as they headed towards the jetty. Ships were being made ready to sail.

Elizabeth had lived all her years in the ambiguous space between settled identities, fashioning an existence from contradictions. Her life had been a tower of playing cards that might be brought down by a whisper. It could stand only so long as no one spoke the truth. Her lover, a Patent Office agent, dedicated to law and the Long Quiet. Herself pulled by the gypsy spirit to cast off anything that might tie her down. She could do all those things the good people of the Gas-Lit Empire thought the province of a man: advance and command and decision and battle. Or she could yield and flow and be guided by the kind of gentle, caring intuition they expected of a woman. And she still didn't know who she really was.

Perhaps Siân had glimpsed the contradiction. Which clothes would Elizabeth choose, she'd asked. The honest answer would have been that she'd choose the clothes to match whichever role she was about to play. And if all other things had been equal? They never were.

Three bodies had been laid out, sheet-wrapped, on the boards in front of the smoking ruin of a house. A teenage girl knelt next to them, her head thrown back, mouth wide, her cry like the wind in the rigging of a tall ship. Elizabeth stared at the corpses. Two were adult sized and one a child. More people were about to die. That was the only certainty. She couldn't weigh the significance of even one life lost. But forces were gathering. A war was about to begin.

Julia took her hand and gently eased her away, on towards the main deckway.

One goal only Elizabeth knew as fixed and certain: to see Julia and Tinker back across the border into the Gas-Lit Empire. When she'd set out, it had been with the intention of bringing herself back also. But now she could feel no such conviction.

It was as if the unresolved strands of her life had been

conjured into two contending armies, each bent on the other's destruction. And she, standing at the meeting point. *Choose a side*, the fates were saying.

They'd arrived at the steps leading to the deck of the Unicorn, but Julia held out an arm to stop her. Elizabeth had been so consumed in thought that she'd almost forgotten that her friend was with her.

"Do you know the story of the queen's daughters?" Julia whispered.

"Tell me later."

Elizabeth tried to get past.

Julia held her ground. "You need to hear this."

"Later." This time Elizabeth pushed through and was up the steps to the deck of the *Unicorn*.

The ship had come through the barrage unscathed. Elizabeth expected to have her pistol taken. It hung from her belt, in clear sight. But the guards just stepped aside, making room for her to pass.

"God keep you," one of them said.

The blessing snagged in Elizabeth's mind. But there was no time to address the questions it raised. Nor Julia's parting words. She ducked through the hatchway into the dark corridor, which smelled of hot candle wax. There were no guards at the throne room door. She opened it and stepped inside. All the chandeliers had been lit. And the brazier.

At first it seemed that only Siân and Gwynedd were present, facing each other across the empty throne. Then something moved among the furs; a skeletal hand, the twitch of a finger. It beckoned. Mother Rebecca was calling her.

Elizabeth hurried to the foot of the dais. "What's happened? Is she ill?"

"No," said Siân, defiant.

"Yes," said Gwynedd, who was kneeling. She covered her grandmother's hand once more.

Siân's glance at her cousin was angry. There could be no doubting it this time.

"I can speak..." the old woman paused to inhale, "...for myself." The light and focus seemed to have gone out of her right eye, which was weeping. But the left eye was bright and fixed on Elizabeth.

"You need to rest," said Gwynedd.

"The gunship got away," said Elizabeth, addressing the report directly to Mother Rebecca.

"Then we act now or die!" said Siân. "We strike before they've time to prepare. If we hit them at dusk, we could take out half their ships and be away before they knew what had happened."

Gwynedd stood and faced her cousin. "Then what?" she demanded. "That's just one fleet. They have other fleets in other oceans. What happens when they all come bearing down on us?"

"We hide and pick them off like we've always done. The more captives we have to sell, the more weapons we can buy."

"We can't hide. They know where we are."

"We abandon the island. We've built it once. We can build it again."

"And feed the people how? We were a dozen the first time. Without Freedom Island, where would we grow the food to feed five thousand souls?"

"The more ships they send, the more slaves we'll have to trade. There'll be more food than you've ever known. And not just fish stew."

"We aren't all warriors."

"Then some of us need to learn!"

"You want Mother Rebecca to take up a gun? Or the children?"

"She's held one before. And killed! You want her to be a

slave? And us?"

The more fierce the exchange became, the less they seemed to notice the woman who was the subject of their argument. Indeed, Mother Rebecca's head had dropped lower than before, but her hand was trying to lift free of the furs.

"She's going to speak," Elizabeth said.

Gwynedd and Siân seemed to realise at the same moment. Both got down on their knees, one on each side of the throne.

Mother Rebecca's good eye was fixed on Elizabeth. "What do you say?"

"Make peace!" The words broke free, as if they had a will independent of Elizabeth's own.

Siân gripped her sword hilt. "It's impossible!"

"Could it be done?" asked Gwynedd.

"Do you know of the Great Accord?"

"A law built by men!" said Siân.

Elizabeth shook her head. "It isn't about the rights of one sex or the other. They framed it to stop nations competing to make ever more terrible weapons. If we – as the Sargassan Nation – ask to sign the Accord, then all the other nations of the Gas-Lit Empire would have to vote to agree or not. If they agreed – then we'd be safe. No one could attack without all the others coming to our aid."

"They wouldn't agree!"

"The Patent Office is terrified of what's out here beyond its sight. They want the Gas-Lit Empire to spread into the ocean. And even if the nations didn't agree, the process of deciding it would take years. It would buy time."

"You're not a fighter," Siân said. "You don't understand. No one votes for peace if they can win by war. If we delay, they'll just gather their forces. They'll choose when to strike. But if we hit first, it'll be us choosing the place and time of it. And once we have power over the whole ocean, there'll be no need of parley. We'll set the terms."

"Do they want to strike us?" asked Gwynedd. "We've taken their ships from under them and they still don't know how. Aren't they afraid?"

Elizabeth nodded. "They are," she said.

"Then we should parley. They'll agree to not sail our waters and we'll agree to not sail theirs. What harm could there be in the Great Accord?"

There were pinpricks of sweat on Siân's brow. Though kneeling, her muscles were tensed as if ready to give battle. Her voice had been the louder. But Gwynedd's face was set calm and resolute. Increasingly, it was her controlling the argument.

"Answer this," said Siân, standing to face Elizabeth. "What harm would your Accord do?"

"It would bring peace."

"At what price?"

"You'd have to agree to not attack their ships."

"And?"

"Nor trade in slaves. But there'd be no more need of slaves once there was peace."

"What else?"

"You'd submit to the judgement of the International Patent office. But only to decide which inventions were permitted."

"They'd ban our weapons."

Gwynedd stood. "We'd have peace," she said. "There'd be no need of weapons."

The furs shifted over Mother Rebecca. "I am... not gone... yet," she said. Her right hand reached out and took hold of the arm of the throne. She rocked once, twice, then raised herself, the furs falling to the ground. Gwynedd and Siân jumped as if to catch her fall. But Mother Rebecca stood. She fixed her one good eye on Elizabeth and said: "What is... their... goal?"

Only one answer was possible. Ever had it been the

statement of the high ideals of the founding fathers. Endless repetition by politicians and schoolchildren had rendered it bland. It was a blade dulled by overuse.

Elizabeth recited the line: "The Patent Office was established to protect the wellbeing of the common man."

Outside the borders of the Gas-Lit Empire, they were words that still had the power to cut. Gwynedd took a half step back. Siân seemed to grow in stature. Mother Rebecca nodded slowly, then lowered herself back to the throne.

"They mean all people," said Elizabeth, understanding the damage too late. "Man means mankind."

"Man means man," said Siân. "We must attack them. Hard and swift."

This time Gwynedd made no protest. Both granddaughters looked to the throne. Mother Rebecca seemed spent by the effort of standing but her eye was still on Elizabeth.

"Do... you... agree?"

"Gather the forces," said Elizabeth. "But don't attack, I beg you."

Julia was waiting in the doorway. "What happened?" she asked. "The colour's quite gone from your face."

"Siân wants war," said Elizabeth, trying not to show the horror she felt.

"And Gwynedd?"

"It's Siân who has the queen's ear."

They were inside now, in the sleeping room, furthest from the deckway, with little chance of being overheard. Elizabeth sat heavily on the edge of her cot, feeling a great weariness pressing down on her shoulders.

"Don't set yourself between Gwynedd and Siân," said Julia.

"I'm too tired for riddles."

"It's what I was trying to tell you before. Their mothers were the queen's daughters, which makes them cousins. But they're half-sisters also."

Elizabeth sat up straighter. "They have the same father?"

Julia nodded. "He was a slave, obviously. Both their mothers chose him to be the father of their children. That was their right. But instead of him being sold on afterwards, he was kept on the island. They argued over him. It ended up in a fight, out on the deckway in front of the *Unicorn*. Siân's mother was killed. But Gwynedd's mother was wounded and died a week later. The thing is, people tell the story to show how love for the Nation makes everything right. The queen's granddaughters are living proof of it because the feud is healed.

"They were just babies when their mothers died. Mother Rebecca raised them. But..." Julia stepped to the door and glanced outside before coming back to sit next to Elizabeth, resuming in a whisper. "...when I see them together, I wonder if they might not remember it. It frightens me to see you working with them so closely. That's what I wanted to tell you. Don't put yourself between them. And don't take sides with one or the other. I don't think it's safe."

CHAPTER 28

No one saw the airship arrive. It emerged from the black as night ended, a grey shape suspended five miles to the northeast of the island. Seeing such things over the cities of England had always been a wonder. But over the wilderness of the ocean there was something alien about it: its vastness and symmetry, its stillness between the pale streaks of dawn and the churning waves. At such a distance it seemed silent, though the trail of smoke proved its engines were working, the propellers turning to keep it from drifting with the wind.

Then, three hours later, a Company steamer was sighted. It took up position below the airship and began to signal. Ekua scrawled out the sequence of long and short flashes as dashes and dots. She'd filled half a page before it stopped. When it started up again the sequence proved the same.

"What do we do?" she asked.

"We use the helio on the *Iceland Queen*," Elizabeth said. "Return three long flashes. That's what they do to show a message has been received."

She ran then, following Ekua and Lena. Back across the island to the jetty. They found the helio in its box and hefted it up to the quarterdeck, fitting the gimballed mounting into its slot.

The signal had continued to flash from the Company steamer. Elizabeth angled the mirror to catch the sun then took aim through the telescope. When all was aligned she pulled the lever three times, opening and closing the shutter, repeating the signal at ten-second intervals. Over and over again until three long flashes came back.

"They've seen it," she said.

Ekua was lying on her stomach on the deck, the helio's instruction book open at the page of codes, a sheet of paper held down under her hand. The corner fluttered against the wind as she transcribed the letters of the message.

"Send negotiator," she said, at last. "That's what they're saying!"

The surge of relief was so intense that Elizabeth felt her legs weaken under her. She held tighter to the railing. "They want to parley!"

"Should I ready the launch?" asked Lena.

"Will it reach so far?"

"Easy. And many miles more."

"Then yes, get it ready!"

More women were approaching down the jetty; a group of armed warriors. Siân was the first of them up onto the *Iceland Queen*, her face set hard and resolute. Elizabeth had seen that expression before. But now, knowing the history of the queen's daughters, its meaning seemed different.

"What are you doing?"

"They want to parley," Elizabeth said.

Siân shook her head. "Make ready the submarines and the long gun."

Lena turned to go, but Elizabeth caught her arm. "They want to negotiate!"

"Do it!" Siân snapped, pointing back down the jetty.

Lena twisted free of Elizabeth's grip and ran.

Ekua still held the book and paper.

"Work out the code to tell them a negotiator's coming," Elizabeth said. Then to Siân: "If Mother Rebecca chooses war, then we go to war. But if she decides we parley, it's not in your power to go against her!"

Anger flared in Siân's eyes. The woman was a killer, sure enough. But she couldn't do a thing once her grandmother's name had been invoked. Elizabeth had positioned herself between the queen's granddaughters; exactly what Julia had warned her against. But the ships of two navies were facing each other; tens of thousands of men and women, millions of tons of iron and wood, a floating island and the leviathan of the mother ship. One spark would set them all aflame.

Most of the lights were out and the throne was empty. At first it seemed that Mother Rebecca had gone, but then Elizabeth noticed Gwynedd kneeling at the top of the dais and a shape lying before her.

"Is she dead?" asked Siân, advancing.

"No," said Gwynedd.

The queen was lying on her back, wrapped in furs, her head propped on pillows. Breath whispered in her throat as it ebbed and flowed. Siân knelt next to her cousin.

"Has she said anything?"

Gwynedd shook her head. "I found her like this."

The guards hadn't crossed the threshold, but were staring in from the open door, aghast. Elizabeth stopped halfway to the dais.

Siân shouted at her: "Get out!"

But Elizabeth couldn't risk leaving them alone. "I'm staying."

Gwynedd gestured dismissal to the guards, who backed out, closing the door behind them.

Siân stared at her cousin. "She's no right to be here!"

If Siân became queen, war would be swift. With Gwynedd

on the throne, there would be parley. Elizabeth couldn't decide which path would be more dangerous. But worse than either would be ambiguity in the succession. If Julia was correct, if there was more to the rivalry than a clash of ideas, then Mother Rebecca would know it also.

"Has the queen written a will?" she asked.

Gwynedd shook her head. "I don't know of one."

"We're at war!" snapped Siân. "She can't lead us like this. It's a fight, so it should be me."

"It's not yet a fight," said Elizabeth.

"Tell that to the dead."

"The Company wants to negotiate."

"They're playing for time!"

The queen took a deeper breath and opened one of her eyes. Half of her face hung slack. Freeing one hand from the furs she pointed to her own mouth. Siân reached for a cup. Raising her grandmother's head, she tipped a few drops between the cracked lips. A rivulet of wine overflowed. The old woman swallowed and coughed.

Siân smoothed her grandmother's hair back from the forehead. "Who's to be queen after you?"

Elizabeth stepped closer for a better view of Mother Rebecca's face. The cheeks were hollowed. The eyes seemed to have sunk deeper into the skull. Beads of spilled wine in the fur near her face caught the candlelight like garnets.

Siân bent closer. "Who should lead us?"

Mother Rebecca's clawed hand struggled free of the furs again. It raised, and for a moment seemed to point towards Elizabeth. Siân's expression changed from shock to disbelief and then fury. "It can't be *her*!"

The queen's arm fell back. She was still breathing but her eyes had closed.

"She can't even see. She doesn't know who's in the room."

Elizabeth said nothing. Her mind was reeling. Siân carried

a brace of pistols at her belt. Two shots. She'd use the first on Elizabeth. Then she'd kill her cousin. The guards would come running. She'd try to make it seem that Elizabeth had shot Gwynedd.

Siân was staring directly at Elizabeth. Her right arm rested by her side. It seemed a casual position, but her fingers were only inches from one of the guns. Elizabeth took a step to the left, bringing herself closer to the throne. If she dived behind it there might be a chance. The throne was made of carved wood. Too thin to stop a bullet at close range. But there was beaten silver in the design, and semi-precious stones. It would give her a chance. She sidestepped again. Siân began to rise.

"There's something in her hand," Gwynedd said.

Siân was the first to break eye contact and look down at her grandmother. Gwynedd eased back the clawed fingers to reveal a crumpled sheet of paper. She flattened it on her knee and read: "Siân, Gwynedd and Elizabeth must agree."

She passed it to her cousin, who read it, shaking her head all the while. "She means we're to vote for the new queen."

"Or she means we're to vote on all decisions," said Gwynedd.

At last Elizabeth found her voice. "Right now, you've one question to answer. Do you send someone to parley or do you start a war?"

Gwynedd regarded her. "And what do you say?"

"Parley."

"She's not one of us!" Siân spat the words. "We should fight! Strike them a blow before they know it's coming. Speed and stealth – that's always been our way. If we parley we cast off all that power."

"But if we parley, there may be no need to fight."

Gwynedd was frowning. "I agree with Elizabeth," she said. "Make a boat ready."

Siân stormed from the throne room, barking orders to the

guards, drawing everyone's gaze so that Elizabeth almost missed the moment when Gwynedd slipped the crumpled sheet of paper into her sleeve. Gwynedd caught her seeing it. For a second they looked at each other.

All the way to the edge of the island, Elizabeth was thinking about that moment of eye contact. It seemed to be an acknowledgment; a common threat shared between unfamiliar allies. But for a fraction of a second she'd thought it might be the other way around: that Gwynedd was sizing up a new enemy.

The jetty swarmed with movement. Crew ran past, and porters carrying kegs of oil. The boards bobbed under the passage of feet and cargo. Siân was shouting orders as they pushed a paddle launch clear of the moored fishing boats.

With the arrival of a Company steamer, the airship had moved closer to the island. Sightings from either end of the boardway triangulated the distance at one mile, seven furlongs. Perhaps they believed themselves to be safe at that range. The airship remained directly above the steamer, from which vantage point they might hope to see any danger that approached from under the surface. How quickly they were adapting to this new kind of warfare.

Standing at the edge of the island, overlooking the jetty with its cluster of fishing boats, Elizabeth pondered a new and disturbing thought. There'd not been time for *Ajax* to carry news of their location so that an airship could be dispatched to reach them so soon. Yet here it was.

There could have been a chance encounter; the airship happening to fly over the steamer, signals flashed up to it. But Elizabeth's dislike of coincidence had made her search for another explanation. She had found one. It seemed fantastical at first, but the more she thought of it, the better sense it made. She was trying to decide whether to reveal her reasoning when a hand touched her shoulder.

"Are we to fight?" Julia asked, then kissed Elizabeth on the cheek.

"It might not come to that."

Steam hissed from the paddle launch. Siân was directing an engineer and a pilot to climb aboard. Gwynedd joined her on the jetty.

"We're still to choose our negotiator," she said. Then she pointed at Julia. "I think it should be you."

"No," said Elizabeth, suddenly alarmed.

"You're to find out what they want," Gwynedd said. "And you're to tell them to leave the Sargasso – ships and airships both. Tell them that for every one of our ships they sink, we'll bring down two of theirs."

"No!" said Elizabeth again. Whoever went to deliver such terms would be seen as a pirate. The punishment for piracy had always been hanging.

"Then have you changed your mind about the parley?" asked Gwynedd.

"Let me go instead."

"Your friend will go under a flag of truce. She'll be safe. Unless you know of some treachery?"

They both looked to Siân. "I agree with my cousin," she said. "Julia can represent the Nation. She'll be faithful – with you here on the island as a guarantee."

The launch steamed away. Coming out of the lee of the island, it turned into the direction of the swell. The hull dipped into the first big trough, then climbed back up the other side and dipped again.

"The crossing will be easy," Ekua said. "Don't worry for your friend."

Elizabeth put her eye to the helio telescope and watched the launch receding. Not once did Julia look back. She'd accepted the challenge without hesitation. Had another woman acted that way, Elizabeth might have thought her ignorant of the risk, or perhaps excessively brave. But with Julia there was something else – an unswerving sense of duty. This was the role she'd been allotted. She wouldn't run from it. She would do whatever it took. Lowering the telescope, Elizabeth felt her eyes prickling with the threat of tears.

Whatever their feelings about the past, Gwynedd and Siân were each dedicated to the Sargassan Nation. Both understood their grandmother's method. They would keep her and Julia and Tinker in different places, each a hostage for the others. And thus would obedience be guaranteed. If only she could find a time and place for the three of them to be together unwatched. They could steal a boat. They might be able to make it all the way back to the Company fleet. She would explain that Julia's actions on behalf of the pirates had been under duress. The Patent Office would pull strings to make sure there was no retribution. After all, Julia had seen things in Patagonia that they'd be desperate to know.

Ekua was packing away the code book in the helio box. The others had gone. Elizabeth felt the sudden lurch of one who realises a mistake.

"Where's Gwynedd?"

"She went with Siân. They were going back to the *Unicorn*."

"Keep watch on that airship," Elizabeth said. "The moment they signal, let me know!"

Then she ran. Gwynedd was in danger. And if Gwynedd died, everything would come to ruin.

CHAPTER 29

The story of an inherited feud had seemed to Elizabeth farfetched. But Siân was so fixated on the need for battle that she might in any case do harm to her cousin. Not for power itself; though power was the crux of it. She would be saving the Sargassan Nation, in her own mind at least. Just as she'd saved the *Iceland Queen* by shooting Captain Woodfall. Elizabeth remembered his blood pooling between the iron floor plates of the cargo hold. There'd been no trace of remorse afterwards. Neither had there been uncertainty.

How precious the gift of doubt that keeps a king from becoming a tyrant.

Women looked to Elizabeth as she sprinted the boardway; not in curiosity as they'd done when she first arrived, but with a kind of confused reverence. They backed out of the way for her. One of them bowed. On the deck of the *Unicorn*, the guards stood to attention.

She ducked through the hatch unchallenged. The door to the throne room was shut. Stopping next to it, she tried to get her ragged breath under control. She could hear no sound from within. It came to her that she should have detoured to pick up her pistol. But it was too late to go back. A few seconds might be the ruin of them all.

The first thing she saw inside was Gwynedd, kneeling on

the dais next to the furs where Mother Rebecca lay. Elizabeth scanned the room, searching for a sign of Siân. It seemed darker than before, though the same number of candles burned. The brazier had been freshly heaped with charcoal and the room felt stifling. She circled to the port side of the throne, peering into the space behind the dais.

Gwynedd didn't look at her, but said: "Siân's not here."

Senses alert, Elizabeth lowered herself to sit on the step of the dais. "I was worried for you."

"My cousin's inspecting the defences. She's protecting us all. There's no one better at what she does."

Gwynedd's voice was little more than a whisper. Elizabeth studied the lines of care and sorrow on the side of the woman's face. It wasn't just a queen who was dying. It was a grandmother.

"Julia will be on board the Company ship by now," Elizabeth said. "Asking them to leave the Sargasso. They might refuse. In which case Siân was right and she'll have her war. But more likely, they'll need to steam back to the mother ship to get instructions. Siân's afraid they'll use the negotiation to delay. But so can we. We could stretch it out for weeks. Months even. They don't want to die any more than we do. If we buy time, we can get a message to New York or London, asking that the Sargassan Nation be allowed to join the Gas-Lit Empire. Then no one will be able to attack us. Not ever. You'll be able to keep your own form of government. Women ruling over women."

"We'd be ordered to give up our weapons," said Gwynedd.

"You'd no longer need them."

"And the Patent Office – you want us to bow the knee?"

"I want us to have peace."

"Do you know these people? These *men* of the Patent Office?"

"I know one of them."

"And?"

"He's the best man that I know in all the world."

Gwynedd turned to look at her directly. Those perceptive eyes, searching. Elizabeth's brow was already prickling with sweat from the heat of the room. But now a heat grew within her as well. The strength of her words had been a revelation to both of them.

"The queen has gone," said Gwynedd, her voice flat.

The statement was so unexpected that at first Elizabeth could make no sense of it. The queen lay before them, wrapped in furs, the skin of her face sagging and loose. There was symmetry in the expression. It had been lopsided before. The lips and the skin around the mouth were tinged with blue. And there was stillness. No rise and fall of the chest. No whisper of moving air.

"When?"

Gwynedd stroked her grandmother's brow. "While we were at the dock."

Elizabeth put her fingers against one side of the queen's neck, feeling for a pulse she already knew wouldn't be there. The skin was still warm. The brazier and the furs would have stopped the body from cooling.

"Did Siân come here before going to inspect the defences?"

"No," said Gwynedd. "At least, I didn't see it. She ran on ahead."

"The guards would know," Elizabeth said.

"The guards had just changed when I arrived."

"Can we find out who was on duty before?"

"Why?"

"There's bruising around her mouth."

"That was her illness," said Gwynedd.

"Or a hand clamped down to stop the breath."

"Siân's a fighter. Not a murderer."

"Just be careful," said Elizabeth. "And... I'm sorry for

your loss."

The moment was broken by an urgent knocking. One of the guards opened the door, but wouldn't step inside. She was very young. Her eyes were wide with awe.

"What is it?" Gwynedd asked.

"The airship's falling," she said. "I thought you'd want to know. It's falling from the sky."

An airship large enough to traverse the Atlantic doesn't go down quickly. But it had started to tilt, so that the nose pointed up at a steep angle. Dark smoke poured from the engines as the motors fought. They would do no good. She could see what the pilots could not: the canopy near the tail fins had already started to fold.

Below, the funnels of the Company gunship were also pouring smoke. It was moving, even as she watched; turning away from them. It was too far distant to see the rotation of the paddlewheels, but they had to be churning the water white for it to be accelerating so fast. And somewhere on it was Julia.

"How?" she shouted as she ran.

The young guard was running next to her. "One of our guns."

Gwynedd was struggling to keep up. "Who fired it?" she called.

"I don't know."

"Who ordered it?" Elizabeth asked, already guessing the answer.

"It was Siân."

The gun was like nothing Elizabeth had seen before. The barrel, long as a mast and thin as a drainpipe, was suspended by chains from a scaffold, and anchored by more chains to the ground. There were wheels, gears and two sighting telescopes, one on each side of the gun. A crew of five were standing in a line, arms over each other's shoulders. They watched the airship as it began to slide backwards, their eyes wide with excitement and pleasure.

Then one of them saw Gwynedd and broke out of the line. "We did it!" she cried. "We ripped through the stern. Isn't it glorious!"

"Where's Siân?"

"She's readying the boats. There'll be salvage to take. And prisoners."

The profile of the Company ship had narrowed as it turned. Steaming directly away from the island it was almost obscured by its own funnel smoke.

"Can you disable it?" Elizabeth asked, fear making her voice shrill.

"The long gun is for airships," Gwynedd said. "It wouldn't scratch the paintwork of a steamer."

"Then send an underwater ship!"

"Too slow submerged. Too vulnerable on the surface. I'm sorry, Elizabeth. Your friend has gone."

They found Siân labouring with a line of porters, heaving cylinders of compressed gas into one of the underwater ships. She'd tied back her hair in a tight ponytail and sweat glistened on her bare arms.

Elizabeth was expecting Gwynedd to call her cousin out, to demand explanation. Instead she stood on the jetty, arms folded, waiting. Siân had seen them, but continued to work until the last of the cylinders was aboard. Then she offered her hand around the circle of women who had been working with her. Each slipped their own palm over hers. Their eyes were shining with the excitement of the moment. And with adoration for Siân. No doubt where their loyalty would lie when news broke of the queen's death.

Siân clambered back to the jetty and consented to follow

far enough away that their conversation not be overheard.

"What of the queen's wishes?" Gwynedd asked.

"She isn't in her wits."

There wasn't a grain of self-doubt in Siân's voice or demeanour. It was the most dangerous kind of delusion.

"Would you be our ruler?"

Siân shook her head. "Only in that one thing. From here we decide together."

"You've put us to war."

"It was always war. I've un-blinded you. That's all."

"They'll send all their gunships."

"You think they weren't already steaming at us? They're out there." She pointed to the northern horizon. "We can't yet defend Freedom Island. Not until we've more shipments from Patagonia. We could pick off two or three of their ships on the way. But most would get through. They'd set a fire to us. You saw how it was last time? And what will happen when they hit one of the gas hulks? It'll tear the island apart. We can't wait for that. Our only way is to attack.

"They're sending their gunships to us. That leaves the rest of their fleet naked. If we sail now, we can take the whole fleet – the mother ship too. The gunships will steam all the way down to the Sargasso before they understand what we've done. Then they'll race all the way back. Their tanks will be empty. They'll have no fuel left to fight us."

"You'd leave the island undefended?"

"The hulks of their fleet will build ten new islands!"

"And our people?"

"We bring everyone with us."

All through the exchange, Elizabeth had been standing back. The two women were so focussed on each other that it seemed she'd been forgotten. But now Siân turned to her.

"We must vote on it, like Mother Rebecca said. What do you say, Elizabeth?"

Two navies. Millions of tons of ships. Thousands of women and men. She had done her best to keep them apart, but they would destroy each other anyway. The only people she could think to save were Julia and Tinker. "Will you take the mother ship or sink it?" she asked.

"We'll take it!"

"And can I be first to board it?"

"You can."

"Then I agree."

Gwynedd regarded her, then nodded slowly. "You'll want to get to Julia before they hang her. I understand that. So I'll agree also. But if we're to let you loose, it's best we keep your boy on a different ship. As a guarantee."

Siân held out her hand. "We have an accord," she said.

Three things came to Elizabeth as she watched Gwynedd slip her palm over Siân's. First, that Gwynedd had accepted the subservient role in the hand ritual. Second, that it seemed now impossible that Julia, Tinker and herself could ever be brought together to escape. And third, that Siân had referred to the queen in the present tense.

CHAPTER 30

From above, it was impossible to see the size of the underwater ship, nor a name plate, nor any means of propulsion. The gangplank flexed under Elizabeth's weight as she edged out from the jetty. But when she stepped onto the back of the craft, it felt steady under her feet; more solid than the edge of the island.

From a distance she'd thought it constructed of wooden staves, like a huge barrel. But the surface she stepped onto was made of copper. The stave-lines were an imprint of the structure within, as if the sheet metal had been beaten and pressed hard over ridges and grooves.

Indeed, this is how it proved, for lowering herself through an opening on the beast's back, she saw the inside surface, which was a wooden construction, braced with iron. The ladder she descended was wooden also, as was the small chamber beneath. A short, heavily freckled woman stood waiting for her, a shy smile on her face.

"Welcome," she said.

Anxiety and distress had been gnawing at Elizabeth since the shooting down of the airship. She wanted to run or to fight. She wanted to do something, anything that might save Julia. But there would be no running enclosed within the limits of this claustrophobic vessel.

She looked around herself, taking in the unfamiliar architecture. It seemed more a drawing room in miniature than an underwater fighting machine. The ceiling was so low that she had to stoop in order to step away from the space below the hatch.

"What should I call it?" she asked.

"*Sea Wasp*," said the freckled woman. "Our newest submarine ship."

"It's... extraordinary."

The skin around the woman's eyes wrinkled as her smile broadened. "My name's Bonny, by the way. Is this your first time? Underwater, I mean. I'll show you what goes where. Come. Follow." All this came in a rush of pride and enthusiasm.

The purpose of the small compartment, Bonny said, was to keep water from flooding the rest of the ship when the hatch was opened in heavy weather. Going in for an attack, the boarding crew waited below until all was in place. Then they swarmed up the ladder and out. Water might crash down to fill the little room, but it would go no further. And being so low to the surface, the ship presented no profile for the enemy to see or to fire on. The doors from the little compartment were watertight. Pumps would make the chamber dry again once the hatch had been closed.

"Why isn't it made of metal?" Elizabeth asked as they edged forward through a narrow passageway. Everything was panelled.

"Condensation," said Bonny. "You breathe down here and iron walls get slick with water. It only takes a few minutes. But this kind of wood absorbs it. It keeps the air good to breathe. Whenever we're on the surface, we blow fresh air through the ship and the wood dries out again. Down here it's all about air, water and carbon dioxide. Get those right and you're good."

She stopped at the end of the passage. The shy expression had returned to her face. "We're really honoured to have you," she said. "On *Sea Wasp*, I mean. And in the Nation."

Before Elizabeth could respond, the woman had opened the door and ducked through.

The chamber in the foremost part of the ship seemed to be a control room. The walls and ceiling curved inwards, meeting at the very nose of the craft, at which point was a circle of glass about the size of a dinner plate.

Other crewmembers hurried about tasks that Elizabeth didn't understand. Banks of gauges to port and starboard connected to a maze of brass pipes running across the inside of the hull, disappearing into the floor and aft wall. She saw a mass of levers and valves, not unlike the controls of a steam engine, but more numerous. The helm wheel stood at the centre of the room. The strangest arrangement was a chair suspended below the crest of the roof. There sat another small woman. Elizabeth had never seen such dark skin. Her bare arms had a sheen like polished ebony in the daylight that shone down from what seemed a small window directly above her.

She spoke into a tube. "Is the hatch made watertight?"

Elizabeth couldn't hear the answer, but the woman seemed satisfied. Looking into the overhead window she called out: "Ahead one quarter."

There was a faint whining sound, and Elizabeth felt her balance shift as the craft started to move.

"Two points starboard."

The officer at the helm adjusted the wheel and they began to turn.

"Straighten out. Engine three-quarters power."

"Would you like to see?" asked Bonny, beckoning her forwards.

Elizabeth had to crouch to look out of the dinner plate

window in the nose of the submarine. All outside was water. Above, the colour was blue with flashes of gold from sunlight refracted through the waves. The colour darkened by degrees towards the black depths.

"What's that?" she asked, looking directly up to a spar that jutted from the front of the submarine like a bowsprit from a regular ship, but somewhat downward in angle. She had to get out of the way for Bonny to see what she'd indicated.

"On the other submarines they call it the saw. We call it the stinger. It's jagged at the top. Sharp and hard enough to cut through a gunship's keel if we aim it just right."

Elizabeth looked through the window again. "And how do you aim it?"

"From up there," she pointed to the glass in the roof above the captain. "It's a kind of lens. It lets you see forwards. When we're out from the island maybe you can have a look."

For all its elegance and the marvel of its construction, the submarine was a killing machine. *The science of destruction,* John Farthing had said. *Weapons are being developed out there beyond our power to stop them. We don't understand what they are. But they threaten to cut Europe from America.* How prophetic his words now seemed.

"You spoke with Mother Rebecca," Bonny said, breaking in on Elizabeth's dark thoughts. It seemed not a question, but the statement of a marvellous fact. "And now here we are – the day we've planned for. I've been twenty-three years in the Nation. All our struggles have been for this."

"For what?" Elizabeth asked.

Bonny seemed taken aback by the question. Then she laughed, as if realising she'd been teased. "The end of hiding. We'll be rulers of the ocean. The *Unicorn* will sail!"

The crew of the *Sea Wasp* were eighteen in number, not counting Elizabeth. They slept in cots rather than hammocks.

But the vessel seemed less thrown about by the waves than a regular ship.

"Two fathoms down, you won't feel them at all," Bonny said.

The ships of the fleet moved at different speeds. The *Iceland Queen* and the other paddle steamers were fastest. The submarines made fair progress on the surface, but were slow submerged. The speed of the sailing boats varied, depending on the strength and direction of the wind.

In anticipation of the Company gunboats taking a direct southerly course to Freedom Island, Siân had set them on a northwesterly path, giving enough space for the two fleets to pass without making sight of each other. That also allowed the sailing boats to take advantage of the prevailing winds, which circled around towards the coast of North America.

With no horizon to gaze on and no sky, one day blended into another. To Elizabeth, the slow passing of time felt unbearable. She lay awake in her bunk, trying to picture the faces of her friends and to remember their voices. When she thought of John Farthing, she cried. He could have used his position as a Patent Office agent to stop her from leaving. But he was the gentlest of men. She longed for his touch.

At last, the rhythm of activity in the submarine began to change. And there were new noises; the sound of a pumping engine working, water and air being forced through narrow pipes. The *Sea Wasp* began to wallow in the swell.

"We're pumping out the ballast!" Bonny said. "It's pushing us higher in the water. Hope you don't get sick."

An unfamiliar light shone through from the dinner plate window in the nose of the submarine as it emerged from the water. Desperate to see the outside world, Elizabeth got down on her knees next to it and looked up at a blue sky streaked with mackerel cloud. Then a wave came and the window was underwater. But only for a second before the blue was above them again, and the dark line of the stinger. The sight of it made her skin crawl. Somewhere ahead Julia was held captive by the Company. Even if she spoke freely, they'd believe she was hiding the truth. Elizabeth's breathing became shallow as she fought back a creeping nausea.

"Did you ever see America?" asked Bonny, who'd come up silently behind her.

America. The very name stirred Elizabeth to the core. The skies were wide there, people said. There was space enough to become lost from the world. It evoked a freedom beyond her reach. The land where John Farthing had been born; a man who might never again hold her close.

"Come on!" said Bonny, taking her hand. "You should look at it. Just to say you have."

There were safety lines to tie before they'd let her up the ladder to the hatchway in the *Sea Wasp*'s back. The harness went around her waist and over her shoulders. Bonny clipped the lines onto an iron loop in the wood-panelled wall before scampering up the ladder. Elizabeth followed more slowly, inhaling the fresh air. As she emerged, the wind whipped her hair against her face and she tasted the saltwater spray. Bonny had shifted a couple of paces down the beast's back. Her feet were planted apart and she'd gathered in the slack of her safety line so that it pulled tight. Doing the same, Elizabeth found she had enough stability to stand.

The light was dazzling after a day and a half in the submarine. Shielding her eyes, she looked around her. Some of the Sargassan fleet had already arrived. More ships were steaming in from the south. Haze clung to the western horizon. Squinting to get a better look, she made out a faint line between the clouds and the sea.

"That's the Carolinas," Bonny said. "Ten miles further and we'd be in their waters."

"I used to dream of going to America."

"We'll not be going there today! This is our furthest west. If the Company's out to attack us, their gunships will be passing way over there." She pointed east. "This is where we make our turn. The rest of the Company fleet is north and east of here. Without any protection!"

Elizabeth had never been greatly afflicted by seasickness. But inside the wallowing submarine her stomach felt unsettled. It was partly the tension of waiting for the battle to begin, and partly that she had no horizon at which to stare. She took to sitting on the floor of the control room next to the dinner-plate window, looking out between waves.

More of the fleet arrived through the afternoon. A few minutes after four bells, she glimpsed a steam launch ploughing its way between two of the larger ships. It appeared again from time to time after that. She began to look out for it, trying to guess the nature of its errand. An hour later it passed close enough to the *Sea Wasp*'s prow to cast a shadow over the dinner-plate window. Its wash splashed over the glass.

When Bonny came from the galley bringing mugs of broth, Elizabeth asked her about it.

"Siân's going from ship to ship with the battle orders."

"Will she come to *Sea Wasp*?" Elizabeth asked.

Bonny beamed with pride. "She's already here. She's talking with the captain."

Elizabeth found them in the captain's cabin, bent low over the small table, consulting the Atlantic chart.

"Did you enjoy the voyage," Siân said, on seeing her.

Elizabeth folded her arms. "What are our orders?"

"Good news," said the captain. "We're to be first into the attack."

"A submarine won't sink the mother ship," Elizabeth

said. "I've seen the hull from the inside. You won't cut that thickness of metal."

The captain seemed embarrassed. "I'll leave you to talk," she said, then stepped out of the cabin.

"We won't be attacking the mother ship," Siân said, when they were alone.

"But we must!"

"You said it yourself – we can't sink it. But they'll surrender once the rest of their fleet is lost."

"You promised I'd be first onto the mother ship."

"The decision's made. But you *shall* be first. After their other ships are ours."

"They'll kill Julia!"

"She won't be the only one to die."

"I voted with you for a chance to rescue her! You cheated me."

Siân shrugged. "You saw what you wanted to see."

Elizabeth's nausea was suddenly worse. The strength went from her legs and she sat heavily on the captain's bunk.

"We're throwing a net," Siân said. "They'll try to escape. They'll send out their fastest ships. But we'll have submarines positioned around their fleet. We'll pick them off until that leviathan is all they've got left. Then they'll surrender. You'll see."

A thought came to Elizabeth; the memory of the unspooling drum. "You're wrong," she said. "There's a cable being paid out into the water under the mother ship. I believe it sends messages all the way back to the Patent Office in England."

Siân angled her head, as if confronted with a curious new creature. "I don't believe you."

"I saw it. It's in the central hull."

"Then why didn't you tell me before?"

"I wasn't sure of what it meant. I'm still not. But it's the only answer that makes sense. It's how they got an airship to the island with such speed. When they see our fleet, they'll use it to call for help. Every gunship in Europe will sail for us. The mother ship won't give up. All they have to do is hold us off for a few days. But if you attack the mother ship first, you'll have the prize by the time their reinforcements come."

Siân didn't answer directly. She looked down at the cabin floor as if considering the question. Then she nodded. "You'd surely make up any story to save your friend. I don't blame you."

"It's the truth!"

"So you say."

Siân turned to go. Elizabeth jumped from the cot to block the doorway with her body.

"Step down!" Siân growled.

"You don't believe me. Nor do I believe you. You won't let me be first onto the mother ship."

"You push too hard!"

"Write it, then. Write it like one of your orders."

They were staring eye to eye, very close in the small cabin. It seemed Siân might barge her out of the way, but abruptly she turned, snatching paper and pen from the captain's desk. Elizabeth watched as she dipped the nib and wrote: *You shall be first to board the mother ship*. Then she signed it with an angry flourish, leaving no room below for any words to be added. There was a dangerous light in her eyes as she held out the paper.

"You push yourself to danger, Elizabeth. One day soon you'll find you've pushed too hard. But then it will be too late."

There was one more ship to arrive that night; one final piece in the puzzle of the Sargassan Nation. Bonny called Elizabeth up onto the back of the *Sea Wasp* to bear witness. Cloud in the western sky had been lit yellow by the setting sun, deepening to bronze near the horizon. The ocean had become strangely calm.

In the golden light she saw the approach of a squat steamer with a tall black funnel. Towed behind it, seeming more like a vision than reality, came the broad curve of a sailing ship, though without masts or rigging.

"What is it?" Elizabeth asked, not believing the evidence of her eyes.

"This is the day," said Bonny. "The *Unicorn* will sail!"

CHAPTER 31

The ships closed with one another as evening came, bringing themselves into a dense cluster of sail and steam and underwater craft. In the centre of it all was the *Unicorn*, as if the fleet was in some way trying to recreate Freedom Island. Elizabeth could see it clearly over the smaller craft that lay between. Once, she caught sight of Gwynedd walking on the deck, but only briefly. Fidelia was there also, and other faces that she recognised.

Bonny seemed transfixed by the sight. She wore a smile that would have looked well on the face of an ecstatic monk in prayer.

"How did they release it?" Elizabeth asked.

"It's the way we built the island," said Bonny, her voice full of pride. "There's a suture line right across the middle. It's just ropes that held the two halves together."

Elizabeth remembered the boards beneath the main deckway, and the ropes like giant stitching. The line ran next to the place where the *Unicorn* had been held. "The island was built for this?"

Bonny nodded. "So the *Unicorn* could sail again. Mother Rebecca knew it would be this way. She saw the future. And now she'll be ruler of all the ocean."

Elizabeth felt the weight of her own knowledge. She'd

told no one about the death. Nor, it seemed, had Gwynedd. If word escaped, the Sargassans would look for a new queen. Whatever reverence they'd shown for Elizabeth's privileged position, they'd be unlikely to accept her alongside Rebecca's grandchildren as part of a triumvirate. If Siân chose to announce herself as leader, the Nation would accept. They were at war, after all. Perhaps that was why Gwynedd had kept quiet, biding her time until the fighting was over and they needed someone capable of making peace.

"Do you see there?" Bonny asked, pointing to a box kite flying above the fleet. Its ropes were too distant to make out, so that it seemed magically suspended below the sky. "It's flying from the *Iceland Queen*."

"It's Ekua, then" said Elizabeth.

"You have good eyes!"

"I'm guessing."

Ekua had been put in charge of minding Tinker. The boy already knew his way around the *Iceland Queen*. Unless they chained him up, he'd find a way to have the run of the place. But he wouldn't be able to escape. If Elizabeth did anything that Siân thought treachery, he would pay the price. Any disobedience. Any attempt to escape or disrupt the attack.

"Ekua was the one who went up in the kite last time," Elizabeth said.

"She's brave, then," said Bonny. "And they say she's a good fighter."

"Do we have a kite?" Elizabeth asked.

"Every ship has one."

"Have you ever been up?"

Bonny shook her head. "I shouldn't like to."

"I want to try it," said Elizabeth, though in truth the idea was horrifying. But seeing the ships alongside each other, and the kite flying, an idea had started to form.

"You're too tall for it, Elizabeth."

"You mean too heavy?"

"Begging your pardon."

"Even on a day of strong wind?"

"Well, then, maybe not. But some get sick from it – the movement, that is. And it's dangerous. Would you really go up?"

"Yes," said Elizabeth, though her terror grew the more she thought that she would. An idea was forming in her mind.

The sailing boats started moving away three hours before dawn. Elizabeth couldn't make out how the operation was coordinated, except that there were shouts in the dark, women calling from one vessel to the next. Space was made between the larger ships, creating channels for them to slip through. Their sails were silhouettes against boat lamps and stars. There were a great number of them, packed heavy with supplies, for Freedom Island had been stripped of food, water and the most valuable materials. They would not take part in the first attacks, she'd been told. But they carried the great mass of the population, who would be ready to board the Company ships once they'd been secured.

When the eastern sky began to pale, the *Sea Wasp* and the other submarines set out to follow. The fast steamers would leave last, catching up with them fifty miles short of the Company fleet. From there they'd head full speed into the attack, approaching from the west so their smoke trails wouldn't show against the pale sky of the eastern dawn.

So much of warfare is waiting. As the day of the fight came closer, the crew of the *Sea Wasp* seemed to bottle up the excitement they had shown before. Bonny's eyes had been wide and her speech full of energy. Now she took to her bunk and slept. But Elizabeth had never possessed such a skill. When she did put her head down and close her eyes, all manner of dark possibilities came to her. She began to imagine the means by which her plan could fail. Chiefly she imagined the deaths of Tinker and Julia.

The only way she could stop the incessant tumbling of ideas was to focus on practical questions. Leaving the bunk, she sought out the boatswain, whose job it was to keep track of all stores and equipment. Elizabeth asked about the box kite, about the lengths of its ropes and the method of steering once it was airborne. The system was simple enough, the boatswain said, but dangerous. No one had died from falling. It was drowning that killed pilots. When a kite ditched in the ocean it was difficult to get free of the harness. The expanse of canvas that had held them aloft became a lid, pressing them down into the water. The ship's movement would pull the ropes, dragging the kite, sometimes taking it so far under the surface that there could be no return.

Elizabeth was woken by the swaying of the submarine. Her first thought was panic that she might have missed the moment of opportunity. She hurried along the narrow passage to the control room where everyone was alert and working. Air hissed through pipes. The dinnerplate window remained black, but the *Sea Wasp* was rising higher in the water.

Bonny was operating the portside controls.

"What time is it?" Elizabeth whispered to her.

"It was four bells twenty minutes ago."

Elizabeth headed back to the small chamber under the hatchway. The captain and another woman stood, braced against the wood-panelled walls, safety lines attached.

"Today's the day," the captain said, dousing the lamp, plunging them into blackness.

Elizabeth could hear her climbing the ladder. The hatch opened with a sharp clinking noise, revealing a circle of stars overhead. The air was suddenly fresh and cold. Elizabeth shivered as she watched the silhouettes of the captain and the other woman clambering out. She couldn't find another safety rope, but followed them anyway, emerging into a keen wind, which cut through her thin clothes.

She could hear the engines of several steamers around them but could see only ghostly shapes in the dark. Gathering so many ships without lamps would be a dangerous manoeuvre. To the east, the sky showed a faint premonition of dawn.

Elizabeth scanned the shapes, searching for a familiar profile. The *Unicorn* and some of the other steamers were yet to arrive, the captain said. There was no sign of the sailing ships. Elizabeth was shivering by the time she found what she was looking for. But at last it seemed that luck was breaking her way. The *Iceland Queen* lay in the deeper dark, perhaps four hundred yards off, but coming closer at a slow crawl.

Elizabeth's teeth were chattering. "Put up the kite," she said.

"Why?"

"The air's clear. The Company fleet will be spread. You'll need to see the outliers before they see you."

The captain held up her hand, as if gauging the quality of the wind.

"And let me fly it," Elizabeth added.

She couldn't see the captain's expression in the dark. But at last there was a nod.

"You're a brave one, Elizabeth."

If preparing a kite had been difficult on the flat deck of the *Iceland Queen*, it was triply so on the curved back of the *Sea Wasp*. But there were lock points that she hadn't noticed before; metal rings onto which ropes were attached to hold the wings as the spars were slotted in place. They couldn't have held it down otherwise. The wind had strengthened and was gusting, licking white spray from the peaks of the waves.

Elizabeth went below, where a quilted coat had been laid out for her.

"It'll still be cold," Bonny said. "But with this on you won't freeze to death."

So she put it on, and while no one was looking, slipped her pistol and a small document case inside the folds, so that when the belt was tightened the gun was held secure against her stomach. Bonny wrapped a scarf around her neck. The last items were a pair of goggles and a leather skull cap, which buckled under her chin.

"Now you look the part," she said.

Climbing the ladder, Elizabeth discovered she lacked the freedom of movement she'd had before. It was with trepidation she stepped out again. The captain guided her to the harness and strapped her in.

"It's going to be a rough ride," she said. "When we release, it'll jolt like you've been kicked. So tuck your chin and keep your arms close."

Two others were there, themselves roped for safety. It could have made for a tangle, but all kept to their positions.

"Are you ready?"

"Ready," said Elizabeth.

The captain stepped in and kissed her on the cheek. Then other women. One placed her kiss full on Elizabeth's lips. There was no time to react.

"Sit and take in the slack!"

She did.

"Pull the port rope to swing towards the port side. Starboard to swing starboard. Pull both and you'll go lower. When you do that we'll haul you in. Pull neither and you go higher. So long as you're going up, we'll let out more rope. Understand? Once you've signalled we'll pull you in anyway."

It was the third time they'd explained it.

"I'm ready."

"One, two, three. Release."

The kite lifted, flipping over above her, righting itself and coming to its limit with a dull thud. The ropes went taut, but she was still attached to the submarine by a safety line. She held up her hand, making a circle with her thumb and first finger, as Ekua had done before her flight.

Then it happened. The safety line was gone. The air was pushed out of her lungs as she catapulted backwards and skywards. She was up thirty foot. Then it was fifty foot. But she was tilting viciously to the side and dropping again. The ocean came veering towards her. In her panic, she'd been pulling hard on one of the steering ropes. She let go and the kite lurched upwards. The ropes angled down steeply towards the submarine, which was only just visible as a darker oval in the dark ocean. She could no longer see the figures on its back, but she could feel the movement as they paid out the rope. Higher and higher she climbed.

The *Iceland Queen* stood off the *Sea Wasp*'s port bow. It was hard to judge the distance. Three ship lengths at least, she thought.

Taking off had been a sudden thing, but now the climb felt slow. As the jolt of panic receded, she became aware of a pain in her cheek bones. It took a moment to realise that the scarf had dropped below her chin, allowing the wind to cut at her skin. Forcing her hands to release the steering ropes, she hitched it up again, this time trapping it in place under the goggles.

The downward slant of the ropes had been kept low as more was paid out. But with all the line used up, the angle became steeper. She climbed to the very highest point of the flight.

The sky on the eastern rim of the horizon showed pale; a perfect line, uninterrupted. But to the northeast there was something that seemed too well defined to be cloud. Looking directly at it didn't help in the low light, but when she shifted her gaze a fraction to the side, it resolved into a column of smoke. And then there were more columns. She counted five of them, scattered across ten degrees of the horizon.

It was time to shift her position, to point the direction for those below. Taking hold of the steering ropes, she eased down with her left hand. The kite tilted. She felt the shift of momentum as it began to slide around and down. She continued to swing through the air until the rope was lined up with the most prominent of the distant smoke columns. Then she eased off, finding the balance so that she could hover, maintaining the aim. Below her, the *Sea Wasp* began to turn until its nose pointed directly towards the distant smoke.

The job was done.

But now came the most difficult part. Impossible maybe. So long as they kept her and Tinker on separate ships, she wouldn't be able to disobey Siân. That meant Julia would be lost. And this was the only way for her to get across to the *Iceland Queen*. Reaching into her boot, she slipped out a knife. Her cold hands felt clumsy.

They'd started to haul her in already. She could feel the uneven pull on the kite ropes from below. She looked across to the *Iceland Queen*, trying to judge the distance against the length of the rope. In steering the kite, she'd already brought herself closer to it.

She knew what she had to do next. But the thought of it made her feel sick. She pictured Tinker's face. He was down there, somewhere, on the *Iceland Queen*. He could even be watching her. Her fingers were so cold that she couldn't tell how tightly she was gripping the knife.

It was time. She pulled down hard with her left hand. The kite tilted and began to swing further around, dropping sharply as it went. The air roared past her ears. The *Iceland Queen* was coming at her. But she'd yet to lose enough altitude. She was going to overshoot the ship.

There were figures on the deck, waving at her. The fall was going to hurt. She began to saw at one of the harness ropes over her head. It sliced through cleaner than she'd expected. She dropped, to hang upside down by the remaining rope. The knife tumbled from her numbed grip. She was spinning. The deck of the *Iceland Queen* swept past below. Then there was ocean, coming up at her fast.

She hit the surface hard and went under, inhaling at the first shock of cold. Seawater flooded into her nose. She blew it out and opened her eyes. Everything was black. Kicking out for the surface, she found her leg snared. Frantic now, she kicked again and again. On the third kick it came free. She put in two strong strokes, expecting to hit the canvas of the kite, but finding only black water. The remaining harness rope was pulling her in the other direction.

Fighting against the urge to breathe, her throat and chest began to spasm. The harness rope tightened. Suddenly she was being dragged back with great force. It came to her that the ship's movement was taking the kite all the way down, and her with it. In the back of her mind she remembered being buckled into the harness. If she could undo that buckle, she might slip out of it. But her fingers were too cold to even uncurl. She couldn't grip the harness strap.

The backward pull became faster. She wondered if, in the end, she would open her mouth and let the water flood in, or if she'd be able to hold what remained of her breath until unconsciousness took her. She hoped she could do that. There was something more peaceful about the blacking out of unconsciousness. She didn't want the violence of water entering her lungs to be the last thing she felt. The rope was not dragging her smoothly. It heaved, pull after pull.

There was a rushing sound; bubbles moving past her ears. She was suddenly heavy again, upside down and heavy, being dragged clear of the water. Pull after pull. She slammed against the side of the *Iceland Queen*. Hands grasped her legs first, then her arms. The deck hit her.

Women were shouting. Someone pulled the goggles from her eyes and the wet scarf from across her mouth and nose. A hand slapped her face. She dragged in a lungful of air, then coughed it out again.

"She's alive!"

"Warm her up!"

She was no longer attached to the ropes. She was sitting, retching. Then she was standing, supported by a woman on each side, her arms over their shoulders. They were hauling her in through the hatch.

She opened her eyes and saw Ekua, yellow lamplight illuminating her face. "You're crazy!" the woman said. "Why did you do that?"

"I've a message..." Elizabeth gasped, stopping to retch again. "Steam northwest. Full speed."

"But... I don't understand. Our orders..."

Pulling her arm free, Elizabeth reached inside the sodden coat and found the document case.

Ekua opened it. The paper was still dry.

You shall be first to board the mother ship.

"Do it," Elizabeth said. "Do it now."

PART FIVE

CHAPTER 32

Nothing impresses the brave more than acts of bravery. Ekua seemed particularly affected by what Elizabeth had done. There had been a moment of confusion after reading the message. It was the strange manner of its arrival that seemed to unsettle her, rather than the plan itself. But it was a message in Siân's own hand, and brought by the new confidant of Mother Rebecca. It could not be doubted.

Elizabeth felt the vibrations of the engine as the paddlewheels started to turn. Only when the ship began to accelerate away did she let go. Her body, which had been numb and still, now began to shiver. And so violently that she was incapable of controlling her own movements. They stripped the freezing clothes from her body and wrapped her in blankets. Then they began to massage her hands and feet. When the first needles of feeling returned, she wished she might be numb forever. The women's fingers felt like hot irons probing at her flesh. She struggled to pull away but they held tighter and worked with renewed vigour as if encouraged by her pain.

One of them said, "She's going to live."

Elizabeth couldn't respond, couldn't even tell who it was had spoken. There'd been relief in the woman's voice. Dry stockings were being rolled up her legs.

"You've gone red," said another voice.

She opened her eyes. Tinker was squatting next to the bunk.

"Your hands," he said.

She looked and saw it was true. Her skin felt tight, as if it was being shrunk over her body.

"How long have I been here?" she asked, surprised to realise the shivering had stopped.

Tinker shrugged.

"Maybe an hour," said the woman who'd been dressing her feet.

"You saved me," she said.

In struggling to reach the surface of the water she'd been swimming away from it. Her instinct for survival had almost killed her. The kite ropes had come to rest across the deck of the ship. The crew had been trying to haul her back and she'd been fighting it all the way, believing down was up and up was down. If only she'd given up her fight, the rescue might have come quicker. And now, here she was, struggling to return to the Gas-Lit Empire, working against a different kind of force; the feeling that she might after all belong with the Sargassans.

She sat up, swinging her legs from the cot, though the woman tried to stop her. Experimentally she placed her feet on the floor, testing for balance.

"What happened to the kite?" she asked.

"The water pulled it down. We had to cut the harness line."

"What if I'd got tangled in it?"

"You didn't, thank God. You must have been swimming clear."

Elizabeth stood, Tinker gripping her hand.

"I need to see Ekua," she said.

Elizabeth's order had been followed. They'd turned northeast and steamed away from the gathering fleet at full speed. The crews of nearby ships might have heard the engine noise and the churning of the *Iceland Queen*'s paddles. But in the near dark, without means of communication, none of them could have guessed what was happening.

At first the change would have seemed like a manoeuvre, an attempt to fish Elizabeth out of the freezing water. From the other ships, it wouldn't have been possible to see where she'd landed. Then the *Iceland Queen* would have straightened out from its turn and begun to pull away. Even then, they wouldn't have known what was really happening. Siân would have been the first to understand it, once news came to her. But far too late.

If association with the queen had won her respect, crossing between ships on the kite had further elevated her station. Several of the crew reached out to touch the blanket she was wrapped in as she shuffled down the passageway. Strength started to return to her legs as she climbed out and then up to the quarterdeck.

Ekua stood, braced against the swaying of the ship. "Thank God," she said, on seeing her. And then: "Look where you've brought us."

Elizabeth did look. First ahead, where Ekua was pointing. The Company fleet was laid out before them in the grey light of dawn, the individual ships clearly visible. Among them she recognised her old ship, the *Pembroke* and the *Vale of Evesham*. And further away, but dwarfing all the others, the unmistakable outline of the mother ship itself. There were no gunships that she could see. She turned and looked out to where the Sargassan fleet was following, perhaps five miles behind.

"Why did Siân choose for us to go so far ahead?" Ekua asked.

"Because we can dock with the mother ship. None of them can. We can board it. We're to hold out until our fleet arrives.

Then we're to let down ropes for the rest of the fighters to follow us."

"But why will they let us approach?"

"We'll signal. We'll say we're the old crew and we've taken back control of the *Iceland Queen*. They'll let us come in to dock. From there, I can show you a way up to the deck." The speech sounded less convincing than she'd imagined when she made it up.

"We don't have enough fighters," said Ekua.

"We'll not be taking the mother ship ourselves. We just have to hold out until the fleet arrives. An hour maybe. And there are places to hide. Aren't there Tinker?"

The boy nodded vigorously.

"But why would they believe our signal?"

"Maybe they won't. At first. But then they'll see a crew of men standing on deck, waving to them."

Ekua's puzzled frown softened. Her eyes widened as understanding came. Then she began to grin. "Then we'll be needing to take the prisoner's clothes," she said.

"We will," Elizabeth agreed. "Though they're not going to like it."

The men of the *Iceland Queen* had suffered all manner of indignities during their captivity. But since the shooting dead of the cook and Captain Woodfall, they'd submitted themselves. Trudging the treadmill or scrubbing barnacles from boat hulls until their knuckles bled. They'd offered no physical rebellion, knowing the consequences of disobedience.

"They refused," Ekua said, as they approached the door of the cargo hold.

Elizabeth put her face to the bars and saw a wall of faces staring back at her. Captain Locklight was closest to the door, his cheeks more hollowed than she remembered.

"You must give your clothes," she said.

"They push too far!" Locklight's breath condensed in the cold air.

"You must do it nonetheless."

"They humiliate us!"

"And they'll kill you also. If you give them reason."

Locklight stepped forwards, pressing his face to the bars: "And you're in league with such tyranny?"

Coming close she whispered, "Soon all will change." Then in a louder voice: "You're to lose the clothes one way or the other. I'd sooner you be stripped alive than dead."

If they'd disliked the order, what followed turned their indignation to anger. For, having given up their trousers and jackets, they were presented with dresses and petticoats by way of exchange. The Sargassans had meant it as an act of humanity, for the temperature was dropping further still. But the men howled in rage and beat their tin cups against the walls of their prison.

Elizabeth set up the helio herself. Four miles from the first of the outlying ships she flashed the message, then handed the controls to one of the other women to repeat it every five minutes. For almost half an hour there was no response. Then an answering message came back from the mother ship, demanding information. Who was in charge? How had they taken back control? And then, what were the number, class, location and speeds of the ships that followed? The smoke columns of the pursuing steamers must have been visible to them for some time.

"Ignore it," Elizabeth said. "Keep repeating."

Retaken Iceland Queen. Fleeing pursuit. Urgent request docking. Captain, signalman dead.

She took a grim satisfaction in the final phrase; an implicit explanation for the clumsiness of the helio work and the lack of proper response.

Most of the crew had come up to see the spectacle of the Company fleet, which the *Iceland Queen* was already drawing in among. A crowded deck was the right image, Elizabeth thought, remembering the way the crew of the *Pembroke* had come up to see the spectacle of the fleet when returning from a whaling trip.

She had instructed that no one be permitted up top unless properly disguised. None of them had questioned the fact that she'd given the order. Her trousers, shirt and jacket were already dry, having been draped over the boiler. For those like her, who'd been wearing male attire, it was simply a matter of binding the breasts and pinning up long hair, or tying it back in the manner of male sailors. Any others wanting to show themselves were obliged to select from a heap of the prisoners' clothes, all of which stank. Tinker's outfit was too big for him, so he folded back the sleeves and trouser legs, tying twine to keep everything in place. He seemed delighted to be rid of the yellow smock.

The storm that had passed to the south of Freedom Island must have curled around the American coast because the western horizon remained dark and a new swell had started to roll in.

Ekua ordered a middle passage between the *Pembroke* and the *Vale of Evesham*, so that as they passed, the ships were a third of a mile distant on either side. Close enough to make out the figures of men waving to them across the water.

"Wave back," Ekua called.

The crew obeyed, too stiffly, Elizabeth thought. It might do from such a distance. But as they docked with the mother ship they'd be observed from far closer range.

The numbers and speeds of the approaching Sargassan ships must already have been calculated and mapped. But not the nature of them. The Company fleet was also on the move; the outliers drawing closer. Two ships had made thick smoke as they steamed south at full speed, no doubt to tell the gunships of the attack. They would have to evade the Sargassan submarines if they were to get through.

Elizabeth stepped close to Ekua and spoke with a lowered voice. "Have you chosen which crew are to board?"

"I've twenty good fighters, armed and ready."

"And me," Elizabeth said.

"You're not a warrior. How many men have you killed?"

"You'll need Tinker. He knows the mother ship better than the commodore himself. And I won't let the boy go without me."

Approaching the mother ship, it was impossible to be untouched by awe. It seemed wrong that human hands could have created a thing of such size, let alone that it could float in the middle of the ocean. The crew fell silent as they watched.

There were Africans among the *Iceland Queen*'s original crew. But all the senior officers were white Europeans and Americans. Therefore Ekua, unable to disguise her skin colour, took up a position on the main deck, next to the starboard wheel housing, to appear as an ordinary sailor. Elizabeth stood next to her.

The water around the mother ship's paddlewheels frothed as it began to turn.

"They're bringing it around for us," Elizabeth whispered.

"They'll just bring us aboard?"

"They'll let us dock. After that, we'll see."

Ekua nodded to a knot of crew waiting at the base of the mast. They hammered the release pins free and then paid out rope through the winch so that it began to telescope down into itself. They stopped only when the crow's nest was low enough to clear the girders and cables that supported the mother ship's deck.

The waves had grown during the approach. They broke

against the iron wall of the mother ship, sending up white plumes. As the *Iceland Queen* turned towards its final approach, the swell began to hit it broadside. Elizabeth held on to the gunwale with one hand and gripped Tinker's arm with the other, though he tried to wrench himself free.

Figures looked over from the mother ship's deck. But it was impossible to see who stood beyond the very edge. It might be a crowd of unarmed sailors, or a full company of marines, muskets loaded and bayonets fixed.

Iron walls towered over the *Iceland Queen*. Coming into alignment, a larger wave hit, tilting them starboard. They swayed back in time to catch the full impact of the next wave. Water rushed in through the scuppers, then sluiced across the deck as the ship pitched the other way. The next waves were smaller, but it still seemed impossible that the ship would make it in through the narrow gap without hitting one side or other.

The paddlewheels were still making maximum revolutions. The ship was too close for such speed. A mist of spray blew over the deck from one of the waves that had smashed itself on the side of the mother ship. Ekua put two fingers in her mouth and whistled. The paddlewheels stopped turning. The prow of the *Iceland Queen* slipped fast between the iron walls.

Ekua whistled again and the wheels powered in reverse. Water churned. Elizabeth fell to the deck, which was suddenly becoming level. But only half the ship was in shelter. Another wave rolled in, catching the stern. A judder ran through the deck and the sickening screech of metal grinding against metal as the *Iceland Queen*'s starboard side pushed up hard against the mother ship. It rebounded as they slipped fully into the calm water. There was a second, smaller impact as the port bow hit. Then the paddlewheels stopped.

Men looked down from doorways in the metal walls high above them, holding mooring ropes at the ready. Elizabeth tensed, willing them to throw down the ropes. Seconds passed. Nothing happened. Somewhere in the shadows above, there were access hatches in the underside of the deck itself.

Elizabeth ducked close to Ekua. "You must raise the mast again."

"It'll give us away."

"They know already!"

Ekua made the signal. The crew began to haul the ropes. The masthead telescoped upwards. Elizabeth slung a coil of rope over her shoulder and ran to the base of the mast.

"Follow me," she said, then began to climb the ladder. Tinker came close behind her. Below him, Ekua and her warriors were following from the deck.

Halfway up, there was the sound of another impact and the ladder began to vibrate. The crow's nest had come up hard against one of the girders that supported the deck. The shifting of the ship swung it away and then back with another clang.

Elizabeth climbed faster. She was above the doorways from which the mooring ropes could have been thrown. Men were looking up at her. She pushed through the hatch into the crow's nest and began lashing the top of the mast to the crossing point of two girders. Turn after turn the rope went around; a quick and ugly binding, but it would hold. Tinker was next to her. And then Ekua, who climbed straight across and began to scale one of the inclined girders, which angled up towards the mother ship's middle hull. The others were following now, in quick succession, heading towards the very underside of the mother ship's deck and one of the access hatchways.

A gunshot rang out from a doorway below. Then another. Elizabeth grabbed Tinker and pulled him below the rim of the crow's nest. Answering shots were coming from the climbing women. They had the numbers for now, but it wouldn't take long for the men to call reinforcements. Two of the women were straining against the hatchway in the deck above them. It didn't open. The men must have locked it from above. If they didn't find a way out, they'd be picked off.

Elizabeth tried to judge the distance to the nearest doorway in the side of the ship. They had ropes. They might be able to get across. But Tinker squirmed free of her grip and started to climb up along a girder angling towards the portside hull. A musket ball hit the mast just above Elizabeth's head, ricocheting away with a sickening whine.

She stood, fired her pistol back down towards the men and climbed out after the boy. He was quick, scampering ahead, up into the shadows.

The gunfire petered out as the men below reloaded. The Sargassan fighters would be finding cover. No one had fallen yet. But the shots had come from ordinary sailors. The marines would take better aim.

"Tinker!"

He was sitting astride a thicker girder, his neck forced low by the underside of the deck itself.

"Come here!" she hissed, beckoning him back down.

He resolutely shook his head, jabbing a finger towards the hull, which lay immediately in front of him. Swearing under her breath, she launched herself up, out of the safety of the crow's nest, to clamber up an angled beam. When she was almost in grabbing range of his ankle, she saw what he'd been pointing at. The girder met the hull imperfectly, leaving a dark hole above, big enough to crawl through. Tinker grinned, then lay flat and squirmed forwards. As his feet disappeared inside, she turned and waved to the Sargassans who were clustered on the other side of the gap between the hulls. One of them gave an acknowledging wave. Elizabeth beckoned and pointed to the hole. But the firing had started up again from below. Turning from the battle, she clambered onto the topmost girder and lay flat, then wormed her way forwards as Tinker had done, and slipped into the black.

CHAPTER 33

Inside, all was dark. She could smell both rust and oil, but see neither. The sound of musket fire had grown suddenly distant. Tinker's hand found hers and he began to lead, though how he could see the way, she had no idea. The floor was metal, studded with lines of rivets, on which she at first stumbled. Feeling to the left she found a metal wall and to the right, the inside of the hull itself. Remembering the kind of space he'd led her through before, she put up her hand in front of her head, and just in time, because it came up hard against a low girder. Tinker might walk underneath it without ducking, but she had to stoop.

"Wait," she whispered, pulling back on his hand. "Where are we going?"

"Where do you want?"

Cocking her unloaded pistol, she said: "Look away," then pulled the trigger. The flint snapped back to the steel, sending out a spark, which lit the space for a fraction of a second. The after-image faded quickly.

"I need to see."

She heard the rub of cloth as he delved into his pocket, then he was placing a smooth cylinder in her hand. It was a candle.

"Tinker, you're a genius!"

He made a sound of pleasure in his throat that could almost have been a purr.

Crouching, she tipped a pinch from her powder horn onto the floor and laid a wad of linen half over it. Then she cocked the pistol and held the flint near the powder.

"Cover your eyes."

She saw the flash through her closed eyelids. But when she looked, the burning linen was hardly visible. Keeping her hands slow and steady, she warmed the candle above the fragile bud of bluish flame. The wick began to smoke, then a tiny yellow flame grew from it. Tinker's teeth gleamed in a broad grin. All candles should be so brilliant.

Next she cut an inch from the base of the candle, carved out a hole for the wick and set it alight also. This stub she placed on the metal floor.

Tinker snatched the stub and snuffed the flame between his finger and thumb. "Can't leave it!" he said.

"I won't abandon the others."

"But they'll follow!"

"That's what I hope! If they don't know where to go, they'll be stuck. They'll be killed. This way they can follow us through the ship." She eased the candle stub from his grip and lit it once more.

Tinker was frowning. He had a right to disapprove. In one compartment of her mind, she knew it. A battle would rage. To save one fighter would be to kill another. Death was the only certainty. As Tinker led her along the narrow fissure next to the hull, she glanced back for one last look at the candle stub. It was a way-marker between walls of riveted iron. But more than that, it was a plea for absolution. It gave a feeble light.

Turning her back on it, she saw that the boy had stopped by a small door on the innerside wall. He was struggling to turn the hatch wheel. Hurrying to catch up, she gripped the metal, adding her strength to his. It turned with an angry screech, then stopped. She tensed as the echo of the noise died. If they'd been seen climbing into the hole in the side of the ship, the marines would be out searching for them.

"Is this the only way?" she whispered.

He nodded.

They gripped the wheel again. This time the screech was followed by a groan of smoother movement and a dull clunk as the hatchway opened. They heaved and it swung inwards. Tinker slipped through the gap, his candle revealing what seemed to be a store room. Shelves lined the walls. She saw brushes of all kinds, tins of grease, paint and turpentine, piles of rags and stacks of folded overalls.

He was heading for a door on the opposite wall, but she grabbed his shoulder and pulled him back. "Where are we going?"

"To my place," he said.

She remembered his secret cupboard, strewn with blankets and tins of jam. "Why?"

"So they won't find us."

"But I need to find Julia."

He frowned again at this.

"Where will they be keeping her?"

"Locked up," he said.

"But where?"

He shrugged.

"Do they have a brig? A prison of some kind?"

A nod. "For men who get drunk."

But Julia wasn't a drunk. She was a prisoner who knew things the commodore wanted to learn. And maybe things he didn't want the rest of the crew to know. What's more, she was a hostage that he might hope to trade in exchange for Fidelia, his lost granddaughter.

"There's a place where the officers have their rooms. When

I was here before, they kept Captain Woodfall locked up there in a cabin on his own, with marines stationed outside the door. Do you know where that was?"

Tinker wouldn't meet her eyes, but stared at the floor between them. "Don't know," he said.

"Look at me and say that again."

He would not.

"Tinker. Listen to me! We can't hide here forever."

"We can."

"Whoever wins the battle, they're going to think us traitors. You and me. And if the Company wins, they'll hang Julia for sure. I've got to find her. We've no choice but to leave the mother ship. Remember the steam launch? That's our way out of here. We'll load it with spare oil, as much as we can. Then we'll steam away. It's small but it's fast. We'll slip through the two fleets. The three of us. Together. And we'll head for the coast. I wouldn't ever leave you in danger, Tinker. Nor can I leave Julia. So if you know where they might be keeping her, you must tell me now."

His nod was a tiny movement, little more than a vibration of the head. She bent and kissed him on the cheek. He turned away briskly, as if there was something important that needed his attention. But she caught him back and pulled him close. This time his arms went around her and he didn't try to hide the tears. She didn't even mind that he wiped his runny nose against her tunic before pulling away.

When she'd been taken to see Captain Woodfall, there'd been two guards stationed outside the door, armed with musket and cutlass, and perhaps more weapons that she hadn't seen. They'd had good sight of her as she approached and had been ready for any attack. With an enemy fleet approaching, they'd likely be gingered up and expecting action.

Tinker held the candle at a safe distance while she reloaded.

Once the pan was covered and the powder horn away, she looked around the room. Aside from her pistol, they each had a small knife; no match for the weapons of the marine guards. Her gaze settled on the pile of blue-grey overalls.

Having searched, the smallest garment turned out to be a one-piece boiler suit. It was still too long for her, so she rolled the legs up inside and gave the cloth belt an extra turn around her waist. An officer's hat didn't fit the disguise. She selected a russet-coloured cloth and tied it as a bandana of the kind the men sometimes wore when shovelling out ash from the fireboxes. The final touch was a dark smear across her cheek from one of the tins of grease. It would serve as the false birthmark had once done.

"You must carry tins," she told him.

So saying, she took a long-handled tar brush for herself and balanced it over her left shoulder in a lazy manner, so that her right hand could grip the pistol in one of the boiler suit's deep outer pockets.

"Ready?" she asked.

Snuffing out the candle, Tinker opened the door an inch, letting in a bar of lamplight. Having peered through the crack, he swung it fully inwards and led the way out into a passageway that looked to Elizabeth like any other on the ship. Most people would have found their way by the letters and numbers stencilled in yellow paint on doors and walls. But Tinker was illiterate. More than that, he despised the written word. Yet he didn't hesitate, turning left and then leading her around a right-hand corner to a stairwell. Three flights up they headed off along another passage, then through another storeroom and out via a different door into sudden, intense daylight.

The shadow of the structure they'd just left lay across the full expanse of the deck in front of them and up the massive buildings above the central hull. A flock of gulls had landed in the middle of the deck. There wasn't a human to be seen. She could hear the crash of waves against the hull and the distant beat of engines reverberating up from below. They were standing in the lee of buildings, but she could hear the ghostly drone of the wind gusting over corners and cables.

Her nerves had been set on edge by a lick of something sulphurous and violent in the air. Her conscious mind only caught up as she followed Tinker out onto the deck. It was gunpowder smoke. She was opening her mouth to call a warning when the air shook. Cannons had fired somewhere close. Four shots in rapid succession. She dropped to a crouch. The gulls had taken off and were wheeling above the deck. Three more detonations followed. Somewhere close. There was no whine of incoming shot. The guns were on the mother ship, firing away from it. Big guns. Billows of smoke were rolling across the deck where the birds had just been.

She followed Tinker out across the open deck, heading for the buildings of the central hull. After ten paces the smoke reached them, thick and choking. Pressing her sleeve over her mouth and nose, she stumbled forwards, half blind but blessing the unexpected cover the smoke had given them. As suddenly as they'd entered it, they emerged from the lee of the buildings and it was whipped away, leaving them exposed. But only for ten paces, for they'd reached the other side. Slipping into a passageway between two of the buildings, they flattened themselves against a wall, panting for breath.

There'd been no answering cannon fire after the outgoing shots. But the mother ship's guns sounded huge. They'd have a far longer range. They were also mounted on a stable platform high above the waves. Their range advantage might be a mile or more.

"Did you know they had cannon?" she asked.

Tinker shook his head.

The main ships of the Sargassan fleet might be cut to pieces before they came close enough to fight back. She peered around the corner. The shots had come from deck level at the stern of the ship. The cannons were hidden from them by the chaotic mass of the superstructure.

Tinker took her hand and pulled. She closed her eyes and thought of Julia, remembering their evening walk by the river Thames, that sapphire dress, the lights on the water. The memory seemed to belong to another life, perhaps another person. She felt the tug at her hand again. This time she followed.

As they were running to cross the wide expanse between the middle and starboard hulls, the cannons fired again. This time it was closer. The impact of the detonation made her stumble. Tinker didn't miss a step. Ballasted by paint tins dangling from his hands, he shot in through a doorway. She followed half a second behind and found herself in a passage that she recognised. Fidelia had led her on the same route on the way to see Captain Woodfall. Back then, she'd imagined the commodore's steward to be a man.

On they went, Tinker leading without hesitation. The stairways and turns were a confusion. But somehow she knew when they were on the last approach. Tapping the boy on the shoulder to attract his attention, she held a finger to her lips. He nodded. She signed for him to put down the tins, then took her knife and eased the lids free so they were merely resting in place. Then she cupped her hands over his ear and whispered. There was no grin this time, but on hearing her instructions, he nodded vigorously.

They both stood. She took in a breath and shouted: "Come back here!"

He nodded once more, then ran towards the turn in the passageway ahead.

"Come back!"

She set off after him, tar brush raised like a club, feet sliding as she rounded the corner. Three guards stood, barring the passage ahead. Why did it have to be three? Tinker slowed as if afraid they might grab for him. Two of the men gripped muskets. One brought the stock around, as if preparing to club the boy. The third man put a hand to his sword belt, ready to draw his sabre.

Tinker turned to face her. She rushed him, swiping with the brush. Though it swung short of his face, he sprawled back, pretending to be hit, and let go of the cans. They landed with a dull thud. Red and green paint spilled out across the floor of the passage towards the guards' immaculately polished boots. They jumped away.

"I'm so sorry," Elizabeth said, her voice only half disguised. "But it's all over your trousers."

She dropped the brush and vaulted over Tinker, who sprawled between the two oozing rivers of paint. Each of the soldiers had looked down to see if it was his own uniform that had been ruined. But Elizabeth was among them. She pressed the pistol into the face of the one with the sabre, for it was that she feared most in the confined space of the passage. And with the tip of her dagger she pricked the side of one of the others. The slowness of their realisation might have been comical if the means of death hadn't been so close. The third man had only just seen the threat when Tinker came for his musket. Indecision and surprise must have made his grip slack, for the boy easily wrenched the gun free.

She made them kneel, facing the wall, hands clasped behind heads. Keys hung from the belt of one. She cut them free with her knife and handed them to Tinker. While she watched the prisoners, he worked his way through the loop, trying each in the door until the lock clicked.

"Done it!" he said.

The door opened. Out came two women: the engineer and

pilot who'd been in the steam launch with Julia. They took up the muskets and sabre and levelled them at the guards. Elizabeth looked inside, searching for her friend. But the cabin was empty.

CHAPTER 34

They moved the guards into the small cabin one at a time, the blade of the sabre held close to remind them of the consequences should they resist. Wrists and ankles were bound with ribbons of ripped bed sheet. The knots wouldn't hold them for long.

"Where's Julia?" Elizabeth had asked as soon as she saw the empty cabin.

"They took her," said one of the women; the pilot.

"Where?"

"I don't know."

"It was the commodore's man who took her," said the other woman; the engineer.

The commodore could be anywhere on the leviathan. But with an attack coming, he'd surely choose his glass-sided control room, at the very apex of the mother ship, with direct communication to the engines and a view over the ocean spread below.

Julia had been the Sargassans' negotiator. He might be keeping her close as a hostage or as a source of information. Perhaps he'd taken her because he imagined she'd be easier to break, not being a warrior herself. If so, he'd surely misjudged. Julia had a stubborn streak wider than the Atlantic. The thought of torture came to Elizabeth's mind. She sat abruptly on the cot in the small cabin, as the others finished trussing the last of the guards in a bundle on the floor.

"That's the best we can do," said the engineer, prodding one of the guards with the tip of the sword. "But they'll worm free in five minutes. Shouldn't we just kill them?"

Hatred glared from the eyes of the men. And animal terror.

"No," said Elizabeth, quickly. "Five minutes will be enough."

She locked the door behind them, then gave the key another half turn and pressed her weight against it, bending the shaft until it was flat against the lock. Then she bent it back the other way, snapping it clean.

"The *Unicorn* will sail," said the pilot.

"Is this the day?" asked the engineer.

Tinker led them back up through the stairwells and corridors. They met no one. It seemed the men were all at their stations. Approaching the main deck, she felt again the shockwaves of outgoing cannon fire.

"What does the queen order?" asked the pilot, as they looked out over the main deck. "Why are they firing?"

"Our fleet approaches," said Elizabeth.

"Then do we attack their guns?"

"I have to rescue Julia. But you go, if you want."

"We might kill the gun crew," said the engineer.

But neither of them moved. And when Elizabeth and Tinker sprinted out across the expanse of open deck, they followed. There was no gun smoke to hide them this time. Behind them, a man shouted the alarm. He kept shouting and other voices took up the cry. Tinker careened through a hatchway into one of the buildings over the central hull. Elizabeth followed and the two Sargassans were quickly after her.

The alarm had been sounded on the starboard hull, but they were running faster than the news of them could spread. The very size of the ship had become their protection. Tinker led them along a lamplit passageway to a storeroom stacked with barrels and smelling of turpentine.

Daylight streamed through the next door. Ahead lay the open deck between the central and portside hulls. A clatter of musket fire made them jump back into cover. Then the cannons thundered again. Everything in the storeroom rattled. With smoke billowing past the door, Elizabeth risked another look. The superstructure of the portside hull loomed ahead like a tower glimpsed through fog. A glint of reflected sunlight came from the glass windows of the control room at the very top.

The rattle and flash of musket fire was coming from a skirmish near the base of the tower. As the smoke cleared, she made out two groups of fighters: a unit of Company marines huddled below a flight of steps and, one level above, a group of Sargassan warriors, taking cover behind a lifeboat. They'd made it up from under the deck but were pinned down. She recognised Ekua among them.

The battle was blocking the stairway. Most of the shots were being fired by the marines, who stood to shoot before ducking back into cover. Return fire from the women was sporadic. They'd be saving their ammunition, Elizabeth thought. She felt queasy. There seemed fewer Sargassans than the twenty who'd left the *Iceland Queen*.

"Should we go to them?" the pilot hissed.

"Go if you will," said Elizabeth. And then: "Is there another way to the top of the tower?"

Tinker crouched beside her in the doorway. He squeezed her hand once, then bolted out onto the open deck. She could only follow. Ten paces out, shots began firing from behind her and above. The deck splintered near her foot. A woman cried out. Elizabeth didn't turn to see if it was the pilot or the engineer who'd fallen. The shots fell silent. They were reloading. Tinker had reached the other side. Instead of heading for the stairs, he sprinted aft. He was making for a ladder fixed to the deck housing; a faint line in the confusion of buildings. She hadn't noticed it before. He was already climbing as she reached the wall. The engineer overtook her, following Tinker. The iron rungs clanged under Elizabeth's boots as she climbed after them to the deck above.

A shot fired and a bullet whined off the wall next to the ladder. More shots. More impacts. A fresh pit appeared in the metal next to her head. She felt a sting on her right cheek. The whine of tinnitus in her ear was like a lathe cutting brass.

She was almost at the top. A hand reached down and pulled her up. She rolled underneath the railings of a narrow walkway and lay flat next to the others. Shots thudded into the wall above them. When the bullets had been spent, she jumped up. Tinker scampered aft again. They rounded the corner, coming straight into the full force of the wind.

"You're bleeding," Tinker shouted.

She touched her cheek, finding the skin numb. Her finger caught on something sharp. Then her tongue probing inside felt it too.

The engineer brushed her hand away and tugged at whatever it was. Pain jabbed like a hot needle. The engineer held up a jagged splinter of metal for her to see. Elizabeth spat blood and saliva.

The aft deck lay below them. The barrels of two great cannons projected from the wall below. They fired. The blast wave slapped Elizabeth in the face. Only then did she look up. Three ships of the Sargassan fleet were steaming full tilt towards them. One of the cannonballs sent up a plume of water. The other hit home. A cloud of dust and debris cleared to reveal a hole in the deck of one of the ships. It heeled over in a tight turn. One of the paddlewheels had been shattered by the impact. The other ships were changing course, trying to throw the gunner's aim.

Tinker had already set off up the next ladder. The engineer was pale with the shock of what she'd seen. If the approaching ships could get close enough underneath the bow, the cannons could have no sight of them. Elizabeth set off up towards the next level.

The submarines were the real strength of the Sargassan fleet. They'd be following on behind, unable to keep pace with the fatal dash that Elizabeth had started. And the Company gunships: how far behind would they be trailing? The musket battle between Ekua and the marines was taking place on the opposite side of the tower. Climbing another level would put them above it. There would be two or three levels more beyond that before they reached the control room.

Clambering under the railings, she followed Tinker up the next ladder. Glancing down, she saw the gun crews rolling out cannonballs and barrels of powder for the reload. The engineer had stayed below. She was taking aim with her musket. She fired. A man in the gun crew fell, clutching a shoulder. The barrel he'd been pushing rolled free.

The other men scattered. But now marines were taking the place of the gun crews. Elizabeth swore silently and climbed faster. The marines began to shoot. They must have been aiming for the engineer but some of the shots strayed towards Elizabeth and Tinker. They'd have little accuracy at that range, but bullets were flying perilously close. One hit the metalwork just to her right. The same side as her lacerated cheek. The whistle in her ear blasted ten times louder.

She could see the top now. Clambering under a railing, she lay flat and looked up at the final climb. The shooters below had fallen out of step with each other. There were no more volleys and no time was safe. A shot broke the outward-sloping window of the control room above. Elizabeth covered her face, but the shards of falling glass were whipped away in the wind.

Tinker was taking cover next to her. Reaching to grab his shoulder, she fixed his eyes with hers. "Do you love me?"

He opened his mouth and closed it again, his brow wrinkled with confusion.

"If you love me, you must do as I say."

He nodded.

"You must stay here. Out of the line of fire. Unless someone comes. Do you understand?"

Another nod. He was crying.

"I'm going to bring Julia. Then we're going to figure out a way to get off this ship. I need you to stay where I can find you. Else it's all for nothing. Because I'll never leave without you."

He was a child who never saw danger and never sought affection. But now he held out his arms to her, himself lying on his side. She pulled him close, her cheek still bleeding. It was her mortality that he'd glimpsed, not his own. She knew it. And she knew too that her heart might shatter if she let herself understand what that would do to him. So she wrenched herself free of his grip, took a series of deep breaths, then launched herself up the final ladder.

The firing started again as soon as she began to climb. She tensed, as if that might stop a bullet. Hauling hand over hand, rung after rung she climbed. A clatter of impacts hit the wall. None of them close. Scrambling under the final railing she rolled onto her back.

She was lying on the highest deck, directly below the outward-sloping window of the control room. They'd see nothing of her from inside. Musket fire rattled somewhere. A man's voice cried out. The battle felt eerily distant.

She could hear closer voices now, coming from within. Men were talking. She could hear urgency in the rise and fall of it, but couldn't make out the words. The cannons boomed far below and the window glass rattled.

Turning onto her stomach, she began to crawl along the narrow gantry. A shadow lay over the metal ahead. A man was standing just around the corner from her. A guard, she thought. With her pistol in one hand and a knife in the other, she wormed forwards. The wind gusted, drowning out the noise of her movement. But he must have seen something, perhaps a reflection in the glass, because he started around the corner. She launched herself at him before he'd properly seen her. Still crouching, she pressed the knife into his groin and held the pistol so he'd see it.

He started to turn towards the glass. She pressed the tip of the knife harder. He flinched to a stop, but raised his hands. They would know, in the control room, as soon as they looked. She stood and began backing the guard up, around the corner. Abruptly the wind was gone. The angled glass showed only reflections. They were level with the door.

"Open it!" she growled.

As it swung inwards, she shifted the knife, stepping behind him. One more jab and they were in. The whole thing had been done in a couple of breaths and the conversation inside hadn't stopped. But as they stumbled through, everyone was turning.

Hatred stared at her from the commodore's desiccated face, and from the faces of two officers, each holding a telescope. Between them stood Julia, her clothes ragged, her face swollen. One of her eyes had closed up and her lip was bloodied. Somewhere in the back of Elizabeth's mind the shock was absolute. But she kept on moving, forcing the guard down to his knees.

She raised her pistol, pointing it at the commodore's chest.

"Come, she said, meaning Julia.

For a moment, her friend didn't move. Then recognition seemed to break.

"Elizabeth? What have they done to you?"

Elizabeth remembered her own face. Her skin and hair would be caked in drying blood and saliva. Her eyes flicked down, taking in the state of her tunic.

"I'm not hurt," she said, though she was. "Take their weapons. All of them."

Julia did, though clumsily, for her hands were also swollen. A broken finger perhaps. Elizabeth shoved the guard around to join the commodore and his officers in the corner of the room.

"Who did this to you?" she asked.

Julia shook her head. But her eyes had given her thoughts away. They'd flicked across to the officer on the left. He was a man of short stature but broad in the shoulder. Elizabeth sheathed her knife and took one of the pistols from the pile of weapons on the chart table. She pointed it at the man's belly and cocked the hammer.

"No!" said Julia.

Elizabeth's finger moved from the trigger guard to the trigger itself. But Julia held out her good hand. "It's my revenge to take," she said.

Elizabeth breathed again. She passed the gun to her friend, who uncocked it and placed it back on the chart table.

"I choose to let it pass," she said.

The commodore turned to look out over the ocean.

The steamer that had taken a direct hit was already upended at the stern. It wouldn't take long to go down. The other two were close in to the mother ship. Only their masts were visible over the edge of the deck. They'd be safe from the cannons. With the *Iceland Queen* lashed in place, they wouldn't be able to come fully into the protection of the docking bay. But they'd still be able to get fighters across, scrambling from deck to deck as the ships were battered by the waves. With the mother ship as a prize, they could wreck all their steamers and still call it a victory.

"You've lit a fire that'll burn us all," said the commodore, his voice crackling with age.

"Get rid of their weapons," Elizabeth said.

Julia took the swords first, carrying them gingerly to the gantry outside, and tipped them over the edge.

"Do your pirate friends know you're working for the Patent Office?" the commodore asked.

"I work for myself."

"Then does the Patent Office know you work for the pirates?"

Julia returned for the pistols.

"Keep two of them for yourself," Elizabeth said.

"You'll hang for this," said the commodore. Then he looked beyond her and his expression changed.

"Put down the guns!" The voice came from the doorway.

Elizabeth turned, but slowly, to see Siân standing there, pistol and sword in hand. Other Sargassans stood behind her. One held Tinker by the collar. There was a knife to his neck. The boy looked more sorrowful than she'd ever seen him.

"The guns," Siân said again.

This time Elizabeth complied. Julia followed suit.

"Traitor!" Sian spat the word at her as she stepped forwards. "You'll pay for the lives you've thrown away."

"I've helped you take the mother ship."

"It's not taken!"

"But it will be."

"They've hundreds of marines!"

The muzzle of Siân's pistol pressed hard into Elizabeth's forehead.

"Your grandmother died," Elizabeth said, managing to keep her voice level.

Siân's expression didn't change, but her finger lifted from the trigger.

Another Sargassan fighter looked in from the doorway.

"We've got to move!" she shouted.

But Siân's eyes were fixed on Elizabeth. "Mother Rebecca lives."

"No. She died before we left Freedom Island. The *Unicorn* carries her body."

"You're a liar and a traitor!"

There was no deception in Siân's face. Only shock and denial. She hadn't known about the death.

"We've got to go!" said the fighter at the door, more urgent this time.

Elizabeth said: "I'm not the traitor. I've saved the fleet. If we'd kept at a distance, those cannons would have picked us off ship by ship. You'd have had to come in close anyway."

"You didn't know about the cannons."

"That's true. All I did was save my friend. And look what they did to her."

"You're still a traitor."

"If you want to find a traitor, go to the *Unicorn*. Gwynedd killed your grandmother."

"No!"

"She smothered her."

"No."

"There are bruise marks around the queen's mouth and nose. You'll see it for yourself. Gwynedd wants us both dead so she can be queen. If you kill me, you'll be doing what she wants."

"Siân! We've got to leave here! Now!"

Siân shifted her pistol to the side and fired. One of the men fell; the squat officer who Julia had spared. Stepping around Elizabeth, Siân ran the others through with her sword.

"You," she said, pointing the bloody sword tip at the commodore. "You'll come with me."

It seemed he might follow. But looking down to the bodies of his men, he said: "What carnage have you wrought?"

"Out!" said Siân.

A calm had come to the commodore's face. He had made his decision. "No woman shall rule me," he said. When Siân cut his throat, his expression seemed almost triumphant.

CHAPTER 35

Fresh Sargassan fighters were rushing up from below. They positioned a strange-looking gun behind a pile of crates overlooking the open deck, slotting its fat barrel onto a tripod. Then it began to fire with a rhythm like a rapidly turning engine. A line of bullet impacts slammed into the wall on the other side of the deck. Three marines fell with the opening burst. Faced with such devilry, others pulled back, taking cover behind doorways. It was one of the guns from Patagonia, Elizabeth had no doubt.

The marines had only muskets and sabres to answer with, but their numbers were great. They had bullets and powder to spare and still held more than half the sprawling landscape of the mother ship. The battle could go either way. All would depend on how quickly the Sargassans could bring reinforcements and supplies from their ships below.

With the marines pinned down, Siân ordered Elizabeth, Tinker and Julia out of cover, pushing them on towards the edge of the deck. When stray bullets whined overhead, she didn't flinch.

Three Sargassans were waiting for them at the steam launch station. The engine was already up to pressure. Siân gestured with her pistols. "Get in!"

Elizabeth was glad to obey, hunkering down with the

others in the middle of the boat, keeping her head low. Next came two of the Sargassan warriors. Siân was the last to climb aboard. She gave the order and the crane lifted them. For a second they hung still, then the boom swung them around. There was a sudden lightness as they dropped towards the ocean. Then the winch brakes screeched and they slowed. The impact came as a heavy slap.

Immediately they were in trouble. The paddlewheels had yet to start turning and the first wave caught them on the beam, pushing them back towards the iron wall of the mother ship's hull. There was a grinding of metal against metal as they started to turn into the swell. They were halfway into the turn when the second wave caught them, pushing them back again. Another impact. A few more like that and the boat would be smashed to pieces. But the paddlewheels were at full speed now, and the turn came sharper so that by the time the third wave hit them, they were straight into it and accelerating.

One of the fighters had grabbed a bucket and was bailing out. Over the waves they went, tipping skywards then pitching over into the next trough. The wind whipped spray from the crests, soaking them through and sending more water into the boat. It gathered at the stern as they climbed, then sloshed towards the prow as they tipped over and descended into the next trough. Two Sargassans were bailing now, and the water wasn't getting any deeper. Elizabeth clung on to the bench behind her with one hand and to Tinker's shoulder with the other. He was pressed into her side and shivering hard. Beyond him sat Julia, staring straight ahead.

Elizabeth caught sight of a steamer through the spray, black smoke pouring from its funnel. Then, as they came around, she saw the swelling bow of the *Unicorn* towed just behind it. A hulk she was, but a totem also. Figures stood on the deck, but with sunlight streaming in from behind it was impossible to see their faces.

Siân drove the launch directly towards the *Unicorn*. Closer and closer until the wooden ship loomed over them and it seemed they'd crash. Then she slammed one of the paddlewheels into reverse and the launch lurched around. The stern hit the *Unicorn* and bounced off, but ropes were clattering down already and they soon had it fast.

Two fighters were left to keep the launch from sinking. The rest of them clambered up the ropes. Elizabeth landed heavily on the deck, finding herself with Julia and Tinker in the centre of a ring of swords.

"Hold those two," Siân said. "Elizabeth comes with me."

The guards outside the throne room stood to attention on seeing Elizabeth. Then confusion clouded their faces, for Siân followed behind, a pistol levelled at Elizabeth's back.

"Where is Mother Rebecca?" Siân demanded.

The confusion of the guards deepened. "She's inside."

A single lamp at the top of the dais was the only illumination in the throne room. Its light fell over the body of the queen, laid out on the floor, wrapped in furs. As the door closed behind them, Elizabeth realised that the brazier had been allowed to go out. The air was cold. Siân jabbed her in the back with a pistol and she stumbled forwards.

"How old was Mother Rebecca?" Elizabeth asked.

"She's no mother to you. And she still lives!"

"Saying it doesn't make it true."

Siân began to circle, all the while keeping the gun aimed. She approached her grandmother's body and knelt. In some part of her mind, she must have known already, or she would have killed Elizabeth when they were still on the mother ship. Elizabeth watched as Siân touched her grandmother's forehead. That's when the pistol lowered.

Elizabeth waited. Only when Siân had placed the gun on

the floor did she approach to sit on the lowest step.

"I'm sorry for your loss," she said.

"You knew this all the time?"

"Yes."

"Why didn't you say?"

"I thought it was you who'd killed her."

Elizabeth tensed as footsteps approached from behind the throne. Siân took up the pistol once more. It was Elizabeth's own gun. There were two more pistols hanging from Siân's belt. And a long knife. Elizabeth and Siân both stood as Gwynedd stepped into the light.

"Why didn't you tell me?" asked Siân.

"I couldn't," Gwynedd said.

"She was my grandmother!"

"And mine. But she was also the queen. You were leading us to war. The *Unicorn* had to sail with her aboard. We've worked all these years for that one destiny. If I'd told you, could you have hidden it?"

Siân didn't answer.

"The people needed to see the queen leading them into battle. After the fight – after we'd won – then I'd have told you. When this is over, we'll announce her passing. We'll dedicate the victory to her."

"You'd lie to the people?"

"It's what they need to hear. She just died a couple of days too soon."

The weight of the revelation seemed to press down on Siân's shoulders.

"How goes the battle?"

Siân pointed at Elizabeth. "This woman betrayed us."

"I've given you a way to win," Elizabeth said.

"If she's a traitor, she'll be punished," said Gwynedd. "But the fight's not over. I need you back out there, leading our warriors. They look to you, my cousin. If anyone can find the victory, it's you."

Siân nodded slowly. She seemed about to leave.

"How did Mother Rebecca die?" Elizabeth asked.

"You'll be drowned," Gwynedd said. "The punishment of traitors. That's all you need to know."

Elizabeth knelt by the body.

"She was old," said Siân.

"There's a mark on her face," Elizabeth said. "A bruise. She's been smothered. Who did it, do you think?"

"Don't try to distract us," Gwynedd snapped. "Your friends will pay the price for your treason."

But Siân had picked up the lamp and raised it over her grandmother's face. She bent low, changing the angle of the light until she'd banished the shadows over the mouth. Her head tilted. She put the lamp down again and stood.

"What did you see?" Elizabeth asked.

"A bruise."

"Then she must have done it," Gwynedd said. Her finger pointed to Elizabeth.

Elizabeth was focussed on Siân. "Ask the guards. They'll know who came and went. And when. I was never alone with the queen. Nor were you."

"Lying won't save you," said Gwynedd.

For a moment, Siân seemed caught between two thoughts, unable to decide. Then she nodded. "You're right. It must have been Elizabeth."

Gwynedd took her cousin's hand. They embraced.

"I should never have doubted you," Siân said, still in her cousin's arms. "The guards will confirm everything you've said."

Then she stumbled. Gwynedd caught the pistol before it fell. Siân sat abruptly on the top step of the dais, an expression of surprise on her face. A tiny mark below her breast began to blossom. She looked down at it. Blood was flowing freely, running onto the floor. She managed to look up one more time before slumping onto her side and falling next to the dead queen.

Gwynedd levelled the pistol at Elizabeth. There was a bloody knife in her other hand. "Shout and I'll tell the guards it was you."

"Why?"

"Because the queen left that instruction – for the three of us to rule. She wasn't in her wits. She told me you were growing to love us. I told her you'd keep trying to escape but she wouldn't listen. And what then? A council of two? It would have been impossible."

"All this so you'll be queen of the Sargassans?"

"I've been ruling for years. I let Mother Rebecca have her little plays. But it was me doing the work – while Siân was out fighting. I always had my way until you washed up. Her new toy."

"I didn't do anything."

"Oh, but you did. Something about you went deep with her. And now you're going to have to die."

"Do you want me to play the murderer?"

Gwynedd nodded. "The Nation needs someone to blame."

"If they find me dead in here, there'll be whispering that it was you who did it. They'll think you killed your half-sister to avenge your mother's death."

There was a telltale hesitation before Gwynedd spoke. "I did it for the Nation," she said.

It was a half-truth, Elizabeth thought. But also half a lie.

"Let me run with Julia and Tinker. Let us get on the steam launch and try to escape. That way no one will doubt your word. And when you sink us, you'll be the hero."

"What if you get away?"

"I'll still be the murderer. And you'll be the queen. And your cousin will be dead."

"You won't escape."

"Then I'll be dead, which is what you want. And this way I get a chance to live – however slim."

Elizabeth held her breath.

At last, Gwynedd said: "You can have three minutes. Then I call the guards and say you knocked me out." Holding Elizabeth's pistol at an angle, she lifted the cover and tipped the black powder from the pan.

Elizabeth accepted it. "I said your grandmother was the queen of all crows. I was wrong. It was you all the time."

"Go!"

Elizabeth slipped through the door without the guards seeing into the room. "Follow me," she said, mustering all the authority she could find. They seemed uncertain, so she added: "This is our great day."

They did follow, then. Back to the deck, where Julia and Tinker waited under guard.

"We have new orders from Mother Rebecca," Elizabeth shouted. "The queen approves our attack on their mother ship. She'll go herself to claim the prize!"

There was confusion among the fighters on deck. They looked to the hatchway.

"Gwynedd and Siân are helping her to get ready. And where is Fidelia? She's to be our pilot."

At first no one moved. Then Fidelia pushed through the crowd on deck. There was a moment of eye contact between them. It was enough. She nodded.

"We need oil," she said. "A spare barrel. And quick now!"

Then everyone was moving. Fidelia let herself down to the launch, making the move look easy, stepping in on a wave crest. She took the helm from the fighter who'd been holding it. Julia and Tinker clambered down next, following a spare barrel of oil. But when Elizabeth stepped towards the gunwale, one of the guards put an arm out to bar her way.

"Yes?"

"You were brought here as a prisoner," the guard said. It was little more than a whisper.

"You doubt the queen's orders?"

"I... that is... I can't accept your word alone."

"Caution does you credit," said Elizabeth. "Go to the throne room. See for yourself."

The guard frowned; she lowered her arm and took a step towards the hatch. But then she seemed to change her mind. Elizabeth was already scrambling over the side. A wave came, bringing the launch up towards her. She let go of the rope and jumped. Her landing was heavy. She fell to one side, her shoulder thudding into the engine housing.

"Go!" she said.

Fidelia dropped the machine into gear. The paddlewheels thrashed the water. The two fighters in the boat half stood. But Elizabeth had her pistol aimed at them.

"Jump!" she said. The ropes were still lying across the launch. They could have gone, but neither did. Fidelia was turning them fast. The ropes slipped into the water. They were pulling away, climbing a swell, then tipping into the next trough.

"Get down!" Elizabeth shouted, pulling Tinker to the floor. Julia dropped. And just in time, for a gun fired behind them. Then a whole volley of shots. Fidelia flinched but remained standing. One of the Sargassans dropped, tipping over the side and into the water. Climbing the next wave, they were fully exposed once more, but the fighters on the ship had yet to reload. Down into the trough they fell. An expression of horror racked the face of the remaining guard.

"What are you doing?" she shouted over the wind and the engine noise.

"We're leaving."

"You can't!"

Elizabeth raised her pistol. "Drop your weapons."

"But there's nowhere to go!"

Behind them, the steamer that towed the *Unicorn* had begun to turn.

As the launch climbed another wave, gunfire rattled again. Bullets whined off the engine and the hull.

The Sargassan fighter unbuckled her sword belt and placed her weapons in the bottom of the boat. Then she sat and took off her boots.

"What are you doing?"

"I can't leave!" she cried. "There is nowhere else."

Then she stood and flung herself into the water.

For a moment she was visible, striking out towards the pursuing ship. Then a wave came between them and she disappeared. When they climbed the next crest, the woman was a speck. And with the wave after that, she was gone.

CHAPTER 36

From her place on the floor of the steam launch, Elizabeth could still hear gunfire. But none of the bullets came close. They were moving faster than the pursuing steamer could hope to match, with the wide bulk of the *Unicorn* towed behind it.

"How far can we go?" she shouted.

Fidelia was no longer standing. Her hand was still on the tiller, but she'd slumped forwards.

Her left shoulder was hanging limp.

"I took a hit," she said, when Elizabeth reached her.

There was a splash of blood on the tunic.

"I need to see the wound."

Fidelia shook her head. "It grazed me. That's all. I'm going to bring us around so we come in close under *Mother*'s starboard hull. The Sargassans won't see us."

"I'm sorry," said Elizabeth. "There's nothing left for you on the mother ship."

Understanding and sorrow grew in Fidelia's face.

"It was quick," Elizabeth said. "Your grandfather was in command until the last moment."

"Who'll win the battle?"

"I don't know."

"Who do you want to win?"

"I'd be hanged, no matter who it was," Elizabeth said. "And Julia and Tinker too if we went back." It wasn't an answer.

Through all the battles and deadly choices, she'd not known which outcome would be best for herself, let alone for the world. If the Company was defeated, communication would be cut between Europe and the Americas. John Farthing had called that the biggest unknown in the Map of Unknown Things. He'd said it would be followed by a perpetual war. Her mind accepted the logic of his words. But in her heart, she still couldn't hope for the Sargassans to lose.

She'd treated Farthing badly. But it was fate that had driven them apart. No good paths had been laid before them. A pang of longing and regret clenched around her chest.

"Hold the tiller," Fidelia said. "Keep us into the waves."

When she bent forwards, Elizabeth saw where the bullet had entered. Not a scratch, but a neat wound. The collar bone looked to be broken. She'd bled enough to soak a patch of her tunic. It had clotted already, on the outside at least. But a bullet can take any course once it enters the body.

"How do you feel?" Elizabeth asked.

"Like hell."

"Can we reach Nantucket?"

Fidelia shook her head.

"Not even with a spare barrel of oil?"

"The wind's pushing us north. You might make Nova Scotia."

"We," Elizabeth said. "*We* will make Nova Scotia."

Elizabeth steered after that. At first Fidelia sat, instructing her. But as the day wore on and the waves grew smaller, a great fatigue seemed to be pulling the woman down. She'd been pale before, but now her lips turned bluish. Her fingernails too. They set a place for her in the bottom of the boat, as comfortable as they could make it. She'd stopped speaking by then, and wouldn't stay awake. Her breathing slackened. Then it stopped altogether.

Many had lost their lives that day, but none of the deaths had so shaken Elizabeth. At first she couldn't accept it. But as the hours passed, Fidelia's body grew cold. At last they wrapped her in a canvas sheet. Elizabeth found a chain with which to weigh down the body. But Julia stopped her.

"We'll bury her in America," she said.

When the sea grew calm enough, they gave the tiller to the boy. He was quiet, but seemed happy to have been trusted with the responsibility.

"How long has it been since you slept?" Julia asked, when they were seated together.

"I don't even know what day it is," Elizabeth said.

"It's a Tuesday."

How like Julia to know such a thing, in the wilderness of the ocean. Elizabeth leaned her head on her friend's shoulder. "Thank you," she said.

"For what? You're the one who rescued me. Twice. I'll never be able to repay it."

"You're not rescued yet," Elizabeth said, quiet enough so Tinker wouldn't hear.

"You came for me. That's what counts – whatever happens in the end."

"Just look at us," said Elizabeth, loud now, for the benefit of the boy. "Blood and bruises. A fine sight we'll be, strolling in New York."

"I trust we'll have a chance to wash before that, and to change!"

"Maybe we'll sail straight into New York harbour – it does have a harbour, I assume?"

"I'm sure it has many."

For months, Elizabeth had been striving for such a moment; the three of them together, with no one else to control their destiny. But however fast she might try to run, fate would always run faster. The oil would run out before they made sight of land, she felt sure of it. They would drift to a quiet death. She remembered the glimpse she'd had of the Carolinas; a smudge on the horizon. At least she'd seen the New World. She thought again of John Farthing. It would have been good to hold him one more time.

Then she slept.

The first time she woke it was night. She was lying in the bottom of the boat, covered in a tarpaulin with Tinker's warm body next to her. He was snoring peacefully. She raised her head and saw Julia's silhouette at the stern, one hand on the tiller. They were riding the gentlest swell she'd felt in days.

The second time she woke, she found herself squinting into brilliant white. Her stomach hurt from hunger. She sat up. They were riding through fog. Gulls called overhead. One swooped close to the boat.

"She's awake!" Tinker shouted. And then: "Look!"

Pulling herself shakily onto one of the benches, she saw that the fog was clearing. A rocky coastline loomed ahead. There were hills behind, covered in thick pine forest. Then the sun broke through and suddenly there was colour; green and turquoise and dazzling blue. An inlet lay ahead, between two cliffs, a river flowing out over a crescent beach. In that moment, it seemed more beautiful than any place Elizabeth could remember.

"We're on the last few pints of oil," Julia called as she steered them in.

There was a grinding of shingle under the keel and they came to rest. Tinker took the rope and jumped over the side, splashing into shallow water. Julia cut the engine and followed him.

Elizabeth was the last to step down and clamber onto the beach. The three of them held hands and embraced. Elizabeth found herself crying, though she was not sad. She knelt and put her forehead to the ground.

"Welcome to America," Julia said.

THE TRUE AND REMARKABLE
HISTORY OF THE FRIGATE HMS *UNICORN*

At the outbreak of the British Revolutionary War in January 1816, the Royal Navy began its blockade of northern ports, hoping thereby to starve out the Republican uprising. Historians have argued about the effectiveness of the action. It is generally agreed that there was a reduction in the number of successful American and French supply runs. But winter storms made it impossible to police the entire length of the coastline with its many inlets and islands. Towards the end of the blockade, the cost of the operation had started to undermine the Royalist cause. As with so many facets of the Revolutionary War, it is impossible to say that either side had come out on top.

The order to build HMS *Unicorn* was signed in 1819, one week before the cessation of fighting. It was to be a Leda-class frigate, agile enough to pursue enemy ships through treacherous coastal waters, but armed heavily enough to be confident of victory in the event of an encounter.

The building process was continually set back by shortages of materials, money and men. Thus, the *Unicorn* wasn't launched until 1824, by which time the partition of the country had been firmly established.

Launched at the Chatham Dockyard in Kent, but not

yet being fitted with masts or rigging, the *Unicorn* was towed to Dartmouth, to serve as a temporary base for the newly established naval training college. When land-based accommodation was found for the college, the *Unicorn* became a floating gunpowder storage facility.

With the signing of the Great Accord in 1821, the Anglo-Scottish Republic had become allied with the republics of America and France. Soon, other countries were adding their names to the Accord and the Gas-Lit Empire began to spread. Trade boomed between signatory nations and their wealth grew. By contrast, the Kingdom of England and Southern Wales remained politically isolated. Commerce withered and the country slid into an economic recession. The government began to search for assets that might be converted into cash to boost its beleaguered exchequer. With the *Unicorn* serving as nothing more than an expensive warehouse, it was one of the first things to be sold. It was purchased at auction by a man of business, who immediately sold it on to Emmet K Wattlington, the flamboyant entrepreneur and fervent Royalist.

A series of financial and diplomatic crises drove the Kingdom of England and Southern Wales finally to sign the Great Accord in 1828. After Accession, Wattlington became a prominent member of the Secessionist campaign. When it became clear that the Kingdom would remain within the Gas-Lit Empire, he announced that he would be leaving the country. In May 1836, he sailed from London with most of the remaining Secessionists in four ships, heading for the New World, where they intended to found a libertarian colony. Calling in at Dartmouth, they towed the *Unicorn* behind their small fleet, leaving British shores forever.

Nothing more is known of Wattlington and his colonists.

The *Unicorn* wasn't seen again until 2012, when it returned to the historic record as flagship of the Sargassan fleet.

Although it served no active part in the Battle of the Grand Banks, its presence galvanised the resolve of the Sargassan fighters, thus influencing the pivotal events that were to follow.

ACKNOWLEDGMENTS

Many thanks to Marc Gascoigne and Phil Jourdan for their insights and feedback, also to Ed Wilson, Mike Underwood and Penny Reeve for their ongoing support. I'm hugely grateful for the advice and encouragement received from Terri Bradshaw, Dave Martin, Jacob Ross and other members of Leicester Writers' Club, particularly Gwyneth and Siân, who allowed me to borrow their names. Last, but really first, thank you to Stephanie, Joseph and Anya, for your patience and love.

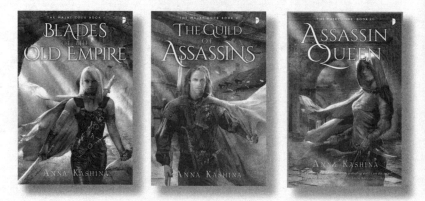